THE ONLY FISH
IN THE SEA

What Reviewers Say About
Angie Williams's Work

Last Resort

"The build up to romance for Katie and Rhys is slow burn but it's like one continuous foreplay and when they finally hit the sheets it very sexy. They also have incredible banter that is fun to read and made their romance even more plausible."—*Les Rêveur*

Mending Fences

"This is not a story driven by angst but more of a sweet (but incredibly sexy) story of finding your way home. ...For her first novel I think Angie Williams knocked this one out of the park. I will be following what she does next very closely!"—*Les Rêveur*

"*Mending Fences* by Angie Williams is a heartwarming second chance romance that highlights the importance of following your heart and being true to yourself no matter how daunting it may seem."—*The Lesbian Review*

By the Author

Mending Fences

Last Resort

Opposites Attract: Butch/Femme Romances

Love and Other Rare Birds

The Only Fish in the Sea

THE ONLY FISH IN THE SEA

by

Angie Williams

2023

ISBN 13: 978-1-63679-444-0

This Trade Paperback Original Is Published By
Bold Strokes Books, Inc.
P.O. Box 249
Valley Falls, NY 12185

First Edition: August 2023

Credits
Editor: Cindy Cresap
Production Design: Susan Ramundo
Cover Design By Tammy Seidick

Acknowledgments

My grandparents have lived on the Oregon coast since I was a little kid. It's a big part of who I am and why I joined the Coast Guard after high school. I've always loved the ocean and dreamed of escaping the desert in Texas to spend my days on a ship at sea. The reality of being on a ship in the Bering Sea, not seeing land for 45 days, wasn't as romantic as I'd imagined, but I wouldn't trade my time on board for anything. There's absolutely nothing like standing on the bridge wings with the icy wind against your face and nothing but open water around you. It was sometimes terrifying, but nothing has ever made me feel so alive.

Thank you, BSB family, for the support, the laughs, and always having my back.

A special thank you to Cindy Cresap and Meghan O'Brien for your patience and guidance.

Every author should be lucky enough to have pals that cheer them on even when said author feels completely in the weeds. I hit the jackpot in that department. Thanks to Jaime Clevenger, Leigh Hays, Aurora Rey, and Paige Braddock for believing in me and encouraging me to go for it.

Finally, thank you for your unwavering support and love, Poodle. You give the best advice, comfort me with the greatest hugs, and are by far the best kisser humankind has ever known. I totally married Meghan O'Brien, and I'm not even going to pretend that isn't the coolest thing ever.

Dedication

For Meghan. I've decided to keep you forever.

And for the moon, who loves the ocean as much as me.

"My soul is full of longing
  for the secret of the sea,
  and the heart of the great ocean
  sends a thrilling pulse through me."

—Henry Wadsworth Longfellow

CHAPTER ONE

Remy Miller pulled the ice pack from her eye and checked the damage in the mirror attached to her truck's sun visor. She ran a finger along the darkened skin and blew out a breath, anticipating the questions she knew were coming from her dad.

This wasn't the first time she'd shown up to work with a black eye, and she doubted it would be the last. Fishermen were a raucous bunch, but this time it wasn't her fault. She knew that wouldn't matter to her dad, though. He had high expectations for her and her brothers, and this would only reinforce his idea that she was still just a punk kid.

She knew for a fact that he would have been the one throwing the punches when he was her age, not just getting caught in the crossfire of someone else's altercation. Growing up, she'd heard enough stories to know the Millers were always trying to prove something. Prove they were better fishermen, tougher fighters, better drinkers, and the best lovers. They walked around the little Oregon fishing village of Elder's Bay like they had something to prove, and they were more than happy to do it.

That game was getting old. The only place Remy wanted to prove herself was out on the water, pulling full pots of Dungeness crab out of the sea to fill up their tanks. Crab and the other fisheries that sustained them between crabbing seasons had been her family's livelihood for generations, and being a good fisherman was the only thing that truly mattered in the world. It was the only thing she understood.

The snap of the sun visor as it slammed back into place against the roof startled Remy and sent a spike of pain through her hungover brain. She was getting too old for this. There was a time when she could spend the night drinking with her crew and show up to the boat before the sun, ready to catch any crab unlucky enough to crawl into the pots they'd set. The years of hard living were already catching up to her, even though she was just twenty-seven. That wasn't a good sign since her days as a crabber had only just begun.

"Hey, ass wipe, nice shiner." Remy's cousin Bill teased her as he handed her a hot mug of coffee. He had always treated Remy like a little sister. As the oldest of their generation of Millers, he took it upon himself to tease the younger cousins relentlessly when they showed up looking like they'd been in the trenches after a night at the bar.

"Where were you, dickhead? We could have used some backup last night."

"Tucked away in my comfortable bed with my beautiful wife so I would be fresh as a daisy this morning. Maybe you should try more of that and a little less time in bars and see how that suits you?"

She flipped him off, but knew he wasn't wrong. In theory, having a wife and kid was something she thought she would want someday, but not yet. Not before they made her captain, and she had her own boat. She wasn't ready to settle down and probably wouldn't be for years. Besides, Elder's Bay was a small town, and most girls her age were either related or Claymans. Her dad would never forgive her if she married a Clayman.

"What did you do this time, kid?" Her dad stepped onto the boat and took her chin in his meaty hand so he could turn her face to see her eye. "Don't let your mom see that. She worries enough about her kids being on the ocean without knowing what idiots you are when on shore."

Frank Miller was a barrel of a man with a white beard and a round face. On land, he was warm and loving, but the moment he stepped onto one of the boats he owned and operated, he was all business. He expected the same seriousness from his crew and, as the youngest of his three children, Remy sometimes took the brunt of his wrath.

"It's nothing." Remy gingerly touched the area around her eye, wishing she could hide the evidence of her night.

"Jay, what happened?" Remy's older brother looked from her to their dad, obviously trying to decide which one he was more afraid of before settling on whether he should tell the truth or come up with a lie.

"Dad, it's nothing. Don't pull Jay into this," Remy said. The last thing she needed was another lecture from him about getting into a fight with the Claymans. The two fishing families had been feuding since her grandfather and his best friend, Joseph Clayman, had a falling out fifty years before. Remy wasn't even exactly sure why the families hated each other at this point, but was told from a very young age that the wealthier, more successful family was not to be trusted.

"Tell me now, Jay, or I'll get someone else to take your place on the boat today."

"Why don't you threaten me for not telling you? You don't have to pick on Jay, Dad."

He rubbed his beard, the first sign he was losing his patience. "Because I don't trust you to tell me the whole truth, Remy. You like to give me just enough to get me off your ass, but not enough to be honest with me."

He wasn't wrong. Remy wasn't one to spill her guts, especially regarding her private life. She knew her dad would find out one way or the other, so she nodded to Jay, letting him know it was okay to tell him what happened. He looked so relieved, Remy almost laughed. When Jay finished his tale, which included details about the night Remy didn't even remember, her dad just shook his head as if he was at a loss with what to do with her.

"Are you sober?" he asked.

She nodded and ran her fingers through her hair. "I'm good. I took a breathalyzer test this morning before I even got in the car."

"Do you feel like dog shit?"

That was an understatement. Between the alcohol and beating she took the night before, Remy wanted nothing more than to crawl back into her bed and sleep off the raging hangover she had. "Yep," she said.

"Good. You're an idiot for going out the night before the season starts, but I can't say I'm surprised. You know, if you'd get your head out of your ass, Remy, you'd make one hell of a crabber."

"I know." Her dad was a hard-ass, but she hated to disappoint him all the same.

He nodded and went back to checking to make sure they had the required safety gear before leaving the dock. "I need you to run this boat today because your brother is sick."

"Yeah? Sure. No problem." Both of Remy's older brothers ran their own boats, and she'd spent her life preparing for the day he'd turn over one of their fleet to her. It was in her blood and she knew deep down that, given the chance, she could make him proud. The only problem had been that he almost never gave her the opportunity to show him she could captain her own boat.

"It's just for today, and I left you instructions for exactly where I want you to be."

"Okay," Remy said, thinking that if she could get through the areas he wanted her to go fast enough, she could move on to ones she knew would produce more crab. Her dad was an amazing crabber, but he'd always been too cautious in Remy's opinion. She knew it was because he'd lost a crewman at sea when he wasn't much older than her, but Remy was careful and knew what she was doing. Her brothers were also good crabbers, but they were little robots who followed everything her dad told them to do using none of the natural instincts she knew they must have. All Millers were born with the sea in their blood. She only needed to show him she could find the crab on her own without his direction.

"Hey, kid," he called to her as he and Jay stepped off the boat.

"Yeah?"

"Be careful out there. This boat isn't yours and I don't want you sinking my property."

"Roger that. Love you, too, old man." Remy shook her head and turned to help her crew prepare to leave.

"We ready to get out of here?" Remy asked her best friend, Andy. They'd been inseparable since her father had moved his medical practice to Elder's Bay when they were in kindergarten.

The Mathesons divorced not long after they moved to Elder's Bay and Remy's parents had treated Andy like one of their own when her mom moved to Portland, leaving her dad to run his business and care for his daughter on his own. They weren't bad people, just couldn't be the parents Andy needed. The Millers were a large family that had plenty of love to go around.

"Sure. Ten more minutes. Corey's running a little late," Andy said.

Andy and Remy's cousin Corey had both been with her at the bar the night before when a fight broke out between Corey's brother and Gary Clayman. Corey's twin brother, Casey, asked a girl to dance, not realizing she was Gary's date since he'd spent the entire night completely ignoring her and drinking with his friends. The girl accepted to teach Gary a lesson, not understanding the hornets' nest she was about to open between two families that were already looking for a reason to fight. The first punch from Gary took Casey by surprise, but by the time he wiped the blood from his lip and looked up to see a Clayman standing over him, Corey and several other Miller and Clayman cousins had joined the fray.

She vaguely remembered Corey taking at least one punch from Gary before she stupidly put herself between the two of them, hoping she could talk them down before someone was seriously injured. Her attempt to defuse the situation was immediately stopped when Gary punched her in the face. He'd gotten a good enough swing that she saw stars for a minute before being rushed outside the bar by Andy.

"Is Corey okay?" she asked Andy as they leaned against the pots stacked on the deck and watched the parking lot for signs of their crewman.

"He's fine. Busted lip and hung over, but fine."

"Then where is he?"

Remy checked her watch and looked toward the parking lot. They needed to get out on the water soon if they hoped to set a few strings of pots before midmorning. Some days they were only out for the day, and other trips would be two or three days. This trip was two days. Her dad had secured a higher price per pound than they would normally get, but they had to have the crab caught and offloaded in the next forty-eight hours. Every minute they sat at the dock was one less they'd have to catch the amount her dad was expecting.

Seven minutes later, a blue Prius came barreling into the parking lot and screeched to a halt. Andy and Remy shouted for Corey to hurry. He leaned over to kiss his girlfriend then ran down the pier wearing only his jeans with his shirt, socks, and shoes nestled under his arm.

"Hold on a fucking minute. I'm coming. Stop being assholes."

Andy playfully shoved Corey to the deck when he jumped onto the boat. "Let's go, Remy. Mr. Sweet Lips over here is finally ready to catch some crab."

Remy nodded and pulled away from the dock. "Hold on, guys, we need to make up for lost time." She could hear Andy and Corey exchanging playful jibes at each other as they made their way toward the spot her dad had told her he wanted her to drop her crab pots. It irritated her that he had to control every aspect of her life. She'd been crabbing with her grandpa and her dad since she was eight years old and knew these waters like the back of her hand. Remy didn't need him telling her where to go every time. She knew the currents and depths the crabs would likely be, and once she had her own boat, she'd prove to him she was at least as good a crabber as her brothers, if not better.

Her grandpa had always told her she had a special connection to the sea and to always trust her gut. She didn't doubt there would likely be crab where her dad said, but she knew deep down that the real jackpot would be two miles north at Sawyer Point. Their recent storm would have stirred up plenty of tiny crustaceans from the ocean floor that the crab would be eagerly eating up.

Several hours later, Remy and the boys had finished pulling their third string of pots. The numbers had been decent in the beginning, but the last string had tapered off. She knew if she called her dad, he would tell her to stick with the spot they were in. He had areas he liked to go, and he didn't want Remy deviating from his plan. In his mind, she was just an extension of him and not someone who could make intelligent decisions on her own.

"Thanks," Remy said when Andy handed her a plate with a sandwich on it. "Hey, what do you think about heading up to Sawyer Point for a few hours to see if we can't fill up our tanks there?"

Andy popped a potato chip into her mouth and shook her head. "You're just dying to piss your dad off, aren't you?"

"This isn't about my dad." Remy set down her plate and pointed to the area on the chart where she wanted to go. "You know they like to hang out on this ridge, and after that storm a couple days ago, they're going to be all over the place. We could fill our tank and wrap this trip up earlier than expected. First beer is on me."

Andy sighed and touched the digital screen displaying the nautical chart of the area. "What about these rocks? You know that's why your dad doesn't like you going over there."

"Dude, it's fine. He's an old ninny who will never trust me. Besides, the weather's supposed to be fine. We'll stay away from the rocks and be home to eat like kings tonight. No risk, no reward, right?"

"We go where you go, so whatever you want to do is good with me."

Remy leaned over the ladder leading below decks where Corey was fixing his sandwich in the galley. "Core? You cool with us pissing off your uncle Frank?"

There was silence for a beat before he yelled back, "What the fuck, I'm game."

"Let's do this." Remy hopped back into the captain's chair and set her course for Sawyer Point. With any luck, her dad would be too busy with his own boat to realize they had deviated from his plan.

"So, what caused that shit last night?" Andy asked. She'd come running to Remy's defense when the fight broke out, but before that, had been flirting with Stacy Wagner and missed the initial argument.

"Stupid Clayman shit. What else? They're all a bunch of assholes. They just can't help it. It's in their DNA or something."

Remy's grandpa and Joseph Clayman might have been the first to start the feud between their families, but it was alive and well in the next generation. Joseph's son, Brian, now ran Clayman Fisheries, which included several high-end restaurants in Portland

and the largest fleet of boats in Elder's Bay. There was no love lost between Remy's dad and Brian, which trickled down through the ranks to the rest of the family.

"You know your dad's buying a new boat, right?"

Remy nodded and popped the last bite of her sandwich into her mouth. "I heard."

"Do you think he's going to let you run it?"

She brushed the crumbs from her pants and looked out the window at the waves as they rolled toward the boat and sent sea spray over the sides when they collided with the hull. "He has to. I've proven to him that I'm more than capable. Besides, my brothers were running their own boats by the time they were my age and I'm twice the crabber either one of them are."

Corey popped his head up from below decks and startled them when he spoke. "I could sure use that full crew pay. Filling in when we're needed here and there is causing havoc on my bank account. Daddy needs a new truck."

"Please stop calling yourself Daddy for Christ's sake, Corey. It's creepy." Andy tossed her crumpled up napkin at his head.

"Brooke doesn't complain when—"

"No," Remy said. "We'll throw you off this boat if you finish that sentence."

Corey shrugged and climbed back down the ladder. She looked at Andy who was still shaking her head.

"Ready to find some crab?"

"You lead and we'll follow, captain."

CHAPTER TWO

The vibration of the mobile phone in her purse distracted Julia Clayman from the discussion she was having with one of their suppliers. Her family owned a large fleet of crab boats in her hometown of Elder's Bay, but the demand for fresh Dungeness crab for not only their own restaurants but several more in the Portland area required them to buy from other local crabbers.

"Excuse me, Toby. I'm so sorry." Julia reached into her purse and switched her phone to silent, as she should have done before the virtual meeting. "Where were we?"

"No problem, Julia. As I was saying, I've always appreciated the price Clayman Fisheries has given us for crab, but we can only provide half of the amount your dad is asking for unless you can give me another few days."

"I appreciate your situation, Toby, but my dad knows what we need and if he says we need more, half just won't do." Julia looked up as her assistant poked her head into her office. She hated interruptions but knew Tessa would never bother her unless it was an emergency. "Can you give me just a minute, Toby?"

"I think we've discussed all we can right now, Julia. Maybe I should reach out to the Millers. They may not give me the same price, but I've heard they're more reasonable. Word is, several boats have signed contracts with them because your dad has been too demanding. At the end of the day, the safety of the crew is all that matters. It's worth losing a little money to know they'll come home safe to their families."

"Don't be like that, Toby," Julia said. "You've worked with us for years and we've always treated you like family. What would it take for you to give us two-thirds of the numbers my dad asked for?"

Calls like this were happening more frequently and Julia knew she'd need to talk to her dad about reining in his unreasonable expectations. Crabbing was an extremely dangerous business, and boat owners weren't always willing to press their luck to haul in the numbers her dad was asking for. Toby was right, and a couple of boats they'd worked with in the past had signed with the Millers because her dad had refused to listen to their concerns. Boats were lost at sea every year, and a little extra money on the load wouldn't bring back the boats or crew that would never return home.

"You're killing me, Julia." Toby sighed and rubbed the few strands of hair left on his head. "Look, I'll get you as much crab as I can. We might be able to hit two-thirds, but I suggest you either buy from the Millers or add more boats to your fleet. You've about hit the limit of what the rest of us can bring in and we're getting tired of your dad trying to bully us into more."

Tessa cleared her throat and pointed to the blinking light on Julia's phone, indicating there was a call waiting on line two. Julia needed to wrap this up quickly and figure out what was so important that it couldn't wait for her to get off the damn video chat.

"Toby, we appreciate your hard work and know you do all you can to help us meet our goals. That's why we pay you above market value for your product. I know all of our suppliers appreciate our generosity and it shows in how willing they are to go that extra mile. Sure, the Millers are an option for the older crews that just can't hack it, but you're still a young man, Toby. You have kids heading off to college soon. The demand for crab is there, and if you can't get it, I'm sure one of the many other boats in the bay would be more than happy to come through for us."

The line was silent for a minute, then Toby sighed. "You Claymans are all alike. Fine, I'll see if I can get the guys to work through the night for another day or two. Talk to you Friday."

"Perfect. I'll talk to you Friday and we'll see where you are at that point."

"I hope your dad appreciates what a shark his daughter is. He got his money's worth when he sent you to that fancy business school."

Julia laughed and held a finger up to Tessa to show she was almost done. "Thanks, Toby, be safe."

"Thanks, Julia."

Julia ended the session and picked up her phone. "This is Julia Clayman."

"Julia, this is Mom. Your dad's had a heart attack." Julia's world stood still as her mother's frantic voice filled her in on his status and what hospital he was being taken to.

"I'm on my way, Mom. Hold tight. Tell him I love him and I love you, too."

"Hurry, Jules, I'm so scared."

Julia updated her assistant as she headed through the office toward the elevator. If the worst happened, and her dad died, she didn't want her mom to have to face that alone.

Two hours later, Julia pulled into the parking lot of the hospital and ran to the desk. They led her to where he was being monitored. The frail man she found connected to the incessantly beeping machines wasn't anything like the sturdy father she knew.

Julia's mom walked into the room with a cup of coffee and fell into her waiting arms. "I'm so glad you're here."

"What did they say?" Julia kissed her mom's cheek and held her close.

"They're monitoring him for the next couple of days, but they think he got here in time. We won't really know until they're able to run more tests."

"How did this happen?"

"How do you think this happened? He works too hard, doesn't eat right, smokes, drinks, and brings the stress of his job home every single night. He can't continue to work like this."

"I thought Charlie was going to take over some of the lower-level tasks to ease Dad's load?" Julia asked.

Her mom stepped back and sank into the chair against the opposite wall from her dad. "Charlie said he would, but you know how your brother is. He doesn't want to live in this little town for the rest of his life. The business was never his plan, and that won't change."

Julia sat on the arm of her chair and took a sip from her mother's coffee when she offered it. "What about Johnny?"

"Your cousin won't be able to run this part of the company. The boy barely graduated high school. You know his parents made a sizable donation to the school to grease the wheels. He's sweet, but he's never held down a legitimate job in his life. And none of your other cousins want the stress of running the company. Besides, you know it's always been your dad's dream for you to take his place. He raised you to be the one. He trusts you above all others."

She knew what was coming next and frantically tried to think of an excuse that wouldn't sound like she was a total asshole.

"Do you think you could reconsider taking over now?" her mom asked.

There it was. Her dad had been trying to convince her to move back to Elder's Bay for a couple of years to prepare for taking over the part of the business he'd always run. The problem was, Julia's life was in Portland. Her apartment, her friends, her life. There were three types of people who lived in their tiny fishing village. Those who wanted to be fishermen, those who wanted to marry fishermen, and the ones who wanted nothing more than to get out and move to the big city. She wasn't sure she was ready to give up the life she'd worked so hard for to come back to this tiny little town and settle down. She didn't want the life her parents had.

Marriage, kids, and a white picket fence were in her future. It was something she thought about more and more, but at twenty-seven years old, there was no rush. The one thing she knew for sure was that she wouldn't marry a fisherman, and in Elder's Bay, there weren't many other options.

Right now, her dad needed her and she could give him that. She'd have to shuffle her duties in Portland around a bit, but she'd make it work. She had to make it work.

"I won't agree to take over forever, but I can shift some things around to spend more time here. I've been training Tessa as my backup, so I'll ask her to take on some of my responsibilities in Portland until we can find someone to help Dad out."

Her mom sipped her coffee without looking at her. "You know he'll trust no one other than you to run the family business."

It was a statement, not a question, and Julia knew she was right. He wouldn't have a choice, though. Julia would find someone who could run the day-to-day here and she could transfer some duties to Portland. It would be difficult, but she'd make it work.

That was a discussion for another day. Right now, she wanted to focus on getting her dad back on his feet. She mentally ran through a checklist of the things she'd need to ask Tessa to handle, as well as what she'd need to do to get up to speed on to take over for her dad.

"Julia?" Her dad's gravelly voice cut through the silence in the room and Julia and her mom rushed to either side of his bed to hold his hands. He'd always been larger than life, and seeing her normally strong, commanding father lying in a hospital bed with all types of tubes and wires connected to him was heartbreaking. It was as if she only just realized he was human and wouldn't live forever.

"Hey, Dad, you could have just asked me to visit. You didn't have to make this dramatic scene to get my attention."

His weak chuckle brought a small amount of relief to an otherwise serious situation. "I…had…to…get…" Each word was obviously a struggle. He cleared his throat and pressed on. "My big shot daughter's attention…somehow."

"We'll discuss how to use a phone to call people once you're feeling better."

He looked at her mom as she smiled through her tears. "Hi," he said, rasping out the word.

"Don't try to speak, you old goat. Julia's here and she's going to take things over for a bit until you're feeling better."

Her dad looked at her, and she nodded. "I've got your back, Dad. Don't worry about anything."

He nodded and closed his eyes. A minute later, he'd drifted back to sleep.

"I'm going to head into the office to see what I can do. Please let me know if he wakes up and is ready for visitors."

Her mom nodded and reached out to take her hand and squeeze it. "Thank you for coming, Julia. I love you, sweetheart, and I know it means everything to him you're here."

"I wouldn't be anywhere else. Where's Charlie?"

"He's out on the new boat your dad bought last month. Your dad's been having a hard time finding a crew for it so Charlie said he'd fill in until someone else can take over."

"I bet he's pissed about that."

"Stephanie's been calling to bitch your dad out every other day. Like he hasn't been working day and night to find a crew already. I don't know why your brother had to marry that woman."

Julia knew exactly why he'd married her. That three-year-old toddler she adored locked her brother into a family and a marriage he wasn't ready for. He was an amazing father, though, even if his wife wasn't a fan favorite of the family.

"Does he know Dad's in the hospital?"

"Yes. He's coming in early, but they were a few hours out the last I heard from him. He should be back any time now."

"Okay. I'll talk to him and go to the office to see what needs to be done. I love you, Mom. He's a tough old grizzly bear. He'll be just fine." Her mom pulled the chair closer to his bed so she could continue to hold his hand.

An hour later, Julia met her brother at the dock as he finished unloading the crab they'd caught that day.

"How'd it go?" she asked him when he was done.

Charlie shrugged and pulled Julia into a hug. "How's the old man? Mom called and said he was stable, but I know you'll tell me the truth."

"He's okay," Julia said, resting her head on Charlie's shoulder as they walked. "You know how Dad is. He's weaker than I've ever seen him, but he'd never admit that. I'm going to take things over until he's back on his feet. Anything special I should know?"

"Hell, yes. You seriously have to find a new captain and crew for Dad's new boat. I can only be here for another few days and the same goes for Craig and Paul. We all have lives we need to get back to."

Julia sighed and threw up her hands. "How am I supposed to find replacements that quickly? You know these things take time, Charlie. Can't you guys give me a couple of weeks?"

"I'm sorry, kiddo, no can do. Stephanie and I are trying to have another baby."

"Really?" Julia hoped the surprise in her voice wasn't too noticeable.

"Yes, really. I wish you guys would give Stephanie a chance. She's changed a lot in the last few years. I think becoming a mom helped soften some of those edges she had."

"I'm sorry, you're right. She's part of our family and she's the mother of the cutest little girl the world has ever seen, so I'll try."

"Thanks, sis," Charlie said.

"Any suggestions where I can find this amazing captain that's just sitting around waiting for a job when the season has already started?"

"Skippers?" Charlie suggested with a smile.

"The crew bar? Really?" Julia smacked him on the chest. "Let me rephrase that. Do you know where I can find a captain that isn't already working on a boat and doesn't hang out in bars?"

"I don't know, Julia. Seems like there'd be plenty of crew that would love a chance at the helm, and just because they blow off some steam in port, doesn't mean they'll be drunk at the helm. Think outside the box, kiddo. It's probably too late to find someone who has a bunch of experience, but if you find the right sailor, maybe it doesn't matter. Just don't let someone sink Dad's new boat because he'll kill you and your new captain."

Charlie was right. Julia knew she'd have to get creative to find someone at this point. She hadn't worked this side of the business and hadn't been around the actual sailors who pulled in the crab in so long that she felt like she was completely out of the loop. Maybe that didn't matter? She might not be a sailor herself, but she knew people. At this late in the game, her instincts about a person might be her only hope.

"Give me one more week to find someone and I promise I'll get you out of here." Julia hated to push her brother, but he was giving her absolutely no time to find his replacement.

"I hate to leave you in the lurch, but I have a life I'd like to get back to and this has already taken way more time than I wanted. You'll be fine, and if you need anything, just call. As long as it doesn't involve me risking my life for a bunch of crab, I'll do what I can to help."

"Fine. I get it. I'm still mad at you, but I understand. Are you going to see Dad?"

Charlie pushed himself off the car and wrapped an arm around Julia's shoulders. "Yep. I'm going there right now. It's good to see you, baby sister. I'm glad you're going to be here to help Dad."

"I love you, too. You better get going before you miss visiting hours."

The sun dipped below the horizon as they both drove out of the parking lot and headed in different directions. Julia's aunt had graciously offered her house to her while she was in Greece for a few months. Julia was thankful she wouldn't have to stay with her parents, but frustrated she wouldn't be in her own apartment, with her own things for what might turn into a months-long stay.

Julia had no idea how she was going to find a captain by Monday morning, but she knew her dad was counting on her. If she hoped to take over the business someday, this was her opportunity to prove to the family that she was up for the task. First she just had to convince herself of the same.

CHAPTER THREE

Remy's black eye had faded a little, but the faint darkness was still there. She touched it and winced when she discovered it was still tender.

"Clayman bastards," she said to her reflection in the mirror. The ridiculous feud between their families had started decades before Remy was born, and she was tired of living in its shadow. It was a waste of time she didn't understand.

"Hey." Andy poked her head into the bathroom. "You're still going to your parents' tonight, aren't you?"

"Duh. Mom would destroy me if I tried to skip out on a family dinner. Have you heard anything else about the new boat?"

"Not exactly, but I heard a little scuttle that your dad's making an announcement, so he wants everyone there. Maybe he's going to name the captain for the boat?"

A thrill of excitement shot through Remy. She'd been waiting for her dad to give her a chance to captain a boat full-time for months, and this could finally be her shot. "You haven't heard anything about the boat other than he bought one?"

"Bill mentioned it's out of Coos Bay and someone is bringing it up here tonight. You know we need it with the new contracts your dad has signed."

"For sure. Our current fleet isn't going to be able to keep up. I bet the Claymans are freaking out that they lost those contracts. Serves them right, the assholes." Remy's mood had lightened considerably, and she was suddenly eager to get to her parents' house to find out what the story was. "You ready? Let's get over there."

Fifteen minutes later, Remy and Andy walked into her parents' backyard to a chorus of greetings and hugs from the Millers and their extended family. It was a close-knit community and when you made your living in such a dangerous profession as crabbing, people considered each other family, blood related or not.

"There she is," Jay said as he draped his arm around Remy's shoulders and pulled her into a one-armed hug. "How's the eye?"

"S'fine." Remy was really hoping to avoid too much discussion about the fight at the bar. Not that she was ashamed of coming to the aid of her cousin, but knowing that a Clayman had given her a black eye was something she wasn't excited to talk about. "Do you know anything about this new boat Dad bought?"

"No. I've only heard rumors. He's been strangely tight lipped about it. I figured he'd tell me if it was something he thought I should know."

"Always the obedient son."

"At least one of us has to do what they're told so Peter isn't the only one named in Dad's will."

"Kiss ass."

Jay smacked Remy on the back of the head, then dodged her attempt to fight back. "You're a jerk, Jay."

He winked at her as he jogged toward their mom for safety. He knew she would protect him from any retaliation Remy might want to dish out.

A warm body pressed against Remy's back before fingers slipped under the hem of her shirt and caressed the skin at the edge of her jeans. She didn't need to turn around to know who those hands belonged to. Only one woman would be brazen enough to touch her like that in full view of Remy's mother.

"What's going on, Brandy?"

There was a soft giggle as Brandy dipped under the fabric of Remy's jeans and made her way toward somewhere Remy definitely didn't want her mom seeing, let alone all the other people at the party.

"Hey, hey, hey." Remy smoothly gripped Brandy's wrist and gently pivoted her around to face her. "Let's keep this PG for the family crowd. I don't think you want my mom explaining to you why it's inappropriate to stick your hand in her daughter's pants in public."

Brandy stuck her lower lip out in a pout. "You didn't have a problem with it on the beach the other night."

"That was different. It was dark, everyone was drunk, and we were between the dunes. Nobody was watching us, unlike right now when I can see my uncle Luke staring right at us from over by the keg."

"Fine. When are you taking me out on another date?"

The sound of Remy's dad's arrival saved her from having to make up an excuse about why she wouldn't be taking Brandy out again. It wasn't anything personal. She was cute, and she wasn't bad in bed, but Remy didn't have time for a girlfriend. She'd explained as much to her many times, but apparently it didn't stick. Besides, Brandy's dad had captained one of the Millers' boats since before Remy was born and she didn't need to give her dad yet one more reason to dismiss her. She kissed Brandy on the cheek before walking away to stand with her family.

A thrill of excitement coursed through her entire body like someone had plugged her into a wall socket. This could be it. If her dad had somehow managed to purchase a new boat, Remy had done more than enough to prove to him she was a capable captain and ready to take the helm. The family business had struggled for years, but she was confident she could turn it around, given the opportunity to prove herself.

Her dad kissed her mom on the cheek before turning toward the gathering crowd of family and friends. The glass clanked as he tapped the ring his father passed down to him against his beer bottle, and a hush ran through the crowd. The anticipation of the announcement made Remy as antsy as a kid on Christmas morning. Her mom reached out and held her arm in a firm grip to encourage her to settle down. Remy smiled at her, but she thought for a moment the smile she returned seemed clouded with sadness.

"I want to thank everyone for coming this evening. It means a great deal to us to have those we love here to celebrate every milestone."

Remy noticed a man she didn't recognize push through the crowd to the front. He tilted his beer and smiled at her dad, who nodded and continued with his speech.

"As some of you have already heard, we've added another boat to the Miller Crabbing fleet. She's out of Coos Bay, and I think she'll be invaluable in helping us meet the expectations of our new customers."

Nervous energy coursed through Remy as she smoothed the wrinkles from her clothes in anticipation of the attention she knew she'd receive when her dad announced she was captaining the boat. This was the moment she'd been waiting for, and she wished he'd just skip to the good part. A million thoughts ran through her head. She didn't know how big this boat was or what they equipped it with, but she knew she'd be the best captain in Elder's Bay.

"And at her helm…"

Remy bounced on the balls of her feet and cleared her throat. She couldn't stop the grin that was straining her cheeks. Her dreams were finally coming true.

Frank Miller reached his hand out in the direction of the stranger Remy had seen in the crowd. "Captain Dan Bratton."

Reality fell away as Remy tried to understand what her dad had just said. The surrounding claps were muffled, as if she were in a dream state. She watched the stranger walk over to her dad and shake his hand. Her dad pulled him into a hug, then guided him around to face the crowd.

"Captain Bratton is Oregon raised but has been crabbing in Alaska for years. He finally thought he'd come back down here to give real crabbing a shot."

Remy blankly watched everyone laugh, but she couldn't understand what they thought was so funny. This was the worst day of her life and they were all going along with it like it was no big deal. She turned to her brothers, who both looked away. When she walked toward her father, her mother grabbed her arm and held her in place.

"Not now, sweetheart." The sympathetic look on her face did nothing to ease the pain Remy felt at that moment.

"Fuck this," Remy said before walking away from her family, the crowd of cheering betrayers, and her dream of ever captaining a boat for Miller Fisheries. She was done. The days of playing her father's game, hoping that he would see her for who she was, were over.

She felt Andy silently wrap a comforting arm around her shoulders as they left the party.

"Hey, where are we going?" Corey called as he jogged to catch up to them.

"Skip's," Remy said. "Get in."

The three of them piled into Remy's truck and sat in silence for a minute. She just needed to gather her thoughts and figure out what the fuck had just happened.

"Did either of you know about this?" she asked.

"No way, man," Corey said from the back seat.

Remy looked at Andy and felt her shoulders relax a bit when she shook her head.

"I'd never keep something like that from you, Remy." Andy glanced back at Corey, who was also shaking his head. "Neither of us would do that to you. You're our captain, and our loyalty will always be with you."

"We need to figure out what we're going to do next. Do either of you know anyone who could get us on a boat in Alaska? We could fish for cod or whatever the hell we need to do to make some connections until we can get on a crabber."

Andy stared at her phone as she scrolled through the contacts, but Remy was pretty sure she'd know if Andy had a connection up there. There was the occasional intermingling, but not much. She looked at Corey in the rearview mirror. "Core?"

"Maybe?" He shrugged and Remy wanted to smack him upside the head.

"You do or you don't, Core. What does maybe mean?"

"I might, but I'll have to feel out the situation first. Do you guys remember that Gretchen chick I dated last year?"

They both nodded. "The one that wanted you to lick whipped cream off of her—"

"Yes, yeah, that's the one. What a fucking idiot. Doesn't she know that's a surefire way to get a yeast infection? All that sugar can't be good for dark, damp areas like that."

"Get to the point, Core."

"So, her brother's on the crew of a crabber out of Kodiak Island."

Finally, a glimmer of hope. It was extremely difficult to get on a crew if you didn't have someone to vouch for you. If this brother would do that, she might be able to save up enough money to buy her own damn boat. Remy wasn't her brothers; she didn't need her dad to hand a boat to her on a silver platter. She'd make this happen on her own. Then she'd come back here with her own boat and prove to them what a mistake they'd made.

"That's awesome, Core. Can you contact her and see if we can get his number?" They both looked at Corey like he held the answer to all of their problems.

Corey gripped his phone in his hand and tapped it against his head. "Yeah, see, that might be a problem."

"What the fuck, Core. Why?"

"It's just that she kinda hates my guts." Corey sunk deeper into the seat and refused to look either of them in the eyes.

"You were an asshole about the whipped cream thing, weren't you?" Remy sighed. This wasn't the first time Corey had been brutally honest with someone and pissed them off. He couldn't help it. It just never occurred to him not to be completely honest with someone. Even when that someone might not like what he had to say.

"It was unhygienic, Rem. I didn't want her to do something that might cause her problems in the future."

"It's okay, Core." Andy ruffled her own hair in frustration. "We'll figure something else out."

Remy started the truck as others left the party. The last thing she wanted was for someone to talk to her, especially her parents or one of her brothers. It was better to just do her own thing and leave the dream of being a part of her family business behind.

CHAPTER FOUR

The noise of the bar drowned out the warning bells going off in Julia's head. What the hell was she doing? Skipper's was the last place she wanted to be on a Friday night, especially when she should be scouring the internet for a captain to run their new boat. Her brother's idea of looking for someone at the bar was the dumbest thing she'd ever heard, but barring any other brilliant options, she decided to give it a try.

"Julia? What are you doing here?" Julia turned to find her Uncle Tommy at the bar with two of her cousins.

"Hey, guys. I heard this is the place to be in Elder's Bay on a Friday night."

Her uncle laughed and opened his arms to invite her in for a hug. "How are you holding up, sweetie? I was down to see your pop at the hospital earlier. It's hard to see him like that, but that old cuss is tough as nails. He'll be just fine."

Apparently, there was a familiar script people said when someone who seemed so strong was ill. Julia smiled at her uncle and allowed him to wrap her in a comforting hug. He meant well. After all, it was his big brother in that hospital bed. Her dad's heart attack had to be difficult for the entire family, and with her grandparents long gone, her dad was the patriarch. He not only ran the family business, but he was basically Poseidon. Gods didn't get sick. They had no weakness. She realized her dad's illness must have everyone feeling a little lost, not just her.

"He's too stubborn to be down for long, Uncle Tommy. Besides, who will give you shit about being the runt of the family if he's not around to remind you?"

Uncle Tommy was by the far the largest of her dad's brothers. At six-foot-five and 350 pounds, he was a monster of a man with the kindest disposition of them all.

He laughed at her tease and hugged her tighter. "You're a chip off the old block, Jules. You know I'm here for you, right? Anything you need. Me and the rest of the family would do anything for you guys. Just ask."

"How about a captain for dad's new boat? Do you know of any that are looking for a job?"

"A captain? Now? The season has already started, Darlin'. Any captains you're going to find available now aren't going to be ones you want running your dad's pretty new boat."

"Be that as it may, that's the situation I'm in. Charlie was running it for a couple weeks, but he had to leave today. Come Monday I either have to have a new captain at the helm or the boat won't leave the dock. I don't want to be the one to explain to Dad why his new boat didn't bring in any crab."

Tommy looked toward her cousins as both of them shook their heads. She could see the disappointment on his face as he turned back to her.

"I'm really sorry, sweetheart. You know I'd do anything for you, but a qualified captain is hard to find on a good day, let alone once the season has started and everyone has already signed on with an outfit for the season."

"I know. It's a long shot, but I have to figure something out fast. I really don't want Dad worrying about this when he should be relaxing and trying to get better."

There was no way Julia wanted to tell her dad she was unable to find someone come Monday morning. She was going to have to pull a rabbit out of a hat on this one, but she'd give it everything she had to make it happen.

"Well, I better mingle. I have a long night ahead of me."

"Good luck, kid. Hey, Calvin." Tommy raised a hand to get the attention of the bartender. "Can we have a drink for my niece?"

Calvin had gone to school with Julia and was the only kid in his family with a debilitating seasickness that kept him on land. He'd gotten a lot of crap about it growing up, but he'd learned early on to make friends with the biggest kids he could find. Pretty soon, all the teasing stopped, and he was everyone's friend. Being a bartender seemed like the perfect job for a guy like that.

"Hey, Cal, how are you?"

"I'm great, Julia. Good to see you back in town. Sorry to hear about your dad. He's a tough old bird. He'll be fine."

"Thanks. Yeah, I'm sure he will."

Calvin brushed a lock of curly brown hair from his eyes. "What can I get you?"

"Put whatever she wants on my tab, Cal," Uncle Tommy said before Julia could speak.

"Thanks, Uncle Tommy. I'll have a whiskey sour, please."

Calvin nodded and pulled out a glass before pointing to the bottles of whiskey on the wall behind him. "Do you have a preference?"

"Buffalo Trace?"

"Good choice."

Ice cubes clanked against the glass as Calvin prepared her drink.

"Here you go, Jules." Calvin set her drink on the bar when it was done. "It's great to see you. I'm sorry it's under these circumstances. Let me know if you need anything."

"Thanks, Cal. I'm sure we'll see each other around." She picked up the glass and held it up to him in a wave.

He waved back and continued wiping down the bar. Julia sipped her whiskey and looked around at the crowd of people. The bar was dark, as always, but they'd added a small dance floor and a stage in the back. A few people were two-stepping to the country song that played through the speakers, but most sat at tables nursing a beer or cocktail. She guessed the majority of them were discussing their boats or the price of crab or the weather forecast. In some strange way, it was comforting.

Without a clear plan, she walked toward the back of the bar until a familiar voice caught her attention. She'd worked with Andy Matheson at the community pool as a lifeguard in high school. They'd gone on a date the summer before their senior year but drove several towns away so Andy's best friend, Remy Miller, wouldn't know she was out with a Clayman.

That Julia's true crush was on Remy, not Andy, made things even more complicated. After their date, Andy dropped her off at her house and explained she'd had a good time, but it couldn't happen again. The burden of keeping something from her best friend was more than Andy could stomach.

She was a loyal friend to Remy, and Julia respected her for that. It had been the only date with another girl Julia had gone on before college, and despite it ending with what could be considered a rejection, that one lovely experience had eventually given her the courage to date more women once she was away from the prying eyes of her parents and their tiny community.

The chance that someone from the Miller crew would help her find an available captain was unlikely, but Julia was desperate, and Andy had always been kind to her. It was worth asking, at least.

Julia followed the voice to a small room where several people stood around a pool table. Andy sat on a stool at a high bar table in the corner, chalking the tip of her cue as she watched Remy Miller line up for a shot. Remy's cousin Corey stood watching from another corner with his arm around a cute blond woman with a red polka dot dress.

Heat warmed Julia's cheeks as she watched the bands of muscle ripple in Remy's arms when she hit the ball with her cue. Two solids dropped into pockets at either end of the table before Remy moved to the other end looking for her next shot.

A lump formed in Julia's throat when Remy looked up from the table and noticed Julia watching her. Embarrassed at being caught, she wanted to turn away, but it was too late to pretend like she hadn't been staring.

With one last sip of her drink for courage, she walked toward the one person her mind told her she shouldn't want, but her hormones had always insisted she needed.

The laughter stopped when Julia entered the tiny room, and all eyes focused on her. They didn't seem angry that she was there, more confused about what was happening.

"Hey, guys, mind if I join you?"

Remy set her pool cue against the wall and folded her arms across her chest. Julia held her breath as they all silently stared at her. Finally, Andy slid from her stool and indicated Julia should take her seat. "Please sit, Julia. It's great to see you. I was sorry to hear about your dad."

"Thanks, Andy." She doubted any of them cared about her dad, but saying that wouldn't make her any friends, so she left it at that. "Who's winning?"

She knew nothing about playing pool but asking about the game seemed like a good way to break the ice. She slid onto the stool and set her drink on the table.

"Remy. As usual. Remy always wins."

"I bet she does." Julia didn't know if flattery would help Remy relax around her, but it was worth a try. "How are you, Remy? It's been a long time."

Remy dropped her arms and retrieved her cue from where it rested against the wall. "I'm fine. I'm surprised to see you slumming with the locals, Julia. Aren't there any cocktail parties you should be at?"

"Remy don't be a dick," Andy said.

Remy bent over to line up her shot and sunk one of her balls in the corner pocket before scanning the table for her next move. "What can we do for you, Ms. Clayman?"

Here goes nothing. "I wondered if any of you knew of a captain that hadn't already signed on with a boat for the season?"

"The season has already started," Andy said. "Why are you just now looking for a captain?"

"True. It's a total long shot, but my brother was running my dad's new boat and can't stay. It was only supposed to be temporary, but my dad couldn't find a replacement. Now he's going to be out at least for a few weeks, and Charlie has to leave. That means it's up to me to find a captain and a good crew, after the season has started, that can start Monday."

"Sucks to be you," Corey said.

"What about you guys? This is exactly what you guys want and you won't have to go to Alaska to do it," red polka dot dress said.

"Brooke," Corey scolded her. "Baby, we aren't an option."

"Why?" Brooke asked.

Remy never took her eyes from the table as Corey and Andy looked at each with expressions Julia couldn't interpret. She honestly had no idea what was happening, but thought it was best if she just kept quiet and let this play out between them.

"A Miller can't go work for a Clayman, honey. It's just not done."

"That's just ridiculous. You've been moaning all night about Remy's dad not giving you guys a boat and how much he's going to regret not giving you a chance to show him what you're capable of and then this pretty lady walks in looking for a captain and crew and you're going to tell me you aren't going to do it because she's a Clayman?"

Julia liked this Brooke chick already. She knew there was almost no chance Remy and her crew would actually come work for her, but the dressing down Brooke was giving them was quite entertaining.

"You don't understand, Brooke," Corey said.

"I don't understand what, Corey? That you'd rather move to Alaska and make me either follow you there or lose you, than you guys take this job she's offering and be able to stay here in Elder's Bay? It's everything you say you want for Christ's sake. I don't understand you idiots sometimes."

Brooke slid from the stool she was sitting on and stormed out of the room with Corey close behind her.

Remy lined up her next shot and sank another ball. Julia cleared her throat and took another sip of her drink, afraid to say anything that might make things even more uncomfortable than they already were.

The room was silent except for the sound of the balls clanking against each other as Remy took one shot after the other. God damn if Remy hadn't grown into a sexy butch. Overactive hormones threatened to derail Julia's thoughts, so she sipped her drink and looked at Andy's friendly face for support.

Remy called the last pocket before sinking the eight ball exactly where she said it would go. She whispered something into Andy's ear before drinking the last of her beer and reaching for her jacket hanging from a hook on the wall.

"Let's go talk," Remy said.

Julia finished the last of her own drink and, with a small wave to Andy, allowed Remy to guide her into the darkened bar. They pushed their way through the crowd toward the front entrance and out into the cool night.

"Take my jacket." Remy held up her black wool naval pea coat and helped Julia slip it on. "Did you forget your jacket in the bar or did you really not come here with one?"

"It's in my car that's parked on the other side of the building. I can go get it so you can take yours back."

"It's fine. You're going to freeze in that tiny dress before you make it to your car. It's winter on the Oregon coast, for Christ's sake. You should know better."

Julia looked down at the black A-line scoop neck knee-length chiffon cocktail dress she was wearing with lace around the sleeves and down the front, exposing just enough skin to tease. It probably wasn't the smartest thing to wear to the bar that night, but she had hoped it might help her convince someone to captain for her. She wasn't above the allure of a sexy dress helping her get what she wanted.

"You don't like my dress?" Julia asked.

"I—that's not—" Remy stumbled through her response before giving up and walking away. "Come on."

A crowd of men were smoking near the corner of building. Normally Julia would have given them a wide berth, but Remy walked past them as if she hadn't noticed they were there. As they passed, Julia heard a couple of them whistle and make lewd comments about her. She rushed to catch up to Remy but before she reached her, Remy stopped and turned to the guys.

"Hey asshats," Remy said as she put herself between Julia and the men. "Didn't your mommas teach you better manners than that?"

"Yeah, sorry, Remy," one of the men said.

"I know most of you are new to town, but I'm sure my dad would hate to have to replace you on his crews when the season's only just started. I think you boys owe my friend an apology."

Julia pressed herself against Remy's back and pulled the jacket tighter around her body. She couldn't remember anyone ever sticking up for her like this and even though it was a tense situation, she was turned on more than she'd been in a very long time. Protective Remy was something to behold.

"We're sorry, ma'am. Put a little beer in us and we forget our manners." The apparent spokesperson for the men stepped forward but didn't make a move to come any closer. "It won't happen again."

"It's okay." It wasn't, but Julia just wanted to leave at that point so she said whatever it would take to bring this confrontation to an end.

"I'd appreciate it if you'd treat my friend with the respect she deserves in the future."

"Of course." The spokesman assured her. "I'm Dean." He reached out a hand to Julia and she shook it.

"Julia," she said.

"It's a pleasure to meet you, Julia. If you ever need anything, you just let me know. The Millers have been good employers and have treated us like family. Any friend of theirs is a friend of ours."

Remy surprised Julia when she reached down to take her hand. "I appreciate you saying that, but maybe try treating all women with respect and see where that gets you," Remy said.

Dean smiled and nodded his head. "You're right. Sorry about that. You two have a nice night."

Without another word, Remy led her toward the back of the parking lot with Julia's hand still cradled in her own.

They finally reached a blue truck tucked away under a tree. Remy opened the passenger door and helped Julia into the cab.

Once she was safely inside, Remy jogged around to the driver's side and climbed in behind the wheel.

"I've had too much to drink to actually drive us anywhere, but at least I can turn on the heat and we can have a quiet place to talk."

"Thanks," Julia said. "And thanks for talking to those guys back there."

It was strange to sit in the relative privacy of the truck cab with someone she'd had such a big crush on as a girl but had thought little about since leaving Elder's Bay. Life was a funny thing.

"My pleasure. I'm sorry they did that. My dad runs a tight crew and most of them wouldn't think about talking to a woman like that, especially with his daughter right there, but those guys are new." Remy reached over Julia's lap and opened the glove box. "Excuse my reach."

The slight buzz from the whiskey and lingering attraction to her stole Julia's breath when Remy rested her body on her lap for a moment while she retrieved something from the glove box.

"Here it is," Remy said as she pulled out a small rectangular tin. The smell of marijuana filled the small space when she opened the box and removed a joint and a lighter. She held it up to Julia with a questioning look.

"Sure," Julia said. She hadn't smoked a joint in years, but if there was a time when she needed something to calm her nerves, it was now.

Remy tucked the joint between her lips and lit the end with the lighter. She took several quick draws before handing it to Julia. The sound of the windows being lowered startled her as she began to take a few hits of her own. Julia held the smoke in for a few seconds before releasing it in a rush. Once she stopped coughing, the tension in her shoulders relaxed and her head felt a little fuzzy.

"Wow. I haven't done this in a long time. I think I forgot how little it takes to affect me," Julia said.

Remy nodded and took one more hit before offering it to Julia again.

"I think I better stop while I'm ahead," Julia said.

Remy put the rest of the joint away and tucked the tin back into the glove box. They both sat there in silence while Julia's mind and body adjusted to the feeling of lightness.

"You know, I used to have a major crush on you in high school," Julia said without thinking.

"No shit?"

"Fuck. I said that out loud, didn't I?" Julia had never meant to let her adolescent feelings slip, but now it was too late. She remembered that this was exactly why she rarely smoked pot. Losing your inhibitions could lead to divulging things you never meant to share.

"I can't believe Julia Clayman, head cheerleader and valedictorian, had a crush on me."

Julia looked over to see a smug smile on Remy's face and regretted telling her even more. Even though she looked adorable. This wasn't the situation she intended to put herself in while hoping to convince a potential future employee to go against their own family and join the other side.

"I was a budding lesbian, and you were a hot, butch, take-no-shit bad girl. Of course, I had a crush on you. It's no secret that I wasn't the only girl at school that had a crush on you. I suspect you're still popular with the ladies." Julia wished she could make herself shut up.

"Wow. I did not expect to have this conversation with you tonight, Julia. Maybe that pot and beer are affecting me more than I realized it would." Remy reached over and gently pinched Julia's arm.

"Ouch. Why did you do that?"

"I barely touched you."

Julia rubbed her arm where Remy pinched it and realized it was more of a shock that she'd pinched her than actual pain. "I just wasn't expecting so much violence from you after professing my teenage feelings."

Remy chuckled and folded her arms across her chest. "So, what's your game here, Julia?"

"What game?" Julia reached down to lower the back of her chair. The movement made her head feel like it wasn't attached to her shoulders.

"Showing up out of nowhere asking Frank Miller's daughter to captain one of your boats. Does your dad know about this? He hates my dad and his children by extension."

Remy was right. Her dad wasn't going to be pleased if she was somehow able to convince Remy and her crew to run the boat for Clayman Fisheries, but Julia didn't really care. The ridiculous feud that kept their families at each other's throats had gone on way too long. Her dad would just have to deal with it. He couldn't find someone to run the boat, so if Julia could make this happen, it would be a win for the company.

"Technically, I asked if you guys knew of anyone I could hire. I never imagined it could possibly be you. No games. Just an honest question. My dad has been looking for someone to run the boat for weeks and my brother was able to fill in for a time, but today was his last day. I need to find a captain and crew that can start Monday morning."

Remy pulled off her boots and leaned her own chair back. "How do you know we're any good? Maybe we don't have a clue what we're doing."

Julia scoffed. "I may not have spent much time in Elder's Bay since I left for college, but I have heard about Remy Miller. I heard my uncle Tommy talk to my dad one time about what an amazing sailor you were. He said he didn't understand why you weren't already running a boat on your own."

She didn't mention her dad's response to Uncle Tommy because it wouldn't help her convince Remy to work for them. Her dad would put his pride above everything and leave the boat moored at the dock rather than hire a Miller. She wasn't glad her dad was sick, but Julia taking over might be the thing that helped their business now.

"I'm no captain, Julia. If someone told you different, they were lying to you. I fill in on one of my dad's boats here and there, but it's only for a trip or two and then I'm right back on the deck with everyone else. That bastard would rather hire a stranger to come in and run his boat than trust his only daughter."

Julia wanted to climb across the center console and wrap her arms around Remy to comfort her. The pain in her eyes broke Julia's heart. Somehow trying to convince her to run one of her boats seemed crass so she just sat silently and listened.

"Do you want to get out of here?" Remy asked.

"I…sure. Where do you want to go? There's no way either one of us can drive, though."

"Are you staying with your parents?"

"No, my aunt lent me her house while she's out of town."

"Can we go there? Andy and I live together, and I really would rather not have to deal with seeing anyone right now."

This night was getting crazier and crazier. Ten hours ago, Julia was at work in Portland and now she was in Elder's Bay about to have sex with the person who had starred in many of her teenage masturbatory fantasies growing up. Life was wild sometimes, but she wasn't going to be the one to question it.

"I'll call us an Uber and text Andy where I'll be, so she doesn't worry. Andy can drop us off tomorrow to pick up our vehicles. Remy opened her door and slid out of the seat. "Julia, are you sober enough to consent?"

The question took Julia off guard. Not that she'd ever thought Remy wouldn't be anything other than a gentleman, or whatever, but it was so unexpected that she gave it due diligence before answering. She was definitely tipsy and a little stoned, but she knew exactly what Remy was asking and she was very willing to be a part of whatever she had in mind.

"Thank you for asking. Let's go to my house."

"You—"

"Yes, sorry, I consent."

Remy smiled bigger than Julia had ever seen her smile and it reminded her just how adorable Remy was.

Julia pulled Remy's coat tightly around herself to stave off the cold air while Remy texted Andy and ordered them an Uber. The idea of Uber being in tiny little Elder's Bay made Julia laugh for some reason. Maybe her hometown wasn't as backward as she'd thought.

"Ready?" Remy asked as she pocketed her phone and reached for Julia's hand.

"As ready as I'll ever be," Julia said. This might be a huge mistake, but she'd deal with the consequences later if it was. In that moment she knew she owed it to her younger self to seize the moment. What a wild night.

CHAPTER FIVE

Remy waved as the Uber driver pulled away. Of course, they'd both gone to school with him, and he had to comment several times on the drive to Julia's aunt's house how crazy it was that Remy Miller and Julia Clayman were in his Uber together. This was probably a huge mistake, but it was too late to back out now.

The lock on the door gave Julia trouble, so Remy offered to try it. Julia stepped back and waved toward the keys that were still dangling from the lock.

"Be my guest," Julia said. "I hate this lock. I don't know why my aunt doesn't just get it replaced."

Remy jiggled the key in and found the sweet spot to turn it. "If you remind me, I'll bring by some graphite lubricant that should fix it right up."

"Okay. Thanks."

Offering to fix doors for near strangers wasn't something Remy normally did. The entire night had been one confusing thing after another, and she still didn't even know what to think of Julia's offer to run a boat for Clayman Fisheries. Her ambition and desire to captain a boat told her to jump at the opportunity, but she still wasn't sure she could trust this offer didn't include strings.

Then there was the fact that she was about to have sex with Julia Clayman. What the actual hell? Not that she was complaining. There wasn't a guy or lesbian at Elder's Bay high school who wouldn't have jumped at the chance to spend a little alone time with Julia Clayman when they were young.

Once the lock gave way, Remy opened the door and waved Julia ahead to enter first. She followed her into the house and dropped the keys on a small table just inside the doorway.

Gray slate tile placed in a herringbone pattern crossed the floor covered by an oriental rug that probably cost more than all of Remy's furniture combined. The dark tone of the tile warmed the light gray walls of the entryway and felt fancier than any of the homes Remy's family owned. It all reminded her that the Claymans were much wealthier than the Millers and made her a little uneasy, like someone would realize she was there and tell her to go back to her side of the tracks.

"Can I get you something to drink?" Julia asked as she slipped off her black pumps and pushed them under the hall table with her foot. Remy toed her boots off and pushed them under the table next to Julia's.

"Sure." Remy followed her through an archway into the kitchen. Granite counters stretched across a gigantic room lined with beautiful cherry wood cabinets. Julia led her to a chair at the island in the middle of the room where Remy sat and waited with her hands folded over the surface. "This is a great house."

Julia peeked around the refrigerator door at Remy and then let her eyes take in the room as if she hadn't noticed it before.

"It is. My aunt completely gutted it and had it redone when my uncle left her for his new wife." Julia pulled a pitcher from the door and held it up.

"Iced tea? I thought we should probably stay away from any more alcohol if we don't want to feel like complete shit tomorrow morning."

"That works for me." Remy watched Julia pull two glasses from the cabinet and pour them each a drink.

"Let's sit by the fire in the den." Julia picked up their glasses and pointed toward another archway.

A giant rug sat at the foot of a stone fireplace that looked like it came out of a lodge from the 1930s. It was the most beautiful room

Remy had ever seen, and she was a little afraid to sit on the plush couches placed in a semicircle facing the fire.

"Let me start the fire and we can talk," Julia said.

Remy set her glass on a coaster that sat on a solid wood coffee table and wiped her hands on the front of her pants before carefully sitting on the edge of the couch. Holy fuck, they were the most comfortable couches she'd ever seen. They were obviously leather, but it had to be the softest leather in existence.

"This couch is amazing."

"It's buffalo," Julia said as she stacked wood in the fireplace and lit a starter with a long match.

"You're kidding me. Buffalo?"

"Yep." Julia closed the metal curtains to keep any rogue sparks from escaping and catching the rug on fire. She turned and smiled at Remy before sitting next to her on the couch.

"You okay?" Julia asked.

That seemed like a trick question. Remy wasn't sure how she felt or if she was indeed okay. She knew she didn't want to have to explain her feelings if she said she wasn't, so she mustered more confidence than she actually felt. "Absolutely. You okay?"

"I'm good."

Julia's small hand rested on Remy's knee, and she realized she'd been nervously bouncing it up and down. Remy took a deep breath and sat back on the cushion. That joint from her truck would be nice right about then. She couldn't ever remember being this nervous before, and it freaked her out just a little. She wasn't sure if it was the house, Julia, or that she was in a home belonging to a Clayman, with an actual Clayman.

"Do you want to talk about this situation with your dad?" Julia asked.

Remy almost laughed. Her dad was the last thing she wanted to talk about. He'd done enough to mess up her day and she didn't want to give him any more power over her that night.

"Do you want to talk about your dad?" Remy asked.

"Nope, not really." Julia winked at Remy, and it was by far the sexiest wink she'd ever seen. Everything about Julia was probably the sexiest thing she'd ever seen.

Remy sat back against the cushions and pressed the heels of her hands against her eyes, hoping that when she opened them again, this night would make more sense.

"Is your offer to let us run your boat for real?" Remy asked.

"It's for real. I need a captain and crew to show up Monday morning ready to sail."

The only sound was the crackling of the fire as Remy ran through every reason she should and shouldn't agree to this cockamamie offer. In the end, she decided she had nothing to lose. She'd rather not have to start over in the Alaskan fisheries, and if this was legit, and she and the crew could get their own boat, she'd show her dad he was a fool for not giving her a chance.

"I'll talk to the crew in the morning."

"I know we're not exactly the family you thought you'd be working for, but we need you and I think you need us right now, too."

"Tell me now if this isn't for real. I'm serious, Julia. Be straight with me because I've had a shit day and if you're just fucking with me, I'm going to burst into tears."

Julia smiled and squeezed Remy's hand. "I'm not fucking with you. This is a legitimate offer to captain one of our boats. If you and the crew come to my office tomorrow, I can show you the contract and we can negotiate the terms of your employment. Do you think Andy and Corey will have a problem working for the Claymans?"

"They'll go wherever I go. They're my crew and we stick together. Besides, it sounds like Corey's going to be sleeping on the couch if we don't take this job."

"It must be nice to have such confidence in your friends."

"You don't?"

The cushions surrounded her as Julia sunk back into the sofa. "Sure. My best friend, Dylan, would drop everything for me, but I think nothing compares to you guys. I can't remember a time when the three of you weren't together when we were growing up."

"You could have hung out with us, too, you know?"

"Really?" Julia laughed. "You think our parents would have accepted that we were friends?"

"I don't care what my parents think about who I date," Remy said.

"Oh, now we're talking about dating. How did we go from friend group to dating so quickly?" Julia pulled Remy's hand into her lap and traced her nail along the creases in her palm. "You wouldn't have given me the time of day."

"You're joking, right?" Julia Clayman had always been on Remy's radar, but she'd known between being a Miller and not achieving the social status that Julia had, she never had a chance. "I would have given you all my days if you'd only asked."

"Really?" Julia turned toward Remy and pressed her hand against Remy's cheek. Their lips were only a breath apart and Remy ached to kiss her. "I wish I'd known."

"Why? You're a Clayman and I'm a Miller. Nothing could ever work between us, especially back then. There's too much baggage between our families."

"I wish you'd been my first," Julia said.

"First what? Andy was your first date with a girl and as far as I know, you didn't date anyone other than football players other than her."

"You know about my date with Andy?"

"She's my best friend. We don't keep anything from each other."

Julia rubbed her thumb across Remy's cheek. "I guess not. I'm glad she told you."

"Why?" Remy asked.

"Because I don't want any secrets between us, either."

Remy leaned forward and gently kissed Julia on the lips. "We aren't friends, Julia Clayman."

Julia closed her eyes and moaned as the kiss deepened. "What if I want us to be friends?" she asked.

"I have all the friends I need." The buzz from the beer and the pot earlier had mostly gone, but the hormones coursing through Remy's body made her feel like she was high.

"That's a shame because I'm a really good friend." Julia climbed onto Remy and straddled her lap. The black lacy dress she was wearing had to be pushed up her thighs to allow her legs to spread wide enough to fit around Remy's body.

Remy slid her hands up the top of Julia's thighs and slipped into her panties to cup her perfect ass. Julia rocked her body forward, pressing her center against Remy's body, her wetness streaking across Remy's shirt.

"Take this off. I want to feel your skin against my pussy." Julia grabbed the hem of Remy's shirt and pulled it over her head to be tossed onto the floor. The warmth from the fire kept the temperature pleasantly perfect in the room.

"Where did you get these panties?" Remy asked as she ran a finger along the edge of their black lace.

"I think I got these at Nordstrom. Why do you ask? I would have pegged you as more of a boxer person." Julia gasped when Remy gripped the thin lacy garment and ripped it from her body."

"I wanted to know where to buy you a replacement pair," Remy said.

Remy's stomach and pants were covered in Julia's wetness as she reached between her legs and slipped two fingers into her pussy.

"Fuck me, you feel so good." Remy looked up into Julia's hooded eyes and smiled at how unexpected this night had become.

Julia's movements became more frantic, and Remy knew she was getting close to coming much faster than she had wanted, so she slipped her fingers out and used their wetness to focus on her clit.

"Oh, God. Remy. Fuck. You feel so fucking good." Julia's words drove Remy to push back into her core. She wanted to be surrounded by this woman who she had always thought was out of her reach.

"Are you ready to come, Julia?" Remy knew she was close and if she pushed just a little bit deeper Julia would fall over the edge.

"Yes. No. I don't know if I'll ever be ready for this to end, but yes. I want to come, so it will have to end at some point."

Remy smiled at her response. "You're mumbling, Julia."

"I can't—oh fuck—I can't help it. Don't stop."

"Hold onto me." Remy was afraid Julia might topple off her lap if she fucked her any harder. She wrapped one hand around Julia's narrow waist and reached inside of her until Remy found the exact spot that made her lose all control.

Remy held on tight as Julia's orgasm shook her entire body. It lasted far longer than most other women Remy had been with before Julia finally collapsed into her arms. She couldn't really believe that any of this had actually happened. Part of her thought there was at least a chance she'd wake up alone in her bed and it would have all just been a fantasy.

"Are you…" Remy held onto Julia as she gasped for breath and clung to Remy's shoulders like she was the only thing keeping her from tumbling to the ground.

"I'm fine. Just…trying to catch my breath. You wrecked me. Let's move this to my room."

"We don't have to—"

Julia slid from Remy's lap and held out a hand to help her to her feet. "Remy, if you say we don't need to do anything else, I'll smack you."

It wasn't that Remy didn't want to do all the things with Julia, but a sudden feeling that they were only making a difficult situation even more complicated came over her.

"Should we be doing this if you're technically going to be my boss?"

"Will you unzip me?" Julia stopped next to her bed and waited, pointing at the zipper on the back of her dress.

Remy helped her remove the rest of her clothes and gasped when the most beautiful breasts she'd ever seen were revealed. "I—Jesus."

"How about we agree that I'm your boss Monday morning, but not tonight? Well, I could be tonight, too, if that's what you want."

Remy admired Julia's perfect ass as she climbed onto the bed. "That so?"

"Does it bother you when the girl you're with takes charge?"

Remy flipped Julia over onto her back.

"Control isn't something I like to relinquish, especially in bed, but I guess we could negotiate those terms, too. I think you'll find I'm a…team player."

"Is that a captain thing? Needing to be in control all the time?"

"I think it's more of a confidence thing." Remy knelt between Julia's legs and leaned forward to pull a puckered nipple into her mouth to give it a slow suck. "I know how to make a woman feel good."

"Oh, fuck." Julia's back arched as she pushed her breasts forward into Remy's eager mouth. "Just like that."

Remy released the nipple and kissed her way across Julia's smooth chest to pull the other nipple into her mouth. She gently caressed the side of her breast with one hand as she reached up to dip two fingers into Julia's warm mouth with the other. The gentle sucking motion as Julia worked her fingers like they were a cock almost sent Remy over the edge before she even got her pants off.

"I want to taste you," Remy said as she ground her hips forward against Julia's pussy.

"I'm clean. I tested after my last girlfriend and haven't been with anyone since."

"Me, too. I get tested regularly and am clean as a whistle."

"Then what are you waiting for?" Julia's question sounded breathless and was almost a plea.

Remy chuckled. "Yes, ma'am."

Julia's perfect body was splayed out in front of her for the taking and Remy had to send up a silent thank you to the universe for making this happen. "Jesus Christ, you're beautiful, Julia."

"Thank you," Julia said. "You're smokin' hot yourself, stud."

Remy looked around and found a small pillow that had been tossed from the bed onto the floor. She picked it up and slipped it under Julia's ass, elevating her hips just enough to open her up. "I need to be honest with you about something before we go any further."

"What's that?" Julia reached down to slip a finger into her folds and circle her clit. "Are you sure you want to do confessions right now?"

"No, but I feel like I should."

"Okay." Julia dipped the finger into her opening and made a noise that Remy was sure would wreck her with want. "What do you need to tell me?"

"I used to fantasize about making out with you behind the bleachers after a football game."

"Did you even go to football games? I don't remember ever seeing you at one."

"No. But I would have if I thought you would have made out with me."

"Well, maybe you should have asked me, Ms. Confidence. I'm pretty sure you would have gotten lucky."

"Seriously? Fuck me, why was I such an idiot?"

"The question is, why are you such an idiot right now?"

"Oh, yeah, sorry."

Julia laughed and directed Remy's head between her legs. "Let's focus more on the things we can do now, and less on the lost opportunities of our past."

Remy was just fine with that idea.

The next morning, light from a large window stirred Remy awake. She rubbed the sleep from her eyes and looked around the room. Julia's still naked body pressed tightly against her own and visions of the things they did to each other the night before flashed through Remy's mind. Christ. Julia was amazing. Far too amazing for the likes of Remy and the smartest thing she could do would be sneak out before Julia had a chance to wake up and find her still there.

That would be the smart thing to do, but Julia's warm soft body fit perfectly against her own and Remy wasn't ready to leave her just yet. What the hell was she doing? Remy sighed and rubbed her hands over her face.

"Good morning." Julia's sleepy voice pulled Remy from her thoughts.

Julia turned to face her and Remy thought once again how breathtakingly beautiful she was.

"Good morning to you. How did you sleep?" Remy pulled her arm from where it rested over Julia's body and left a little space between them.

Julia stretched and scooted back into Remy's arms. "Better than I have in a very long time. How about you?"

Remy gently kissed Julia's neck, just below her ear. "I slept well." They had to stop this before things got even more out of hand. "Julia—"

"Shhh. Please let me have this perfect moment with you before you bring the real world into it. Do you mind?"

"Um, I guess not." Remy rested her head on the pillow and pulled Julia tight against her body. Soon, they'd both fallen back asleep.

"What the hell is that?" Julia asked when the guitar solo from the Van Halen's song, *Eruption* blared from Remy's pants on the floor.

"Sorry." Remy hoped out of bed and fished the phone from her pocket. "It's Andy."

She swiped to accept the call and silently mouthed sorry to Julia once more. "Hey, dude, what's up?"

"I'm just making sure the Clayman girl didn't drop your lifeless body somewhere off the coast."

Remy chuckled and reached down to retrieve her jeans. "No, I'm still alive. Would you mind picking me up? We need to talk."

"Sure. Where?" Andy asked.

She heard the slam of a car door and the rumble of an engine from the other end of the line.

"I'm still at Julia's." Remy slid into her jeans and tucked both her socks and her underwear in her pockets. Julia startled her when she wrapped her arms around her from behind, caressing her abdomen with her soft fingers.

"Interesting. I'll be there in a couple of minutes. I want all the details. You're playing with the devil, but she's smoking hot. I'll give you that."

Remy cleared her throat and hoped Julia hadn't heard the other side of the conversation. "I'll see you in a minute." She ended the call and slipped her phone into her back pocket.

"Do you know where my shirt is?"

"I guess this means going out for brunch isn't a possibility?"

Remy followed Julia into the living room, where her shirt and bra still sat on the couch from the night before.

"No. I need to talk to my crew and make sure they're cool with this new plan."

"Okay. When can I see you again?"

"Um, I'm not sure." The reality of the entire situation came into focus, and Remy felt a little lost on what to say. Did she want to see Julia again? Of course. Was it the best idea? That was something she needed to figure out.

"Okay, here." Julia dug through her purse and pulled out a business card. She wrote something on the back and handed it to Remy.

"My office number in Portland is on the front if you ever need anything. While I'm in town, please call my personal cell. That number's on the back. If you want to have dinner or something, you know how to reach me."

A car horn honked from in front of the house, interrupting the awkward moment.

"That's Andy," Remy said.

"I assumed," Julia said. "Did you forget anything?"

Remy looked around the room, then checked her pockets to make sure her wallet and phone were there. "No. I think I got everything."

"Very well. I guess I'll see you in the office. Are you guys coming by later today to sign the contract?"

The horn honked again. Remy looked toward the door, then back at Julia, and nodded.

"Probably. Yeah. I'll text you."

Another honk from Andy and Remy was ready to smack her upside the head. "Jesus Christ, Andy." She turned to Julia and wasn't exactly sure how to walk away. She had an urge to kiss her one last time, but wasn't sure if it was appropriate, and giving her a hug seemed like a real dick move. "Julia, I—"

Julia reached up on her tiptoes and pulled Remy down for a kiss. What began as a gentle brush of lips soon became more passionate. For a moment, Remy forgot she was supposed to be leaving until Andy honked the horn once again, this time with a sustained sound that showed she was losing her patience.

"I better—"

"Yeah. I'll talk to you later," Julia said.

Remy picked up her boots from under the bench and looked back at Julia. She'd pulled on flowered pajama pants and a thick knit sweater. Soft brown curls hung in unruly locks around her face, and Remy had to force herself to turn away. Since when did leaving a girl after a night of sex become such an impossible task? This was so not good.

"Bye, Julia." Remy walked away while she still had the strength to do so. When she climbed into the truck, Andy stared at her silently before backing out of the driveway and heading toward the house they shared.

Remy called Corey on the way home and asked him to meet them at the house so they could talk. By the time they reached their porch, Corey pulled up in his girlfriend's car.

"What's going on?" Corey asked as he jogged to catch up with them as they entered the house.

"Let's get a beer and head out to the deck so we can talk," Remy said.

"It's nine in the morning, Remy," Andy said.

Remy pulled three beers from the fridge and held one up to each of them. "We're going to need beer to get us through this conversation."

They sat in the lawn chairs Remy and Andy kept on the deck. There was still a bit of a chill in the air, but nothing the three of them weren't used to.

"What's going on?" Andy asked. "You seem a little shaken. Did something happen with Julia?"

"She didn't take advantage of you, did she?" Corey seemed ready to go to war for her and she appreciated his misguided loyalty.

"No. Nothing like that. I wanted to talk to you guys about the job she offered us." Remy sipped her beer and waited for their chatter to die down.

"She wants us to start Monday."

"My dad would kick my ass if he even knew we'd talked about this, let alone the freak out your dad will have."

Remy looked at Andy, who just shrugged. "I'm here for you, Remy. I don't give a shit what anyone else thinks."

"Brooke made it pretty clear how she felt about the whole situation last night. Are you more afraid of what our family will think or losing your girlfriend?"

Corey sipped his beer then focused on pulling the label from the bottle. "I'd do anything to make Brooke happy. Even disappoint my dad."

"I don't see any other options unless we're willing to keep working for my dad and give up any dreams we've ever had of running our own boat. I can't do it anymore. I won't do it anymore, not when we're given an opportunity to run this boat for Clayman Fisheries. Once we prove to my dad what we're capable of, he'll either reconsider and give us a chance, or he'll at least learn to regret not believing in us."

"I hear you." Corey covered his face with his hands and groaned. "I know you're right. It's just this could mean—"

"I know what it means, cousin. I've thought about it for hours and I can't imagine doing it, but I also can't imagine walking away from an opportunity like this."

"How do we know this isn't some joke?" Andy asked.

"I know I shouldn't, but I believe she's sincere."

"Is this your brain talking or something else?"

Corey sat forward in his chair and stared at Remy. "What's she talking about? You didn't…please tell me you didn't—"

"This has nothing to do with that." Remy knew the fact that she'd slept with Julia wouldn't sit well with Corey.

"What the fuck, Remy? You're fucking kidding me. You let a Clayman fuck you into submission. She must have been one hell of a lay." Corey was angry and Remy knew lashing out at him wouldn't help the situation, but she was on the verge of putting him in his place. Giving her shit about this was one thing, but saying something about Julia was more than Remy could abide.

"Corey, I'm going to say this only once. Julia is off limits. I love you like a brother, but I will beat the ever-loving shit out of you if you even utter her name in a funny way." She hadn't yelled, but she knew she'd made her point when he sat back in his chair and sipped his beer. "What'll it be, guys? Are we going to run our own boat and make our own fortunes, or are we going to be our family's bitches for the rest of our lives?"

"I'm in," Andy said. It wasn't her family, so she didn't have the same stakes as Corey, but Remy appreciated her loyalty all the same.

"Corey?" When he shook his head and looked up to the sky in defeat, she knew she had him.

"What the hell, let's do it. They'll forgive me when I eventually give them grandchildren."

"You guys aren't—?" Both Remy and Andy almost fell out of their chairs in shock.

"No, no, no. I'm just saying. At some point, that's going to happen, and my dad can't stay mad at me when my mom tells him to stop because she wants time with her grandbabies."

"Okay. Weird, but whatever. To our futures," Remy said as she held up her beer.

The others tapped it with their own and in unison repeated, "To our futures."

CHAPTER SIX

The coffee pot beeped, alerting Julia that it was ready. She'd never been much of a coffee drinker, but mornings after late nights became harder and harder the older she got. Not that twenty-seven was old in the grand scheme of things, but it was old enough that she didn't spring back quite as quickly as she had in her early twenties.

She sorted through her aunt's mugs until she found a travel one with a lid so she could take it with her on the drive to the hospital. Visiting hours would start in half an hour and she wanted to be there to see her dad as soon as they'd let her in. Seeing her big, strong dad so weak and vulnerable was difficult, but she knew he'd worry about the business if she didn't at least update him now and again.

The parking lot was full by the time she arrived, but she found a spot that was vacated by a nurse leaving from her shift. Julia admired people who dedicated their lives to the care of others. She wasn't sure she'd be capable of such a sacrifice. Everyone wanted to believe they would step up if someone they loved needed them, and she would, but it would be difficult to maintain the level of selflessness they possessed for complete strangers day in and day out.

"Hey, sweetie." Julia's mother sat up in her chair when she entered the room.

"Relax, Mom. There's no need for you to get up."

"If you don't mind, I think I'll go to the cafeteria and get a bite to eat while you stay with your dad."

"Yeah, of course. Take your time."

Her mom slowly stood and Julia realized just how old they'd actually gotten. When you were around someone on a fairly regular basis, you didn't always notice the changes they were experiencing, but she could see it now.

"Is that my baby girl?" Her dad still sounded weak, but she was happy to hear he was at least awake and coherent. That had to be a promising sign.

"It's me, Dad," Julia said as she stood next to his bed and held his hand.

"I'm going to get some food, Brian. I'll be back," her mom said.

He nodded and she left Julia alone with her dad. He'd regained some of the color in his face, but he was still pale. Years at sea had left him with golden brown skin, but now he looked washed out and haggard. Julia stared at where their hands intertwined. Her dad always had big, powerful hands. When she was a girl, he'd convinced her he descended from giants and she'd believed every word he said.

"Mom said they're going to keep you a few days longer to monitor you." Julia pulled a chair from the corner of the room to sit next to him so they could continue holding hands.

"That doctor's a worrywart. I told him I was fine and could go home right now, but he refused. You know they charge you by the day to stay here?"

Julia knew the conversation would come around to money at some point. "I know, Dad, but you have insurance that's going to handle most of that."

"That's exactly why he wants to keep me here. They milk every dollar from the insurance companies they can. Do you think it's them that gets shafted?"

"I'm guessing your answer will be no." This wasn't the first time Julia had heard her dad complain about insurance companies.

"You're darn right. It's you and me that pay the actual price when our premiums go up. It's all a scam to milk more money out of hard-working people."

This insurance conversation would go round and round unless Julia changed the subject.

"I saw Charlie."

Her dad grumbled and pulled the sheets up to his chest.

"Did he come by to see you yesterday?"

"That boy. He lets that woman run roughshod over him. I'm all for women's lib and you know I consider myself a feminist, but he lets her play him like a marionette. I can't stand to see it. He had responsibilities to this family, and she tells him to leave and he can't get there fast enough."

Every time her dad told her he considered himself to be a feminist, she had to hold back the laughter. He wasn't terrible. She'd definitely met much more misogynistic men in her life, but he was still an old white man with old white man views of the world. She didn't bother arguing with him about that stuff unless she knew he was going to make a fool of himself or embarrass her.

"I think I found someone to run the boat now that Charlie's gone, and she has a crew already so I won't need to hunt for additional people."

"She?"

"Yep. We're lucky she agreed to do it."

"Who is it? Janet Baker runs the *Lucky Strike*, but she owns her boat. I can't imagine she'd leave that to someone else to come run a boat for us."

"No. It's not Janet."

"I don't know any other women around here running a boat. You better not give my boat to someone you found on a random internet site. That just won't do."

Julia was hesitant to tell her dad who she'd found because she knew exactly what his reaction was going to be. She wished she could have just kept it all to herself and let him know once Remy had been able to fish for a few weeks and establish numbers that would be difficult for her dad to dispute. He wouldn't wait that long to know who she'd found, though.

"She's local. Don't worry. I wouldn't let a random person take over one of your boats."

"Local? Now I'm really confused. There aren't any local women except Janet. Who the hell is it?"

"Remy Miller."

"Remy Miller?"

Julia could see the gears turning in his mind while he tried to picture who she was talking about. He probably knew who Remy was, but she wouldn't be on his radar at all.

"Frank Miller's youngest kid," Julia said. As soon as Frank's name came out of her mouth, her dad sat up straight in bed and turned a deep shade of red.

"Julia Elizabeth Clayman, please tell me you didn't hire a God damn Miller to run one of my boats. That kid can't be more than twenty years old."

"She's my age, Dad. We went to school together."

Her mom walked in at that moment with a cup of coffee in one hand and a magazine in the other.

"What's going on in here?" her mom asked.

"Your daughter thought it would be cute to hire a Miller to run my boat." Her dad was mad. She knew he'd be upset but he'd had his chance to find someone and now that it was down to the wire, Julia didn't have the luxury of hiring someone her dad would approve of. He may not have been happy about it, but there wasn't much he could say.

"Remy's a great sailor, dad. She's been working on her dad's boats her entire life and her crew is her cousin and her best friend. They're reliable, smart, and willing to sign on with us at the last minute. The contract is as good as signed so don't upset yourself about it at this point. If they don't work out, I take full responsibility."

"Really?" Her dad got an evil glint in his eye and Julia was afraid to know what he was thinking.

"Really," she said.

Her dad coughed and her mom stood to pat him on the back. She looked at the monitors nervously and gave Julia a look that told her it was time to go.

"I'm going to trust you on this, kiddo, but this girl better be as good as you say."

"She is." God Julia hoped Remy was as good as she was building her up to be. Her dad would never let her live it down. She had to be good, right?

Having Remy come to work for the Claymans could actually be a positive move toward putting the stupid feud between their families to bed. The memory of that particular Miller in Julia's bed that morning came to her mind, and she felt the heat of a blush warm her cheeks.

"Are you feeling okay, sweetheart?" her dad asked.

"Yes. Yeah. Sorry. I'm fine. It's just a little warm in here."

"They always keep it too warm or too cold in these hospitals, depending on whether they want you to stay or go."

Julia rolled her eyes and glanced at the time on her phone. She noticed a text from Remy saying they were ready to meet her to sign the contract. A wave of relief settled over her.

"I have to go, Dad." Julia picked up her jacket from the chair she'd draped it over and kissed him on the forehead. "Mom will take good care of you."

"I'm not a child, Julia. I can take care of myself."

Her mom rolled her eyes at her dad's comment. "I wouldn't be so sure about that, Brian Clayman. You better stop being so cantankerous or your daughter's going to pack her things and go back to Portland."

"Love you both." Julia kissed her mom on the cheek and walked out of the room while she could.

Once she was alone in the hall, Julia sent Remy a reply to her text asking if she and her crew would be interested in signing the contract over a late lunch at her place. She wasn't in the mood to go into the office and doing it at her house would give her an opportunity to get to know them a little better. She didn't have many friends left in Elder's Bay and wouldn't mind spending time with them off the clock. Especially Remy although that probably wasn't something they should make a habit of. No matter how satisfying that sounded.

Two hours later, Remy and her crew arrived at her door and Julia got them settled on the back deck with cold beers and a tray of cheese and crackers to hold them off until lunch was ready. The smell of tomato sauce filled the air as Julia dropped pasta into a pot of boiling water. A gentle kiss on her neck startled her as she fell back into Remy's muscular arms.

"Sorry," Remy said. "I know I shouldn't have done that. This whole domestic scene I walked in on was just unexpectedly hot."

Julia turned in Remy's arms and kissed her lips. "You like this, do you?"

Remy nodded and nibbled on Julia's skin below her ear. "Mm-hm. I didn't know I had a fetish for beautiful women in aprons."

"I'll have to invite you over more often. Play your cards right, and next time I'll wear the apron and nothing else."

A groan rumbled in Remy's chest and she rested her forehead on Julia's. "We shouldn't be doing this. My brain is telling me we're steering this boat way too close to the rocks, but I haven't stopped thinking about you all damn day. It turns out you're like a drug, Julia Clayman. A drug I shouldn't want if I know what's good for me, but one I'm finding hard to resist."

Julia glanced at her timer and stirred the pasta in the pot. "I agree. Although, letting this play out to see where it goes is awfully tempting."

The sound of the sliding glass door opening and closing pulled them from the moment. Remy stepped back to lean against the opposite counter as Julia turned off the burner and poured the pasta into a colander she had waiting in the sink.

"Mind if I grab a couple more beers?" Corey asked when he walked into the kitchen.

Remy glanced at Julia and cleared her throat. "I think we're almost ready to eat. Right, Julia?"

"Yep. I'm just going to toss the salad once more, put everything on platters, and we'll be ready." The cabinet creaked as Julia opened it to pull out a stack of plates. "Would you mind grabbing utensils from the drawer and taking both them and these plates out to the table on the deck? Remy and I will be right behind you with the food and more beer. Unless you want wine? I'm going to have wine with dinner if you want some."

"Um. No. Thank you, Julia. I think we'll just have beer."

"I'll have wine," Remy said.

"You will?" Corey looked at Remy like she'd suddenly grown a horn from her forehead. "I've never seen you drink wine once."

Remy picked up the bowl of meatballs with pasta sauce and the plate of bread. "Let's go, wise guy. I have a life when you aren't around."

Julia smiled at their banter and followed them out the door with the rest of the meal. Once they were all settled on the deck, they passed around the bowls and silently started eating their meal. She wasn't sure exactly what to say to them but felt rude about not starting a conversation.

"Remind me how long you guys have known each other? I don't remember a time when you weren't together." Julia knew them in school and they'd talked here and there, but to say they hung out in different crowds would be an understatement.

Remy wiped her mouth with the cloth napkin and took a sip of her wine before answering. "You know Corey's my cousin, so I've known him my whole life."

"Remy and I have been best friends since kindergarten. She stuck up for me when some older boys were teasing me about being so much taller than the other kids. Tiny little Remy shoved a kid three times her size down in front of his entire second grade class. He punched her back, and they both ended up in the principal's office. She's been looking out for me ever since."

Julia poured more wine for both herself and Remy, then sat back in her chair. "I totally remember that. I think it was my cousin Teddy, wasn't it?"

"Yep," Remy said. "He's never been a big fan of mine."

"He's an asshole. He's my uncle Ted's only son, and he's trained him to be just as much of an asshole as he is. My parents gave me a bike for Christmas when I was ten and Teddy used to let the air out of my tires, so I had to keep a pump with me and air them back up every day before I could ride it home. I can't stand him. I guess the one good thing he's ever done is facilitate you guys becoming friends."

"Hear, hear! To Teddy Dipshit Clayman," Remy said as they all tapped their glasses together.

"What ever happened to Teddy? I haven't seen him around in a few years," Corey said as he added another meatball to his plate. "This food is freaking amazing, by the way."

"Thanks." Julia wiped her mouth and dropped the napkin on her plate. "He lives in California with his wife and four kids. Personally, I think his dad may have pulled a few strings to get him in, but he graduated from UCLA and is now a chiropractor. The family wasn't super happy that he didn't go into the family business, but nobody complained too much since everyone thinks he's an asshole."

"Good riddance," Andy said. "Speaking of the family business, we should probably talk about the job. I know Corey's going to need to get home to his girlfriend before long."

"Sure," Julia agreed. "Let's leave this here and sit by the fireplace. It's more comfortable over there and I'm getting a little cold." They all picked up their drinks and moved to the sitting area her aunt had set up near a beautiful stone fireplace.

An hour later, they'd worked out the details of the contract and signed on for the next two seasons. It took all of Julia's negotiating skills to add that second season, but the last thing she wanted to do was go back to Portland and her dad get rid of them just because they were Millers. Hopefully the guaranteed two seasons would allow them to establish a good enough recommendation that they'd either stay or get hired on with someone else.

"Thanks for indulging me in letting me cook for you guys. I'm going to miss my weekly dinners with my Portland friends while I'm here, so this helped. It was also nice to get to know you better."

Corey and Andy both gave Julia a hug and thanked her for the incredible meal and the opportunity to be in charge of their own boat. Julia made to-go packages for each of them and walked them to the door.

"Hey, can you guys give me just a minute?" Remy asked.

Corey checked the time on his watch and shook his head. "I really have to get back to Brooke, Rem. It's date night and I still have to iron my shirt."

"You own an iron? I didn't think you knew what an iron was, let alone how to use one." Andy seemed sincerely shocked by his disclosure.

"Well, technically, it's Brooke's iron, but I know how to use it, wise ass."

Remy turned them both toward the door and gave them a gentle push. "I'll be right there. I just need to talk to Julia for a couple of minutes. If I take too long, you can leave me and I'll walk home."

"Let's just leave her," Andy said.

"For sure," Corey answered.

"You better give me a few minutes, assholes. Don't just leave me for the fun of it. It's freaking cold out there and walking home would suck."

"I could always take you home." It wasn't exactly a completely innocent offer since she'd hoped for some time alone with Remy to do more than just talk for a few minutes, but Julia knew as soon as she looked at Remy's face what her answer would be. "Or not."

"Thanks for the offer, but I really need to get home, too. I just wanted to ask you a couple questions and these dorks dragging this out is only prolonging things." Remy glared at her friends until they turned, held up their hands in surrender, and left them alone.

Remy pushed the door closed, then leaned against it, shutting out the rest of the world. The confined space of the entryway left very little room for them to move, and Julia wasn't sure if Remy wanted time to blow her off or get one last kiss in private before she left, so she just stood there.

The pained expression on her face told Julia that now that they were alone, Remy wasn't sure what she wanted to do either. Bands of muscle rippled in her forearms as she visibly struggled to hold herself back from reaching out.

When Julia couldn't take it any longer, she stepped forward and cupped the sides of Remy's face. "What do you need? Just tell me what you want."

Without hesitation, Remy turned to press Julia against the door and kissed her. She knew what they really needed to do was talk about what was happening between them, but that discussion would have to wait. Right then, Julia allowed herself to revel in the feel of Remy's body against her own. Far sooner than she was ready to stop, Remy stepped back and out of Julia's reach.

"You're going to be the death of me, Miller," Julia said when they stopped to catch their breath.

Remy rubbed her face with her hands and released a groan that sounded like both agony and frustration. "We can't keep doing this. My family's already going to be furious about us working for the Claymans, they may disown me if they find out what I want to do to Brian Clayman's daughter."

The muffled sound of a car horn reminded them that the others were still waiting for Remy in the truck.

"I need to go," Remy said.

Julia stepped forward and tugged on the front of Remy's jacket. "I know. I don't want you to go, though."

"This is nuts."

"What's nuts?"

"The way you make me feel," Remy said. "You show up out of nowhere after years of being gone and suddenly I'm acting like a teenager again. Ugh. This is so embarrassing."

"Don't be embarrassed. You're not the only one who feels a little like they're losing their mind. I'm going to miss you tonight when I'm all alone in that big bed."

The sound of another honk followed by Andy and Corey yelling for Remy to hurry up made them both laugh.

"I'm going to murder them." Remy leaned down and placed a gentle kiss on Julia's lips. "Call me later. I'll read you a good night story."

"Go now before I drag you back to my bedroom."

Remy hesitated long enough to let Julia know the thought of staying had crossed her mind. She watched as Remy ran to the truck and jumped inside to the sound of Andy and Corey giving her shit for taking so long. Julia folded her arms across her chest and watched them drive away, realizing that she missed Remy already.

CHAPTER SEVEN

Puddles formed in the road as Remy drove through the pouring rain, already ten minutes late to her family's regular weekly get-together. She wasn't looking forward to the conversation she needed to have with her dad, and being late to dinner would already put things on a bad footing.

They hadn't spoken since the day her dad blew all her hopes and dreams out of the water and Remy wasn't sure she was mentally prepared to speak to them now. No matter how much the conversation was going to suck, she knew it was better that he learned the news from her instead of finding out when everyone was preparing to go out Monday morning.

She'd spent the entire day working through how she would explain to her dad and the rest of the family why working for the Claymans was something she needed to do. Her dad had left her no choice, and if his pride and the stupid feud weren't involved, he would see that. He'd had his chance to hire her as a captain and he'd missed the boat, so to speak. It wasn't Remy's fault he didn't see what a great captain she knew she would become. Julia had made her an offer she couldn't ignore. It was her dad's loss. Maybe if she kept telling herself that, it would make things easier.

Andy and Corey stepped from Andy's truck when she pulled in behind them. They both looked as scared as Remy felt and she almost suggested they leave and just send her dad an email explaining what happened. It might be safer for all of them that way.

"We have to face him, Remy." Andy knew her far too well.

"I know. I know we do. Are you guys ready? It won't be pretty."

Corey adjusted the hat on his head and blew out an exaggerated breath. "You could have at least been on time, so we wouldn't have pissed off Aunt Carolyn, too. She's going to murder us before your dad can even get his hands on us. Way to go, Remy."

"I know. I'm sorry."

They fell into step next to each other as they threaded through the rows of raised flower beds her mom meticulously kept in their front yard. Remy remembered the summer she'd helped her dad build them and a pang of regret for what she was about to do threatened to send her back to Julia's house to beg her to let them out of the contract they'd signed.

"This is really going to suck," Remy said.

Andy wrapped a comforting arm around her shoulders and pulled Remy into her side for a quick hug. "We made the right decision, Rem. This isn't something he should be all that surprised about. You've never made what you wanted a secret, and he has done nothing to nurture the talent I know he sees in you. Now let's do this. We're right beside you."

Corey stepped up to her other side and the three of them walked into the backyard, where the family gathered. They were a united crew, ready to face whatever happened together.

The first to notice them was Remy's brother Jay. The moment he saw them walk into the yard, he excused himself from the conversation he was having with Liliana Navarro, set down the beer he was drinking, and made a beeline for them. Remy could tell by the look in his eyes that their secret had already leaked.

"Hey, brother—" Jay cut off her greeting by wrapping his large hand around her arm and pulling her around the corner and away from the crowd.

"What the fuck, Remy? Please tell me you didn't do what I think you've done."

Remy jerked her arm away from him and pushed against his chest to make room between their bodies. "Keep your hands off me, Jay. I'm not a child."

"Could have fooled me."

"What's that supposed to mean?" She expected grief from her family, but she had hoped it would at least be after she'd talked to her dad. Revealing what she'd done and withstanding his anger and disappointment was already going to be hell. She didn't need Jay screwing with the little of courage she'd mustered.

"You know exactly what I'm talking about."

"Look, Jay—"

"A Clayman, Remy? Really? You couldn't keep it in your pants? They're our mortal enemies. Do you know what it's going to do to Dad when he finds out you're fucking Mr. Clayman's daughter? He's going to lose his mind."

"What? How the fuck did you know I was with Julia?" Remy suddenly realized Jay was talking about Julia and not the fact that she'd accepted a job with the Clayman's.

"It doesn't matter how I know. If I know, it's only a matter of time before the whole town knows. Dad's going to freak out. I wish you would just try to get along with him. You don't always have to go against everything he wants, just because he hasn't given you a boat to run, yet."

If Jay was this worried about their dad's reaction because she slept with someone, he was really going to hate it when he found out the whole story.

"It's none of your business who I spend my time with, Jay. It's not Dad's business, either. This is my life, and I'm sick and tired of being under his thumb."

Jay frustratingly combed his fingers through his thinning hair and sat heavily on the bench her mom kept next to the house where she could sit to put on her gardening shoes. He was the spitting image of their mother with his fine features and blond hair, but the older he got, the more she saw their father in him as well.

"I just don't want things to get even more complicated between you two than they already are. I love you, Rem. You're my little sister and I want what's best for you."

Remy sat next to him on the bench and rested her head on his strong shoulder. "I know and appreciate that. I have to make my own path and it's not always going to be the one Dad thinks I should take. That's his problem."

Jay wrapped his arm around her shoulders and pulled her closer. She welcomed the comfort and protection of being in his arms, even if she knew he was really going to freak out once he knew the extent of the new path she was about to take. For a moment, she contemplated telling him, but she knew she had to speak to her dad first. Jay would only try to talk her out of it, and that train had already left the station.

"Is she worth it?" Jay asked.

"Who?"

"Jesus, Remy. The Clayman girl. Is she worth pissing the old man off?"

"I don't know. I don't know her all that well yet, but so far, yes, she's worth it. She's not like the other women I've dated."

Remy hadn't meant to talk about Julia, or open up to her brother about feelings she'd not really even admitted to herself, but here they were. He was asking, and she found talking about it felt good.

"So you're actually dating, and not just fucking?"

"Again, not your business. But, yes, I think I'd like to get to know her better. She's funny, and smart, and way too good for this shithole town."

"You are this shithole town, Rem. If she's too good for it, don't you worry she's too good for you? You belong here. It's in your blood and she's only a visitor."

"She grew up in Elder's Bay, you know." Remy knew Jay might not know much about Julia, but he had to know that if she was Brian Clayman's daughter, she grew up there, just like the rest of them.

"And she left, Remy. She left because this town wasn't good enough for her and she's not planning to stay after her dad is feeling better."

"How do you know all this? Are you suddenly the town mayor and I hadn't heard about it?"

Jay laughed and playfully tugged on her hair. "You wish I was mayor so I could get you out of all those parking tickets you have.

Liliana lives across the street from Julia's aunt and told me she saw you over there. Late."

"Fucking small towns." Sometimes Remy wished she could just pack up and get out of this town that knew every single detail of her and her family's lives. It would be such a relief to start fresh and not worry about what everyone was going to think. Maybe Julia had the right idea, living in Portland. She doubted her neighbors even knew her name, let alone the brother of someone she slept with. The idea of Julia sleeping with another woman sent a pulse of jealousy through her, which was absolutely ridiculous since they weren't really even dating.

"Well, tell Dad before he finds out from someone else. If Liliana knows, others will know soon enough."

"Thanks for the warning, but it's honestly the least of my worries right now."

Jay sat up straight, a look of concern on his boyish face. "What's wrong? Are you okay? Are you sick?" He looked her up and down as if he'd be able to tell she was dying just by looking at her.

"No. Stop. Nothing like that. I'm fine. Look, I appreciate the chat, but I have to go talk to Dad."

Jay nodded and patted her knee. "Yeah. Good idea. It's better to get ahead of this thing before he's blindsided."

She paused a moment and wondered how their relationship would change once he knew what she'd done. He was the closest in age to her of her two brothers, and he'd always been her protector. She loved him for that but knew this news would force him to take a side, and she had no illusions he would go against their father. It would affect his livelihood since he captained one of the family's boats, and it just wasn't something they did. The Millers were faithful to a fault, and going against Frank Miller was to betray the very essence of who they were as a family. This wouldn't be pretty, but it was her only option. Her family would have to understand that or live without her in their lives.

Remy stood and pulled her brother to his feet. She wrapped her arms around him and took a minute to savor the feeling of being his little sister and having the love and devotion that came with that title. Maybe he'd surprise her, but she wouldn't know for sure until it was all out in the open. She wouldn't hold his decision against him, whatever he did going forward. This was something she was doing for herself and she would accept whatever came of it.

"I love you, brother. Never forget that."

"I love you, too. Seriously, Remy, you're freaking me out. Are you okay?"

Laughter from the crowd of people in the yard pulled her attention from him for a moment. She really loved her family. "Yeah, I'm going to be just fine. I'll see you later."

She turned away from him before he could see the tears that had pooled in her eyes. She couldn't let them detect any weakness or they'd question how confident she was about what she was doing. If they suspected any doubt, they'd use that against her, and she couldn't have that.

Andy and Corey were both sipping beers near the firepit. She could see the fear in their eyes and wished she'd convinced them to skip this family dinner so they wouldn't have to deal with what was about to happen. They'd never have let her do it alone, though. Leaving her side wasn't an option, just like leaving theirs wasn't for her. They were a crew and nothing would ever change that.

She gave them a quick wave and silently pointed toward her dad. He was standing in a group of older sailors, laughing and drinking beer. Remy had to get him alone because the last thing she needed was this to all play out in front of these people.

"Hey, Dad," Remy said. He smiled when he saw her and wrapped an arm around her shoulder to pull her close.

"Did you boys see the shiner my kid got?" He pointed a finger at the eye that still bore the faint evidence of her fight. "She kicked some Clayman kid's ass. She doesn't take any shit from those assholes." Her dad failed to mention it pissed him off when he first learned how she got the black eye or that Remy was actually just a casualty of someone else's fight, but that was beside the point.

Remy touched the bruised skin around her eye and wished she'd had Julia put some makeup or something on it to hide the fact that she'd only given her family more reason to believe she wasn't ready for the responsibility of being a captain.

"Hey, Dad," Remy tried again. "Can I talk to you privately for a minute?"

"I'm the host of this party, Remy. Can it wait until our guests have gone?"

That was probably exactly what she should do if she knew what was good for her, but the longer she waited, the more she lost her nerve. "No, I really need to talk to you now. Sorry, boys." She gave the men her dad was drinking with an apologetic smile.

"Okay, kid. Come on. Let's go find your mom."

"No!" The last thing Remy needed was the look of disappointment she was sure she'd see on her mom's face. Her dad's anger would be difficult enough to deal with. "No, I need to talk to you alone, if that's okay?"

"What's wrong?" Her dad looked concerned, and that only made her feel even more guilty.

"I'm fine. I just need to talk to you," Remy said. "Can we sit in your office?"

He looked at her like he was trying to puzzle out what this was all about by reading it on her face. "Let's go sit and talk and I'll explain everything," Remy said.

She followed him through her mom's garden to the small office she and her dad had built when she was eleven. A photo her mom had taken of the two of them, in matching overalls, ball caps, and each with a pencil tucked behind an ear, hung on the wall and stung her with a moment of regret. Remy's relationship with her dad had always been the best and worst thing in her life. On one side of the coin, he was a loving, kind, protective dad who had made her feel like she could do anything because she had him on her side. On the other, he was controlling, moody, and verbally abusive when she dared to stray from what he deemed the best thing to do. It was exhausting, but she'd known nothing else. He was her dad, and he loved her. This was going to suck.

The one-room building smelled of cigars and whiskey. Remy sat in one of the guest chairs across the desk from his while he turned on the air purifier so it wouldn't be as stuffy in the room while they talked. She looked around at the various drawings she and her brothers had done throughout their lives that he'd proudly framed and mounted on the walls where everyone could see. None of them had a lick of artistic talent, but he never seemed to notice.

Her dad poured them each two fingers of scotch and handed Remy the glass before taking his seat in the comfy leather office chair across from her. They both took a slow sip, and Remy allowed the liquid to swirl around her mouth before giving a slight grimace as it burned her throat on the way down.

"This is nice," Remy said. She held the glass up to the light from the window and watched it illuminate the swirl of golden color as it settled.

"Tommy Jensen gave it to me for my sixtieth birthday. He took a tour of the distillery when he was in Scotland a couple of years ago."

"That was nice of him to bring a bottle back for you," Remy said. The small talk was only delaying the inevitable, but part of Remy wanted to savor this moment while she could. The future was unknown, and she needed these last few minutes with her dad to look back on if things went south.

"It was. Tommy's a good guy." He tossed the last of his drink down his throat and reached into the cigar box on his desk. He held one up for Remy, but she declined. She occasionally smoked with him when they were having a father-daughter moment, but she'd never really been a fan of smoking and wanted nothing in her hands if she had to leave quickly.

He lit the cigar and took a couple of puffs before leaning back in his chair and training his gaze on her. "So, what's going on, Remy? I would worry you'd gotten yourself pregnant, but for some reason, it would make more sense if you'd been the one knocking the poor girl up." He chuckled and ashed his cigar into a tray on his desk that her brother Peter had made him in high school.

"Come on, Dad. Don't be weird." Remy downed the last of her drink and sat forward in the chair. She rubbed her sweaty palms on her jeans and steeled her nerves. Remy felt like she was standing on the edge of a cliff, about to dive into a future she couldn't exactly see. She'd had much more confidence when she signed the documents with Julia.

The memory of Julia's sleepy face the morning they'd woken up together crossed her mind, and she felt some of the tension in her body relax. Julia was absolutely right. Her dad would never give her the opportunity the Claymans had given her, and if she wanted to captain her own ship, she'd have to suck it up and seize this opportunity. She had to dive off that cliff or she would spend the rest of her life just standing there wondering what was at the bottom.

"Let's get on with it, then. What's on your mind, Remy?"

"Someone offered me a job as a captain and I'm going to take it. We start tomorrow."

Her dad sat there quietly, staring at her like he was waiting for her to continue. So she did.

"I appreciate all you've taught me, but I think it's time for me to take those lessons and put them to good use. I know I can be a great captain like you someday, and I'm more than ready to prove that."

He stubbed out his cigar and tucked it back into the box with the others. "So, you think you're ready, do you?"

"I know I'm ready."

"And who is it that's giving you this golden opportunity?"

"Does it matter?"

"It matters to me," he said.

"Clayman Fisheries."

Remy had played out in her mind how he'd react to the news for so long that she was sure she knew exactly what would happen. The calmness of this moment was never a scenario she'd considered, and it freaked her out more than the yelling she had expected.

"And you've signed a contract with the Claymans for this season?"

"This season and the next, yes."

"Of course." He tapped his fingers on the desk as if he'd decided about something, then stood. "Let's go tell the family your good news," he said. Remy's heart sank as he swiftly walked toward the door.

"Dad, we don't have to—"

"Don't be silly. You know what you're doing. Everyone's going to want to know about your success."

Remy trailed after him, scrambling to process what exactly was happening and how she'd so quickly lost control of the situation, assuming she'd ever had control.

Everyone hushed and crowded around when he stepped onto the stage they'd built in the corner of the yard for when they had a band. Her dad raised his hands to stop the indistinct murmur of the guests and get their attention.

"I wanted to thank everyone for coming out tonight," he said.

Remy frantically searched the crowd for Andy and Corey as the guests clapped for her dad. She finally spotted them near the beer kegs and rushed to their side.

"What happened?" Andy asked.

"I—" Remy began before her dad spoke again.

"My youngest child, my baby girl, Remy, has something she'd like to share with you all. Remy, why don't you come up here and tell everyone the great news you just told me?"

They all turned to Remy, and she'd never been so scared in her life. Why was he doing this? It was so much worse than the two of them just having it out in private. Of course, she knew exactly why he was doing it. Telling the family like this would be much harder, and he had a tendency to make her feel the full effect of her mistakes. Or at least, what he thought were mistakes.

She turned toward Andy and Corey and found sympathy in their eyes. She knew they would stand up there with her if she asked, but she wouldn't do that to them. She was the captain. This was her decision to own, and she took full responsibility for her actions.

Remy stepped onto the stage and focused on Jay. She knew he thought her admission would be about Julia and she wished it was that simple. It would be difficult to explain, but this... This was going to be bad.

She stuffed her hands in her pockets and worried her bottom lip. Her dad nodded at her, prompting her to say something. Fuck it. She'd made the right decision, and she wouldn't give him the satisfaction of making her second-guess herself, not this time. Remy cleared her throat and stood as straight as she could. Her confidence grew with every second and with her head held high, she removed her hands from her pockets and acted like the leader she'd always wanted to be.

"First, I wanted to thank Dad and everyone for raising me to be a sailor. The sea is in my blood and I wouldn't want to be anything else. It's where I belong, and for that reason, I've accepted a job offer to captain a boat."

Confusion crossed her family's faces as they all turned to her dad for an answer. She knew they were trying to work out in their heads what boat she meant since Dan Bratton had taken over the only boat they knew of that was available.

"My crew and I will start running a boat for Clayman Fisheries first thing Monday morning, and we'll take with us every lesson we've learned from each one of you."

A murmur rose as questions spilled from everyone's mouths. Remy looked at her mom, who stood silently next to her grinning father with red-rimmed eyes. This was exactly what she'd feared would happen. The guilt and fear of what came next were inevitable, but the look on her mom's face broke her heart.

Her dad raised his hand to quiet the chatter. "Tell them about your contract, Remy. What kind of commitment have you made to the family that is our direct competition?"

"I—" Remy faltered as the words stuck in her throat. She swallowed around the pain and owned up to what she'd done. "We've signed a two-season contact with them." Time seemed to stop as she watched her brothers process what she'd said. Jay turned and stormed away as Peter stared at her in confusion.

"I think you've done enough, Remy. You and your crew should probably get going. This gathering isn't for Clayman employees."

"Whatever, Dad." Heat from her anger burned her face as she stepped off the stage and walked toward Andy and Corey. They met her halfway and the three of them headed for the side gate, ready to leave the nightmare behind.

"You okay, cousin?" Corey asked.

Andy wrapped an arm around her and one around Corey as they walked toward their trucks. "She's going to be fine, Core. We'll all be fine. We're together and that's what matters. Right, Rem?"

Remy looked at Andy and let herself soak in the comfort she offered. This was her true family, no matter what blood said. They were the ones she'd bet her life on, and that's all she needed. They believed in her and that's more than she could say for her dad right then.

"Right," Remy said. "You guys ready to show the Claymans what we can do?"

"Hell, yeah," Corey said.

"Hell, yeah is right." The sun took that moment to peek through the clouds and Remy took it as a sign from the universe. They were going to be just fine.

CHAPTER EIGHT

Julia drove straight to her office when she got to Portland on Monday morning. Being away for a week had left her behind on her normal workload. One of her first tasks would be to offer her assistant, Tessa, a temporary promotion as the lead until Julia could get the situation in Elder's Bay under control until her dad was ready to go back to work.

The thought of stepping away from the relationships she'd so carefully cultivated with their clients and contractors made Julia's stomach ache. She wouldn't have to step away completely, but there was a limit to the time she'd be able to dedicate to her duties in Portland. Her dad typically took care of the fisheries side of the business while Julia dealt more with the customer side of things. She'd spoken to most of their contracted fishermen, but her dad did the bulk of managing them.

The conversation she'd had with Toby McKenzie on the morning of her dad's heart attack was something he usually handled. She wondered for a moment if he'd asked her to call Toby because he knew something was wrong or if it was pure coincidence. She made a mental note to ask him when she was back in Elder's Bay. If he hadn't been feeling well, but didn't tell anyone, she was going to kill him. It was almost certainly what happened because, of course, he'd keep something like that to himself, but she was still going to kill him.

"Hey, Julia, you wanted to see me?" Tessa Jacobson was young, beautiful, and ambitious. Julia had almost fired her the first week she'd worked for her when she'd taken it upon herself to contact a client without getting approval first. It took the wind out of Julia's sails when, in the middle of the reprimand she was doling out, the client called and agreed to double their order for the season. Tessa apologized for overstepping, and Julia learned she needed to trust the people she hired to do their jobs.

"Have a seat, Tessa." Julia offered her a chair in the comfortable sitting area she kept in the corner of her office. "How were things while I was away? Any problems come up?" Julia poured two cups of coffee from a carafe on the cart near the door. She added cream and two sugars to each of them and handed one to Tessa before sitting across from her on the large azure blue couch.

Tessa sipped her coffee and set it on the coffee table before slipping off her heels and taking a moment to stretch out her legs. Julia knew things had been hectic with her gone and she hoped Tessa was up for what she was about to ask of her.

"It's been busy, but good. I spoke to Steven Hicks at Willie's Seafood Bar about committing to a bigger order instead of coming to us at the last minute expecting us to find him crab we weren't aware he would need. He said to apologize to you for being a pain in your ass and agreed to double his order for the next six months. He'll look at the numbers later and decide if he should continue with that amount or not."

"Perfect," Julia said. Steven had been a thorn in her side for years, and not having to deal with his constant flirtation was a welcome relief. She hoped he hadn't just taken his inappropriate behavior and transferred it to Tessa.

"He didn't—"

"Talk to my boobs and then ask when you would be back? Yes, that's exactly what he did."

"Ugh. I'm sorry, Tess. I'll call him and tell him again that he needs to back off. Maybe if I threaten to no longer do business with him, he'll get the point. We aren't the only ones selling the product, but he'll struggle to find the quality in the quantity he wants anywhere else."

Tessa took another sip of her coffee and shook her head. "No need. I basically told him the same thing. I also mentioned that the Claymans were a respected family in Portland, and he'd find it difficult to find anyone who would do business with him in the future if he didn't learn to behave like a professional."

Julia lifted her mug in a silent salute. Tessa was ready for whatever this job could throw at her.

"We need to schedule a meeting to discuss the contracts we've lost recently. I talked to Caleb Svenson and he said the Millers weren't offering as much for the product, but close enough to not want to deal with my dads moods. I can't help but wonder if dad wasn't feeling well for longer than he's letting on and it affected his people skills."

"Maybe. I've heard similar rumblings from other crews, too. He's pissed a lot of people off," Tessa said.

"Let's see what we can do to change the tide and get people back on board with Clayman Fisheries."

"You can count on me, Jules."

Julia set her mug on the coffee table and folded her hands in her lap. "On that note, I wanted to talk to you about a temporary promotion."

Tessa sat forward. "Promotion to what?"

"It looks like my dad's going to need me in Elder's Bay a little longer than I expected. I appreciate you stepping in this last week and I'd like to ask you to continue doing that for the next couple months. It doesn't feel right asking without compensating you appropriately, so this will be a temporary promotion, instead of just dumping all my work on you with nothing extra for your trouble. I know I'm asking a lot of you, so please be honest with me if you aren't interested."

Tessa smiled and leaned back in her chair. "I'll do it on one condition."

"Name it." Julia was desperate, and Tessa was savvy enough to understand she had her over a barrel.

"If we open a Seattle office, I want to run it, or take over Portland for you if you leave. I don't expect you to commit to it right now, but if I do a good job covering for you now, you'll at least put me at the top of the candidates list."

"I had already planned on offering you the job, my friend. You're the only one I trust. We have a little time before that's going to happen, but the job is yours when it does."

"Then, yes, I'm very interested. Thanks for the opportunity. I know I was a cocky know-it-all when you hired me right out of college, but you trusted me and I'll always be grateful for that."

Julia stood and held out a hand to pull Tessa to her feet. "Best thing I ever did," she said as they hugged.

The clatter of rain against the window meant Julia had waited too long before leaving, but she picked up the box of things she'd collected to take back with her to Elder's Bay and said her good-byes to everyone before braving the walk to her car. She'd be back in now and again to check on how things were going and get face time with some of their higher end clients, but she'd be spending most of the next couple of months in Elder's Bay.

The memory of the last kiss she and Remy had shared in the entryway of her house flashed through her mind. The pulse of arousal in her core made Julia laugh. What the hell was Remy doing to her? She'd dated plenty of women, and the occasional man, in her life, but none of them had ever been like Remy. They'd only spent a little time with each other, and most of that was having sex. They'd known each other for years, but hardly knew anything about each other. Tell that to her hormones, though. Every time she thought of Remy, she felt like a teenager getting attention from the star quarterback. It was absolutely ridiculous.

When she arrived at her apartment, she noticed her roommate's car parked in one of their two assigned parking spots. The idea of a tiny little Dylan driving the gigantic pickup always made Julia smile. She didn't understand why Dylan didn't get something more reasonable for driving around the city, but the heart wants what the heart wants, she supposed.

"Dylan? You here?" Julia asked as she rolled her suitcase into the shared apartment. "I brought you the saltwater taffy you love."

"Hey." Dylan quietly slipped out of her bedroom, pulling a robe around her naked body. She tiptoed over to Julia and wrapped her arms around her like they hadn't seen each other in months instead of the week they'd actually been apart. "I missed you. We have to keep it down. I had someone over last night."

"Oh, really?" Julia looked around the room for the first time since she'd arrived and noticed boots, a flannel shirt, and jeans strewn across the floor. "Looks like you had a great time. Boy or girl, this time?"

Dylan rolled their eyes and waved off Julia's comment. "Shut up. A very sexy masculine-of-center lesbian hottie, I'll have you know. Want some coffee?"

"No thanks. I've already had two cups today. You realize it's noon, right?"

"So glad you're home, Mom." Dylan sniffed the day-old coffee that was left in the carafe and shrugged before pouring it into a mug and sticking it into the microwave to heat.

"You're disgusting. If I come home someday and you've died from some stupid thing you've put into your body, I'm going to be pissed."

"Yeah, yeah." The microwave dinged, and Dylan added creamer to her cup and took a sip. "Why are you here, by the way? I thought you'd be with your family for another couple of weeks. I could have sent some clothes instead of you driving all the way up here."

Dylan followed Julia to the sofa and sat next to her when she dramatically collapsed in a heap. "Ugh. My dad needs me to stay for longer than I thought."

"Is he okay? I talked to your mom the day after his heart attack, but she didn't seem like she knew for sure what was going to happen at that point." Dylan and Julia had been roommates since college, and the Clayman clan adored her. "Shouldn't Charlie be the one taking over the stuff in Elder's Bay so you can do your job here?"

The whole thing gave Julia a headache. "You know Charlie. He's decided he no longer wants anything to do with crabbing. Besides, he and Stephanie are trying to have another kid."

"No." Dylan almost choked on her coffee in shock.

"Yep. Apparently, Stephanie's a new woman now that she's a mother."

"Mm-hm." Dylan shook her head and reached out an arm, inviting Julia to snuggle into her side. "So, what does this all mean for you? Are you finally going to move back to Elder's Bay and take over the business, just like your daddy always wanted?"

"I hope not. I'm not ready to let go of my life in Portland."

"And what happens when your dad really is gone? Someone has to run that part of the business. Are you just going to give the whole thing to a cousin and call it a day?"

"I...no, I'm not leaving things to my idiot cousins. No one is as invested in the company as Dad and I are. They'd try to run it for a year or two and then sell it off to some giant company that won't care about the product they're selling or the people who risk their lives to catch it. We'd lose our customers and everything my family has built for generations. I can't do that. I won't allow it to be my legacy."

The question of how she would handle things once her dad was gone had kept her up at night for a couple of years. Having the main office in Elder's Bay where they had daily contact with the fishermen and their catch was the main reason Clayman Fisheries had been so successful for so long. Most other fishermen sold their catch to processors who paid the middleman. Technically, they still did that with part of the crab they caught, but Clayman Fisheries purchased them for their own restaurants and others in the area, ensuring they were serving their customers the best product they could.

Since her brother Charlie had said he wouldn't be the one taking over for their family once her father was gone, it was up to Julia to decide how they would move forward. A Clayman had been running the company in Elder's Bay for generations and she didn't want to be the one to break that tradition. Besides, the last thing Julia wanted was to work for one of her cousins.

"I can't deal with that right now. My dad's doing better and hopefully he'll be back on his feet in a couple of months and will be ready to take over. I'm trying to just deal with what's in front of me right now, and the rest is tomorrow's problem."

The look on Dylan's face said she was skeptical of that answer, but Julia knew she wouldn't push for more. Dylan had a habit of saying just enough to make Julia voice the things she'd been desperately trying to avoid, but not push the point so far it made her feel bullied into saying something she wasn't ready to put words to. She realized how much she appreciated having Dylan to talk to. Yet one more reason to get back to Portland as soon as possible.

"What about you?" Julia asked, turning the conversation away from her own stressful life. "What have you been up to while I've been gone? Apparently, not watering the plants."

They both turned toward the plants on their deck that were a shared responsibility but had always fallen more to Julia. She never thought she'd be a plant person, but having that little extra bit of greenery helped ease the negative things about living in a big city. If Julia could, she'd live outside the hustle and bustle of Portland but close enough to meet friends for dinner or catch a show. She'd grown up in a small town and there would always be a part of her drawn to the quiet peacefulness of being away from honking cars and concrete.

"Yeah, the plants have been a little needier than I'd realized. I'm trying to put myself on a schedule, but you know how I am with schedules."

"Oh, the life of a starving artist."

"Well, maybe not so starving. I sold a piece to the Chapman Gallery, and they've commissioned three more from the series."

Dylan was an incredibly talented artist in a community that seemed to take forever to recognize how special she was. Julia knew the moment she saw Dylan doodling on her science homework in college, she had a bright future ahead of her. That she got a business degree, instead of going to art college, would hopefully benefit her once she had to do things like negotiate contracts. It also appeased her parents, which meant they were happy to not only pay for her education but help to support her for five years after graduation while she tried to make it as a professional artist. Graduation was four years ago, so the news of the commission meant her dreams might just come true after all.

"I'm so proud of you, Dyl. It's about time people recognized what an amazing artist you are."

"Thanks. Hey, are you going to be here next weekend?"

"I hadn't planned on being here, but I can if you need me to be. What's up?"

Dylan scrolled through her phone, then held it up so Julia could see the invite to an art event. "I want you to go to this party at the Chapman Gallery with me. Cameron can bring her sister, so you won't have to look like the sad sack that doesn't have a date."

"First, who is Cameron? Second, you're an asshole. I can get a date, thank you."

"I'm Cameron." A disheveled looking blonde appeared from the hallway that led to their bedrooms, wearing Dylan's much too small lacy robe and socks. "I look like a fool, Dyl. Do you know where my clothes are?"

Dylan climbed into Cameron's lap when she sat next to them on the couch. "You look adorable."

"Mmm." Cameron grumbled. "Is that coffee?"

"Yep." Dylan handed Cameron a coffee and laughed when she puckered after her first sip like she'd tasted lemon juice.

"It's old," Dylan said. "Sorry."

"Yeah. I see that." Cameron offered a hand to Julia in greeting. "I'm Cameron."

"I'm Julia. Nice to meet you. How long have you guys been seeing each other?"

Cameron checked the time on her watch. "Oh, I guess ten hours."

"Cameron valet parks at the gallery."

"Oh, that's nice," Julia said, trying not to sound like she wouldn't kill Dylan for bringing random women she'd only just met back to their apartment when nobody else would be home. She worried about her judgment sometimes.

"It's only a side thing for extra cash. I'm in a band, but we're between gigs right now."

"Of course you are."

"So, will you come up next weekend for the party? Cameron's sister is a few years younger than us and more on the femme side than you're usually into, but I've seen pictures and she's hot."

Cameron nodded vigorously, and it creeped Julia out just a little that she would be so enthusiastic about how hot her own sister was.

"Thanks for the offer, but if I'm able to come up, I think I already might have a date."

"Where in the world did you meet someone if you've only been in Elder's Bay, and why haven't I heard about this mystery person before now?"

Julia shrugged and scrolled through Facebook on her phone, looking for a picture of Remy. She found one of her and her crew standing on a giant stack of crab pots and turned the phone so Dylan and Cameron could see.

"Holy shit, which one are we talking about? They're all gorgeous."

"The guy on the left is Corey, and he has a girlfriend named Brooke. The girl on the right is Andy. I don't think she's seeing anyone, but I'm not sure. The middle one is Remy, and I'm hoping that one is off limits."

"Really." Dylan took Julia's phone so she could pinch to zoom in on Remy. "She's a fucking stud, Julia. I don't blame you for wanting to lock that one down."

"Hey," Cameron said. "I'm right here."

"Oh, honey, we just met a few hours ago. It's much too soon for you to get all possessive. Besides, look at her." Dylan held the phone up closer to Cameron's face.

"Not my type, but I get it. She looks pretty cool."

Julia took her phone back and looked at the photo once more. "She's dreamy. I had a huge crush on her in high school, but we ran with different crowds and our families are kinda mortal enemies, so we didn't really hang out much."

"Jesus. That sounds dramatic. Elder's Bay sounds like such a soap opera," Dylan said.

"It can be." Julia pocketed her phone and pulled her legs up to press her thighs against her chest for comfort.

"Do you want to talk about it?" Dylan asked.

"Not yet. I'm still figuring out how I feel about everything. I don't think I'm ready to explain it all to someone else."

Dylan nodded and reached out to squeeze her hand. "Bring that stud home with you next weekend and let me size her up."

"It would be nice to spend some time with her, away from the stress of our families. She's not exactly ready to let anyone know we're…whatever we are. I'm not even sure what that is, but it's a secret."

"That's not cool." Dylan was obviously ready to stand up for Julia's honor, but the last thing she wanted was for her best friend to have negative feelings about someone she hoped to spend more time with.

"No, it's fine. It's all new and there's an entire history we're fighting against. Let me ask her if she can come and you can size her up. Just please be nice. I really like this one."

Dylan placed a hand against her chest as if she was shocked Julia would even suggest she would be anything other than nice.

"I know you get protective of me, but you don't need to with this one. I really, really like her. Hopefully, that goes both ways, and it's enough to overcome the obstacles in front of us."

"You know I'm pulling for you, sweetie. Always."

"Same. I love you, Dyl. It was great meeting you, Cameron. I better get back before it gets too dark. I hate driving on the windy roads out to the coast. The fog comes out of nowhere and it can get scary, fast."

"Text me when you get home. I love you, Jules."

Julia stood and kissed Dylan on the cheek before going to her room to pack up the things she needed to take with her. This visit with Dylan was exactly what she needed to get her through the next week.

CHAPTER NINE

The sun crowned the horizon as Remy and her crew began dropping their pots over the side. They were up way before dawn so they would be ready at peak low tide, or slack water, when the crabs would forage and be ripe for the picking.

A horn beeped every few seconds to let the crew know Remy was ready for them to dump a crab pot over the side, feeding it to the depths of the ocean. They'd done this process so many times in their lives that it was like second nature to them. They didn't need to communicate with each other; they just listened for the sound, then tossed the pots, over and over, until they'd emptied the deck. Then they waited.

"Hey, Andy, drop the anchor and let's have some breakfast."

"Aye, aye, Captain."

"Shut up, dork. Hey, Core, what's for breakfast?"

Corey walked below deck, then came back with a small insulated cooler. They had always relied on coffee and donuts to get them through the morning, but Corey's chef girlfriend made it her mission to provide them all with something more substantial. None of them complained.

"It looks like one thermos of hot coffee and another with oatmeal."

"I'll grab bowls and cups." While Andy went below, Corey and Remy unpacked the rest of their breakfast items.

"Holy shit, brown sugar, pecans, blueberries, milk. If you don't marry this woman, I will." Remy was only half kidding. She'd never been interested in relationships and all their frustrations, but knowing someone loved you enough to care that you had a warm meal seemed like a pretty good deal.

"Hey, Core, are you happy being with Brooke?"

Andy stopped making her bowl of oatmeal and looked from Corey to Remy. "What's happening?"

"You can't have my girlfriend, Remy," Corey said. "Besides, I heard you already have one of your own."

"I'm not trying to move in on your girlfriend, dumbass. Having a girlfriend just never seemed like it was worth the inevitable heartache and frustrations, but I don't know. You seem pretty happy. Maybe it wouldn't be horrible. That's all I'm saying. And Julia isn't my girlfriend. We spent one night together, and that's it."

Corey and Andy both looked at each other and smiled while they finished preparing their bowls of oatmeal.

"Sure, Rem. Whatever you say," Andy said.

"You guys are assholes." Remy leaned back in her captain's chair and dug into her warm bowl of food. She watched the seagulls search for fish scraps on their deck and wondered what Julia was doing at that moment. They'd left so early that morning that the office staff hadn't arrived yet. Remy checked her watch and imagined she might be on her way to work just about then.

"Remy?" Andy pushed Remy's chair with her foot, which caused it to spin. The motion jerked her arm enough that she spilled oatmeal on her shirt. "Fuck. Why'd you do that, dickhead?"

"Sorry. I was trying to get your attention but didn't mean to make you spill." Andy handed her a napkin and took her bowl so she could clean up her mess.

"Use your words. You guys are a bunch of animals."

"We'd been talking to you for five minutes, but apparently you'd drifted off somewhere else," Andy said.

"Wonder where that could be?" Corey asked.

"I think she was in the land of thinking about someone who isn't her girlfriend," Andy said. Corey snorted a laugh, which sent them both into giggles.

"You guys are impossible. Let's pick up our pots and see what we got. Unless you two need a nap since you're acting like children."

"I'm sorry, Rem. We're just kidding around." Andy handed the bowls to Corey and pulled on her jacket. "I'll pull the anchor while Corey washes the dishes."

"Again?" Corey complained.

Andy swiped the cap from Corey's head and smacked him with it before putting it back.

"She's right, you're an asshole, Andy."

Remy couldn't help but smile. They were a huge pain in the ass, but she couldn't imagine doing this without them. The teasing was constant, but the three of them had been there for each other as long as she could remember. She loved them, even when she wanted to toss one of them overboard now and again.

A few hours later, Remy watched the numbers on the scale as the dock workers weighed their catch. They caught just over their quota for the day and had offloaded before anyone else had even pulled into port. Clayman fisheries gave them a quota they expected each boat to bring in, depending on the length of their trip. A trip could be one, two or even three days, and the fact that Remy and her crew had finished faster than any of the other boats meant they were off to a good start. Hopefully Julia and the others in the administration building would recognize that and feel good about hiring them to run one of their boats.

She nodded at her dad as he walked past her on his way down the pier, but he refused to even look her way. He could be such a dick sometimes.

"Remy," her brother Jay called as he stepped off his boat.

"What's up, Jameson?"

"Not much, Remington."

"Looks like Dad's still pissed," Remy said.

Jay glanced toward where their dad was talking to another fisherman.

"Yeah, well, what you did was kinda a dick move. I don't really blame him for being pissed."

"Whatever, Jay. You would have done the same thing if he'd strung you along like he has me. All of you were running your own boats by the time you were my age. I've busted my ass to prove to him since I was ten that I could do anything you boys could do, and I can, sometimes even better."

"You're right," Jay said.

"Then why? Why the fuck won't he trust me?"

"Jay." Their dad called and waved for him to come over.

"Just a sec, Dad," Jay answered. He turned back to Remy and wrapped his arms around her to pull her into a hug. "He loves you, Remy. Probably more than any of us, but you can be reckless and you're shit at taking orders. You know how he is. If he says he wants you to do something, he wants you to do it exactly like he said. He's been doing this a lot longer than us and he's lost a lot of friends out there."

"Working on the ocean is dangerous. It's part of the job. Risk and reward. He can't protect me by micromanaging me. I know that works for you guys, but it just doesn't work for me."

Jay nodded and looked back toward their dad. "I know. And that's the problem. You're an amazing crabber, Remy. You have instincts that the rest of us just don't have. It's like you can anticipate where the crab will be before they even know it. That's a gift. But you take too many risks. You're like a dog with your nose to the ground, and Dad's just afraid you're going to walk right off a cliff because you weren't watching where you were going. If he didn't love you so much, he wouldn't be so scared."

She knew he was right. Their dad was cautious with his children and the boys had always followed his every command. That wasn't who Remy was and her dad knew it.

"Well, that's why I moved on. I can't keep waiting for something that's never going to happen. You have to understand that."

"I understand. We all understand." Jay checked the time on his watch. "Look, I have to get back to Dad, but what you need to understand is that it's not only about you moving on, you moved on with the Claymans. You basically lit a match and threw it at your already strained relationship with him. He'll get over it, but you're going to have to give him some time. He feels like you've betrayed the family."

"That's bullshit," Remy said. "That stupid feud is ridiculous."

"It's not only about the feud, and you know it."

"Jay, what the fuck?" their dad yelled.

"I gotta go." Jay gave Remy one more hug. "I love you, little sister. You be safe out there."

"You, too. Tell Mom, I love her."

"Why don't you tell her? She's still talking to you, even if the old man isn't. It would be good for her to hear from you. She's hurt by all of this, too. It sucks to be in the middle of your war with Dad."

She hadn't really thought about how her mom felt. He was right that she should reach out to her when her dad wasn't around. None of this was her fault.

"I will. Love you, Jay. I'll catch you later."

He waved and jogged toward their dad. A pang of sadness stung her when he wrapped an arm around Jay and pulled him into the conversation he was having with the fisherman. She remembered what it felt like to have his approval and she wished things were different between them.

"Hey, sailor," a warm, sultry voice called from behind her. She turned to find Julia strolling her way.

"Hey there. What brings you out here with us ruffians?" Remy couldn't help but notice that the moment she saw Julia, any lingering frustration she was feeling about the situation with her dad melted away. At least for the moment.

"I wore pants today. I'm just like the rest of you."

Remy took Julia's hand and spun her around so she could see her entire outfit. "I hate to tell you, Ms. Clayman, but wearing slacks and a beautiful blouse doesn't make you one of us. Do you even own jeans?"

"Of course I own jeans," Julia said with slight indignation.

"Want to prove it?"

"You want me to prove to you I own jeans?"

That she was having a friendly conversation with Julia, right in front of her dad, probably wasn't helping her relationship with him.

Rubbing it in his face wouldn't win her any points. Hoping Julia would follow, Remy turned and starting walking toward her truck.

"How about you and your jeans go out on a date with me and my jeans?"

Julia smiled and leaned her back against Remy's truck when they reached it. "No one has ever asked my jeans out on a date before."

Remy looked around the parking lot to make sure someone wasn't watching. Then she leaned in and kissed Julia on the cheek. Her warm skin was so soft against her lips Remy felt like she would melt into a puddle at her feet. Remy cleared her throat and tried her best to regain her cool.

She leaned in to whisper in Julia's ear and smelled the faint scent of lilac. Exquisite. "I hope you'll allow both of our jeans a little floor time together before the night is over."

Julia snorted, then moaned. "This jean thing is super weird, but I get what you're saying, and I approve. What do you think about getting away this weekend? The two of us, and our jeans, of course."

"It would be nice to not feel like we have to be looking over our shoulders."

"I—" Julia started before shaking her head and stepping back to put space between them. "This isn't something where we will constantly have to hide, is it? Because I'm a grown woman and that's not really my thing. I know your dad is upset. Mine won't be happy when he finds out either, but I don't really give a shit."

"Hey," Remy said. She reached out and took Julia's hand, pulling her closer. "I'm sorry, that's not what I meant. I want to be able to spend a little time with you without people all up in our business. That's all." Remy stuck out her bottom lip in a pout. "Please forgive me?"

"Stop. You can't use your cuteness as a weapon," Julia said.

Remy smiled and pulled Julia back into her arms. "Aye, aye, Captain. No more cuteness."

Julia rested her head on Remy's chest and sighed. "You're going to be trouble. I can tell."

"No trouble. I promise," Remy reassured her.

"Hey, stop making out with not your girlfriend in the parking lot, Remy. I'm tired and I want to get home."

"Jesus, Andy." In that moment, Remy regretted carpooling with her roommate. "Please don't be a dick around not-my-girlfriend."

"What's happening?" Julia asked.

"Nothing. Sorry. Andy's giving me shit." She tossed the keys to Andy and wrapped an arm around Julia. "Get the truck started and I'll be right back. I'm going to walk Julia to her car."

"Okay." Andy unlocked Remy's truck with the remote. "Bye, Julia, it was lovely to see you."

"Bye, Andy," Julia said over her shoulder as she and Remy walked toward her car.

"Sorry about that."

"It's fine," Julia said. "I'm going to need a better explanation of the not-your-girlfriend thing over the weekend, though."

"Deal. So, should I make reservations somewhere?"

"Here's the thing. How do you feel about spending the weekend at my apartment in Portland?"

"Okay. Won't Dylan be there?" Remy asked.

"Yes. She has this party she wants us to go to at a gallery that's going to show her work."

"What kind of party?"

"I'm not exactly sure, but it looks like a fancy party. Do you have anything to wear to a fancy party?"

Remy thought about the dress-up clothes she had in her closet. She usually wore her least faded jeans without holes and a button-down shirt when she needed to dress up. Not that she wouldn't like to have fancy clothes, she just didn't know what to buy, and it's not like she spent much time in stores that sold nice things.

"Not really."

Julia clapped her hands together and made a joyful little noise. "I was kinda hoping you would say that. Can we go shopping before the party? Pretty please?"

"I'm a little scared, but okay. You'll go easy on me, right?"

"Where would the fun be in that?"

"I should probably get my hair cut while we're at it. Andy's mom usually cuts my hair, and it's fine for being under my hat, but probably not the best for a fancy party."

"Perfect. I'll call my ex-boyfriend Sean. He works at the barber just around the block from my apartment."

"Ex-boyfriend Sean? Should I be worried about ex-boyfriend Sean cutting more than my hair?"

"No, silly. He left me a long time ago for his now husband, Travis. You'll absolutely love him and he's going to go gaga over you."

When they reached Julia's car, she pulled her keys from her purse and waited for an answer. Spending the weekend in Portland sounded great, and Remy had wanted to see where Julia lived, but meeting her best friend was a little nerve-racking.

"I hope Dylan likes me."

"The problem is going to be keeping Dylan off of you. She's a flirt and you're a big sexy stud."

Remy placed a kiss on Julia's forehead. "This big sexy stud already has a date to the party."

"That's right, she does," Julia said. "You should probably get going, stud. Andy's waiting for you."

Another kiss, but this time Remy slipped a hand into the back of Julia's blouse and skimmed her fingers across the soft skin she found there. "I kinda don't care what Andy's doing right now."

Julia placed her hands on Remy's chest and gently pushed her back a step. "If we don't stop, I'm going to end up taking you home with me and you won't get any sleep. Sleepy captains aren't safe captains and I kinda like having you around."

Remy rubbed her face with her hands and blew out a breath. "Ugh. I know." She looped a finger into Julia's belt loop and pulled her closer for one more quick kiss. "You know, these slacks really are amazing."

"Well, you've already invited my jeans, so you're just out of luck," Julia said.

"You're a goofball. I like it." Remy bopped the tip of Julia's nose with her finger. "Text me tonight? Maybe you and your jeans can send me a pic?"

"Why did I ever allow this jeans thing to go this far?"

Remy kissed Julia's hand and stepped backward toward her truck. "Because you think I'm charming?"

Julia shook her head. "Humble *and* good-looking. That's a dangerous combination."

With a last wave, she turned and got into her car. Remy watched her drive away and, for the first time in her life, she hoped the week out on the water would go quickly so she could hang out with Julia again.

CHAPTER TEN

The rain pelted the windshield of Remy's truck as they navigated through the congested streets of Portland. They'd spent the day shopping for clothes and Julia was excited to show off the smoke show that was her date.

She couldn't wait for Dylan to meet Remy, but she knew Dylan would spend the evening flirting with her. She wasn't jealous. Julia knew Dylan would never do anything other than flirt, but she had a tendency to be forward enough to embarrass the faint of heart and Remy was already nervous about the event.

Thankfully, they were meeting Dylan and Cameron at a bar across the street to get a pre-party drink and she could warn her to tone it down while they're there.

"Text Dylan and ask her to meet you out front," Remy said as they pulled onto the street. "I don't see any parking spots that are close and I don't want you to have to run through the rain in that beautiful dress with those super hot, but pointy shoes."

Julia looked down at her black lace bustier midi dress and Louboutin's. "Thanks, sweetie. I probably should have expected the rain and not worn something quite this nice. I think I got excited about going out to a fancy event with my hot date and overdressed."

"Hot, huh?"

"You have no idea." Julia reached over to trail a red fingernail along the inseam of Remy's pants to the noticeably warm space between her legs.

"God, Jules, you can't do that to me right now. I'll just keep driving and take you back to your apartment. Who needs this fancy party anyway?"

Julia patted Remy's thigh and slipped into her wool coat that she'd slung over the back of her seat. They both watched out the window for Dylan to appear, then she jumped out and ran around the truck to help Julia out so she didn't fall on her face. They probably should have driven Julia's car to Portland, but Remy felt more comfortable in the truck since the forecast said there would be a big storm blowing in.

Dylan gave Remy a quick wave as she pulled Julia under her umbrella and ran for the door. The crowded bar was full of young people dressed up for a night on the town. Julia thought about the difference between this bar and Skip's in Elder's Bay, and it made her smile. They were about as different as they could be, but she realized that both had their own charm.

"What'll you have, Jules?" Cameron asked when they finally made it to the bar.

"I'll have a glass of red wine and Remy will have whatever amber ale is on tap."

The drinks arrived just as Julia saw Remy making her way toward them. The press of the people in the relatively small space left little room to move, but Julia spotted a group leaving a table in the back and guided everyone there before someone else could take it.

Remy helped Julia remove her jacket before offering her the spot in the corner where she wouldn't get clobbered by drunk people trying to move from one place to another.

"Dylan and Cameron, this is my date, Remy Miller."

"Hey there." Dylan gave Remy an appraising look that made Julia laugh. So predictable.

Cameron and Remy shook hands, then Remy pulled her chair closer to Julia so she could hold Julia's hand under the table while she held her beer in the other.

"Do you only catch crab on weekdays, Remy?" Cameron asked. "I thought you guys were out for months at a time."

"You're thinking of Alaska. They do much longer trips up there because the crab they're catching is in much deeper water. Dungeness are closer to shore, so we're home most nights, although we do occasionally stay out for two or three days at a time. Depends on what the weather is like, or what state the fishery is in."

"That's super cool."

"What do you do, Cameron?" Remy asked.

"I'm in a band," Cameron said.

"No fucking way." Remy pulled her chair closer to Cameron and Julia realized that she'd lost her date for at least the next few minutes.

She looked over at Dylan to find her watching Cameron and Remy intently.

"You okay?" Julia asked.

"I'm fine." Dylan scooted her chair closer to Julia. "Remy is fucking hot."

"I know, right?" Julia looked at her talking to Cameron and took a minute to appreciate the fitted white button-down shirt, black slacks, and black oxford dress shoes. The small splash of color from the socks with crabs on them that peeked out below her pants leg warmed Julia's heart. They were the one thing Remy picked out when they were shopping and she was so cute when she asked if they would work with her outfit that Julia didn't have the heart to say no.

"How are things going with you two?" Dylan asked.

Julia shrugged. "Good. Complicated."

"What do you mean? One sec." Dylan held up a finger at Julia to stop her answer. "Would you sexy beasts mind getting us both another glass of wine?"

"Right now?" Cameron asked.

"Of course." Remy stood immediately and kissed Julia's cheek. "We'll be right back. Do you need anything else?"

"No, thanks, just wine."

Dylan and Julia watched as Remy grabbed an obviously irritated Cameron by the shirt and pulled her toward the bar.

"What's that about?" Julia asked when they'd disappeared into the crowd.

"Cameron's great. She's funny, and hot, and decent in bed, but Cameron's biggest fan is Cameron. It's the me show with her unless she wants something from me, and I have to be honest, I'm over it."

"Why did you bring her tonight?"

Dylan looked toward the bar to make sure they weren't within listening distance. "Because I'm weak. I've been trying to figure out all day how to break this thing off, but she acts like we're engaged or something. We've barely been seeing each other a week."

"Jesus, Dyl. Do you think she'll be shitty about it?"

"I don't think she'll be thrilled, but hopefully she'll put on her big girl panties and be cool about the whole thing."

"I'm glad Remy and I are staying the night."

"Me, too. Perfect timing on your part."

Remy and Cameron came back to the table with their wine and asked if they minded them leaving again to play darts. Apparently, they met a couple of guys at the bar and, after brief introductions, followed by shit talking about their dart skills by Cameron, the guys challenged them to a game.

"No, that's fine with us," Julia said. "Don't let those boys take your lunch money."

Remy pushed Julia's hair aside to expose a bare shoulder, then placed kisses from the tip of her shoulder, up her neck, to the delicate curve of her ear. She knelt down next to Julia and spoke close enough that she wouldn't have to yell over the noise of the crowd. The vibration of her low voice sent goose bumps across Julia's skin.

"You sure you don't mind if I leave you? I promise I'll make it up to you after I teach these guys a lesson in humility."

There wasn't anything explicitly sexy about her words, but Julia's body certainly responded as if they were.

"I don't mind," Julia said. "It's nice to talk to Dylan."

Remy leaned in and kissed her temple. "I'm glad. Sorry I keep touching you. This dress is doing all sorts of things to me and I'm finding it very difficult to keep my hands off of you."

Where did this woman come from? Remy never failed to make Julia feel like the most beautiful, treasured woman in the room. She could definitely get used to this.

"Play your cards right, sailor, and you can help take this dress off later tonight."

The low groan that elicited from Remy made Julia laugh.

"When are we going over to the gallery?"

"Soon, I think. I'll talk to Dylan."

"We'll be back in a few." Remy placed one last kiss on Julia's lips before nodding to Cameron. "Let's go, dude."

When they were alone again, Julia rolled her eyes as Dylan watched Cameron walk away.

"You aren't breaking up with her tonight, are you?"

Dylan bit her bottom lip like someone had caught her doing something naughty.

"No?"

It sounded like a question, even though Julia knew it wasn't. She shook her head. Dylan had never been the best at resisting an attractive butch woman.

"When do we need to head over to the gallery?"

"About eight. It starts at seven thirty, so that'll give it a minute for others to arrive. I don't want to stay long. Eat some fancy hors d'oeuvres, enjoy a few cocktails, dance with the hot butch I'm about to break up with, then head home."

"Sounds like a good night to me. Except the breaking up part. I'm enjoying my hot butch too much."

"I don't blame you one bit. She's smoking hot, Jules. I'm doing my best to keep my cool and not climb her like a tree, but it's a struggle."

Julia laughed and almost spit out the wine she was drinking. "You're preaching to the choir, my friend. I've got it bad for her."

Dylan raised her glass. "To hot butches."

"Hear, hear."

"Back to what you said before, why are things complicated? You seem pretty into each other."

"I don't think it's us. We've only just started hanging out, but so far, so good. It's more about everyone around us that makes it so very complicated," Julia said.

"What's the story with your family?"

A waitress stopped by their table at that moment and they both ordered more wine.

"This has to be our last glass or I'm going to make a fool of myself at the gallery party," Dylan said.

"Same," Julia said.

"So, family drama?"

"It's not as much my family as it is hers. I mean, my family is definitely part of the problem, but I just don't care as much as she does."

"If her family doesn't love you, they must be complete idiots. There's no way any reasonable parent wouldn't be trying to marry their child off after spending ten minutes with you. Hell, I never plan to get married, and you're too girly for my taste, but I'd marry you."

"Thanks?" Julia giggled and sipped her wine. Nobody made Julia feel more like a rock star than Dylan. She wished everyone had a friend like that in their life and it was precisely why she'd never let this friendship drift apart. No matter what direction their future took them, Dylan was her sister, and she loved her for it. "It's not about them not liking me. I've met them casually, but as far as I know, they aren't aware I'm dating their daughter. It's not like we've been super careful hiding it and it's a small town that likes to gossip, but we haven't even officially discussed what's happening between us with each other, let alone our family."

"Then what's the problem?"

Julia sighed and picked up a cardboard coaster from the table to fiddle with. "I won't bore you with all the details, but for years, our families have been embroiled in a ridiculous feud. It started with our grandpas and each generation has carried on the tradition."

"Are you serious?"

"Yep. It's stupid and embarrassing."

"So this is like a Hatfields and McCoys situation?"

"Mmm, maybe not quite that violent, but pretty intense."

"Sounds like it. So what does that have to do with you guys seeing each other?"

Julia wished more than anything that she could say it meant nothing and this ridiculous tension between their families wasn't enough to derail a relationship with someone she was growing fonder of every day, but that wasn't the reality. This thing that ultimately had nothing to do with either of them was like a dark cloud over everything they were building.

"It shouldn't mean anything. The issue isn't with us, though, and Remy's a sailor who has dreamed of running a boat in her family's fleet since she was old enough to know what she wanted to be when she grew up. Her brothers both work for her dad, and Remy expected to do the same someday. Her dad wasn't ready to give her the chance to prove herself, and I did. Clayman Fisheries hired her, and the last thing her family needs is to find out that she's not only sailing for the enemy, but also potentially dating their future leader. Remy is hesitant for her dad to find out about us, but it's inevitable. Like I said, we're not exactly sneaking around."

Dylan perked up at this new information. "So you're like Romeo and Juliet?"

"Umm, I guess, except we're not doing that whole suicide thing at the end. That was a real bummer."

"Agreed. I support your decision. That seems a little too extra, anyway."

They both launched into giggles, and when Remy and Cameron returned and asked them what had happened, that only made them laugh harder. It was probably a great time to stop drinking wine, especially since they still had to go to the gallery and look dignified.

"Ready to head across the street?" Cameron asked when the laughter had settled enough for her to be heard.

"Yep."

The four of them spent approximately an hour at the gallery before they decided it was boring as hell and they were ready to head back to the apartment. Dylan had made an appearance, and that was the important part of the reason to go.

By the time they made it home, Julia could tell that Dylan had reached the end of her rope with Cameron. They were bickering when they walked into the apartment and Dylan's door slammed when they retreated there for more privacy. Julia and Remy went into their own bedroom to avoid getting caught up in any of the drama.

"What's going on there?" Remy asked.

"I suspect Cameron is being broken up with."

"That makes sense."

"You aren't going to ask me why?" Not that Julia had a burning need to gossip about Dylan and Cameron, but she found it odd that Remy hadn't asked for any reason or details.

"Is it because she's a selfish ass?"

"That bad, huh?"

"She almost got our asses kicked at least twice at that bar. She basically seemed put out if she had to do anything or even acknowledge Dylan most of the night. Did you see her at the gallery?"

"When Dylan was trying to talk to people and Cameron kept checking her watch and asking when we were going to leave like she was a child and it was her bedtime?"

"Exactly," Remy said. "She's an ass."

Just then, the yelling got louder, and Dylan's bedroom door slammed again, followed by the front door slamming. Julia held up a finger, telling Remy that she would be back, and knocked on Dylan's bedroom door.

"Dyl, it's Jules, can I come in?"

"Sure."

"Hey, you okay?" Julia asked when she found Dylan lying face down on her bed.

Dylan held out an arm and Julia slipped off her shoes and crawled in next to her. Julia was small at five-foot-three, but Dylan was even smaller, with long auburn hair and bright green eyes. She was a knockout, and Julia understood why Cameron must not have taken the rejection well.

"Do you want to talk about it?" Julia asked. She wanted to get back to her room to spend time with Remy, but first she had to double-check that Dylan didn't need her.

"No. That sucked. I hate breaking up with someone. I'd almost rather be the one getting her heart broken because then I don't have to feel so guilty."

"If it makes you feel better, I think Remy's on your side."

"That does make me feel better. Thanks."

"Any time." Julia pushed a lock of hair away from Dylan's face and wiped tears from her cheeks with her thumbs. "There are plenty of fish in the sea."

"I don't know if I believe that. I think there's plenty, but I wish I could find the one."

"The only fish in the sea?"

"Exactly. The only one for me, I guess."

"She's out there, sweetie. You're just going to have to toss back a few duds before you find her." Something in the back of Julia's mind wondered if Remy was her only fish. It was a ridiculous thought since they hadn't been dating very long, but at some point, if you were lucky, you found the one. Maybe that one was Remy?

"You need to get back to your date," Dylan said.

"Can I get you anything? Did you want us to hang out with you and watch a funny movie or anything?"

"Nah. I'm good. You guys enjoy your time together. I know with her schedule you don't get all that much time to bone."

"Jesus, Dylan."

"What?"

"I love you," Julia said.

"I love you, too. Remy is amazing, by the way. She's quite the gentleman, or however you say that for butches."

Julia looked toward the door and thought about the millions of little things Remy had done for her that day that meant she cared and wanted to make Julia happy. She held doors, brought her drinks, held her hand, kissed her cheek every chance she had. It wasn't that Julia thought Remy *wouldn't* be like that, but her attentiveness surprised her in a very good way. "She really makes me happy."

"I can see why. And she's smoking hot. Did you pick out her outfit?"

"I did. Simple but stylish."

"I don't think Cameron even noticed that I was staring at your date's ass all night. She doesn't notice much that doesn't have to do with herself."

"I noticed," Julia said.

"You don't count. You know I'm harmless."

"I wouldn't say you're harmless, but you're not the date stealing type."

"Well, I call seconds if you and Remy break up."

"In your dreams." Julia shoved Dylan until she rolled over.

"I had to try. Now go before we start making out and poor Remy is left high and dry."

Julia kissed Dylan's cheek, then tickled her until Dylan shoved her out of the bed.

"Leave me with my misery," Dylan said. "I'm going to drown my sorrows in the second season of *Love is Blind*."

"Isn't that the crazy season where the guy goes off the rails at the end?"

"Yes, I love it so much."

"Well, enjoy. We'll see you in the morning. Want to go out to breakfast with us before we head back to Elder's Bay?"

"For sure. Wake me up an hour before we need to leave."

"Sounds good. I love you, Dyl."

"Love you, too."

Julia returned to her room to find Remy already out of her dress clothes and lounging on her bed in boxers and a white undershirt. She was disappointed she wouldn't be able to take the sexy outfit off of her herself, but she was awfully cute looking so relaxed and at home, too.

"Whatcha' doin'?" Julia asked.

Remy turned her phone so Julia could see that she was streaming the movie *The Perfect Storm* with Mark Wahlberg and George Clooney.

"Of course, that's what you're watching." Julia slipped out of her clothes and crawled into bed next to Remy.

"What does that mean?"

"You sailors are just predictable. Doesn't watching that tragic movie freak you the hell out?"

Remy shrugged and turned off her phone. "Not really. I mean, the risk is a part of the job and that scares me sometimes, but the alternative is not being out on the water, and that's not an option."

"What if you couldn't go out anymore? My dad almost never goes out anymore."

"He doesn't go out, but he's constantly down at the dock talking to the others and giving the Millers dirty looks."

Julia laughed and smacked Remy's chest. "No, he doesn't."

She didn't argue, but Julia could tell she wasn't joking about her dad. It didn't exactly surprise her all that much. He really hated Frank Miller, and Julia knew her dad was likely giving him dirty looks on the regular.

"Sorry."

"It's fine," Remy said. "Someday there will be a new sheriff in town and my plan is to program you to think the Millers are awesome and then we can all move on with our lives."

"That's my plan. Not the part where you program me, but the rest of it. I can't be manipulated so easily."

"Oh, really." Remy rolled onto her side and slid her hand under Julia's T-shirt to cup her breast. The warmth of her palm as she massaged Julia's sensitive flesh made her moan. She felt her pussy tingle as wetness slipped onto her thighs.

"You think this is going to make me do your bidding? It won't work."

"You're probably right." Remy moved between Julia's legs and pulled her panties over her hips and down her legs to be tossed onto her bedroom floor. "Let's just do a little experiment and see if that's true. If you don't feel you would do anything I wanted you to do, I'll apologize and admit your superior willpower."

"This doesn't seem like a fair test." Julia threw back her head in ecstasy as Remy's mouth found her clit and sucked the nub into her mouth. "Not that I'm not willing to be your subject. Feel free to experiment with me anytime you'd like."

CHAPTER ELEVEN

Remy shut down the last of the navigational equipment and stepped out onto the deck to help the others secure the pots so they could leave for the day. She'd told Julia she would pick her up for their date at six p.m. sharp, and it was going to take a minor miracle to keep her promise at that point.

A line had caught in the prop on their last string of the day, and untangling it took a couple of hours. Time they didn't have to spare since they'd been a little late to start that morning.

Spending her nights at Julia's the past week had been amazing, but the lack of sleep from their extracurricular activities was catching up with them both.

"Pick up the pace, Miller," Andy said as she tossed a coiled line at Remy's chest. "I'd like to get out of here before my date decides I'm not worth the wait."

"Me, too, asshole. I'm moving as fast as I can." Remy knew she was dragging. She'd always been the hardest and fastest worker on the crew, so she knew she'd have to have a talk with Julia about stopping their escapades earlier so they could still get a full night's sleep. If the exhaustion on Julia's face that morning was any sign, she wouldn't argue with the request.

"Maybe you should spend more time sleeping and less time fucking that Clayman—"

"Hey, guys." Julia's dad interrupted before Corey could finish his sentence. Jesus Christ. This was the last thing Remy needed. The panic was like being punched in the gut and she wasn't exactly sure how much he'd heard or what she should say. A time machine to take her back an hour would be nice.

"Hello, Mr. Clayman." Remy stepped off the boat and down to the dock. She brushed her hands across her jeans to clean them as much as she could, but the cleanly manicured hand he offered her was more than she could manage.

"Miller," Brian Clayman said. "How are things going?" He waved his hand toward the pots that were now neatly stacked on the pier, ready to be stored for the night.

"Good, sir. Great." Remy folded her arms across her chest and stood ramrod straight, showing confidence she didn't actually have in that moment.

"I've been watching your numbers. They aren't bad."

Remy glanced toward her crew as they pretended to secure a boat that was, in reality, already done.

"Thank you, sir. I appreciate the opportunity and the faith you have in us."

Brian nodded and checked the time on his wristwatch. "That would be my daughter's faith. Not mine."

"Yes, sir." Clearly Brian Clayman wasn't happy that Julia had hired them to run his boat. Remy couldn't decide if that should worry her or not, so she decided to just let it go for now.

"Would you mind walking me back to my car? I'd like to discuss something with you in private."

Andy and Corey both stopped what they were doing and looked at Remy.

"Um, sure." Remy handed the line she was holding to Andy and turned toward the end of the pier. "I'll be right back, guys."

As she walked toward the parking lot with Mr. Clayman, she looked back at Andy and Corey, still on the boat. They were both wide-eyed and Corey gave her a shrug like he didn't know what situation she was walking into. A thousand possibilities flew through her mind about what he could want to talk to her about.

When they reached a stone wall that separated the dock from the parking lot, he stopped to rest against it. "Sorry. I'm still regaining my strength."

Mr. Clayman was pale and seemed weak, but Remy wasn't sure what to say. She doubted he was the type of man who would appreciate empty reassurances from her. Instead, she stood there with her hands in her pockets and patiently waited for his breathing to slow.

"I apologize for pulling you away from your crew like this, Remy," he said after a couple of minutes of rest.

"No problem at all, Mr. Clayman. They know what they need to do."

He nodded and reached out a hand for her to help him stand. "They seem like a good crew. They're obviously very loyal to you. That kind of loyalty is hard to find."

She nodded in agreement but wondered where that statement came from. Andy and Corey would have told her if someone had approached them with any job offers. She'd mention the comment to them later to see if they knew what he meant, but it wasn't worth asking him. For all she knew, he could try to plant a seed of doubt in her mind about them. That wouldn't happen. Especially from something said by Brian Clayman.

They finally reached his car, and he leaned against it, arms folded across his chest, and silently studied Remy. The appraisal made her uneasy, but she'd be damned if she would show him any weakness. There wasn't anything for her to lean against where she could still face him, so she stood with her feet shoulder width apart and folded her arms across her chest in a mirror of his position.

Remy could tell he was hesitant to voice the reason he'd brought her there now that he had her alone. She was just about to tell him good night and go back to her boat when he finally spoke.

"I understand you've been seeing my daughter." It wasn't a question. He was stating the facts and then waited to hear how Remy would respond. There were several ways she could approach this, and she wasn't sure which would be the best course. If she denied it, then she'd just look like an ass because he obviously knew something was going on between them. She could tell him it was none of his business who she dated, but that would only piss him off more and he was her boss. Finally, she went with her gut.

"Yes, sir, I am."

"Do you believe that's the best move when you're her employee? Not a good look, Miller."

The last thing Remy wanted to do was get into this discussion with Brian Clayman in a parking lot when she had her crew waiting and was going to be late with the very woman he was apparently warning her to stay away from.

"I like and respect Julia very much. So much that I'd rather you talk to her about this and not pull me away from my crew to ask me about it behind her back. I understand you're her father and my boss, but this is something you should discuss with her."

The tension between them was thick and Remy wanted to be out of this conversation as soon as possible, but she waited. She stood her ground and only allowed herself to exhibit confidence. Inside, she wanted to curl into a ball at the thought that she might throw her newly found chance to realize her dream as a captain away over a girl, but she'd never let him see that.

"What do you think of this car?" he asked. The question was so unexpected, Remy stuttered for a moment, not sure what kind of trap she was falling into. Mr. Clayman ran a finger along the polished roof of the brand new, Mercedes-Benz AMG GT Black Series Coupe. Remy knew it was worth over three hundred grand. She'd never seen one in real life, but Corey had pointed the same car out to her in *Car and Driver* magazine only a couple of months before. It was otherworldly beautiful, but she knew that opinion wasn't something she should share with Mr. Clayman. This was the trap she was expecting him to set.

"It's nice. Is this a midlife crisis thing for you?" Julia was probably going to kill her for riling her dad up, but she was tired of the games.

The question obviously took him off guard because he stood to his full height, which was about three inches more than Remy's five-foot-ten and stepped into her space. With very little distance between them, she could smell the slight stench of the cigarettes she knew he wasn't supposed to be smoking on his breath.

"I bought it for my wife on her sixtieth birthday. It's worth more than you'd hope to make in two seasons out on the water. The life Julia has had is very different from yours, Miller. Do you honestly believe you can provide her with the future she deserves?"

Seconds passed as Remy struggled to believe he had actually just said that. Sure, the very things that he said had crossed her mind, but that this asshole would say it to her face was something out of a movie. Ridiculous. Anger pushed the surprise from her mind, and she knew that the way she responded to him would mean everything. Not only for her future as a captain of his boats, but for her future with Julia, whatever that might look like.

As Remy gathered her thoughts, a vision of Julia curled up in blankets with her hair all mussed and the early morning light giving her an ethereal glow crossed her mind. It grounded Remy enough to fight back the anger. A calmness settled over her as she cleared her throat and took a step back, moving their interaction from confrontational to conversational.

"You're probably right, Mr. Clayman. I'll never be able to give someone a car like that. What I can offer is respect and love. The person Julia spends her time with isn't up to you, or me, for that matter. She's an intelligent, funny, remarkable woman and you should be proud to have her as your daughter. I can't presume to know what would make Julia happy, but at the moment we're enjoying our time together and I won't risk that by allowing her father to pick a fight with me. Besides, I have no doubt that Julia will someday be able to buy her own three-hundred-thousand-dollar car if that's something she wants. Her success has nothing to do with me."

Remy checked the time on her watch and glanced back toward the boat to see Andy and Corey pushing a cart with their supplies toward the warehouse. "If that's all, I'd like to help my crew finish up for the night. I have a date with a beautiful woman that I'd rather not be late for. Have a good night, Mr. Clayman."

Without waiting for a response, Remy turned and jogged toward the dock. She fought the urge to look back. After that interaction, she knew this might be her last day as a captain for Clayman Fisheries, but she wouldn't shirk her responsibilities just because her boss was a grade A asshole.

The cart of crab pots was halfway up the ramp to their storage space as she fell in next to Andy to help push it the rest of the way. This was exactly what she needed. Work. Muscle burning, mindless, physical labor that took her mind off the emotions that were swirling in her head.

"Do you want to talk about it?" Andy asked after they secured the warehouse door.

"Not really," she said.

Corey wrapped his arms around her from behind and squeezed her. "Are you okay, Rem?"

"I'm good. It was more about Julia than the job, but there's a chance I fucked this all up for us. I'm really sorry if I did."

Andy shrugged and joined the cuddle, sandwiching Remy between them. "Whatever happens, happens. You've done nothing wrong. I know we give you shit, but that's because we love you. Julia's a great girl, and you actually seem happy for once in your life."

"Right?" Corey added. "You're usually a lot grumpier."

"I've even seen her smile a few times. It's nice. Creepy, but nice," Andy said.

"You guys are dicks. I love you, but you're dicks."

Both of them backed away, and Andy wrapped an arm around her shoulder as they walked out to the parking lot.

"We love you, too, cousin," Corey said. "See you guys tomorrow."

They waved good-bye as Corey walked toward his truck.

"Where are you guys going on your date tonight?" Andy asked.

Remy mentally calculated how much time she had left before she was supposed to pick Julia up. An hour and a half should be plenty of time for her to get home, shower, and change into something that didn't smell like the ocean.

"Mini golf and dinner," Remy said.

"You suck at mini golf. Are you sure that's the best move to impress this girl? You're going to lose, and you can sometimes be a grumpy loser."

"That's not true." The truck chirped as Remy remotely unlocked the doors. They both toed off their boots and reached into the mounted toolbox in the truck bed to pull out slip-on shoes to wear home. She'd learned long ago that it was impossible to remove the smell of crab bait from the cab of a vehicle if you wore your boots inside the truck every day. Most fishermen didn't care, but thankfully Andy indulged her and changed her shoes, too.

"You don't think you're a sore loser?" Andy asked once they were both in the truck.

"No. I don't love to lose, but I'm not a baby about it."

"I'm not saying you're a baby. You just get a little…intense."

Remy didn't know what Andy was talking about. She had never freaked out over losing a game in her entire life. She wasn't a baby. "What are you talking about, dude?"

"Remember our freshman year when we played darts with Caleb and Jonathan and you hit the board so hard it fell off the wall?"

"Hey, someone hadn't nailed that board securely to the wall. That's not my fault," she argued.

"Fair enough, but I doubt it would have happened if you hadn't thrown the dart so hard. It seemed like you were trying to drive it through the board."

Remy remembered the night she was talking about and still hadn't forgiven Caleb or Jonathan for being such assholes about winning. It didn't help that she'd gotten into it with her dad earlier that night before going out and was already about three beers in by the time they'd played darts.

"One time," she said. "You can't judge me for the one time I lost my cool."

"No judgment. They were being dicks. You're just going to have to control that impulse to need to win when you're on a date."

"Duh. This isn't my first time going on a date, Dad."

Andy laughed. "You rarely take girls on dates where things get competitive. That's all I'm saying."

"I'll be fine."

"Need another example? Remember when you hit Kevin in the balls with your pool cue because he was trying to explain to you why you'd never make the shot because you weren't hitting the ball at the correct angle?"

"I—" Maybe Andy was right. She could get a little intensely competitive. "Fine. I'll be on my best behavior."

The difference between the games Andy mentioned and playing with Julia was that she didn't feel like she had to prove herself to Julia in that way. Being the youngest child and the only daughter of an overbearing father who constantly underestimated her abilities had obviously made her a bit overly competitive.

Things with Julia didn't make her feel that way. It was like she could allow herself to relax and enjoy their time together and didn't feel like she was being judged. It was different. She could really get used to that kind of different.

CHAPTER TWELVE

"C ome in!" Julia hoped she wasn't inviting a murderer into her house as she searched her aunt's closet for the right shoes to play mini golf in. She wanted to be comfortable but look stylish, and nothing she'd brought from Portland would do the trick. Even though she was much older, her aunt was better at the casual thing than Julia was, so she hoped since they were the same size, she could find something that would work for their date.

"Julia?" Remy called from the hallway.

"In here."

"I could have been a murderer, and you invited me right in."

Remy wrapped Julia up in a hug from behind and enveloped her in a cocoon of warmth and comfort. Their busy lives had kept them apart for a few days, and she'd missed her touch.

"Or a vampire," Remy said.

"What?"

"I could have been a vampire, and you just invited me into your home." Remy pulled Julia's hair away from her neck and placed several gentle kisses, followed by a delicate press of her teeth.

"Agh! No. Seriously. Vampires seriously freak me out." Julia giggled and rubbed where Remy had placed her teeth on her neck.

"You know—"

"Yes. Of course, I know. It's irrational, but they've freaked me out since I was a little girl."

"You're adorable." Remy left a trail of kisses from Julia's neck to her shoulders and around to her back.

"You aren't trying to cheat me out of a date, are you?"

Remy chuckled and stepped back. "I can't help it. All I think about when we're apart is when I'll get to touch you again. You can't blame me for being smitten."

"Smitten?" Julia turned in her arms so they were facing each other.

"Big time smitten."

"I didn't think big tough butches admitted when they were smitten."

"I'm so far past trying to hide my mushy center from you. You know my secret shame, and I swear you to secrecy."

"I don't know," Julia said. "We're all full up on secrets at this point."

"Well, it's not that secret." Remy's entire energy changed as she plopped down on Julia's bed.

Julia crawled in next to Remy and draped an arm around her middle. "What's going on?"

"Nothing. Sorry. I'm not trying to bring the mood down."

"It's okay. Did something happen today that upset you?"

"Your dad knows about us."

Julia wasn't expecting that answer. It was no surprise that her dad would find out. They hadn't exactly been hiding their attraction to each other in the parking lot the other day.

"Is that a problem?"

"No. I'm not afraid of your dad."

Julia sat up and studied Remy's face. That comment made it sound like her dad had confronted her. The man just can't help himself.

"What did he do?" Julia tried to keep her tone even and not reveal to Remy how frustrated she was with her dad.

"Nothing. He's fine."

"Remy. Please tell me."

Remy pulled Julia back down to lie next to her on the bed. "It's nothing." She brushed her thumb across Julia's cheek and then kissed her lips. "I'm sorry I brought it up."

"Please talk to me, Remy. I can't fix it unless I know what happened."

"There's nothing for you to fix. I'm sorry I brought it up. Please excuse my moment of sad-sackery."

"I don't think that's a word." Julia wanted to force Remy to talk to her but could see this wasn't the time to do it. "When you're ready to talk, I'm here. Always."

"Thanks," Remy said.

Julia kissed her once more before leaning down to slip her shoes on. "Are you ready for me to beat your ass at mini golf, sailor?"

"As if." Remy allowed Julia to pull her to her feet. "You're about to get schooled. I figured we'd stop for Mexican food at the place near there afterward. Does that sound good to you?"

"You never have to ask me if I want Mexican food. Just assume the answer will always be yes."

The nearest mini golf place was a couple of towns over, and by the time they had played a round, spent a half hour in the batting cages hitting balls, and an hour in the arcade, Julia was starving. They'd been seeing each other for a couple of months, but with their busy schedules, they hadn't had many opportunities for an actual date. It was nice.

"I enjoy hanging out with you," Julia said while they waited for their food to be delivered to their table.

"Really?" Remy reached across the table and took Julia's hand in hers. "Even though I'm an evil Miller?"

"Well, maybe not all the Millers are evil. Unless you're playing the long con, and you're waiting for me to let my guard down before revealing your devil horns."

"It's exhausting hiding those things from you. I'm so glad we're finally talking about it."

"I noticed your head was a little misshapen." Julia laughed when Remy tried to smooth down her hair.

"Hey, I have a couple of cowlicks that misbehave. I thought you liked my boyish good looks."

"Oh, I do. A lot. I was hoping you would stay the night at my house so I could show you how much I like you."

"Hmm. Check, please!" Remy pretended to get the attention of the server.

"Hold on. I'm not leaving without pastor tacos. Just warning you."

"Fair enough. I would never dream of coming between a girl and her tacos."

The server arrived with their food, and the conversation lulled while they dug in. Julia had been in relationships before and knew that things that might be adorable in the beginning would, at some point, sour and drive her crazy. As she watched Remy meticulously add salsa to her taco before delicately cradling it in her hand and then cramming as much as possible into her mouth, she laughed. It was inevitable in their relationship Remy would do things that drove her crazy. Still, right then, she was utterly adorable.

"I could eat like ten of these," Julia said.

"I don't know how you stay so tiny. You eat man-size portions, but you're so freaking fit."

"I work out, and I try not to snack. During the workday, I eat healthy food. Mostly vegetables, cottage cheese, and stuff like that. And I drink lots of water. The first thing I did when I took over for my dad was to add water coolers all over the building."

"I noticed they seemed to be everywhere."

"Hydration is essential. Besides, the more water I drink during the day, the less guilty I am about a couple glasses of wine in the evening."

"Or beer?" Remy held up her Dos Equis Ambar Especial bottle to tap against Julia's.

"Especially beer."

"Tell me about the first time you got drunk." Remy flagged down the server and asked for two more beers.

"First time I got drunk? Let me think...do you remember Garret Chambers?"

"Um, yeah, that guy was a dick. I was so glad when his family moved out of town our freshman year."

Julia took another bite of her taco and nodded. "Do you know why they moved?"

"His dad got a job up in Alaska, right?"

"Probably, but that wasn't the only reason."

"What do you mean?" Remy asked.

"You know Garret had always been a partier, right?"

Remy nodded. "He got naked and tried stealing Bob White's boat once. I thought Bob was going to take him out to the middle of the bay and drop him over the side tied to a crab pot."

"I remember that. My dad had to convince Bob it wouldn't be worth the legal fees trying to fight an attempted murder charge." They both laughed so hard that tears came to their eyes. "A few months later, Garret convinced his older brother to get him a bottle of vodka. Kayla Moore, Leslie Adams, and I got drunk with him in the little shelter on top of the tornado slide at Boynton Park."

"Seriously, how old were you?"

"Thirteen, almost fourteen, maybe? Way too young to be getting drunk."

"Jesus. I'm never having kids," Remy said.

The admission wasn't something Julia should have cared about. Still, she hated to admit that she was disappointed to hear Remy say that. They were so far from any serious discussion, like having kids, but Julia was passionate enough about wanting them herself that she couldn't let her say something like that without at least a follow-up question.

"You don't want kids?" Julia asked. She tried to toss it out there in as much of a casual way as she could, even though Remy's response was important to her.

Remy shrugged. "Maybe?" She drank the last of her beer and switched to her glass of water.

"Just maybe?" Julia needed more than that.

"I haven't really thought about it, I guess."

"Do you like kids?"

"I love kids. I have two nephews and one niece. All Peter's kids. The boys are great, but my niece Sailor. Oh, my goodness. She's the light of my life. Everyone says she looks and acts exactly like me when I was that age. It explains why my mom's hair grayed early, but something about that kid just makes my heart melt. I'd do anything for her, and she knows she has me wrapped around her little finger."

Julia's treacherous mind allowed her to imagine Remy carrying around a little toddler of their own, and her heart almost exploded. She thought she could work with that as long as Remy wasn't dead set on not having children. The important part was that the door didn't seem to be shut.

"She reminds me of my three-year-old niece, Haley. I'd do absolutely anything for that kid. She's smart as a whip and keeps her parents on their toes. My poor brother has his hands full with that one, and I love her to bits."

"Didn't Charlie marry Stephanie Turner?"

"Yep. They'd only been dating a couple of months when Stephanie got pregnant."

"That's rough," Remy said. "I used to work with her younger sister at the pool. She wasn't a big fan of Stephanie. It sounds like she bullied Kelly a lot when they were growing up."

Julia sighed and sat back in her chair. She didn't want to gossip about her sister-in-law, but she definitely had opinions about her. "I'm not surprised. I've met Kelly, and she seems like a nice woman. She's been to several family events, but I don't remember her from school."

"She went to a boarding school during the year and was only home in the summer. She was some sort of genius or something."

"That makes sense because I think she's a neurosurgeon now. I try to speak to Stephanie's family as little as possible."

Julia remembered the first time their families had gotten together after Haley was born. You could have cut the tension in the room with a knife. Her brother had already pulled away from his own family, and it was hard not to hold Stephanie at least partly responsible for that.

"Kelly's a good egg. If you see her again, tell her I asked about her."

Julia nodded and watched as Remy gave the server her credit card, and he hurried off to charge her for the meal.

"Thanks for a lovely evening. I had a really great time. Next time it's on me."

"Nope. You make me incredible meals at home. Taking you out on a date is the least I can do to thank you for taking such good care of me. The best I can do is chili. I'll make it for you at some point, and you'll see that I know how to chop things and what a pot is."

Julia laughed. "Deal. I'll provide the cornbread and dessert."

"That sounds amazing. What about next weekend?"

"Dylan's going to be in town. Are you okay with a plus-one?"

The server returned, and Remy signed the check and held her hand to help Julia to her feet. She slipped her arm through Remy's as they walked toward the parking lot.

"Would you mind if I invited Andy over, too? I've kinda been ditching her a lot, and I feel bad. Besides, we usually make chili together, anyway. Let us make dinner for you both."

"That sounds like an offer we can't refuse. I'll need to run it by Dylan first to ensure she's okay with the plan change. I'm sure it'll be totally fine. She's feeling neglected since I've spent so much time in Elder's Bay. I don't want to commit to something with you guys if she wants to be alone with me."

Remy held the car door open for Julia, then jogged to the driver's side. She knew some women would complain about the old-fashioned gestures Remy did, but Julia was eating them up. They made her feel cared for, and she hoped this was who Remy was, not just the early relationship version that was trying to impress her.

"I appreciate all the little ways you make me feel special," Julia said when Remy had gotten into the truck.

She backed out of the parking space and looked at her before she put it in drive. "You don't mind my hovering?"

"I don't think it's hovering at all. It tells me you care about me and express that in more ways than just with words. You're a catch, Remy Miller."

Remy held Julia's hand while she drove them toward Elder's Bay. "I appreciate you, too. Remember the other day when I stayed at your house, and you'd set the coffeepot to start at four a.m. so there would be a fresh pot for me before I left? And you left the little note on the counter telling me to have a good day, and it had the kiss with your lipstick?"

"I do. I wanted to wake up early and kiss you before you left, but I was being realistic and assumed that wouldn't happen. The note was the best I could do."

Remy let go of Julia's hand and pulled her wallet from her pocket. "Look where my driver's license is."

Julia opened the wallet and found the note she'd left Remy folded up and tucked away where she kept her license. It was adorable, and Julia's heart exploded a little. "You are definitely swoon-worthy, my friend. I think you just might be my favorite person."

"Ditto." Remy reached for Julia's hand again, and they were content to listen to the music on the radio the rest of the way home. There weren't many times in Julia's life when she truly felt content. She wasn't worried about work, her family, or her future. At that moment, all she needed was to hold Remy's hand.

CHAPTER THIRTEEN

The mood at the Miller family's weekly get-together was more subdued than their usual jubilant celebration. Remy thought it might be her, but even her brothers seemed distracted. She hadn't been brave enough to show up to a family event after they'd stormed out of the last one, but her brother Jay had texted her asking that she at least stop by to see their mom. Having the family together meant everything to her, and Remy didn't have the heart to keep disappointing the one person she knew loved her, no matter what.

"Hey, Mom," Remy said, wrapping her arms around her and kissing her cheek before turning to her dad. "Dad."

"Remy," he said before walking away to join a group of older men standing around the grill.

"Looks like he's still mad at me," Remy said to her mother.

"You knew he would be, honey. It won't be forever, though. You're his baby girl, and he'll always love you, no matter how angry he is."

She hoped her mom was right, but she couldn't be sure. As far as things that would piss her dad off the most, leaving the family business to work for their biggest rival had to be at the top of his list. The second on the list would probably be dating the heir to said rival family. Oh, boy.

"How are you?" Remy turned back to her mom and vowed not to allow her dad's dismissal to derail her visit. "Has your knee been bothering you?"

Her mom sighed and rubbed the knee in question. "Don't get old, sweetie. One star, would not recommend."

Remy laughed and pulled a chair over to sit next to her. "I'll do my best, although the alternative seems like a bummer, too."

"I guess you're right." Her mom squeezed Remy's knee and she marveled at how different their hands were. Remy's hands were large and square, like her dad's, while her mom's were delicate and small.

Genetics were such a funny thing. One would think her brothers would take after their dad, and Remy, their mom, but it was the opposite. Peter and Jay were slightly taller than her, but they both had a slight build, like their mom, while Remy had strong, broad shoulders and well-defined muscles. She was glad it wasn't something that caused tension between the three siblings. Her brothers had never made her feel like she was anything other than perfect just the way she was.

"How are things at work?"

Remy looked around to ensure no one else was listening to their conversation. It wasn't like she was sharing Clayman company secrets or had done anything wrong. Still, it felt strange to discuss aspects of her other job while surrounded by people who would love nothing more than to see the Claymans' business fail.

"They're good. Pretty great, actually. We've been catching our quota quickly enough that we're supposed to get more next week. The boat they've given us is the nicest I've ever run. The Claymans certainly don't spare any expense."

Her mother's eyes flicked toward her father and brothers, who huddled around each other like they were discussing the next play in a football game. Remy caught Jay's eye, and he gave her a sad smile before turning back to whatever their father was saying. Being the only girl, she'd sometimes felt a little separate growing up, but never as much as she did at that moment.

"Are you happy there? Are they treating you well?" her mother asked.

"Yeah. Sure. They're fine. I mostly deal with Brian's daughter, Julia. She's taken over things until he's back on his feet." Remy hoped her casual mention of Julia gave nothing away about how much more she was to her than just the boss's daughter.

"Didn't you go to school with her?"

"Hmm?"

"Julia Clayman, didn't you go to school with her?"

Remy hadn't been sure if the news that she'd been seeing Julia had reached her mom, but apparently, it hadn't.

"Umm, yeah. We were in the same grade but weren't friends growing up."

"Why not? What's wrong with that girl?"

Her mom was the best in the world. That someone wouldn't be friends with Remy was a mystery to her. She wasn't sure how to explain that it was mostly because they ran in different circles without making it sound like Julia was rich and she was poor. No matter how much they struggled, she knew her mom would never have considered them poor. And maybe she was right. Maybe rich and poor weren't the right way to classify their differences back then.

"We were very different people, Mom. I don't think it was something that either of us consciously did. We just never really hung out. Besides, she's a Clayman, and I'm a Miller. It was taboo for us to even acknowledge each other's existence."

Remy's five-year-old niece, Sailor, interrupted their conversation. She was the youngest of her nieces and nephews and was the spitting image of Remy at that age. She acted so much like her that her brother and his wife warned that if she became half the hellion teenaged Remy had been, she would be responsible for their therapy.

She loved all of her brother's kids, but she and Sailor obviously had a special connection.

"Hey, kiddo, what's going on?"

Sailor started the special greeting they'd choreographed, which never failed to make Remy's mom laugh. Once complete, she hugged them both and sat in front of them on the grass.

"Nothin'," Sailor said.

The sour mood was hard to miss. Remy reached out to smooth a cowlick from the crown of her head.

"What's wrong, sweetie?" Remy asked.

"Why haven't you been at Grandma's lately?"

Ugh. Remy hadn't thought about how avoiding her dad would affect Sailor. She'd always been a bit of an outlier since the older boys didn't want to include her in their games, and she wasn't interested in doing the things the other girls were interested in. Remy understood that feeling all too well, and she'd always tried her best to spend time with her when the family was together.

"I'm sorry, kiddo. I'm sure you probably heard, but I got a new job, and it's just kept me super busy."

"I heard." Sailor nodded. "Daddy said you work for Darth Vader. I don't think Darth Vader is real, though."

Remy rolled her eyes and reached out to welcome Sailor onto her lap. She curled into Remy's arms and rested her head on her shoulder. Remy glanced at her mom, who was sending Peter a look that had him squirming from across the yard.

"You're right, sweetie. Darth Vader is just in a story, and your dad was only kidding. He doesn't like the man I'm working for, but he isn't evil. He's just your dad's competitor. Do you know what that means?"

"Competitor?"

"Yeah, do you know what that is?"

Sailor looked toward Remy's mom for help, but she let Remy handle the explanation.

"No," Sailor said.

"You know how we always go to Sally's for fish and chips, but we never go to Nico's?"

Sailor nodded, and her soft brown curls bounced around her head.

"It's not because Nico is bad. He's a nice man and makes excellent fish and chips, but Sally is our cousin, and Nico is her competitor. They compete for the same customers, so they're competitors. We support cousin Sally and not Nico, but that doesn't make Nico an evil man."

A group of kids ran by, chasing each other, and Sailor watched them for a minute before nodding her head. "So you work for Nico's?"

Remy's mom chuckled.

"No. I work for the Claymans. They catch crab, just like our family does. They offered to let me be the boss on one of their boats, and since Papaw didn't have a boat where I could be the boss, I went to work for the Claymans. I want to be a captain, just like your dad and Uncle Jay. This was the only way I could do it right now. Does that make sense?"

Sailor wrapped her arms around Remy's neck and kissed her cheek. "Yep. I understand. So that means you aren't part of our family and can't come on Sundays. I want to be a Clayman, too."

Fuck. This all went off the rails quickly. "Hold on, missy. I'm not a Clayman. I'm still a Miller, and I promise I'll come every Sunday that I can, okay? Please never tell your dad that you want to be a Clayman. He'll really hate me."

She tickled Sailor until she fell off her lap in a fit of giggles. "He'll never hate you, Aunt Remy. He's your brother, and sometimes brothers get mad at their little sisters, but they never hate them. They love them very much."

"You're absolutely right. I'm glad you reminded me. You're pretty smart for only being five."

"I'll be six in two months, silly," Sailor said.

The number of kids had increased as they made another round through the yard and past where Remy sat.

"Hey, Caleb." She called for Sailor's oldest brother to come over.

"What's up, Aunt Remy?" At ten, Caleb was the leader of the group.

"Do you think you can include my friend here? She has some skills. What she lacks in stature, she makes up for in agility."

Caleb reached out a hand to pull Sailor to her feet. "Let's go, sissy. You can ride piggyback on me. We'll still be faster than those other slowpokes."

"Good man, Caleb," Remy said.

"Love you, Aunt Remy." Caleb waved as he pulled Sailor onto his back and took off toward the other kids.

Remy and her mom sat silently for a minute, just watching everyone. Her mom had always been an observer, and she understood the appeal. Her instinct was to dive into the fray, but sometimes it was nice to watch from the sidelines.

"So, this Clayman girl…."

Remy knew nothing would distract her mom from probing for more.

"Yes," Remy said. "Julia. Her name's Julia."

"Can I ask you a question, sweetie, and you won't be angry with me?"

Alarms sounded in her head, but Remy didn't have it in her to deny her mom anything so she reluctantly nodded and braced for whatever she would say next.

"Why did Julia reach out to you about this job? Do you think it might be a little suspicious that Brian Claymans daughter shows up out of nowhere and offers you your dream job."

Remy held her breath and counted backward from five to stop her instinct to spring to Julia's defense. Her mom was only asking questions. She could be a bit nosey at times, but she was never rude or intentionally hurtful.

"I understand why you might think that without knowing Julia. I wondered about that very thing in the beginning, but that's not who she is. I know she's a Clayman and my gut reaction is to not trust them, but these past few weeks I've gotten to know some of them, especially Julia, and they aren't bad people."

"I know that," her mom said. "I've never bought into the whole us against them thing, but I don't trust Brian Clayman as far as I could through him which is admittedly not very far. It would be more of a push, and I doubt he'd even budge."

"Just because Mr. Clayman isn't a good man, doesn't mean his daughter isn't trustworthy."

"What do you know about her besides the fact that she's quite beautiful and obviously intelligent?"

Remy couldn't stop herself from smiling when she thought about Julia. "Well, she's funny."

"You're funny, too. It's one of my favorite things about you."

"Thanks, mom. Julia's a different kind of funny, though. I'm more of a goofy funny, but she's so dam—er, darn smart and has the best come backs. She makes me laugh every day and she says these hilarious things while maintaining a straight face. I don't know how she does it."

Her mom picked up her glass of lemonade from the small table next to her chair and sipped it. She watched Remy babble about Julia quietly and it made Remy panic a little because she suspected her mom could see right through her. She had to end this Julia's amazing promotional speech as soon as possible.

"Anyway, I trust her," Remy said. "Besides, Dad hasn't left me with much of a choice, has he?"

"Are you and Julia dating each other?"

She was sure her mom had picked up on the complete panic she felt when she asked that question. She didn't know why. It wasn't exactly a secret that they were dating, especially in a small town like this, but admitting that to her mom who would likely tell her dad, left a ball of stress in the pit of her stomach.

"It's okay if you are, sweetie. I'm not judging you. I'm only trying to know more about your life. You've pulled away so much since you've started working at Clayman Fisheries and I guess I want to know if it's just about the job, or if there's more to the equation."

A crushing guilt settled over Remy. Her mom had always quietly been the rock of the family and sometimes it was easy to forget that even though her children were all grown, she still worried about them.

"I'm sorry, mom. I'm going to be better about not disappearing on you." Remy rubbed her thumb across the sun-bleached plastic armrest of the chair she was sitting in and tried to gather her thoughts. "Yes, Julia and I are dating."

"It's nothing to be ashamed of, Remy."

"No. I'm not ashamed at all. Actually, I think it's all kinda amazing. She's amazing. I just worry about Dad's reaction and what it will mean to my future in this family."

"Don't, Remington Miller. Don't think for a minute that your dad will not love you, or that your place in this family will be any different than always. He's an old man that's stuck in his ways, but he loves you so much."

"Hate the sin, but not the sinner, I guess." Remy's thumb was beginning to hurt from rubbing the rough plastic of the chair. Her nervous energy felt like it would burst out of her and the chair arm was her only outlet for the moment.

"That's not true," her mom said. "It isn't a sin to take a job that's good for your career and it will never be a sin to fall in love with someone that treats you well and loves you back."

Remy's gaze darted to her mom. It wasn't love. She and Julia didn't love each other, they were just enjoying this time together until Julia went back to Portland.

"It's not like that, Mom. She's only here until her dad is better and then she'll be back in Portland. This is only a temporary thing between us."

Her mom squeezed her hand. "I'm sure you're right, sweetheart. It's just that I can see a spark in you when you talk about Julia that I'm not sure I've seen in you before. It's nice."

"Yeah. Well. It's more complicated than I'm ready to deal with right now, so I'm just trying to enjoy the time we have together."

Laughter from the group of men her dad was talking to caught their attention. She knew he would never accept Julia as part of their family. Not that they were thinking long term, or even wanted more than they currently had, but if they did, he wouldn't be the one to let past prejudices go just because his daughter had a thing for her.

That thought made Remy mad even though he didn't know she had feelings for Julia yet. She knew she should allow him to prove her wrong, but everything inside her said he wouldn't understand.

"I know Dad won't be happy." She said the words out loud, but not necessarily to her mom. She just needed to voice them.

Her mom sighed and shook her head. "He can be a stubborn."

"You got that right."

"But sometimes he surprises me. Give him a chance before you decide how he'll feel. If you really love this girl, he loves you, and he'll understand. My parents didn't want me to marry your dad, but they eventually came around, and he will, too."

The conversation skipped about twenty steps, and Remy suddenly felt the need to escape.

"We're nowhere near talk of marriage or love, so we'll cross that bridge if we get there."

"Don't get in your own way, sweetheart."

"Remy," her dad called from the other side of the yard. "Come over here, kid. We want to ask you something."

She sighed and kissed her mom on the cheek. "Wish me luck."

"Don't let him bait you, Remy. He's in attack mode right now because he's hurt. Don't fall into his trap."

Remy shook her head. "I don't understand how you've been married to him for as long as you have. He can be such an ass."

She smiled and tugged on Remy's hand. "He can also be a sweet old bear. You take the good with the bad."

"You should be sainted. I love you, Mom. See you next week."

Remy knew that whatever was about to happen with her dad would be her cue to leave. She walked toward him and the group he'd gathered around him when her brother Jay stepped into her path.

"Hey," Jay said.

"Jay, what's up? Dad wants me," Remy said.

He looked toward their dad, shook his head, and then waved a hand to get his attention. "Hey, Dad, I need to talk to Remy about something."

Her dad nodded and waved a dismissive hand in their direction.

"Come on," Jay said. "Let's go sit in your truck and talk."

"You're being weird."

"Just come on," Jay said.

Once they were safely in the truck, Jay looked around, ensuring nobody else was around. The realization that he might be worried someone saw them together cut her deeply.

"Look, I didn't ask you to come out here, so if you have a problem being seen with me, just get out and let me leave."

"What?" Jay seemed genuinely surprised by what she said. "Dude, this isn't about that. I wanted to ask you something and didn't want anyone to overhear us talking."

This day was getting stranger by the minute, and Remy just wanted to go to Julia's and pretend none of it happened.

"Ask me what? Are you in some kind of trouble?"

Jay pulled his phone from his pocket and scrolled through the photos. When he found the one he wanted, he held it up for Remy to see.

"This is probably nothing, but does this log of Bratton's seem a little off to you?"

Remy looked at the photo of a standard log they kept to record their daily activities while underway. It was used to document vital information for each string of pots like their depth, the number of pots on the string, their soak time, the location of the string, estimated pounds caught, what bait they used, etc. They were required to turn in a yellow copy of the logbook pages for each month to the Oregon Department of Fish and Wildlife. This helped Fish and Wildlife track not only what the commercial fishing fleet was doing, but how much they were hauling in.

The captain kept the original logbook on the boat so they could refer to it later when they were trying to find a good spot to drop their pots. For the copies to be different, they would have to be intentionally altered and this might indicate to Fish and Wildlife that the boat's captain was hiding something or knowingly misrepresenting to the state agency what they were doing.

In the photo, Remy could see the yellow and white copy of a page from the logbook, which should have the same information listed, but there were a few discrepancies, like the estimated pounds and locations of the strings. They weren't significant differences, but enough to possibly get the logs flagged. Fish and Wildlife officers could then ask the captain to explain the discrepancies.

"That's super weird. I don't understand how this could even happen unless someone deliberately changed those numbers. Has Dad seen this?"

Jay shook his head and slipped his phone back into his pocket. "No. I only noticed because Dad asked me to compare the logs from all of our boats to get ahead of the crab. Things have been pretty spotty lately, and I think the old man's a little nervous."

The urge to share any information she had about where she'd successfully found crab was hard to keep to herself. Still, she knew it would be unethical of her to tell her employer's competition, so she kept her mouth shut.

"Do you think Bratton did this on purpose? I don't really understand how it would be an accident, but why would someone do this on purpose?" Remy asked.

"I don't know. I'm trying to give him the benefit of the doubt, but I'm also keeping my eye on him. He acted like he didn't know how it happened when I asked about it. There's no proof he did anything wrong. I caught the mistakes before we turned it into Fish and Wildlife, so nothing will come of it. I hope I'm just making a mountain out of a molehill."

The last thing Remy felt like doing was sticking up for the ass hat sitting in the captain's chair that was rightfully hers, but none of that was Jay's fault. She wouldn't take her beef with her dad out on him.

"Maybe it's nothing, but I would watch that guy if I were you. Fish and Wildlife don't have a sense of humor about incorrect logbooks. That's a headache you don't need," Remy said.

"Should I tell Dad?" Jay seemed antsy, and she couldn't tell if the idea of telling their dad about what happened or not telling him made him more nervous.

"I wouldn't tell him until I could see if something else happened. If it was just a one-off thing, and somehow an accident like he said, Dad won't be happy that you bothered him with what is essentially paperwork issues."

Remy felt her phone buzz in her pocket and pulled it out to see a message from Julia asking when she would be home. Referring to her house as home to Remy made her heart beat a little faster. She smiled and sent off a quick message, telling her she'd be there soon.

"Sorry," Remy said as she pocketed her phone and turned back toward Jay. "That's me, though. You have a better relationship with Dad, so maybe it's better for you to talk to him. Or at least mention it to Peter. It wouldn't hurt to have someone watching Bratton, and Peter won't hesitate to tell Dad if he thinks it's serious."

Jay nodded. "Yeah. You're right." He pointed toward her pocket and smiled. "Are you still seeing Julia?"

This was different. The last time they'd talked, Jay had scolded her for fraternizing with the enemy.

"Yep. I…" Remy hesitated, then looked Jay right in the eyes. "I think I might really like her."

"Wow." Jay looked shocked. "I don't think I've heard you say that before."

Remy shrugged and looked out the window to hide her embarrassment.

"It's good," Jay said. "I'm happy for you, Rem." He pulled her across the center console and into a hug.

"We aren't getting married or anything, but I like her, and she likes me, so it's a start."

"A fantastic start," Jay said. "I love you, sis."

"I love you, too, brother. Good luck with that dipshit Bratton."

"Yeah, thanks." Jay hopped out of her truck and jogged toward the yard, where the party was still in full swing. Part of her yearned to go back and be with the people she'd spent her entire life with. A bigger part of her just wanted to get back to Julia.

She watched as her childhood home grew more distant in her rearview mirror. They'd always be a part of her life. She wouldn't want it any other way, but things were different now. Remy was different, and there was no going back to the lost kid she once was.

CHAPTER FOURTEEN

The timer dinged and Julia pulled the fresh-baked dinner rolls from the oven. Remy texted to say she would be home soon, so hopefully that meant before the food was cold. Julia had left her parents' house two hours before and stopped by the store to pick up everything she'd need to make Remy a nice meal. Cooking had always been something she enjoyed doing, but making something for Remy felt special.

She wasn't ready to give up her job and stay in an apron all day like Remy's little woman, but it was nice to make her something that she obviously appreciated so much. Making Remy happy made Julia happy, and that felt nice.

"Honey, I'm home," Remy said from the entryway. Julia had given her a key to the house so she could let herself in. Another first for her as far as relationships went.

She met Remy on her way into the kitchen and kissed her. It had started to rain a few minutes before and Remy's hair was still wet and mussed. She looked rugged like a lumberjack. Julia hadn't realized how into lumberjacks she was.

"Hey, baby, is it too cheesy to tell you I missed you today?" Julia asked.

Remy lifted her up onto the counter and pressed her body between Julia's legs. She rested her head against Julia's breasts and wrapped her arms around her for a tight hug. "I missed you so much. This is exactly what I needed."

"Is everything okay?" Julia asked as she combed her fingers through Remy's hair.

Remy shrugged but didn't answer. Julia knew she'd been dreading going to her family dinner and if she had to guess, things didn't go well.

"Do you want to talk about it?"

"Not now, if you don't mind." Remy's words were muffled from speaking with her face buried in the fabric of Julia's shirt. "Is it okay if you hold me for a minute and then we have a nice evening? I promise I'll talk to you about it, but I need a little comfort first."

"I get it and it's perfectly fine. Whenever you're ready to talk, I'll be here."

Remy nodded then moaned in appreciation. "Mmm. This is possibly the best place on the entire earth."

"Pressed against my boobs?"

"Exactly. This whole situation is almost orgasmic. Your fingernails grazing my scalp as you play with my hair, my face buried in the cushion of your bosom…heaven."

"All for you, sweetie." Julia kissed the top of Remy's head and gave her a gentle squeeze. "You almost ready to eat?"

"Almost."

Remy released the buttons of Julia's shirt and kissed down her chest to the sensitive skin between her breasts. They would never eat if she didn't get things under control right now, but she wasn't sure how much she cared about eating when Remy made her feel like this.

"Remy? Should we pause this to eat dinner?"

"Mm-hm."

When there was no sign of stopping, Julia pulled Remy's head away from kissing her way toward the point of no return and pressed their foreheads together so she could catch her breath. "You slay me."

"That's a good thing, right?"

"Mmm. That's a really good thing," Julia said.

Remy stepped back and helped Julia down from the counter. Over the next hour, they enjoyed the meal she had prepared and talked about Julia's day. She told Remy about her brother and his family being at her parents' and how they announced they were expecting a baby in late spring. It all seemed so domestic and Julia had never realized how much she would enjoy that aspect of being in a relationship with someone.

She'd dated women before, but never to the point that they talked about intimate details of their family. It was nice. She wouldn't have guessed how nice, but she could get used to this.

"Hey, can I ask you a question?" Remy took her hand and pulled her toward the living room once they'd put the food away and washed and dried all the dishes.

"You can ask me anything," Julia said.

Remy sat at one end of the couch and pulled Julia down to snuggle next to her, almost covering Remy's body with her own.

"Are you my girlfriend?"

"I want to be your girlfriend. I know we haven't really labeled what's happening, but neither of us are seeing other people and I basically want to be with you all the time. That sounds like girlfriend status to me."

Remy's smile left no question as to how she felt. "Good. Same."

Julia rested her head on Remy's chest and enjoyed the warmth she felt there.

"I want this forever," Julia said.

"What's that?"

"This feeling. Contentment."

Love? They hadn't talked about feelings that serious, yet, but Julia knew she was falling in love with Remy. She turned in Remy's arms and allowed herself to be cradled. They kissed and when she pulled back, Julia knew from the hunger in Remy's eyes that she had noticed her black lacy bra.

"That was supposed to be a surprise for later," Julia said.

Remy shifted to lie Julia flat on the ground and knelt beside her to unbutton her shirt and toss it to the side, leaving her gorgeous upper body exposed. Remy hadn't been wearing a bra, but with her small, athletic breasts, she rarely needed one.

"You're so fucking hot." Julia grazed her manicured nails down Remy's chest and across the hard peak of a nipple.

"You wreck me," Remy said. She groaned as she unhooked the front clasp of Julia's bra and watched her full breasts spill out. "Fuck me."

Soft lips enveloped Julia's nipple and gave it a slight suck. The feeling shot to her pussy, and she felt her wetness coat the inside of her thighs.

"What do you want, baby?" Remy asked.

"Your fingers deep inside of me." Julia moaned as Remy unbuttoned her jeans and stared deep into her eyes as she pulled Julia's zipper down.

"Is that all?"

Julia lifted her hips as Remy grasped her jeans and pulled them and her panties down her legs, leaving them bunched just below her knees.

"I want all of you." Julia's clit throbbed with the anticipation of what she hoped was about to happen. The vision of Remy without a shirt but still in tight jeans and a wide brown belt was enough to push her toward the edge.

A low chuckle rumbled in Remy's chest. "You can have anything your little heart desires." Remy moved behind Julia and pushed her legs forward, still bound by her jeans and panties. "Spread your legs as much as you can and pull your knees as close to your chest as is comfortable. I want to look at your beautiful pussy."

"Remy, this can't be a sexy position."

"That's where you're wrong, Julia Clayman. Every position you're in, especially when you're so vulnerable, is the sexiest thing I've ever seen." Remy opened Julia's folds with her thumbs and stared at her pussy.

"Remy, what are you—?"

"Shh. Relax and give yourself to me, sweetheart." A single finger rubbed the tight circle of her entrance, and Julia felt a rush of wetness ease its way. Her pussy contracted, trying to pull the digit inside.

"Beautiful. Absolutely beautiful," Remy said.

The pounding of her heart was almost deafening as she watched Remy gaze upon her like a painter falling in love with their masterpiece. She knew that whatever made Remy look at her that way wasn't her doing. It was all Remy. Every time they were together, it was as if Remy had created her and knew exactly where to touch and kiss to make her melt into a puddle at her feet.

"Remy, I—"

"It's okay, sweet girl. Do you want me to stop? Yes or no?"

Julia shook her head and pulled her knees closer to her chest. "No."

"Good." Remy leaned forward and placed kisses everywhere but where Julia wanted her mouth the most.

"I love being inside of you."

A nod and a gasp when Remy's fingers dipped into her eager hole just enough to register that it was there was all Julia could manage. Remy added a second finger, still only an inch or two inside, and used them to stretch her eager entrance.

"Remy—"

"Shh."

Remy kissed Julia's clit before pulling it into her mouth for a gentle suck.

"Yes, fuck. That feels so fucking good, Remy."

Two fingers pushed deeper into her core as they started a slow rhythm, in and out. Remy scooted up to lift Julia's bottom and rest it on her lap. She wrapped one arm around Julia's legs to hold them against her torso while she rubbed her clit with her thumb.

"I'm close," Julia said.

"Are you ready to come, baby?"

"Yes, please, yes. Make me come. I want to feel you inside me while I come."

Remy changed her position slightly and curled her fingers against Julia's G-spot. The change in pressure immediately sent her over the edge. She came and came until her throat was sore from screaming. When she couldn't take any more, she gently pushed

Remy's arm. Remy slowed her movement, and carefully removed her fingers from Julia's depths.

Out of breath, Remy collapsed next to Julia and cradled her in her arms.

"I need to either pull my pants back on or remove them completely."

"Let's take them off." Remy helped Julia remove the rest of her clothes.

Julia kissed Remy and tugged on the button of her pants enough to express her intent but not follow through with the action yet. "You look incredibly sexy in jeans, but these will have to go."

"You're bossy."

Julia watched as Remy removed her pants and boxers before straddling her face.

"Is this okay?" Remy asked.

Julia nodded enthusiastically. Remy's knees were on either side of Julia's head as she opened herself up and lowered her pussy to Julia's waiting mouth.

"Fuck, yes, Julia. That feels amazing." Remy rocked back and forth, and Julia used her tongue to alternate between rubbing her clit and slipping inside her tight hole. "I'm already close. Jesus Christ, I can't believe how good you are at that."

"Come in my mouth, baby."

Julia loved that sex with Remy was always different and a little dirtier than in some of her past relationships. She was tired of sex always being this precious thing that had been so loaded with emotion. She was all for that. Sex with someone you loved was amazing, and having sex was the best way to express those feelings to each other, but sometimes she wanted it raw and hard, and Remy was game for all of that.

Remy collapsed forward and held her pussy open for Julia to suck while still supporting her body from falling over. Julia caressed Remy's muscular body as she felt her clit getting harder and harder in her mouth.

"I'm coming," Remy said as she groaned, a guttural cry that sounded like a wild animal. Their sweat slicked skin glistened in the low light of a lamp. "You've ruined me for anyone else. Nothing could ever compete with this."

Julia pulled Remy next to her and snuggled into her side. "So, you're telling me that you've found at least one redeeming quality in a Clayman?"

Remy laughed and covered Julia's mouth with her hand. "Let's just keep that one between us."

CHAPTER FIFTEEN

Remy pulled off her glove and ran a finger across her lips. They were still tender from a morning filled with kisses and so many more things she should not be thinking about while piloting a boat that close to the shore. She smiled at her memories of Julia, then cleared her throat and looked around to ensure Corey and Andy hadn't caught her being a lovesick sap.

Ugh. This was so not her. She'd never, ever been like this in her entire life. Of course, when she got all googly over a girl, it had to be a girl from the family she'd always been told to stay far away from. After her run-in with Brian Clayman in the parking lot, she couldn't argue with the stories she'd heard about him, but not all the Claymans were terrible. Julia was certainly an exception to the rule.

"We're here," Remy said as they arrived at the coordinates she'd mapped out that morning for where they'd drop their first string. "You ready?"

"Ready," Andy and Corey called from the deck.

"Here we go." Remy marked the start of their string on her navigation unit and touched the button to signal to the crew it was okay to toss the first buoy, followed by the pots secured to a line and spaced two hundred feet apart.

Remy leaned out the window to watch the pots plunge into the ocean as her crew tossed them over the side. When the string was complete, she noted the last location in the log.

"Okay, guys, take a break. We've got about forty minutes to the next coordinates."

Andy and Corey both went below deck to hang out in their bunks. They'd be on the boat for the next forty-eight hours, so she did her best to give them alone time when possible.

She had planned the location of her following two strings beforehand, but after that, she hadn't decided where to go yet. As a refresher of previously suitable areas, she pulled out her logbook for reference. Then she opened the navigation software on her computer to show historical data. The logbooks were invaluable for understanding where the crab liked to gather. She thought back to her brother, mentioning their new captain possibly altering the entry on the copy of the log.

A discrepancy like that could cost her dad a hefty fine and bring negative attention to his business, that was extra time and money they didn't have to spare. Remy was glad Jay caught the error before he had turned the logs in to Fish and Wildlife.

Some fishermen found it an annoyance to have to do things like keep accurate logs, but Remy understood how important it was for the future of their fishery to have some kind of accountability. Her grandpa had always told her to take care of the ocean and she'll take care of you. Small things like keeping accurate logs were one way to do that.

Even captains that thought the logs were a waste of time, knew better than to screw with them and report inaccurate information. That was inexcusable. The fact that Dan had the correct information on one sheet and what should be the duplicate had been altered was unfathomable. She couldn't help but wonder how the hell it happened.

Losing the boat to some other captain was hurtful enough to drive her away. Still, she'd never wish that kind of careless behavior on her dad. She might not be happy with them, but they were family.

"Hey," Andy said from behind her.

"I thought you were taking a break?"

Andy shrugged and sat in the other chair. Remy watched as she pulled a box of Nerds candy from her pocket and poured some into her mouth. She reached out her hand, and Andy handed her the box. They'd been friends long enough to not care as much about things like germs.

"What's on your mind?" Remy asked as she crunched on the strawberry-flavored bits of candy.

Andy took the box back and poured more into her mouth. "I don't know. I guess I miss you, jackass."

"Aww. You're such a charmer. You're still helping me make chili for Dylan and Julia this weekend, right?"

"Yep. Who is this Dylan person? Have you met him before?"

"*She* is Julia's roommate and best friend. They share an apartment in Portland. They went to college together. I met her when Julia and I spent the weekend there for that art thing Dylan had to attend."

Andy struggled to get the candy out of the box and finally blew the dust from an empty coffee cup on the table and poured the contents from the package into the cup. "Is that when you got the fancy clothes Julia helped you pick out?"

"Yep." Remy watched Andy pour candy into her mouth like she was drinking it from the cup. "Dude. Did that cup have crusted up old coffee in it?"

Andy inspected the cup, inside and out for some reason, before shrugging. "Yeah. I guess so. It was dry."

"You're disgusting," Remy said.

"Not all of us can be fancy with our fancy girlfriends and fancy clothes we wear to fancy art shows in the city."

"Don't be a dick."

Andy laughed and handed Remy the cup of candy. Remy hesitated for only a moment before tipping the contents into her mouth and crunching on the strawberry candy that now had a hint of coffee flavor.

"Tell me more about this Dylan woman."

"What do you want to know?"

"Come on, Rem. Don't be like that."

Remy picked up her phone and searched through her chat history for a photo she remembered Julia sending her. She clicked on it once she'd found it and showed it to Andy. It was of Julia and Dylan hiking the Pacific Coast Trail together a few years before. Both girls looked exhausted but happy with their arms wrapped around each other and hats raised in the air to celebrate the conclusion of their journey.

"She's cute. How long have they lived together?" Andy asked.

"They shared a dorm room together at Stanford and remained best friends after graduation. Julia moved to Portland to be with some girl who eventually broke her heart. I guess Dylan came up to help her move out after the breakup, and they ended up getting a place together. Dylan's an artist and can basically live anywhere."

An alarm sounded and Remy called down to Corey to have him check the engine room. Occasionally things shifted, or sensors misfired, but it was always best to check, just in case something was wrong.

Remy and Andy silently watched the waves while they waited for Corey to check on the boat. The navigation program showed they were approaching their next location just as Corey stepped into the pilothouse.

"That alarm was nothing, Cap. I checked everything, and it all looks good," Corey said.

"Good. You guys ready to earn your money?"

"Yep." Andy stood and followed Corey toward the deck. "Hey, what do you think I should wear to the dinner? Does Dylan like a snappy dresser or is she into the casual but studly type?"

"Get out of here, lover boy. Stop stalling and get to work."

"I was just curious."

"Mm-hm." Remy laughed and pushed the buzzer to indicate they could start dropping the next string.

She watched them work and wondered why anyone would want any other job. Hanging out with your best friends, spending days on the ocean, and perfect sunsets every night, it didn't get better than this.

Julia didn't exactly spend her time out on the water, but Remy wondered why she would ever want to live away from the coast.

She seemed so happy in Elder's Bay right now, but eventually, she'd have to return to her life in Portland. What would that mean to whatever thing they had going on between them now? Whatever that was. It might not be anything. Although the more time they spent together, the more it felt like something.

And if it became something, could Remy move to Portland? Julia made much more money, and the last thing she'd ever want to do is expect her to leave the life she'd worked so hard for to just come back to tiny Elder's Bay.

Remy moving to Portland seemed like a reasonable choice, but the thought of leaving this—giving up her dream of being a captain—made her sick to her stomach. It was all she'd ever wanted. Hell, she'd pissed off her entire family to chase that dream. Was Julia worth giving all of that up? Probably.

She knew that if she ever let herself actually entertain those feelings, she'd decide Julia was worth whatever it took to be with her. The bigger question was, could Remy be happy without her dream? Could she walk away from the ocean and become one of those who visited on the weekends? Not to be dramatic, but that would kill her. She knew it would eventually cause resentment and frustration, destroying her relationship with Julia.

Life was so much more complicated when relationships were thrown into the mix. Whatever was going on between them, thoughts of moving and futures shouldn't even be a blip on their radars right now.

When the string was complete, and she'd logged the information in the logbook, she asked Corey to watch the helm so she could give Julia a call. Sometimes the service was total shit when they were underway, but they were in a pocket of good reception at that moment, and she wanted to hear her voice before she lost the opportunity.

The motor's hum was comforting as she headed for her rack for some privacy. She stripped out of everything other than her shirt and thermal pants, climbed under the covers, and selected Julia's name from her contacts list.

"Hey, baby, I wasn't expecting to hear from you tonight. Is everything okay?" Julia's voice made her homesick for the shore for possibly the first time in her life.

"Yeah, everything's great. I had four bars and crawled into my rack to call while I could."

"It's so weird that sailors call their beds racks. Why is that?"

"No idea. I think it's a navy term or something. It's just what we call it."

"It sounds like a torture device," Julia said.

"It can sometimes be." Remy shuffled around, trying to find a more comfortable position on the thin mattress. "How was your day? Did you do anything fun?"

"I don't know if I'd call it fun, but I had a nice day. I think I might actually have a genuine talent for this stuff."

"What stuff?" Remy asked. "Working?"

"Well, yes, but specifically managing the boats and crews. The things you've shared about what you do and your daily routine have helped me better understand the captains that work for me. Thanks for that."

"My pleasure," Remy said. "For what it's worth, I think you're doing an amazing job, and I have heard nothing other than positive stuff from the others. Maybe that's because they know you're my girl, but I don't think that would stop sailors from complaining if they had an issue with someone."

"No, you're right about that." There was a rustling of fabric on Julia's end of the line, followed by a contented sigh.

"What was that for?"

"Nothing. I just got under the blankets. Hearing your voice always makes me feel all warm and cozy," Julia said.

"I wish I was warm and cozy right next to you."

"Me, too, sweetheart. Me, too."

Remy could have closed her eyes right then and gone to sleep, but she didn't want to miss a minute of being able to talk to Julia, so she forced herself to stay awake. "Tell me a story."

"A story about what?" Julia asked.

"Anything. I just want to listen to you talk."

"Well, Dylan called earlier and said she'd be here by noon on Friday."

Remy rolled over to face the wall on one side of her rack. She hoped it would help muffle the sound of her voice in case Andy was near.

"Hey, is Dylan seeing anyone?"

"No, not that I know of. Why?"

"I showed Andy that picture of you guys on the trail, and she seemed...interested."

"Interested, huh?"

"I know, right? We're regular little matchmakers."

"This could either be amazing or terrible."

"Why?"

"Well, if they hit it off and everything goes well, our best friends are dating, and that's awesome for us. If they don't and there's tension, that would be a bummer at future get-togethers."

"True," Remy said. "I think they'll hit it off and live happily ever after."

"You're such a romantic. I love it," Julia said.

Corey stuck his head into the room and pointed up to indicate it was time for her to get back to work. She nodded and lifted a finger to show she'd be one more minute.

"Hey, I have to get back to work, baby," Remy said.

"Boo," Julia said. "I can't wait for this weekend. It's hard when you're out for so long. My poor little feet get cold at night."

Remy laughed. "Yeah, you'll have to wear socks because the next time you press those ice cubes against my leg while I'm sleeping, you will leave me no choice but to punish you."

"What are you going to do to me?"

Unsure of where this was going, Remy remained silent.

"Remy? Did I lose you?"

"No. I'm here. I'm just wondering if you're asking me for what I think you're asking me for. Because if you are, um, yeah, I'm totally down with that."

"I'm sure you can devise many pleasurable ways to punish me." Julia almost purred, and Remy felt it down to her clit.

She cleared her throat before she spoke for fear that it would only come out in a croak. God, this woman made all her dreams come true.

"I can think of something appropriate. Don't feel you need to put your cold ass feet on my leg to deserve a punishment, though. That's just cruel."

"You got it. Now, get back to work. Those crabs won't jump in the boat on their own. I'm your boss, and I shouldn't be distracting you."

"You distract me whether or not we're on the phone. I'm going to go. I l—iked talking to you. See you Friday night."

Remy hung up the phone in a panic before Julia could question her about what she had almost said. What the hell was she thinking? They'd barely decided to be girlfriends. It was way too soon to bring out love talk. She'd never said that to anyone romantically and assumed she never would. Man, this woman was going to be the death of her.

CHAPTER SIXTEEN

Julia watched Dylan pull into her driveway and rushed out the door to greet her. They'd lived with each other for years, and she hadn't realized how much she had missed her until now. She'd been living two separate lives between Elder's Bay and Portland, and the visit was like having her worlds collide.

"You made it." Julia wrapped her arms around Dylan and placed kisses all over her face.

"Man, isn't that girlfriend of yours giving you enough attention?"

"Shut up, or I'll tell you exactly how much attention she's giving me," Julia said.

"No thanks," Dylan said. "Well, maybe. Let's drink wine first."

Julia picked Dylan's bag up and slung it over her shoulder. "Let's get you inside."

The spare bedroom was on the opposite side of the cottage from the master Julia had been staying in. At first, she'd felt a little sheepish about using her aunt's bedroom, but she had reassured her it was too nice to not enjoy while she was gone. The bathroom alone made her swoon with the large soaking tub of her dreams.

She'd started a fire in the fireplace and lit several candles around the room to make it smell warm and inviting. Julia loved this little cottage and could see herself living somewhere exactly like it someday. It was so different from their apartment in downtown Portland in all the best ways.

There were neighbors, but the house had a yard big enough to accommodate a vegetable garden on one side and a brick patio with a seating area on the other. The backyard had a massive fireplace at the edge of another patio, covered by a beautiful wooden pergola. A large table that could seat ten people sat under it. It reminded Julia of the many family dinners they'd had there when she was growing up.

"This place is amazing, Jules. You're seriously never going to want to leave."

"I know. It's honestly perfect." Julia couldn't hide the sadness in her voice when she thought about having to abandon the place that had begun to feel like home in such a short time.

Dylan looked at her quizzically, then wrapped an arm around her shoulders and guided her toward the kitchen. "I brought you Gilda's for dinner and the ingredients to make an old-fashioned."

"This is exactly why I love you so much," Julia said. She'd been craving her favorite Italian restaurant, and Dylan made the best version of her favorite drink. God, she'd missed this.

"I'm happy to supply you with all the trappings of civilization while you're roughing it in the boondocks."

Julia pulled plates out of the cabinet and popped the food containers in the microwave to heat them up. Friday nights at Gilda's had been somewhat of a tradition of theirs for years, and even though eating it here wouldn't be the same as being in the restaurant, she was excited to have a small piece of that life in Elder's Bay.

"Here you go, my dear," Dylan said, handing Julia her cocktail.

She took a sip and sighed. "I don't understand how you do it, but your old-fashioned is the best I've ever had anywhere. You have a gift."

Dylan kissed her cheek and carried the heated bowls of food into the dining area. Julia followed with the plates and a bowl of salad. They both sat and dished up portions of the food.

"How are things going?" Dylan asked.

Julia wiped her mouth with her napkin and nodded her head. "Good. You know. There's a learning curve, but I'm figuring it out."

"Do you still like dealing with the stinky fishermen, or has the sparkle of that part of your job worn off?"

A memory of Remy in the rain gear she wore on the boat came to Julia's mind. She looked so disheveled and sexy, like some sailor version of a warrior. Julia wouldn't have guessed how much that turned her on, but she was into it.

"Julia? Where did you go?"

"Sorry." Julia tried to hide her smile, but she knew Dylan would see right through her. "Working with the fishermen has been fun. They seem gruff, but once you get to know them, they're a great bunch. Mostly. Some of them don't like that I'm in charge instead of my dad, but I'm dealing with them."

"Any serious problems?"

Julia shook her head and sipped her drink. "Nothing I can't handle. They aren't violent, just grumpy. I've lived with you long enough that I can handle grumpy."

Dylan laughed and kicked Julia under the table. "Shut up, asshole."

"Speaking of sexy fishermen..." Julia started.

"I didn't recall saying anything about them being sexy, but go on."

"Remy asked if we wanted to meet them at the local bar tonight. I know they're coming over tomorrow night to cook us dinner and watch a movie, but this would give you a chance to meet her crew."

"Crew? Is Andy part of that crew?" Dylan asked.

"Yep. Remy, Andy, and Corey run the boat together. I take it you liked the photo I sent you of Andy?"

Dylan wiped the last remnants of sauce from the plate with her piece of focaccia, then sat back and rubbed her stomach. She shrugged, and Julia could have sworn she saw Dylan's cheeks flush. That was definitely new. "Maybe."

"Playing hard to get?" Julia winked at Dylan, who answered with a roll of her eyes.

"I know nothing about her other than that she's a total hottie, and she works on a boat. That's not much to go on, Jules, even for me."

They both picked up their empty dishes and started for the kitchen.

"I grew up with her, but she's always been kinda shy. We worked at the pool together one summer. She seemed like a responsible, kind person. Patient with the kids at the pool. Respectful of the adults. I like her. Remy loves her like a sister, and that's high marks in my book."

"Well, she doesn't sound like a serial killer. That's a start."

Julia took a freshly poured old-fashioned from Dylan, and they both walked toward the living room to sit in front of the fire.

"They've been out for a few days but should pull into port about now. They'll need to unload the boat and then go home to get cleaned up, so we have a little time to hang before they're at Skipper's."

"What are you getting me into, Julia?" Dylan asked. "This girl lives hours away from Portland. I'll kill you if I end up falling for her, and nothing can come of it because of logistics."

"You're getting a little ahead of yourself since you haven't met her, but if you fall for Andy, I will take responsibility. Besides, it's not that far from here to Portland. Remy and I make it work."

Dylan drained the last of her drink and set the empty glass on the coffee table. "Sure you do. You're mostly in Elder's Bay and only occasionally drive to Portland every couple of weeks. I thought the arrangement would change once your dad was back at work. You told me it was why things have remained casual between you and Remy."

Julia focused her attention on a string that had come loose from the stitching of her leggings. She couldn't argue with anything Dylan said, but she'd been happy to block all of that out until it became an issue.

"Julia?" Dylan reached out to take Julia's hand and squeeze it. "You remember that this little fairy tale won't last forever, right? Things will have to change."

She finished the last of her drink and picked up both of their glasses to take to the sink. "I know. It's just…more complicated than I had expected."

"Complicated, how? Has Remy knocked you up? Is there some secret baby you haven't told me about yet? Can we name her Audrey? I've always wanted to name a little girl Audrey."

"Slow down, crazy town. Don't be weird. If Remy got me pregnant, a long-distance relationship would be the least of our worries since they would whisk us off to some government facility to be studied ET-style."

Dylan followed Julia toward the kitchen. "Well, I'd totally rescue you on my bike, but you will have to be the one in the basket. I don't like that look for me."

Julia handed the last of the dirty dishes to Dylan to place in the dishwasher and hugged her. "I'm so glad you're here."

"Okay, let's do this. Give me a bit to clean up, and I'll be ready."

Julia started the dishwasher and slipped her arm through Dylan's as they walked out of the kitchen. "I missed you so much."

"I missed you, too. I can't wait to see your hunk of a girlfriend again. Did she miss me?"

"Be nice. I really like this one."

"I haven't forgotten you never answered my question about what's happening when you have to leave Elder's Bay." Dylan leaned against the wall outside the guest room. "You can't avoid thinking about it forever."

"I'm not avoiding anything." The reality of their situation gave Julia a headache, not to mention what it did to her heart. "I'm just choosing not to think about it until I have to. I want to enjoy our time together while we have it."

They'd agreed from the beginning that things would just be casual, but they were way past that point. Julia wanted Remy to be part of her life, but she couldn't imagine how that would ever work out. Remy spent most of the week out on the boat, so maybe she could work something out with her dad to come back to Elder's Bay on Fridays and then be here for the weekend. Would that be enough? No. Maybe?

"Isn't there some kind of off-season?" Dylan asked. "They don't catch crab all year, do they? Maybe she could spend the time between the seasons with you in Portland?"

"When crabbing season is done, they rig the boat for other fisheries like rockfish or salmon. They're always chasing the catch. It's not a life that's conducive to long distance relationships. The ocean is already a fisherman's mistress, then add the fact that I wouldn't be home during the week on the nights when she's in port, and you have the makings of a life spent mostly apart."

"What if you were here full time?" Dylan asked.

Julia's phone dinged with a text notification. She looked down to see a selfie Remy had taken of the three of them standing on the dock together with Sherlock Holmes style pipes in their mouths. They each wore serious expressions, but the rain gear and mussed up hair ruined any chance of looking dignified.

She smiled and showed the picture to Dylan before pocketing her phone. "Can we talk about this later? I just want to enjoy our time together this weekend and pretend none of these difficult questions will need to be answered. At least they don't right now."

Dylan hugged her. "I'm pulling for you, Jules."

"Thanks. Now, go get all fancy. You might just have your own sexy fisherman pretty soon."

Two hours later, Remy and Andy met them at the door of Skipper's. They'd only been apart for a little over forty-eight hours, but her heart still pounded when she saw Remy leaning against the brick wall of the bar. Black jeans that hugged her body in all the right places, boots, and a white Henley with enough buttons undone to tease without exposing too much. A hint of the pirate ship tattoo on her chest peeked out from the edge of her shirt.

Remy smiled when she saw Julia approach and leaned down for a kiss.

"Hey, baby," Remy said when they came up for air.

"I'm glad you're home safe." Julia cradled Remy's face and rubbed her cheeks with her thumbs.

"Always. I'll always come home to you," Remy said.

A throat being cleared pulled their attention from each other, and they looked over to see Andy giving Remy a look she assumed was irritation.

"I'm so sorry," Julia said. "Dylan, this is Andy Matheson."

"It's a pleasure to meet you," Dylan said.

"Dylan." Andy took Dylan's hand and kissed the back of it. Julia thought she saw Dylan swoon just a little. "You look beautiful this evening. I've heard great things about you from Remy. I'm glad we'll have a chance to get to know each other this weekend."

"Yes, um, me, too. Hanging out, that is. With you."

Julia struggled to hold back a laugh. She glanced at Remy, who seemed equally amused.

"Let's head inside," Remy said. "Corey and Brooke are holding a table for us."

"Corey is Remy's cousin and their crew's third and final member."

The music bumped as they made their way to the table where Corey and Brooke were waiting. Remy did the introductions, then pulled Andy and Corey away to order drinks for everyone. Once they were alone, Julia turned to Dylan.

"What do you think of Andy?" she asked.

Dylan shrugged, then covered her face with both hands while Brooke scooted closer to them. "Are you dating Andy?"

"Not yet," Julia said. "I see a little sparkle in Dylan's eyes, though." Julia hadn't seen Dylan react to another girl like this in a long time. Attraction, sure. Flirting, absolutely. But this was something different.

"I've known her like five minutes, but so far, fishermen seem like a pretty sexy bunch." Dylan pulled lip gloss from her bag and touched up her lips.

Brooke and Julia busted out laughing.

"I told you," Julia said. "Although, don't get the wrong idea. These fishermen are special. Normally, they're smelly and not nearly as handsome."

"Well, I'm glad you found the cute ones."

"My pleasure," Julia said.

Remy and the others returned to the table and passed drinks around. Julia watched as Andy casually draped an arm over the back of Dylan's chair and leaned in so they could talk. She was happy to see Dylan and spend time with her, but having someone there to entertain her so she could still spend time with Remy was nice. She felt terrible for feeling that way, but the last couple of days apart had been hard.

"I missed you," Remy said, placing a trail of kisses along Julia's jaw and up to the spot just below her ear.

"Mmm, I missed you, too. Terribly. It's going to be hard to not spend the night with you, knowing you're in town."

Remy looked toward where Andy and Dylan were talking and shook her head. "At this rate, Dylan might otherwise be occupied, and me staying with you won't make a difference."

"They seem to be hitting it off rather quickly."

"Did you guys eat?" Remy asked.

"Dylan brought dinner from my favorite Italian place in Portland. I'll take you there when you go home with me next time."

"Sure. Yeah. That would be nice."

"What's wrong?"

"Nothing. I'll miss you when you're gone. That's all," Remy said.

A casual relationship wasn't supposed to feel like this. There was a part of Julia that wanted to stop herself from going down this road any further, knowing it could only lead to heartache. A larger part of her knew there was no turning back.

CHAPTER SEVENTEEN

"You ready for this?" Remy asked as she hefted the bags of groceries in her arms. They'd agreed to make chili for Dylan and Julia, so while they spent the day at the beach, Remy and Andy had gone shopping and were going to cook at Julia's house while they were out.

"I think so. I can't believe Julia gave you a key to her house." Andy carried a six-pack of beer in one hand and a cast iron skillet in the other. They'd gone back and forth about how important it was to cook the cornbread in cast iron, and Remy had insisted there was no other way to do it.

"I think she originally gave me the key because I woke her up way too early for her liking when we came back from a trip at six in the morning. She smiled and pretended she wasn't upset, but I saw the murder in her eyes, and the next day she gave me a key to the house."

Remy unlocked the door, and they carried everything inside. She didn't cook often, but she'd spent enough time in Julia's kitchen to have a general idea of where everything was. It was strange to be there without Julia, but she was excited to have a warm meal waiting for her when they got home.

"You start chopping, and I'll gather the spices," Andy said.

"Roger that." Remy put on the University of Oregon basketball game to play in the background while they worked. They'd both opened beers, and Remy looked over at Andy. It all filled her with so much happiness she thought she would burst. Everything about that moment made her happy. "Hey, I love you, bud."

Andy looked confused, then grabbed her beer and tapped it against Remy's. "I love you, too, dipshit."

Remy shook her head and laughed. "You just have to ruin everything, don't you?"

"Yes." Andy tossed a chopped piece of onion at Remy's head.

"Don't play with your food," Remy said. A cheer from the TV caught their attention, and they both watched the game as they finished prepping the ingredients for their chili. They'd made the dish so many times that they no longer needed a recipe. It was their thing, and Remy couldn't wait for Dylan and Julia to try it.

Three hours later, the chili was simmering on the stove, and the cornbread cooled on a rack while Andy and Remy watched the game in the living room. Laughter from the doorway caught their attention.

"Hey," Julia said when Remy met her at the door.

"How was it? Did you have a good time?" Remy asked before kissing Julia. Seeing Dylan and Julia together was a reminder that Julia wouldn't be in Elder's Bay forever. Before long, she'd be back in Portland, eating her favorite Italian food, living her real life. She was happy that Julia loved her job and living in the big city, but Remy could no longer imagine what her own life would be like once Julia was gone. She fought the urge to fall into a funk, thinking about it, but it was hard.

"We had an amazing time. I haven't done the touristy thing since I've been back, and I hadn't realized how much has changed."

"Downtown Elder's Bay is freaking adorable," Dylan said. "The art galleries were amazing. I never imagined a little town would have such appreciation for art."

"We get a fair number of tourists in and out of here, and our retirement population is growing. People want to escape the city's congestion, and once they don't need to live there to be near their jobs, they find quiet little towns to escape to," Remy said. "It's a blessing and a curse because the extra foot traffic is awesome for things like restaurants and art galleries, but the rising cost of housing makes it difficult for people with lower-paying jobs to find a place to live."

"I guess I never thought about it that way," Dylan said.

Remy picked up Julia's bags from the floor and carried them into the living room. "The chili and cornbread are ready whenever you are."

"I'd like to freshen up before we eat if you don't mind."

"Please do. Andy and I can set the table while you guys get ready," Remy said.

When they returned, everyone sat at the table and dished up their portions of the meal. Remy had picked up a bottle of wine that Julia mentioned she enjoyed so she poured a glass of it for her and Dylan while Andy grabbed fresh beers for the two of them.

"Tell me what it's like to be a fisherman," Dylan asked. "This chili is delicious, by the way. Absolutely stunning."

"Thanks," Remy smiled and tapped her bottle to Andy's in salute. "Being a fisherman can be a freezing cold and torturous job, but we wouldn't have it any other way."

"Says the captain in the heated box, out of the elements." Andy loved to tease her about going soft now that she was a captain and didn't have to do the grunt work the others did.

"To be fair," Julia said. "The captain has the most stressful, mentally taxing part of the job and is ultimately responsible for not only ensuring you get the amount of crab you're supposed to get in the small window of time you have to do it but also keeping both the crew and the boat safe in some of the roughest waters in the world."

Everyone knew that was the truth, but hearing Julia stick up for her like that was nice. She knew for someone who didn't work on boats, like Dylan, Andy's teasing might have seemed like a valid point. Andy knew that wasn't the entire story and was only kidding. Still, Julia coming to her defense made Remy want to find a private spot to show her appreciation.

"Exactly right," Andy said. "I couldn't handle the stress of the captain's job, and there's no one I trust more to bring us home safely than Remy. We love her, and she loves us. We appreciate Julia for believing in us and allowing us to run this boat for the Claymans."

Julia blushed and shook her head. "We have some great crews working for us, but you have quickly become one of our highest producers. I should probably have someone make sure there's plenty of food on the boat before every trip. Who knows what you guys could do with full tummies?"

"We do all right. Corey and I take turns making meals, and Brooke is a chef, so she sends lots of yummy things. Remy mainly eats and bosses us around," Andy said.

Everyone laughed, and Remy recognized the dreamy look in Dylan's eyes as she watched Andy speak. They both had it bad, and Remy couldn't wait to tease Andy about it.

"Let's clean this up and move to the living room to watch a movie," Julia said.

Everyone got up and cleared the dishes from the table. Remy pulled out a container to transfer the leftovers into. She watched as the others cleaned everything up like a choreographed team. The scene reminded her of being at home when her mom had her and her brothers cleaning like a well-oiled machine. It was nice. They were like a little family. Her family of choice, and it made Remy's heart full to be with them.

CHAPTER EIGHTEEN

Julia watched Remy tuck her shirt into her pants for the tenth time since they'd started getting ready for dinner at her parents' house. She knew this wasn't something Remy was excited to do, so she appreciated the effort she was making to be part of her life.

The talk Julia had had with her parents just the day before about how to behave with Remy there and what not to bring up would hopefully keep her father at bay. She wasn't worried about her mom or brother, but her dad was another story. She knew he saw her as a Miller and, therefore, the enemy. It was ridiculous, and she was prepared to leave dinner at any moment if he didn't behave.

The large home Julia grew up in was built on a cliff that overlooked Elder's Bay and the town below. The stained wood and stone house was the largest in town, and everyone in the area knew it belonged to Brian Clayman and his family. What her father saw as a reflection of his status in the community was one more thing to separate her from her friends and classmates. She'd hated living in that house growing up and spent hours sitting on the deck, perched high above everyone else, wishing she could have a normal life.

She realized the idea that the privileged rich girl in the beautiful house, whining about her situation, was pretty pathetic, but it was true. Her parents loved her. She got along with her brother and never wanted for anything. These things were all the makings of a perfect childhood. Still, she couldn't help feeling distant from most of her classmates whose parents struggled in the small fishing community.

Everything for her parents had been about status. They had the nicest cars, the biggest house, and the perfect children. Her brother was the captain of the football team and homecoming king the year he graduated. Julia was a cheerleader, homecoming queen, and valedictorian of her class the following year. She'd been accepted into Stanford University, and there was never a question of how her family could afford her college education.

These things made her feel incredibly guilty when she pulled up to her parents' house with a feeling of dread. It could only come from someone embarrassed by what they were about to subject the person they cared deeply for through. If she didn't think it would only be more embarrassing to do so, she would turn around and take Remy back to her aunt's house and curl up in front of the fireplace with her.

That wasn't an option. If Remy was going to be in her life, she needed to make it clear to her parents that this was for real. She wasn't sure exactly what was happening between them, but she knew she wanted Remy. Introducing her to her family was the first step, no matter how much she dreaded their reaction.

"You ready?" Julia asked.

Remy stared out the window at the perfectly manicured landscape and high-end fixtures on the house with anxiety written all over her face. She clutched the bottle of wine she'd picked up to give her parents like it was a life preserver and she was about to be pulled out to sea.

She cleared her throat and brushed the wrinkles from the blue slacks she wore that framed her body perfectly. "Yeah. Let's do this."

The night air was crisp, and Julia wished she'd remembered to wear a jacket as she climbed from the car and met a waiting Remy on the other side. Before they made their way up the path, she straightened Remy's tie and kissed her. If it was possible to transfer reassurance to someone through a kiss, she was determined to do it.

"Hey," Julia said. Remy looked at her like a scared child. It pulled at Julia's heart, and she almost called the whole thing off and took her home right then. This was inevitable, though. It had to happen at some point, and it was better to pull the bandage off now and get it over with. "It's going to be fine. Remember that I'm on your side, no matter what. If things get too uncomfortable, signal me, and we'll get out of here."

"What signal?"

Julia wasn't expecting that question and laughed when Remy asked it like they were a SEAL team about to go into battle. "I'll know when you give it. Try not to be too obvious, but I'll watch for it and know if you need an extraction team."

Remy nodded and looked at the bottle in her hand. "I don't know if wine was the best idea. Are you sure they're going to like this one?"

"Baby, my mom will love it. My dad doesn't drink wine, but this is my mom's favorite."

Bugs circled the bulbs in the lights that illuminated the path to the front door. Julia could feel goose bumps prickling her skin from the cold, but she didn't want to rush Remy. It was the least she could do for putting her in this situation.

"Okay. Should I have gotten something for your dad? I should have gotten something for your dad."

"Remy." Julia wrapped her arms around Remy's middle and rested her head against her broad chest. "You're good. My dad can't have alcohol or cigars right now because of his heart attack, and there isn't anything else you could have brought that would have been appropriate. You're the reason I agreed to come to this dinner. Forcing me here will be enough for him. Trust me. He gives me hell for not coming home more often."

Julia shivered, and Remy rubbed her bare arms. "God, I'm an asshole. Let's get you out of the cold," Remy said.

Charlie, Julia's brother, pulled up with his family at that moment, and she'd never been so happy to see him as she was right then. Hopefully, her father's disdain for Charlie's wife, Stephanie, would be just the distraction they needed to keep his focus off Remy.

Soon after Charlie's car came to a complete stop, Julia's niece released herself from the confines of her car seat and came barreling toward them at full speed. Julia knelt next to Remy and opened her arms to embrace her. She was a spitting image of Julia.

"Aunt Julia!" she said as she leapt into her arms and wrapped herself around her like a baby monkey.

"Hey, sweetie," Julia said as she stood, still holding Haley in her arms. "I want you to meet someone very special to me." Julia placed a hand on Remy's shoulder. "This is my friend Remy. She works on one of Papaw's boats. Remy, this is my favorite little girl in the entire world, Haley."

"It's a pleasure to meet you, Haley. I've heard so much about you." Remy gave Haley a regal bow that made Julia's heart melt.

Haley hid her face in Julia's chest but giggled at the overly dramatic gesture.

"What do we say, Haley?" Charlie asked as he walked up to them with Stephanie.

Without hesitation, Haley straightened up in Julia's arms and reached out a hand to Remy. "It's a pleasure to meet you, Remy. My name is Haley Clayman, and I'm three years old."

It was the cutest thing Julia had ever seen, and for a moment, she imagined what it would be like to have a little girl just like Haley with Remy. It was too early in their relationship to think about anything like that, but she smiled and kissed Remy's cheek.

"I'm Charlie, and this is my wife, Stephanie." Charlie held out his hand for Remy to shake.

"Remy Miller, it's a pleasure to meet you both."

"Oh, right, you're the captain running the boat for us, aren't you?" Charlie asked.

"The one and only. Thanks for trusting me with one of your boats," Remy said.

Charlie shook his head and wrapped an arm around Stephanie. "That was all my little sister's doing, but I'm glad it worked out."

"Are we ready for this?" Julia asked. She noticed Stephanie roll her eyes, and for the first time, she felt a kinship with her sister-in-law she'd never felt before.

"Into the breach," Charlie said. Julia allowed Charlie and Stephanie to lead the way while she and Remy followed, with Haley still wrapped around her.

Julia's mother answered the door and immediately asked for Haley before greeting anyone else in the group. The woman had priorities, and Julia was more than okay to no longer be the baby of the bunch. She was so thankful for her mother's love, but it could sometimes be a little much. Julia handed Haley over to her mother and followed the crowd as they entered the house and removed their shoes. Julia had forgotten to mention her mom didn't allow shoes in the central part of the house and was glad to see that Remy had worn black dress socks that she wouldn't be embarrassed for anyone to see.

"Hi, Mom," Julia said as she kissed her. "This is Remy Miller. She and her crew are running Dad's new boat."

"Oh, right, the Miller girl. I remember seeing you with your dad at the crab fest every summer. You've grown into a strapping young woman. How tall are you?"

"Mom," Julia said, embarrassed that her mom was commenting on Remy's height after only knowing her for a few seconds.

"It's fine." Remy smiled at Julia and turned back to her mom. "I'm five-foot-ten. Still shorter than my brothers, as they like to point out at every opportunity."

"I'm sure they do," her mom said. "Poor Julia and I weren't blessed by the height fairy, but we make up for it with our beauty."

Good God, this woman was embarrassing her.

"I agree," Remy said. "Julia takes my breath away every time I see her. I can see where that beauty comes from now that I've met you."

Her mom studied Remy for a moment, then smiled. "You're dangerous. Don't let your father chase this one away, Julia."

Without another word, she led them into the den where everyone else had gathered. Her dad stood at the wet bar, pouring whiskey for each of them, including himself. Julia knew he wasn't supposed to drink alcohol, but she didn't want to call him out for it in front of everyone. She looked at her mom, who gave her a nod of understanding.

"Here you go," he said as he passed the glasses around. When he reached Remy, he noticed she had a bottle of wine in her hand and traded her the glass of whiskey for the wine. "Are you trying to butter my wife up with a bottle of her favorite wine, Miller?"

Remy's eyes went wide, and she started to respond, but Julia took her hand and gave it a tug. This was only his first volley to rile Remy up, and Julia wanted to head him off at the pass.

"It's a traditional hostess gift, so don't start, Dad."

"Where's the gift for the host?" he asked.

Her brother pulled Stephanie to the couch, making it clear he wasn't willing to get involved. Coward.

"The host recently had a heart attack and shouldn't be drinking, so the host's gift is the pleasure of spending time with his family."

"Hmmff," he said before raising his glass in a toast. "To family."

"To family," everyone repeated as they sipped their drinks.

"The Clayman family, that is," her dad said, pointedly looking at Remy. "What do you think of our home, Miller?"

Remy cleared her throat and started to answer, but was thankfully interrupted when Haley came running into the room with a puzzle Julia's mom had given her. She asked Remy if she would help her put it together, and Julia made a mental note to get her an extra scoop of ice cream the next time they were out together.

"Do you mind if I…"

"Nope. Not at all. You guys have fun and I'll see if mom needs help with dinner."

She watched as her two favorite people found a table in the corner where they could spread the pieces out. Julia had never seen Remy around kids and she shook her head and smiled at how happy it made her to realize she was good with them. At some point she needed to get control of the emotions swirling around in her heart, but watching Remy and Haley look so adorably serious as they hunched over a unicorn puzzle, now wasn't going to be the time to start.

The next hour was quiet as Julia, Stephanie, and her mom worked on dinner. At the same time, Charlie and her dad drank whiskey and talked about the company. She knew she should be with them since, technically, Julia was the one running the company at the time. After the tension from earlier, she wanted to avoid her dad at all costs.

"Remy seems nice," her mom said as she handed Julia the heated cream and butter to add to the mashed potatoes.

"She is nice. Very nice."

"You seem quite taken with her." It was more of a statement than a question, so Julia decided to leave it without trying to respond.

"She's good with kids, too," Stephanie added. "Haley would love some little cousins to play with."

"Whoa," Julia said. "It's a bit early to be thinking in that direction."

"Is it?" her mom asked. "From the look on your face when you keep glancing at her with Haley, I'd say those thoughts have already crossed your mind."

Julia picked up the potato masher and focused on her task. She wasn't ready to dig into those feelings, let alone with her mom and Stephanie.

Remy's and Haley's laughter pulled her attention away from her task, and she looked over to see Remy on all fours with Haley on her back. Haley's little fingers were grasping Remy's ears since her hair was cut too close for her to use as reins. It couldn't be comfortable for Remy, but she didn't complain as she allowed Haley to lead her around as her faithful steed.

"I'd say she would make a wonderful parent. Wouldn't you?"

Julia looked at her mom, ready to scold her for continuing with the baby discussion, but she stopped and turned back to watch Remy and Haley play some more. "Yeah. She would. We're…I'm going back to Portland soon, and I have no idea what that means for whatever we have going on here. We haven't really talked about any of that yet. I'm unsure how that would work or if it's even what I want."

Her mom touched her arm and gave it a reassuring squeeze only a mom could provide. "I think you should talk about it. I haven't ever seen you look at someone the way you're looking at her, and that has to mean something."

"Yeah," Julia said. Her mom was right, and she knew they needed to talk. The question was how to start that conversation without possibly freaking Remy out. It was all happening so fast, no matter how much they'd sworn to take things slowly. There was nothing slow about how Remy made her feel, and she owed it to her to ensure she knew that.

CHAPTER NINETEEN

A week later, Remy and her crew prepared the boat for a three-day trip. They rarely stayed out that long, but a friend had given her a tip about a hot spot that she just couldn't resist. One of Julia's other boats had broken down the day before, and she offered their quota to Remy and her crew. They'd burn a lot of fuel to get there and back, but if the information she received was good, and with the extra crab they were now able to catch, they would make a killing.

She hated to admit it, but a small part of her couldn't wait to show Brian Clayman how good of a captain she was. He might not think she was good enough for his daughter, but he couldn't deny the fact that she could make a lot of money for him. At least, that was something.

Hell, maybe she wasn't good enough for his daughter. That was for Julia to decide, but she vowed she would enjoy every minute of their time together until Julia returned home to Portland.

She'd done her best to not let her alarm wake Julia that morning when it went off at three a.m. Still, Remy wouldn't complain about the visitor she had in the shower a few minutes later or the orgasms Julia was kind enough to give her as a going-away gift.

Remy knew Julia worried about her when she was out on the boat, but these longer trips were especially difficult for those left on the shore. The weather report was clear, but they expected a storm to hit the West Coast within the next few days. Winter in the Pacific

Northwest was unpredictable, but it was also when the crabbing was at its best.

She remembered watching her mom pace the floor when she was a kid, waiting for the phone to ring with any news of her dad. The wives of all the fishermen in the area had a good communication network. They shared every tidbit they heard, but Remy knew the stress of waiting for information took years off her mother's life. She wondered if her dad would retire while they could still enjoy themselves or if he would end up working himself to death like so many crabbers before him.

Crabbing was a dangerous job and a risk they were prepared to take every time they left the dock. It rewarded them with a life at sea, which Remy knew was the only thing that would ever make her happy.

"You guys ready?"

Remy stowed the last of the safety equipment she'd inspected as part of her duties. She was responsible for the lives aboard the boat and took that task seriously. Not only because she was the captain and leader but also because Corey and Andy were more than friends to her. They were more than any family member. The three of them were so close they were almost an extension of each other.

"We're ready, skipper. Let's get the hell out of here," Corey said.

They pulled in the lines that attached them to the dock and were off. Elder's Bay had one of the most dangerous passages on the West Coast, from the safer waters of the bay to the turbulence of the open ocean. Long sand bars jutted out on either side of the entrance to the bay, which made navigating through the small opening between them extremely tricky. Remy contacted the Coast Guard to alert them they would sail through and waited for the required escort.

Commercial fishermen had sailed into and out of Elder's Bay for hundreds of years, and the Coast Guard no longer allowed boats to pass without their watchful eye. Remy could tell the seas were high as they passed out of the bay and into open water. Fifteen-foot seas did their best to knock them off course, but Remy turned into them enough to stay on her course.

This was exactly what she loved about being a captain. The more nautical things got, the more alive she felt. Making a living on the ocean wasn't for the weak of heart, and knowing she was one of the few brave enough to do it was like a drug.

The door to the pilothouse opened as Andy joined Remy at the controls.

"How's it looking?" Andy asked.

Remy checked the gauges, then tapped on the old-fashioned barometer she kept on the boat with her at all times. It was a gift from her granddad when she was a kid, and he'd convinced her not to solely rely on anything that needed electricity to run. She'd never actually been in a situation where it was her only way of predicting the weather. Still, the connection to him was a comfort.

"So far, so good. Hopefully, the weather will hold out until we can fill our tanks and get home."

Corey stepped into the room and handed Remy and Andy a hot coffee.

"I hope so," Corey said. "I'm going to propose to Brooke when we get home."

"What?" Andy pulled Corey's arm and almost caused him to spill his cup of coffee. "Are you serious?

"As a heart attack," Corey said.

"Holy shit," Remy said. "I never thought I'd see the day."

"Me, either," Corey said.

Andy wrapped her arms around Corey and hugged him. "I'm so happy for you, man. You're a lucky guy. Brooke is great."

"Thanks, Andy." Corey cleared his throat and tried to covertly wipe a tear from his cheek. "You'll both stand up with me and be my best men or whatever, right?"

"Hell yeah, we will. You're our brother," Remy said.

The emotions in the room were more than any of them were comfortable with, so Andy drained the last of the coffee in her cup and excused herself to go below to make their breakfast. Corey sat in the chair on the other side of the room and watched the seagulls play in the wind currents ahead of them.

"How do you know you're ready to get married?" Remy asked, finally breaking the silence.

Corey shrugged and stared into the depths of his coffee cup like he would find the answer there. "I just know, I guess. I've never felt like this about anyone, and all I want to do is get started on our lives together."

"You have to get married to do that?" Remy asked. She wasn't trying to be an ass. She just really wanted to know. The idea of attaching yourself to one person for the rest of your life had always seemed horrifying.

On the other hand, the thought of Julia leaving physically hurt her. Like an ache in her gut that she wasn't exactly sure how to fix. If that was love, why was everyone so eager to fall into it?

"No. I don't think you have to get married to love each other, but I want her to be my wife. There's something temporary about saying someone is your girlfriend. I've had lots of girlfriends, and Brooke is more than any of them ever were. She's my everything. I'm ready to share my life with her. I want to have babies with her—"

"Babies?" That seemed like a bridge too far. Sure, there'd been a moment when she'd seen Julia with Haley that she wondered what it would be like if they had a kid of their own, but having babies with someone seemed like a huge commitment when you put yourself at risk daily to make a living.

"Yes, babies, you dork. People have them, you know?"

"Don't you worry about dying out here and leaving your family alone?" Remy asked.

"Jesus, Remy. Of course, I worry about that. Everyone who works out here worries about that, but I won't let it keep me from having a family. Our dads are crabbers, and they had families. Granddad had a family he loved very much and still worked on the boat practically until he died. Besides, I'd walk away from this in a heartbeat if I had to choose between the boat and having a life with Brooke."

Remy tried to hide her hurt at his admission, but she knew he'd seen right through her. They'd always put each other above everything and everyone, but she didn't fault him for prioritizing Brooke. It was only natural, and knowing he had that kind of love in his life was a gift.

"I'm happy for you, cousin," Remy said.

"When are you going to tell Julia that you love her?"

Her instinct was to deny her feelings and tell him she didn't know what he was talking about. That would be a lie, and he would know it.

"I don't know that I will," Remy said.

"You're an idiot."

"Wow, okay, asshole. You decide to ask someone to marry you, and suddenly you're the authority on love?"

Corey slid off his chair and walked over to where Remy sat. He wrapped an arm around her and ruffled the hair on her head. "Don't be chicken, Rem. I have a feeling she loves you, too. You guys are both just too stubborn to say it."

"We haven't even been dating all that long, Core. Isn't it a bit early to profess our love for each other? Besides, she's going back to Portland, and long-distance shit never works," Remy said.

"Look, I'm not suggesting you propose marriage. I'm just saying you should be honest with her about how you feel. It's called communication. You should try it."

"You're an asshole," Remy said and pushed him away.

"But I'm a right asshole. That's what matters."

"Breakfast," Andy called from below decks.

"You go first," Remy said. "Bring me a plate when you guys are done, please."

"You sure?" Corey picked up his empty coffee mug and twirled it on his finger. "I can watch this while you eat, then you can relieve me."

"Nah," Remy said. "I wouldn't mind a little time alone."

"Roger that." Corey walked toward the ladder that would take him below decks but stopped before climbing down. "I love you, Rem. I wouldn't want to do this with anyone else. This life with you and Andy, being a part of this crew, means the world to me. I don't want you to think that I wouldn't follow you both to the ends of the earth just because I said that about choosing Brooke and a family over everything else. You guys are my family, too."

Remy didn't remember a time in her life before Corey. She was older than him, but they were so close in age that they'd always been together. The older they got, the more their lives would change, and responsibilities would adjust the dynamic between them. She knew that no matter what life threw at them, they would always have each other's backs.

"I love you, too, cousin. With all my heart. Now stop being a sappy dumbass and get breakfast so I can have a damn minute to myself."

"Aye, aye, skipper." Corey gave her a mocking salute. "Oh, hey, did you hear the latest on your dad's new captain?"

"No. Why?"

Remy wasn't surprised that Dan Bratton was causing more problems. She wanted to be the bigger person and not find a little satisfaction that he wasn't the perfect captain her dad must have thought he would be.

"Kel told me that he was on Bratton's crew last week with a couple new guys Dan had brought to the boat that had only been on one other trip. He wasn't supposed to be on there, but Jay had asked Kel to go out with them to see if he noticed anything weird going on with Bratton."

"And? I know I have a chip on my shoulder about Bratton, but besides that, I don't trust the guy. There's something about him that makes the hair stand up on the back of my neck. I know Jay has his suspicions, too."

Remy wished her dad would wise up and stop putting so much trust in this almost stranger. She knew Bratton had worked with someone her dad knew and that guy had vouched for him, but something was off with that guy, and she knew it would take more than a couple mistakes and a bad feeling to convince her dad to get rid of him. Besides, whatever Remy said about him her dad would only brush off as her being upset he got the boat instead of her.

"I guess they started pulling in the pots and Kel couldn't find the crab gauge to measure them before they were added to the tank. Bratton had told the new guys some nonsense about using their hand to judge the size. Kel confronted the captain about it, and he said it was a waste of time to use a damn tool to do something a good sailor could do with the hands the Lord gave him."

When a boat offloaded their crab at the dock, the crab would be spot checked by an official and if one crab was found to be smaller than the minimum requirements, the entire load was subject to inspection. Depending on how many were found to be out of compliance, not measuring each crab before they were put into the tank could lead to thousands of dollars in fines not to mention the bad reputation a careless mistake like that can put on the boat. Between this and the log mistake, it seemed obvious to Remy that Dan Bratton didn't know what he was doing. Either that or he was intentionally trying to sabotage the boat but that didn't make any sense. It would not only leave a bad mark on the boat, but on him as a captain.

"What did Jay say when Kel told him?"

Corey shrugged. "I'm not sure exactly what he said, but unless they could prove he's intentionally doing something wrong, he has a contract with your dad to protect him. I think he was told he had to use the crab gauge from now on. Your dad's just lucky they didn't get caught with small crab before this. Jay put Kel on there permanently to make sure Bratton is doing what he's supposed to do."

"I need to talk to Jay. I'd meet with my dad but he's not going to listen to me. The guy who recommended Bratton to my dad sure has a lot to explain. I don't know how he could have gone from a good captain to a complete fuck up overnight," Remy said.

"Me either. Hopefully your dad can get through the season without him causing too much damage. What are you going to do if Bratton is out of the picture and suddenly your dad wants you to captain the boat?"

That was the million-dollar question. She had signed a two-year contract with Clayman Fisheries so she couldn't just break that if a boat became available with her dad. She wasn't even sure she wanted that. Her dad had his chance to make her the captain of that boat. Maybe it was an immature attitude to have, but at that moment she didn't think she'd work for her dad even if she could.

"I'll be right back with your breakfast, Rem."

"Yeah. Thanks." A million scenarios of what could happen with Dan Bratton and that boat swirled in Remy's mind. She just hoped he didn't do something so stupid that someone got hurt. No matter how angry she was with her dad, she'd never want anything to disrupt the family business or for someone to be hurt.

The rest of the day dragged by as they made their way toward the coordinates given to Remy by her friend. Since Dungeness crab fishing on the Oregon coast was a derby fishery which meant there was a start time and a finish time and you had to squeeze everything in between those parameters, wasting time steaming an entire day away from your home base was a tremendous gamble. It was a gamble that would either pay off with a boat full of crab, or she would crash and burn, having used three days' worth of fuel and wasted days on the water they could have been catching closer to their home port. It was a risk she was willing to take.

Before dawn on day two, the crew was on deck tossing pots over the edge in long strings. They would spend the morning dropping every pot they had into the sea, hoping when they saw them again, the pots would be full of Dungeness crab, or dungies, as they called them.

Remy sighed as she checked the latest weather report. It said the same thing it had the day before, but her trusty barometer and an uneasy feeling in her bones, told her there might be a shift in the weather sooner than they expected. She carefully read each report from the national weather service for any sign they should head home early.

By evening , the latest alert worried her, so she'd moved them into quick recovery mode. Each pot was expensive, and leaving any behind would not only cut into their profit but litter the ocean floor.

"How many more strings?" Andy asked. The boat jerked as a wave crested over the side rail and drenched the crew as they held on for dear life.

"This is the last one," Remy said. "Let's get this shit on the boat and get the hell out of here."

"Thank God you had your weird intuition thing and we started hauling in before the weather service pulled their heads out of their asses and told us what was coming," Andy said. "I don't think we could have pulled everything if we were just starting now."

"More hauling and less talking," Remy said. The wind had picked up, making it a challenge to keep them out on deck. Remy did her best to point the boat in a direction that would reduce the impact of water coming over the side, but that left them vulnerable to being tossed by the waves that were building by the minute.

"Come on, guys." Remy watched out the side window as Andy and Corey used the crane to pull in the last string of pots. The rough seas were like hills and valleys where the boat would sink into a trough at its lowest point in the cycle, then shoot up to its highest crest and over the edge to plunge back into the next trough.

She'd never been seasick in her life, but the constant jerking of the boat as the waves tossed it around gave her a massive headache. Remy counted the pots as each one in the string came onto the boat. The crab were removed, then secured to the rest of the pots on the deck. She could see a thick layer of ice as it accumulated on the windward side of the vessel. A collection of ice on one side of the boat could quickly become a nightmare because it made that side heavier than the other and could essentially cause the vessel to roll over if pushed hard enough by a wave from the other direction.

Remy wiped her sweat-soaked bangs out of her eyes and kept her head on a swivel between her crew on deck, the navigational instrumentation in front of her, and the ocean ahead. Built for this kind of situation, Remy only needed to stay calm and trust her instincts to get them safely through this.

For a moment, the world stopped as she watched Corey lean too far over the side with the buoy stick they used to retrieve the line attached to a pot just as a rogue wave crashed into them. Her stomach turned as she stared into the darkness, waiting for the water to clear so she could see if her crew was still on the deck.

"Corey! Andy!" Her voice was almost a plea as she watched for any sign of them. Leaving her post at the helm wasn't an option, so all she could do was wait and hope they'd made it.

"Here!" Andy yelled back as the wave receded, and two figures appeared huddled together on the deck.

"That's it. We're done. Cut the line and let the last two pots go. Get your asses in here. It's not safe."

Andy cut the last two pots free as Corey secured the rest of their equipment, and then they both ran for the safety of the pilothouse.

"Fuck, that shit came out of nowhere. I mean, it's been picking up for a couple of hours, but that got nautical fast."

"No shit. Are you guys okay?" Remy searched them for any sign of injury while still keeping an eye focused out the window on the beast ahead of them.

"We're good," Andy said.

Corey nodded and gratefully wrapped his arms around Andy. "Thanks for having my back."

"Always." Andy held Corey tightly. "I thought I'd lost you for a minute. You started to go over, and I reached out to grab any part of you I could. I'm lucky I got a hold of your belt and pulled you back in."

"It was close. I owe you my life. Again."

Remy would have given anything to join them in their hug, but things were getting more treacherous by the minute.

"What the fuck happened to the weather?" Corey asked.

"Fuck if I know. They said this was coming, but it wasn't supposed to hit us for a few more hours. I knew they were wrong. I just knew it. You guys get—"

"PAN-PAN, PAN-PAN, PAN-PAN. All stations, all stations, all stations." A transmission over the radio interrupted Remy. "This is the United States Coast Guard Sector North Bend. United States Coast Guard Sector North Bend. At 18:45 Local. In the vicinity of the North Jetty in Coos Bay…Coast Guard has confirmed…three persons in the water. We request all mariners to keep a sharp lookout. Assist if possible. And make all reports to the Coast Guard."

The pilothouse went silent as the information set in. Another boat had gone down in their sector, and its crew was fighting for their lives in the raging sea. Remy understood how quickly that could be them, and her blood felt like ice in her veins. She had to get them home and fast.

"I need to radio in our position and let the Coast Guard know we're safe. You guys go below and put something warm on. Find some dry life vests and keep them on until we're out of this mess. Got me?"

"Roger." Corey and Andy turned toward the ladder when a giant wave hit them so hard it knocked them both off their feet. Remy watched out the window as anything that wasn't tied to the deck was pulled out to sea.

"You guys okay?" Remy asked.

"We're good," they answered simultaneously.

"Get below. I'm going to call in."

"Come on." Andy tugged the sleeve of Corey's shirt toward the ladder as they both disappeared below.

Remy blew out a breath and checked the control board once more for any alarms or indications something had happened after that last wave. Everything seemed okay, so she picked up the mic to call the Coast Guard.

The radio unit had power, but there was only static when she pushed the button to speak. She checked the screen to ensure she was on the correct channel and noticed it showed no signal.

"Fuck." She wasn't much of a betting woman, but she'd put her money on the antenna being broken. She'd seen a wave take out the antenna on one of her dad's boats she'd crewed for a few years before. They'd been able to climb up and reattach it, but with the weather like it was, she was hesitant to investigate.

Andy and Corey returned bundled up and dry and handed Remy a life vest to wear.

"Did you reach the Coast Guard?" Andy asked.

Remy held up the mic and clicked the button to show her the radio wasn't working.

"Well, shit," Corey said. "What are we going to do?"

There was only one option, and no matter how loudly the voice in her head told her it was too dangerous, she knew she had to at least try.

"First, I'm going to climb up to see if it's something I can fix. Can one of you take over the helm for me?"

"Remy, we won't let you go out there." Another enormous wave crashed against the side of the boat and jolted them all.

"I don't have a choice, Andy. You guys keep watch in here. I'll be right back."

"Remy—"

Remy walked out onto the deck and closed the door behind her before they could try to stop her. The boat jolted violently as more waves crashed against the side. Remy knew this was a royally stupid thing to do, but communications were worth the risk. She couldn't allow something to happen to her crew without even trying.

Rain pelted her face as she found the ladder that would take her up to the roof of the pilothouse, where she could evaluate the situation with the antenna. Growing up, her dad taught her the skills she'd need to be a great captain, which included a little knowledge about everything. She might not be an electrician, but she knew enough to fix just about anything electrical on the boat. That would have to be enough.

She found a rope attached to the railing and wrapped one end around her body, and the other end she tied to the boat. If she did end up going over, hopefully she'd be able to pull herself back up and not be lost to the sea forever.

The wind almost pulled her off her feet as she crested the roof line and stepped onto the slick metal surface. She held onto the railing for dear life as she navigated her way to the other side of the structure where the antenna should be mounted. Her heart sank when she realized the cable to the antenna was almost completely severed with only a single strand of wire holding it together.

"Fuck." Remy searched for any sign of the bolts that connected the antenna to the bracket that held it in place, but they had been lost when the wave struck them and ripped it from its cradle. She slid across the metal roof as another roll of the boat slung them around.

The seas were getting worse and every warning bell in Remy told her to get back into the relative safety of the pilothouse, but she was here, and she was the captain. Her crew and their safety were her responsibility and she had to at least try to do something to fix this problem.

The rain made it hard to see anything as she held onto the rail with one hand and slipped the other under her rain gear and into the pocket of her jeans beneath them. Fridged water seeped beneath her gear and soaked her clothes as she exposed them to the elements in her effort to reach the multitool she always kept with her. The gloves she wore prevented her from getting her hand far enough into the pocket to reach the tool so she pulled one off. As she tried to stuff it into the big pocket on her rain jacket, a wave rolled the boat. In her haste to grab the rail, the glove dropped out of her hands, slid across the deck, and over the side into the ocean.

"There goes sixty-five dollars." Remy chuckled when she realized how silly it was to think about the cost when her bigger worry should be the fact that her hand was now exposed to the freezing elements. Andy and Corey were going to give her shit when she told them about this later.

Her gloveless hand was now able to reach the tool in her pocket. Years of practice had honed her skills with the item she'd never step onto a boat without. She thought of her seventh birthday when her grandpa first gave it to her and explained it was something a good sailor always kept handy.

"Thanks again, grandpa." Maybe the winds that kept the sound of her voice from reaching her ears would be enough to carry her words to wherever in the ocean she was sure her grandpa's spirit lived.

Remy checked that the rope she had secured around her waste was still there then opened her tool to click the wire cutters into place. One by one she carefully snipped the ends of each wire then reached up to snip the ends from the other end of the break. Frayed pieces of broken wire were carried off with the wind.

Once each one had clean ends, Remy used the knife to strip the plastic sheathing from each wire, exposing the copper below. This wasn't going to be pretty, but if she could get them connected enough to at least get a signal out to Coast Guard, she'd be happy.

Every twist of the metal stung her fingers as the fridged air slowly froze the exposed body parts. Her cheeks burned from the biting wind and her eyes felt like tiny little pellets of ice were being thrown at them. She was miserable and knew she couldn't keep this up for much longer.

When they were all connected, she used what little strength she had left to jam the antenna between the bracket where it should be mounted and the metal surface it was attached to. She wrapped the little bit of extra cable around the mount a couple times to help secure it and hoped doing that wouldn't cause more problems if it interrupted the signal.

She didn't have the luxury of second guessing herself at that moment, so she went with her gut and hoped her grandpa was right about her instincts. She was counting on them now to regain communication with the outside world, and she hoped they were enough.

There was nothing else she could do from up there, so she held onto the rail and guided her body back to the side with the ladder.

Another jolt almost took her over the edge as it tossed her forward and back, but she hung on. The weather was only getting worse, and she was worried that the waves would pull her out to sea if she didn't get inside the pilothouse soon. She thought of Julia and wished they were together, curled up in front of the fire.

"Come on, kid. If you don't get back, she'll kick your ass for getting yourself killed," Remy said out loud to herself.

The roof's metal was freezing cold, and her exposed hand had lost most of its feeling, so holding onto the metal railing was almost impossible at that point. Remy scooted toward the opening as carefully as possible, knowing the ladder would be waiting. She reached out with her foot and found the first rung as another wave jerked her backward. She gripped the rail for dear life but felt her shoulder pop. Intense pain flowed through her body, and she knew she'd screwed up.

One final jolt of the boat was too much for her injured arm to withstand. She felt herself sliding across the roof and over the side before her head slammed against metal, and everything went dark.

CHAPTER TWENTY

Julia paced her office as she waited for word from Remy and her crew. It had been hours since the Coast Guard reported that another boat, the *Lady Jane,* had gone down near Coos Bay, Oregon. They'd tried to contact Remy around that time, but there was only radio silence.

She couldn't lose her. Julia refused to believe the universe would rob them of a future together so soon after finding each other. Everyone who loved a sailor knew this was a possibility. Especially as someone who came from a family that made a living in this industry, she understood the risks. Remy was different, though. Every life lost was a tragedy, but losing Remy would break her. Not Remy. Not now.

"Jules, are you okay?"

Seeing her dad gave her the slightest amount of hope. "Did you hear anything?"

He crossed to where she stood by the window that overlooked the raging weather outside and wrapped his arms around her. "No. I haven't heard anything, sweetie. I'm sure they'll let me know if they find it. It's only one boat. It would be an unfortunate asset to lose, but the company will be fine."

"Do you honestly think I give a shit about the boat?"

"I know. I didn't mean it like that. They're my employees, and I want them to come home safe."

"Remy is everything to me, Dad. Everything."

"Hey now, I'm sure you're concerned for your friend."

This wasn't the time to hash something out with her dad, but Julia couldn't stop the words from spilling out of her mouth. "You aren't listening to me. Remy isn't just a friend. I'm in love with her."

"Look." He stepped back and waved a hand toward her. "You care for Miller. I wasn't trying to say you didn't. I just meant—"

"I know what you meant."

"Look, Julia, you're upset right now. Let's discuss this once we hear from the crew and they're safe at home."

Julia shook her head. Her dad would never accept Remy. The funny thing was Julia realized she didn't really care what he thought.

"Just leave me alone, Dad. You'll accept no one for me who doesn't come with a trust fund. No more begging for your acceptance. I'm in love with Remy, and you can get on board with that or leave me the hell alone. I don't need your money."

Julia knew she was making him angry, but this was the time to make it clear to him that her relationship with Remy was vital to her. He'd continue to disregard its importance in her life if she didn't.

"You certainly haven't complained about my money before now. The same money that paid for your braces, cheerleader uniforms, your first car, college... Should I continue?"

Julia's secretary poked her head into her office and looked like she wanted to slink away when she realized they were arguing. "What's going on, Cindy? Did you hear anything?"

"Umm, no, sorry, I just wanted to let you know they found one of the guys in the water in Coos Bay."

"Is he alive?"

Cindy shook her head. "They weren't able to find him in time. His injuries were too severe, and he'd been in the water too long. No word on the other two crew members, including the captain."

"Thanks, Cindy," her dad said. When they were alone again, he turned back to Julia. "Where is this all coming from? Did Miller say something to you?"

"Say what to me? What are you talking about, Dad?"

He shook his head and walked toward the door. "Forget it. I'll let you know if I hear anything."

"Stop. What are you talking about? Is this about Remy?"

Julia folded her arms across her chest and waited for an answer. Something about her dad's behavior told her she wouldn't like his response, but she was sick of his bullshit regarding Remy.

"Yes. It's about Miller."

She hated he wouldn't even say her name. This stupid prejudice toward her just because she was a Miller was more than ridiculous at this point.

"Her name is Remy, and she's the best captain you have on your payroll, and you know it. The numbers her boat has pulled this season consistently outnumber any of our other boats, and she does it burning less fuel. Her crew has far less drama than the others and works efficiently and professionally. You should thank your lucky stars they agreed to run that boat for us, and you know it."

"This isn't about her work performance, Jules; you know it."

Julia sighed and slumped into the chair behind her desk. "This whole class war bullshit you're clinging to is so old, Dad. I mean, seriously. Do you think you're better than her because you have more money?"

"Is that what she told you?"

There was something he wasn't saying, and she knew it must be pretty bad if he was dancing around it this much. "What are you talking about? What is it you're so afraid Remy has told me?"

He must have realized that Remy hadn't told Julia anything because a slight smile lifted the corners of his mouth.

"Nothing," he said. "I have to get back to my office to finish some paperwork. I want to be home at a decent hour tonight. Your mom doesn't want us out on the road with the weather like this."

"Just tell me." Julia was emotionally exhausted and no longer had the energy to do this verbal dance with her father. "Please, just say it so I can get on with my day."

"Nothing, Julia. Why don't you go home for the day? I'll let you know if we hear anything."

Julia didn't have the energy to argue with him when it took everything not to fall apart with worry over Remy and her crew.

She knew there was nothing her dad would tell her that would help things at that moment, so she cut her losses and told him to leave.

"Please get out of my office."

He seemed surprised by her directness. She couldn't look at him as he walked out of her office and shut the door behind him. He would never change. She loved him. He was her dad, but his behavior disappointed her.

The buzz of an incoming call to her cell phone pulled Julia from her thoughts. She quickly sat up and noticed Brooke's name on the screen.

"Brooke, have you heard anything?"

"Yes," Brooke said. "The *Lady Angeline* heard a distress call from them over the radio. My cousin is on the *Angeline* and said the signal was terrible but they reported that one of them was badly injured."

"Who was injured? Where are they now? Has the Coast Guard been notified?"

Brooke's voice was muffled like she had her hand over the phone. Julia did her best to patiently wait for a reply, but she felt like she was coming out of her skin she was so anxious.

"Sorry, Julia, they called the Coast Guard, and they're sending boats out to escort them into the bay. My cousin didn't know who was injured. The call came in only a few minutes ago so I think they're all still trying to figure out what's happening. I'm heading down to the dock now. Want me to pick you up on my way?"

If she rode with Brooke, she'd be able to ride back with Remy in her truck. Julia refused to believe she wouldn't be able to drive away with Remy, safe and sound. When she did, she didn't plan on letting her out of her sight anytime soon. If ever.

"That would be great. I'll meet you out front."

"Give me ten minutes."

Julia grabbed her coat and purse and ran for the door. Cindy told her the Coast Guard had called to tell them they'd gotten a distress call, but they didn't have any more information than Brooke had regarding the condition of the injured crew member or who that person was.

Julia wanted to tell Cindy that it wasn't Remy. If anyone had been out on the deck, it seemed like Remy would be the last one of the three of them. Knowing her girlfriend, if someone put themselves in danger, it was her.

Brooke arrived a few minutes later and they drove to the dock together. Neither of them spoke on the drive there, fear of the unknown stealing all of Julia's focus.

They found several other vehicles in the parking lot with other families sitting in their cars, watching the bay for any sign of their loved ones. This was the life these people lived when their husbands, wives, fathers, sons, daughters, and anyone who made their living on a boat were away from the shore. Julia wondered if she could do it. Could she be a sailor's wife, never knowing for sure that the person she'd built her life around would come home safe to her at the end of a trip?

"How do you do it?"

"Do what?" Brooke asked. Julia hadn't realized it before, but they'd been holding hands for support for she didn't know how long.

"I just can't imagine watching someone you love more than anything constantly leave to do a job so dangerous there's a good chance they might not come back. My dad and brother have been out on boats, but neither of them did it enough to make me this scared."

Brooke rolled down the front windows just a crack and pulled a joint from her purse. She held it up to Julia in question, and when Julia nodded, she lit one end and took a deep drag. She blew smoke out with a cough before she handed it to Julia, who did the same. A calmness came over her and was exactly what she needed. Not enough to lose her mental sharpness, just enough to take the edge off her anxiety. She watched as Brooke dabbed the joint out on an empty cup and tucked it back into the small metal box to be returned to her purse.

"Thanks," Julia said. "That helps."

Julia let her head drop back against the headrest.

"I guess you do it because you love them, and they love being a sailor. Corey would do something else if I asked. I know he would, but he wouldn't ever be happy. Sure, he's happy when we're together, and I know he loves me with everything he has. He tells me every single day. But he loves being on the ocean, and if I tried to take that away, he'd only be a shell of who he is. It's scary and dangerous, but it's who he is, and I've known that since we met. He'd do whatever I wanted him to do to make me happy, but sacrificing who he is isn't something I'm interested in. I love him, and his love of the water is part of that."

Brooke leaned her chair back a bit and closed her eyes. "If you can't do that for Remy, you need to walk away now. That girl was born to captain a crab boat, and nothing will change that."

A black boat came into view over the horizon, and Julia saw movement in several cars to her right. Women with kids in tow piled out of the vehicles and scrambled toward the dock. When the waves were too big, the Coast Guard would close the passage into the bay because the entry would be too dangerous. The appearance of the black boat meant that at least some vessels were making it through, which was a good sign.

"I love her," Julia said.

Brooke reached over and squeezed Julia's hand, where it rested on her lap. "I know you do," Brooke said. "Have you told her?"

"Not yet."

"She loves you, too."

Julia looked at Brooke for a moment before turning back to the water. "I hope so."

Lights appeared over the horizon, and a Coast Guard vessel came into focus, followed by the blue hull of Remy's boat. Brooke and Julia released their seat belts and crawled from Brooke's tiny car. Other doors shut behind them, and Julia saw the Miller family get out of their own cars and walk toward the dock. She looked to Brooke, unsure whether she should hang back and give the Millers space, but Brooke didn't hesitate to grab her arm and guide her along with the rest of them.

The scowl on Remy's dad's face was difficult to miss, but her mom gave Julia a warm smile that helped reassure her she belonged there. The crowd of people waited patiently as they tied the boat up. A group of Miller family members climbed on to help secure everything and assist the crew off the boat.

Julia's heart sank as she got her first glimpse of Remy, arm cradled in a makeshift sling and a bloodied bandage wrapped around her head. Brian Miller was the first to reach her as someone carried her off the boat and practically set her in his arms. Julia wanted to run to her but gave Remy's dad space to be with her first.

The moment Remy's gaze settled on Julia, time seemed to stop. She reached her hand toward Julia, and she was by her side in a second. She said something to her dad, who nodded and carefully placed her on a gurney someone had wheeled up to them. Julia hadn't even noticed an ambulance had arrived or the paramedics hovered around her as they checked her vitals. Everything faded away as Remy pulled Julia to her and wrapped her good arm around her. A sob wracked her body as waves of relief washed through her. Remy was injured, but she was alive.

"I love you," Remy said into Julia's ear. It was only a whisper, but Julia heard the words clearly.

"I love you, too, baby," she said. "I think we should let them take you to the hospital now to get checked out. You look like you got a little banged up."

"I'm okay," Remy said before Corey and Andy flanked them.

"Don't be an idiot, Rem," Corey said.

Julia stepped back so the paramedics could maneuver the gurney down the dock to the waiting ambulance. Mr. Miller stepped into the back with her, and Julia wasn't sure if she should force her way into the back of the ambulance with them, or let this go.

Before she could decide, the doors were shut, and the ambulance was on it's way with lights flashing and the sound of a siren breaking through the sound of the storm still raging around them.

"Remy would have wanted you with her. She'll make that clear to her dad and in the future, you'll be in the back next to her," Andy said.

"I wish I could say she'll never be injured again, but I know that's not reality."

"She's going to be okay." Corey rubbed Julia's back with one hand as he cradled Brooke in his arms with the other. "She either broke or dislocated her shoulder. She got a pretty nasty knock on her head but that thing's too hard to have any lasting effect. I think she just got her bell rung pretty good. Maybe a concussion? The best we can tell, that's about all that happened. We couldn't see any broken bones, but they'll know for sure at the hospital."

"Was she unconscious?"

"You fill her in and take her to the hospital, Andy. "Brooke and I will follow in the car."

Andy nodded and reached out to take Julia's hand in her own. She'd never sought comfort from Andy before that moment, but as Julia wrapped her arms around Andy's solid frame and allowed herself to be led to the truck, it was as if a part of Remy was there to support her through this.

Once they were both in the truck and driving toward the hospital, Andy continued to tell Julia what happened. She never let go of her hand as the storm intensified.

"Looks like it's finally hitting shore," Andy said.

"I didn't think it was going to hit until early tomorrow morning. The weather service said we had more time."

"Well, they're all just guessing, aren't they? We all are. Mother nature has her own plan and we're just along for the ride."

Trees swayed dramatically and threatened to fall into the road. The road was littered with branches. It was far too dangerous for them to be out there if this wasn't an emergency.

"Was it this bad out on the water?" Julia knew the answer was going to be yes and she didn't actually want to hear that, but she had to know.

Andy glanced at her for a moment before quickly turning back to the road. She cleared her throat and Julia knew she was trying to decide how much to share.

"Keeping things from me, won't help, Andy. I appreciate you wanting to protect me, but I need to know."

"You'll protect me if Remy tries to kill me for telling you everything?"

"Why wouldn't she want me to know everything?" Julia felt bad for putting Andy in this awkward position, but she knew Remy would do her best to play down the severity of what happened.

"It was just…"

Julia reached across the console and squeezed Andy's arm. "It's okay, Andy. I'll make sure she knows that I forced you to tell me."

Andy nodded and gripped the steering wheel even tighter. "The weather had been picking up for a bit. It was gradual at first but thankfully Remy's Spidey senses and that old barometer her grandpa gave her, told us to start wrapping things up way before the weather service pulled their heads out of their asses. We were able to get most of the gear on the boat but things got nautical so quickly that we had to cut the line and abandon two pots. It wasn't safe for us to be out on the deck and Remy could only do so much to protect us before calling it and bringing us inside."

"She's a good captain."

"The best," Andy said. "She's the best captain I've ever sailed with by far. No matter how crazy things get out there, I know she'll get us home."

The fact that things on this trip could have easily gone very differently and even the best captain isn't able to beat the odds every time wasn't something she needed to mention. Andy knew the dangers far better than Julia ever would and yet she still went out there almost every day and put her life in Remy's hands. That's a unique kind of trust that Remy had earned from her crew.

"What happened once you were all back inside? How the hell did Remy end up so injured?"

Andy swerved around a branch that had fallen into the road from the high winds. "You okay?"

Julia nodded. "I'm good. Now, tell me what happened."

"It was wild. We lost the signal to the radio and she figured the wind had done something to the antenna so she insisted on climbing up there to investigate. We needed to send a message to the Coast Guard to let them know where we were and tell them we'd be coming in. We had no idea if the channel was open or not. We tried to stop her, but you know Remy. We could hear her on the roof.

The wind was howling past us and it took everything I had to keep control of the boat. She was up there far longer than we liked and Corey was gearing up to go check on her when we saw her body fall from the roof of the pilothouse and land on the deck below with a loud thump. Corey and I almost lost it. I couldn't leave the helm so he ran out there and found her unconscious with blood oozing out of a gash on her head and her arm bending in a direction it really shouldn't. He has some EMT training so he stabilized her as best as he could then brought her into the pilothouse. The rest of the story is just us trying to get the boat back into port. She was in and out of consciousness. Corey did his best to keep her awake and talking with us, but he was very nervous of a serious head injury."

"I'm sure that will be one of the first things they look at when she gets to the hospital."

"She'll be okay." Andy meant it as a reassurance to her, but Julia could hear the question in her voice.

"We'll make sure she's okay," Julia said. She'd never been as scared as she had been that day, but this experience had made a few things very clear to her. One was that she was in love with Remy Miller. Another was that no matter what it took, she couldn't see a future that didn't include Remy in it.

CHAPTER TWENTY-ONE

A faint beeping sound pulled Remy from a deep sleep. She'd spent six hours in the hospital getting every test known to man before they released her under Julia's watchful care. Other than the few times Julia had woken her up to check on her and help her to the bathroom, she'd slept.

Her head and arm complained as she sat up to reach for her watch that someone had removed from her wrist and placed on the nightstand. Remy pressed the button on the side to stop the incessant beeping and checked the time. The room was too bright for it to be nighttime, but it surprised her to discover she'd been out of it for about thirty-six hours.

Remy heard voices from the other room and thought her mother was speaking to Julia. She knew that couldn't be right but decided she'd been in bed long enough and would investigate. Her legs were heavy as she slid them over the side of the bed and wobbled a bit as she stood. Julia had helped her into sweatpants the day before, and she put on the house shoes she'd left for her.

Once she was up and moving, the room spun a bit more than she had expected.

"Julia?"

Her mom appeared at the bedroom door and took Remy's uninjured arm to help her into the living room.

"What are you doing here, Mom?"

Her mom helped her into the recliner in front of the fireplace and placed a blanket over her lap. "I stopped by to check on you, and Julia asked me to stay for coffee. She's a lovely girl, Remy. I couldn't be happier for the both of you."

"Don't let Dad hear you say that. You'll get the boot from him, just like me."

Remy could hear the refrigerator door open and close, then the microwave beeping. "I brought you some homemade chicken soup. The pills they gave you for shoulder pain can upset your stomach, so I made something gentle."

"Thanks, Mom. Where's Julia?"

"She had to run to the store," her mom said. "I expect she'll be back any minute. She hasn't left your side since you came home, so I told her I'd be happy to stay with you while she picked up groceries."

The smell of chicken soup filled the room as her mom placed a towel on her lap and set the bowl on top of it. She'd always made chicken soup when Remy was sick as a kid, and even the smell felt like a warm blanket.

"Thanks for this, Mom."

"You bet." Her mom sat on the couch near her and quietly watched the fire as Remy ate her soup. "The doc called and said your shoulder should feel better in a week, but you'll need to go easy on it for a while."

Remy vaguely remembered the doctor talking to her about her shoulder and concussion in the hospital. Still, she'd already missed a couple of days of work as it was. She couldn't blow the season by missing over a week on the water. Especially as a new captain, she needed to prove to them she was tough enough to bounce back quickly and show up to work. None of this was something she was prepared to argue with her mom about, so she kept her mouth shut and continued to eat her soup.

"Julia's brother has taken over until you're back. Andy and Corey have been asking how you are, so call them this evening when they're back in port."

She nodded and looked toward the front door, hoping to see Julia walk through it. "Dad's never going to accept my relationship with Julia, is he?"

Her mom crossed her legs and brushed the wrinkles from her skirt. She knew the signs of avoidance, especially when the subject was her dad, so Remy wouldn't push her to answer. It didn't really matter. She needed nothing from her dad, and he evidently wasn't interested in any kind of relationship with her.

"You scared the daylight out of him, Remy. I've known that man my entire life, and I can't say I've ever seen him that scared."

Remy dropped her spoon into the empty bowl and handed it to her mom. She used the towel to wipe her mouth, and her mom took it and the dirty dishes to the sink.

"I don't get him. One minute he acts like he doesn't give a shit, er, crap, about me, and the next, he acts like I'm this delicate gem that he wants to protect. I just don't get it."

Her mom handed her a mug of tea with honey and sat back on the couch. Remy sipped the hot liquid and enjoyed the warmth that spread through her body. This was exactly how her mom cared for her when she was sick as a kid, and nothing made her feel more loved than chicken soup and a hot cup of tea.

"Thanks for taking care of me, Mom," Remy said. "I'm sorry. You seem to always get caught up in my arguments with Dad. I know it can't be easy for you to be in the middle."

She squeezed Remy's knee and gave it a comforting pat. "It's okay, sweetie. Your dad can be a lot to deal with. I knew he would be a difficult man when I married him, but I love him. He loves his family more than anything, and you may not feel it right now, but you're special to him. You're both very much alike in some ways, good and bad."

"Hey." Remy half-heartedly protested, but she knew her mom was right.

"I know it's difficult to hear, especially when you seem so far apart right now, but I hope you're able to take the good parts you share with him, like your work ethic and love of your family, and learn from the bad parts like his stubbornness and short-sightedness. You have the best parts of your life ahead of you, and I hope you don't allow old wounds to fester and hold you back from becoming the amazing person you can be."

Remy knew she was at least partially talking about the beef between the Millers and the Claymans and hoped her mom might finally give her some insight into why her dad and Brian Clayman stubbornly refused to act like adults and let the anger go.

"Why can't Dad and Mr. Clayman just get over this stupid feud between our families? I know Grandpa was partners with Julia's grandpa, and hers screwed mine over, but why is this still a thing? Are they really just that ridiculous?"

Julia came in at that moment with several grocery bags. Remy moved to help her, but her mom pushed her back down into the chair and went to take a couple of bags from her.

"Is this everything, Julia?"

"It is. Hopefully, this will get us through the next few days," Julia said.

They placed the items on the counter, and Remy's mom put the refrigerated ones in the fridge while Julia put the non-perishables away in the pantry. When they were done, Julia kissed Remy's head and checked her temperature. When she seemed satisfied that Remy would be okay, she knelt beside the chair and kissed her cheek.

"How are you doing, baby? It's nice to see you up and around. You had us worried to death."

Remy cradled Julia's face and traced her cheek with her thumb. She was such a beautiful woman. Remy had noticed her in high school, but as the head cheerleader and a Clayman, she never imagined Julia would be hers one day.

"I love you," Remy said.

"I love you, too. Sorry I interrupted your talk with your mom. I'll go into the other room and read to give you more time together."

"No." Remy reached out and held Julia's hand as she stood. "Please have a seat. We were just talking about the whole Clayman and Miller thing."

"Sit with us, sweetheart," Remy's mom said. "This has just as much to do with you as Remy. I don't know why you both haven't been told before, so it's about time you were."

"Okay."

Remy's mom scooted down the couch to let Julia sit closer to Remy. She smiled when Remy held out a hand for Julia to hold. Having her mom's approval of their relationship meant the world to her.

"What do you know about the family issues, Julia?" Remy's mom asked.

"Well." Julia cleared her throat and seemed a little uncomfortable talking about it. "I was told that it started with our grandfathers, who were partners. Someone offered my granddad, Papa Joe, an exclusive contract to provide fresh crab to a few big restaurants in Portland for a fixed price per pound. He then went to Edward Miller with the offer, but Edward didn't think it was fair for the other fisherman who could no longer compete with those vendors. The contract prices were slightly below the market. Still, Papa Joe believed it would be a good deal in the long run because at least the contracts would guarantee those prices, no matter the fluctuation in the market. In the long run, I think he was right since the Claymans eventually signed contracts with other restaurants while the other fishermen fell victim to an unstable market. It led to our ability to open our first restaurants where we exclusively provided product. Edward Miller felt slighted by Papa Joe, but as far as I know, it was purely a business opportunity he didn't want to be part of."

Remy had heard some of what Julia said, but her father's version made the Claymans out to be the story's villain. She was curious about what her mom knew and where the truth was in the middle of everything.

"That is mostly true, except what I know, Joseph Clayman didn't come to Edward and offer him the opportunity to be a part of the deal. Joe signed the contract and formed Clayman Fisheries, then told Edward about it after he had already signed it. He offered to sign a contract with Edward, agreeing to pay slightly less than Joe would make when he sold them to the restaurants, but that was a guaranteed price. It would essentially dissolve their partnership and make Edward one of Clayman Fisheries' suppliers. Maybe it would have been a good deal for Edward, maybe not, but he took it as a betrayal, and the two families have hated each other ever since."

The pieces of the stories filled in some gaps in the mumblings Remy had been told growing up. But it didn't explain everything.

"Why do Dad and Brian Clayman hate each other so much? You would think that after all this time, they would be adults and let this stuff go."

"Are you sure you want me to talk about all of this? Sometimes it's better to just leave stuff in the past and move on. Especially when you're trying to start a life together."

Julia turned toward Remy's mom and placed a hand on her knee. "Please, Carolyn. I think some answers might help us understand the obstacles ahead of us regarding our families."

Her mom nodded and patted Julia's hand. "I understand. You're right." She cleared her throat and then took a sip from the mug of tea on the coffee table. "Have you heard of your uncle David, Julia?"

"My dad's brother?" Julia asked.

Remy's mom nodded.

"I've heard a little about him, although nobody talks much about him. He died before I was born, but I saw pictures of him and my dad when I was young. I think he was in an accident on a boat."

"Davy was a great guy. I went to school with him and your dad, but Frank was the football team's quarterback and paid little attention to anyone who wasn't in that circle. Davy was different, though. He was artistic and funny and wanted nothing to do with boats or crab fishing. He and Remy's dad, Frank, were best friends, and when Joe wouldn't pay for Davy to go to art school, he joined the crew of a boat Frank was skippering for his dad."

Julia shook her head. "I've heard none of this. Nobody would ever talk about him, and I guess this explains why. I feel terrible for Uncle David."

"Yeah," Remy's mom agreed. "Davy worked his butt off all season and saved enough money to get him through his first two years at the Pacific Northwest College of Art in Portland. He was supposed to leave to start classes in January but agreed to make a couple more trips with Frank's crew for a little spending money before he left. The entire crew had been on a three-day trip up the coast and went out drinking the one night they were home before heading back out the next day. Your dad was already at the University of Oregon, so Davy was celebrating that he would finally leave Elder's Bay. They were young and stupid and drank way too much to be out on the water without giving themselves time to sober up more than they were. Frank swears he stopped drinking before the others and was fine to pilot the boat the next morning. The boat rolled over when caught between the sand bars on the way out of the bay. Frank and two crew members hung on until the Coast Guard could reach them, but they lost Davy to the sea. Frank passed a breathalyzer test when taken to the hospital immediately after the accident. Still, Brian and the other Claymans needed someone to blame for Davy's death, and Frank seemed like the best choice."

Julia wrapped her arms around her body like she was seeking comfort. Remy wasn't sure if she should feel ashamed of her dad or angry that the Claymans blamed him for something that wasn't his fault.

"Why haven't you ever told me this story before?" Remy asked.

"You never asked," her mom said. "It's not something I particularly enjoy discussing, so I never brought it up. Please mention none of this to your dad, Remy. He loved Davy very much, and a part of him still blames himself for what happened. It's also partly why he's so scared of you being out on the boats."

"Why me and not my brothers? Doesn't he worry about them?" Remy asked.

"He does, but there's always been something about you that reminds us of Davy. Not the art school part, but something about your personality and your kindness reminds us of him. Your dad and I have talked about it since you were little. It's like a little bit of Davy's spirit is in you, and it terrifies him he might lose you, too."

The three of them were silent for a few minutes while they processed everything. For the first time, Remy understood her dad in a way she never had. It frustrated her he'd never talked to her about any of this, but it helped to explain why they'd been so close when she was growing up. He'd loved all his kids very much, but they'd had a special relationship that now came more into focus.

She also felt sorry for Brian Clayman. Losing a brother was unthinkable, but losing a twin had to be beyond agonizing. She hadn't even realized Brian had a twin or that any of the Claymans had died at sea, which was amazing since all their little town liked to do was gossip. Some things were too painful to talk about, and she imagined the death of such a bright young man would be one of those things.

"I should let you both get some rest." Remy's mom stood and kissed her on the cheek. "You take care of yourself, my little bug." She reached over to take Julia's hand. "You take care of each other."

"I love you, Mom. Thanks for talking to us and for the soup."

"You bet," her mom said.

"I'll walk you out." Julia stood and walked with her to the door, then closed it and turned back to Remy. "You okay, baby?"

Remy nodded and pulled the blanket a little tighter around her body. "Do you mind if I just close my eyes and sleep here for a bit?"

"Not at all." Julia tucked the blanket around her feet and tossed another log into the fireplace. "I'll be here when you wake up."

CHAPTER TWENTY-TWO

Julia was startled when Remy hugged her from behind. "You scared the crap out of me," she said as Remy placed sweet kisses along her jaw and neck. "You're lucky I didn't flip you over my back and body slam you to the ground."

"Can you do that?" Remy asked.

"No, which is why you're lucky." Julia turned in Remy's arms and winked at her before kissing the lips she'd been thinking about since she'd woken up before the sun that morning.

The timer beeped, and Julia pulled a tray of hot biscuits from the oven and set it on top of the stove.

"Can you carry that skillet of sausage gravy to the table while I put these biscuits in a basket?" Julia asked.

"Wait." Remy looked around the kitchen as if she had just realized Julia had been cooking something. "How long have you been awake, and are you telling me you made fresh biscuits and sausage gravy for breakfast?"

Julia cradled Remy's cheeks and placed another quick kiss on her lips. "I've been up for two hours, and yes, my maternal grandma was from Texas. Whenever we'd visit, she'd always make biscuits and gravy for us on Sunday morning. After yesterday's revelations from your mom, I needed a little Memaw comfort food."

Remy nodded, clearly understanding precisely what Julia was saying. Once they set the table and dished the food onto their plates, they both ate their breakfast in comfortable silence. The previous conversation with Remy's mother had shaken them, and Julia wasn't sure she was ready to discuss her confusing feelings with Remy just yet. Not when it would be so easy to say something that might put Remy on the defensive or cause her to feel like she needed to stand up for her family. At the moment, Julia wasn't blaming either side of the conflict. She wanted to gather more information before forming opinions.

This feud between their families wasn't going away soon. She felt like as the third generation affected by it, and someone quickly falling in love with an enemy agent; she needed to have a clear picture of the battlefield if they were going to survive.

"How are you feeling today, honey? You seem like you're getting around better," Julia said after they'd cleared the table and put away the leftover food.

"I am. The pills the doc gave me sucked, so I cut back on them. I can deal with the pain, and I didn't like how foggy they made me." Remy reached over with her good hand and rubbed the shoulder she had injured.

"Don't forget to keep ice on it and gentle stretches," Julia said. "The doc said that would be essential in returning your normal movement."

"I won't forget. Thanks again for taking care of me." Remy pulled Julia over to the couch and down next to her to cuddle. "I'm sorry I scared the shit out of you."

"I think you scared Corey and Andy even worse. You should stop by to see them today. Andy cried when she told me about them finding you unconscious on the deck, bleeding from the gash on your head and an injured shoulder." Julia tried to covertly wipe a tear that had fallen onto her cheek at the memory of him recounting his version of events.

"I'm just lucky they were there and could get us back into port." Remy turned away from Julia, and she knew she was still struggling with the guilt of being too out of it from the pain caused by her fall to safely get them home. Andy had taken over while Corey tended to Remy's injuries. They'd told her repeatedly that they didn't see it as her abandoning them, but Julia wasn't sure Remy would ever forgive herself.

"Hey, why don't you invite them to hang out? I know the boat isn't out today because my brother had to take Stephanie to an ultrasound appointment. They'd probably love to eat pizza and watch the Trail Blazers game I recorded for you while you were recovering."

"Are you leaving?" Remy asked.

"Yeah. If you don't mind, I'll call my mom to see if she wants to go out for lunch. I've been so busy we haven't seen each other much, and I'd like to talk to her about a few things."

Remy squeezed Julia with her uninjured arm and kissed her forehead, obviously understanding what Julia wanted to talk to her mom about and trying to wordlessly give her support.

"I love you, baby," Julia said before getting up and helping Remy to her feet.

"I love you, too. You know Andy's a Golden State Warriors fan, right?"

Julia mimicked a shocked expression and clutched her imaginary pearls. "And you allow her to be your best friend?"

"It's been a process." Remy kissed Julia's cheek and pulled her phone from her pocket to call her friends. Julia appreciated being with someone secure enough to feel they didn't have to be together every moment of the day. She hadn't always been that lucky in past relationships, and it was just one of the many things she was thankful for about Remy.

An hour later, she and her mom were sitting on the patio of her mom's favorite seafood restaurant, watching the water crash onto the rocky Oregon shore. Julia had been fortunate enough to travel to many places around the world. Still, she rarely saw anything as beautiful as the coast of her home state.

"So, what did you want to talk about?" her mom asked.

"What makes you think I want to discuss something specific, Mom? Maybe I just missed you and wanted to spend time with you?"

"Have you talked to Remy about what will happen when you return to Portland?"

The conversation was quickly heading away from where Julia had hoped, so she knew she needed to suck it up and just bring up the subject of the Miller family. Her dad had always been very blustery about them, but the more she thought about it, her mom hadn't said much. She hoped that meant she wouldn't tow the family line and bullshit any answers Julia needed about what happened.

"No, not yet. The accident happened, and we haven't talked about it. We will."

"You better do it soon before someone gets their heart broken," her mom said. The arrival of the food interrupted them, but Julia plunged forward once the server had left.

"Mom, what do you know about the issues between the Millers and us? The stuff with Papa Joe and Edward Miller."

Her mom picked at her food for a minute, then sipped her wine and dabbed the corner of her mouth with her napkin. "Why do you ask?"

"I'm just curious. I know the story that Dad has always told us, but I want to know what you know."

"Tell me what you think you know, and I'll tell you if it's correct," her mom said, sipping her chardonnay and peering at Julia over the rim of her glass.

"Mom. Come on. Don't do this. I deserve to know. Someday, I'll take over Clayman Fisheries. I think that gives me the right to know exactly what happened." Julia was sick of getting the runaround from her family. Why did they need to hide the truth if they had done nothing wrong?

Her mom waved her hand as if brushing away an irritating fly. "I don't know what to tell you, Julia. Why don't you ask your father about it? Why do you have to come to me?"

"Because Dad won't give me a straight answer, either. Why is what happened such a fucking secret?"

The wine gave Julia the courage to speak her mind and might have convinced her she was invincible.

"Look, Mom, I just want to know what happened. It'll be my company someday, and I'll need to know about all the skeletons in the closet."

The server stopped to check on them, and Julia's mom asked him to bring back an entire bottle of chardonnay. Apparently, this talk needed more alcohol than one glass could provide.

"Everything happened before your dad was born, so none of us know exactly what happened. The story I've always heard was that Joe asked Edward if he wanted to be a part of the deal, but Edward declined, so Joe went ahead without him, forming Clayman Fisheries in the process. When it turned out to be a sound decision, the Miller family was upset and tried to sue your grandfather for half of his profits for the first five years of business because he had violated a partnership they had verbally agreed upon. The case never went to court, and they dropped the lawsuit."

She hadn't heard that same story before, especially the part about the lawsuit, but it was basically what her dad had always told her. There was something in how her mom acted that made Julia believe there must be more to the story, and her mother was hesitant to tell her.

"What are you not saying, Mom?"

"What?" Her mother's innocent act was terrible. Hopefully, the woman would never be accused of a crime because she'd incriminate herself just with the look on her face.

Julia didn't even have to push. Her mom blew out an exasperated breath and poured herself another glass of chardonnay.

"Fine. When your father and I were first married, I overheard him talking to his uncle Calvin. Apparently, Calvin had threatened to testify for Edward Miller that he had proof his brother, your grandfather, broke his agreement with the Millers when he signed the contract with the restaurants."

"That's a real dick move, but legally, would it matter? Unless they had a legal partnership and the restaurants intended the deal for them both, but Papa Joe signed on his own, it doesn't seem like any wrongdoing happened. I don't even know if that would have mattered. I'm not a lawyer, but it seems like Papa Joe was an asshole but didn't break any laws."

The server took away their empty plates. Julia wasn't sure what to do with this new information. While she felt like the whole thing put her grandpa in a terrible light, he was also a shrewd businessman. Julia wondered what she would do if she were in his position. She liked to think she'd handle the whole situation better, especially with a friend and partner, but who knows? Going behind his partner's back and signing a contract that essentially shut him out of the deal without allowing him to be included was a dick move.

If her Papa Joe really had talked to Edward Miller before he signed the contract, that was on Edward if he didn't decide to sign. Was Julia horrible for feeling that way, or was that just the businesswoman they had trained her to be? Business and emotions rarely made good bedmates.

"It's water under the bridge now," her mom said, interrupting her thoughts. "Things played out like they did, and nobody died."

"Except Uncle David." Julia hadn't planned to mention her uncle, but her mind was spinning so much over her mother's admission about her grandpa, that it just slipped out.

"Yeah," her mom said. "Except David. Someone has been spilling the tea and sharing family secrets, haven't they?"

"Is that also water under the bridge?" Julia asked.

Her mom shrugged and poured the last of the wine into her glass. "So, don't you think you should at least start the conversation with Remy about Portland? Your father is feeling much better, and you'll return to your real life before you know it. It's better to work these things out before you're forced to deal with them later."

Julia shook her head and signaled the server for the check. Her mom knew exactly how to shift a conversation, and she wasn't falling into her trap this time.

"I'll drop you back at the house, then I need to get home," Julia said.

"It's not your home, sweetheart. Your aunt should be back in a few weeks, and everything will return to normal."

Lunch with her mom was a mistake. She could be the kindest woman in the world one minute and a deadly viper the next. Julia suspected things with her father weren't going well at the moment. Her parents' relationship had always been complicated, but she knew her mom would miss him very much when her dad was gone.

Julia was curled on the couch with Remy an hour later as she and the others watched the game. The comfort of being in Remy's arms settled her mind like nothing else could, even with the three of them yelling at the television when big plays happened. Even amid the chaos, she could focus on everything she'd learned in the last couple of days and evaluate what that meant for her and the future of Clayman Fisheries.

Her grandpa may or may not have been honorable, but as far as she knew, her dad hadn't followed in his footsteps. He was a successful business owner and would do what he needed to do to ensure his company thrived. Still, she'd never seen him do that underhandedly or do something that would bring shame to the company's reputation.

At some point, her dad would step down as president of the company, and she would take his place at the top. She couldn't erase the past, but maybe she could help level the playing field in favor of the smaller fishermen trying to feed their families.

"You okay, baby?" Remy asked.

"I think I will be." She might not be in charge of the company yet, but she was excited about her envisioned future. Something she would be proud to pass down to her own children someday. The thought that those children might have the name Miller made her chuckle. Talk about everything coming full circle.

CHAPTER TWENTY-THREE

For once, Remy was awake before her alarm. She'd finally been cleared to return to work and was more than ready to get out on the water. Andy would pick her up before dawn, so she quickly showered and dressed, doing her best not to wake up Julia. She'd gotten good at using the dim light from her phone to navigate through the darkness of their room, and she was ready and waiting in the driveway before Andy arrived.

"Holy shit," Andy said when Remy handed her a travel mug full of hot coffee. "Someone is eager to get back to work."

"You bet your ass I am," Remy said. "Don't let me forget that I'm supposed to take my clearance letter from the doc to HR when we get back this evening. They wouldn't let me go out this morning without it, but I convinced them to accept an emailed copy until I could bring the original at the end of the day."

"Couldn't you just have given it to Julia?"

"They're weird about HR stuff. I guess someone decided it could be a conflict of interest," Remy said.

"'Cause you're boning her?"

"Jesus, Andy. Don't be an ass."

Andy just smiled, and Remy couldn't help but smile back. Sex with Julia had been more than she had ever imagined. She hoped that now that she was cleared for work, Julia would be up for something a little more athletic than the gentle lovemaking they'd had since her injury.

"That good, huh," Andy said.

"Just drive."

They stopped to pick up Corey, and the three of them were prepped and underway just as the sun crested over the mountains to the east of town. Remy loved this part of the day; being on the water was the best place to witness it.

Once they were clear of the coast and in open water, Remy stood on deck and sucked in a deep breath of the crisp ocean air. There was nothing like it; she'd been a little depressed when she was stuck on land and couldn't be out on the boat.

Julia had asked her the night before if she was nervous about going back out after being injured, and the thought hadn't even occurred to her before it was mentioned. The answer was a confident no. She understood what being out there could do to her, and it was the price you paid when you made your living as a sailor. It wasn't anything personal. They were trying to take their bounty from the sea, and sometimes it put up a bigger fight than usual. Remy was just fine with that.

A beep from the pilothouse told her they were approaching where she'd plotted out to drop their first pots, so she took one last deep breath and returned inside.

"Time to work, guys. Look alive out there."

Six hours later, they'd finished up for the day. Julia had made them promise not to overdo it on Remy's first trip out. The fact that she had to be back in port to go to human resources before the office closed forced her to comply with Julia's rules.

"Give me a few while I turn in this paperwork, and I'll be back," Remy told Andy and Corey when they secured the boat.

"Roger that," Corey said. "We'll wait in the truck."

The offices of Clayman Fisheries weren't all that big, but Remy still felt a little lost roaming the halls searching for human resources. The vast warehouse was close to the dock, so crews could store equipment on the bottom floor, and the top floor held a maze of hallways, offices, and conference rooms. Julia worked in one of the offices, but Remy wasn't exactly sure which one.

After wandering aimlessly for a while, she found a young man in an office who directed her through the doors at the end of the hall and to the back of the building. Signs would be helpful. She needed to remember to mention to Julia that signs directing you where to go to find HR would be a great employee benefit.

Remy finally found the office she was searching for and dropped her documents off with HR. The three ladies working there were very sweet and insisted she have a piece of cake they'd brought in for one of their birthdays. Remy happily ate the chocolate cake with chocolate frosting and giggled at how mad Andy and Corey were going to be when they found out they had to wait extra long so she could eat the cake. It would have been rude of her to refuse their offer. At least that's what she would tell them.

When she finally escaped, she thought she might as well see if Julia was still there on her way back through the maze and out of the building. Maybe she'd even be able to convince her to leave a little early and escort her out herself. Remy was excited at the prospect even though she was fully aware of how sappy that was.

She wasn't entirely sure where Julia's office was, but she assumed it would be near her dad's office. Or she could be using her dad's office since he wasn't there to use it. Surely the acting CEO wouldn't be pushed into some cubicle somewhere. Without direction, she followed her instincts and looked for higher-end furniture and larger offices.

The strategy seemed to work, and before she knew it, she found a door with a nameplate on it that said Brian Clayman, CEO. She didn't see an office near there that had Julia's name, so she took a chance and raised her hand to knock on the partially open door. She stopped short when she heard a male voice on the other side. She didn't want to interrupt Julia if she was in a meeting.

She started to turn away when she heard Brian Clayman say, "And what did Jay Miller say to you when he found out?"

The world seemed to stop spinning for a moment and Remy's lungs felt like all the air had been sucked from them. Why was Brian Miller talking about her brother and who was the man in the office with him? Remy didn't know if she should storm into the room and confront him, or not. The man was telling Brian something, but his voice was too quiet to distinguish what he was saying. Had she misheard what Brian said? She'd heard him pretty damn clearly.

If she did confront him, he'd only deny it and she could be out of yet another job. Andy and Corey would kill her if she blew this up and it turned out to be nothing. She couldn't do that to them. If she wasn't going to confront him right now, she needed to figure out how to leave without him seeing her.

"Is someone there?" Brian asked.

There goes that idea. Before she could think of what to do, Brian opened the door the rest of the way and stood between Remy and Dan Bratton like he hoped she wouldn't notice who he was with.

"Hey, Remy," Brian Clayman said. "What brings you to my office at this time of day?"

"Mr. Clayman." Remy stood stunned as she watched Dan Bratton, bow his head and quickly walk down the hall.

"Call me Brian, please," Brian said, wrapping an arm around Remy so he could turn her away from Bratton as he left.

"How do you know Dan Bratton?" Remy asked.

Brian cleared his throat and poured each of them whiskey from a liquor cart in the corner of his office. Remy took the offered glass and sipped from it, too stunned to process what was happening.

"Oh, I used to fish with Dan's father, Jerrod, years ago. He stopped by to tell me his pop wasn't well and asked if I'd mind checking in on him. He's a nice boy. Good son."

"Hmm." Remy peered at Brian from over the rim of her glass. "I hadn't realized you guys knew each other."

"Well, it's a small world." Brian sat in his office chair, pulled a cigar from the humidor on his desk, and lit it up. Remy ridiculously thought at that moment that Julia would kill him if she knew he was smoking and drinking against the doctor's orders. That should have been the last thing on her mind, but at the end of the day, he was her girlfriend's dad, and she loved her girlfriend.

"I could have sworn I heard you say something about my brother, Jay."

Brian looked her right in the face then took another puff of his cigar. She could have sworn she saw him smile.

"What brings you here today, Remy?" Brian asked once more. "Is there anything I can help you with? Julia left early today to do some shopping. I sent her home and told her to make you a nice dinner."

Remy looked out the window and saw Dan emerge from the first-floor doors and jog toward the parking area. She didn't know what the hell was happening, but she knew that Brian wouldn't tell her a damn thing. She needed to think carefully about what she should do next.

"Yeah. Julia's an amazing cook." Remy checked her watch and downed the last of the whiskey. "Well, I better get home before she wonders what happened to me."

Brian leaned back in his chair and watched Remy place her empty glass on the cart. "We're all so glad you're back at work, Remy."

"Thanks, Mr., umm, Brian. You take care."

The maze didn't seem as confusing as Remy practically ran from the building. The events of the last few minutes were a blur, and she wasn't exactly sure how to interpret them. If she made false accusations and had nothing to back them up, everyone would just assume she was bitter about the captain job, or stirring up shit because she's a Miller and Brian is a Clayman. She wanted to talk to Julia, but who was she going to believe? Remy or her father? She didn't think for a minute that he would admit to Julia that he was a conniving asshole that was involved in some shady shit with Bratton. It even seemed far-fetched to Remy now that she was thinking it. But what other explanation was there?

She was almost surprised to see Andy and Corey waiting for her when she finally got to the truck. She'd taken way longer than she would have had the patience for if one of them had been in her place. The injury she'd just suffered had shaken them all to the core, and she had no doubt they would be cutting her some slack for a bit.

"Hey, guys." Remy climbed into the truck's passenger seat and fastened her seat belt. "I'm sorry it took me so long. That place was a freaking maze."

"Sure." Andy put the truck in reverse and backed out of the parking spot. "You still have chocolate frosting on your lip."

"Shit." Remy wiped her mouth with her sleeve and wanted to die at the realization that Brian Clayman had seen her with chocolate frosting on her face. Ugh. She'd never be cool.

"You couldn't even bring us any?" Corey asked.

"Any what?"

"Whatever had chocolate frosting," Andy said.

"Oh. Yeah. Sorry. Next time," Remy said.

"Are we going to Skip's to celebrate your return from near death?" Corey asked.

"I didn't almost die, drama queen." Remy chewed her fingernail and watched out the window as buildings passed by. "I think Julia might have made me dinner. I need to go home and check with her before I can commit to going out tonight."

"Home, huh?" Andy glanced at Remy and then back to the road. "You do remember that the house belongs to her aunt, and she'll be returning to Portland at some point, don't you?"

"Yes." Remy was irritated that Andy was being a dick. Of course, she knew that. It didn't mean she couldn't enjoy the time they had together right now. It did feel like a home. More of a home than she'd had since she was a kid. "Get off my ass, Andy."

Andy raised her hands in surrender and pulled up to the curb outside Corey's house.

"If you guys decide to go out, give me a call. Brooke's working on a new recipe, so she wants me out of the house because I make too much noise and bother her."

"Roger that," Andy said. "Even if mother hen over here doesn't go out, I'll call you. The house is too quiet without her big mouth yappin' it up all the time. I should probably thank Julia for taking you off my hands, now that I think about it."

"Dude, you're just on my ass for some reason."

"She misses you, Rem. We both miss you. Julia's brother was a nice guy, but he wasn't you. It sucked being out there without you."

Remy looked at Andy, who refused to look in her direction. She'd felt it while stuck on land but hadn't considered how much it would have affected them.

"Look, I have to see if Julia made me dinner, and then I'll give you guys a call. It might be late, but we'll meet up for one drink at least. That work?"

"Yep. That works. See you guys later." Corey slapped the truck door and jogged the path to the house he shared with Brooke. Remy was so proud of him. He hadn't had the easiest childhood, and nobody deserved to be happy more than her cousin.

"You okay?" Andy asked when they pulled away.

"I don't know." Part of her wanted to tell Andy what had happened, but she wasn't sure getting her involved before Remy had time to think about what happened was the best idea. She'd call Jay and talk to him as soon as she could. He would know what to do. "I'll be okay. Just take me home and I'll see you guys tonight."

Thankfully Andy didn't push for more and she silently looked out the window while they drove to Julia's house. This had been the first day back from hell and she just wanted to put all this out of her mind for a few hours.

CHAPTER TWENTY-FOUR

Julia watched Remy grumble about the ice pack the doctor suggested she place on her shoulder when her pain got worse. After a week out on the boat for what was supposed to be light duty, Remy struggled to put her shirt on that morning. She was sure Remy's version of taking it easy and the doctor's idea of what that meant were two entirely different things.

Thankfully, her crew had a couple of days off, so Remy had time to finally relax and allow the swelling in her shoulder to calm back down. Remy had been acting strange around her all week. Julia wanted nothing more than to spend the day with her, trying to figure out what bothered her, but she had an appointment in Portland that afternoon she couldn't miss.

"Hey, babe. What do you think about going to Portland with me? I want you to be able to rest your arm, so if it's too much, I totally understand."

"No. Let's do it. It would be nice to get out of town for a bit."

Julia knelt next to where Remy sat in the recliner and brushed a stray lock of her hair away from her eyes. Remy was a strong and capable woman when she was around others, but Julia was privileged enough to be allowed to see the vulnerable side of her, as well. Both were equally sexy, and Julia's heart bloomed each time she looked at her.

"If you want, we could pack a bag and stay overnight. I need to grab a couple things while we're there, and I'm sure Dylan would love to see us," Julia said.

One of the things Julia hoped to accomplish on their trip to Portland was a talk with Remy about what'd been bothering her.

A few hours later, Julia had finished meeting with the vendor she had promised to see in person. She returned to her apartment with enough Chinese food to feed an army. They'd gone back and forth about whether to go out to dinner or bring something home, but the weather ultimately decided for them. Rainy nights were best spent at home under a blanket with the person you loved.

Dinner was shared while sitting on the floor in the living room watching old episodes of *The Golden Girls*. Julia had missed evenings like this with Dylan and having Remy there only made them even more fun.

After eating, they shared clean-up duties and retired to their bedrooms. The long day had worn Remy out, and when Julia came out of the bathroom, Remy had already fallen asleep. Julia thought about knocking on Dylan's door to see if she was still awake, but the temptation to snuggle up to Remy and go to sleep early was too much to deny.

It seemed like they'd only just fallen asleep when she felt Remy get up to go to the bathroom then returned to bed.

"Good morning," Julia said.

"Morning."

"Did you sleep well?"

Remy shrugged and then winced from the pain it caused in her shoulder.

"I'm sorry, baby. This trip probably wasn't the best idea. You aren't resting your shoulder as much as you should."

"I'm fine."

Julia traced the edge of Remy's lips with the tip of her finger and gazed into her beautiful blue eyes. Remy Miller was hot, and Julia was getting wet just thinking she was lucky enough to be there with her. Before things escalated too far between them, Julia knew this was the best opportunity to talk to her about a couple of things, one being why Remy seemed so distant the last few days.

"Can I ask you something?"

"Sure." Remy leaned forward and placed a gentle kiss on Julia's lips. One that wasn't rushed and promised more to come.

"How should we handle things once I'm back in Portland?"

"What do you mean, handle?" Remy shifted uncomfortably, and Julia started to massage her shoulder.

"This trip was too much, too soon. I never should have suggested you come."

"It wasn't. I'm fine," Remy said.

"You're stubborn." Julia knew she'd never get Remy to admit it if it had been too much, so she'd just have to do her best to make her take it easy until it had more time to heal.

"Are you excited to be back in Portland? I can tell you're happy here," Remy said.

Julia helped remove Remy's shirt and squirted some lotion on her hands from a bottle on the nightstand. Remy rolled over to lie on her stomach, and Julia sat up to straddle her hips so she could lean over her body and massage her sore shoulder and back.

"I am excited to be back here, but it's weird," Julia said.

"Weird, how? Mmm."

"Feel good, baby?"

At Remy's nod, Julia continued her massage.

"It feels so familiar, but something about it no longer feels like home."

"Really?" Remy started to turn around, but Julia gently pushed her back onto her stomach. For some reason, she felt like she couldn't be looking at her to have this conversation.

"I'm not sure if it's because I've become so used to the house in Elder's Bay or because that's where you are."

Remy cleared her throat but otherwise kept quiet.

"This apartment almost seems like another person lives here, not me. It's all my stuff. I have years of memories here, but it no longer feels like me."

"What about your job?" Remy asked.

"What about it?"

"I know you have to come here occasionally for meetings or whatever, but how do you feel about the job you're doing in Elder's

Bay for your dad. Do you miss the business suits and corporate muckety-mucks?"

Julia slid off of Remy's hips and snuggled up next to her. She took a moment to consider her answer carefully before responding. The life Julia had built in Portland was all she'd ever thought she wanted. She'd spent her teenage years dreaming of getting out of Elder's Bay and vowed to never end up there, no matter what. Now the idea of coming home to this apartment, and her empty bed, after a grueling day at work seemed depressing.

When had that happened? When had the vision of what she wanted from life changed so dramatically? It wasn't only her relationship with Remy. That might have significantly affected what made her happy in Elder's Bay, but it was more than that.

Instead of feeling ready to kick the world's ass every morning, she couldn't wait to see everyone at the office and hear about what their kids did the night before. She loved to walk around the docks in the afternoon and chat with the fishermen while they unloaded their catch and joked with each other about some goofy thing one of them did or bragged about how many crabs they had pulled in that day.

They made her feel like she was part of something bigger than herself. Like she was family. Her job in Portland had always made her feel important. She had the biggest and best office. Clients came to her when they thought they needed the big boss to get involved. She fixed problems. Evenings were often spent at fancy restaurants where instead of enjoying her meal, she would turn on her charm to convince the chef they needed to get their crab exclusively from Clayman Fisheries.

It was fun. Julia wouldn't lie to herself and say she didn't enjoy what she did. And she was damn good at it, but that life didn't seem as appealing as it once had. The question was, what could she do about that?

"No. Honestly, I don't miss that aspect of being in Portland. I really thought I would, but I don't. I will miss working in Elder's Bay, not only because I've enjoyed working there but also because I've become quite fond of a certain sailor."

"Really?"

"Does that surprise you?" Julia asked.

"No. I guess not. You seem much happier now than when you first got to Elder's Bay."

Julia nodded and played with the fuzz on the blanket Remy had pulled over them. "I think I am happier."

"You think?"

"I just have no idea what to do about that. I don't want to completely give up my life in Portland. It's something I've worked for my entire adult life. I can't just walk away from that."

"Can't you?" Remy asked. "Isn't your assistant handling things here just fine?"

Julia nodded and snuggled closer into Remy. "Yeah. She's great. I told her this would be a temporary position, but I'm sure she'd jump at the chance to make it permanent. It's worth asking. I need to stop by the office before we leave, and I'll talk to her."

"What do you think your dad's going to say?" Remy asked.

"I don't know." Julia knew he would be happy to have her around more, but worried he might feel like she was usurping his throne before he was ready to give it up. She'd have to figure out the best way to present the idea to make him think it was his. That was the only way to get him totally on board. "I'll figure something out."

"Speaking of your dad...."

Remy used her good arm to push herself to a sitting position and scooted back to lean against the headboard. She pulled Julia's head into her lap and gently combed her fingers through her hair. Yeah, Julia could get used to having this more regularly.

"Let's not talk about my dad anymore," Julia said.

The gentle caresses stopped as Remy cleared her throat and seemed to tense up.

"What's going on? Are you okay, baby?"

Remy looked down at her momentarily, anxiety and indecision clouding her eyes. Julia knew this must be why she'd been so distant lately. Some of her suspected it might be related to her dad somehow. Every time she mentioned him, Remy would tense up and look uncomfortable.

"Tell me, Remy."

"Do you remember the other day I had to drop off the doctor's note with HR?"

"Yes. I remember." Julia remembered her dad had sent her home early that day so she could make dinner for Remy. It was a strange suggestion from him since he'd never seemed happy that they were dating in the first place. Still, she had hoped it meant he was coming around and taking their relationship seriously.

"That place is a maze. It took me forever to find HR, and then I was trapped there for a bit."

"This is the birthday cake thing, right?"

"Yeah. The cake," Remy said.

"You know they can't make you stay for that. If they pressured you to stay—"

"No, no, no. They were just fine. Fran is hilarious. That's not what this is about," Remy said.

Julia wanted to shake the story out of Remy. She had this way of taking forever to get to the punchline, and this story was no different than the rest. It drove Julia nuts, but she usually also thought it was adorable. Right now, she just wanted to know what had upset Remy.

"Tell me what happened, sweetheart," Julia said.

Remy looked everywhere except at Julia. This wasn't going to be good. "What did he do?" Julia was already pissed at her dad even though she didn't know what he had done yet. Just making Remy feel this way was enough to make her angry. As soon as they were back in Elder's Bay, she would talk with him about what Remy meant to her and how she expected her to be treated going forward.

"I thought I'd see if you were still in the office before I left. I didn't know your dad sent you home at that point."

Julia nodded, encouraging Remy to continue.

"I found your dad in his office instead, and he wasn't alone and I heard him say something that I'm very confused about."

"Oh, God, please don't tell me my dad is having an affair. I don't want to know if you found him with someone. I knew it was strange that he sent me home early. He seems so in love with my mom, though. Fuck." Julia felt her mind start to spin out. Her dad was a lot of things, but she'd never pegged him as a cheater. How could he do that to her mom? Charlie was going to freak.

"He wasn't with a woman," Remy said.

"Okayyy. That's even more surprising, but I guess sailors spend so much time on the water, away from their family, it's inevitable."

"Julia, no. Your dad isn't having an affair," Remy said. "That I know of, at least."

"Thank God. That was going to be too much to deal with right now."

Remy still seemed hesitant to explain, so Julia squeezed her hand for encouragement. "Go on. I'm sorry I started to spin."

"It's okay." Remy rubbed her eyes and pressed forward. "Do you remember me telling you about Dan Bratton?"

"The asshole your dad hired to captain the boat you thought you were getting?"

"Yes. Yeah, that guy. I haven't mentioned this because it didn't seem like something I should tell you, but he's done a few very questionable things that have caught Jay's attention. Nothing that couldn't technically be explained away as mistakes, but things that any self-respecting captain wouldn't have done."

"Like what?" Julia asked.

"Like he screwed up some logbooks that could have been a big problem if my brother hadn't caught the mistake before they were turned in, for one."

"It could have just been an accident. It can't be easy to take over a new boat. Mistakes happen."

"Sure," Remy said. "But there's more. Jay sent my cousin Kel to crew with Bratton, and he found out the new guys on board had been told they didn't have to measure the crab. If it was bigger than their hand, it was fine."

"Ugh. That's a dangerous game to play with a hefty fine if you're wrong."

"Exactly. I don't trust this guy as far as I can throw him."

"Okay. What does this have to do with my dad?" Julia was struggling to follow how these stories would merge.

"The man talking to your dad was Dan Bratton."

"So?" Julia said. "My dad knows lots of fishermen. Why does that have you so worked up?"

"Because I overheard your dad ask Bratton what Jay Miller said when he found out?"

"Found what out?" This wasn't making any sense and even though Julia could tell Remy was getting frustrated, she couldn't exactly get angry about something she thought she overheard her dad saying.

"I don't know. Maybe about not measuring the crab?"

"So, it could have been about anything?"

"Don't you think it's awfully suspicious that this Bratton guy shows up out of nowhere and is doing all these things that could cause my family a lot of problems then I find him having some secret meeting with your dad where he mentions my brother's name? Your dad acted suspicious like I'd caught him doing something he wasn't supposed to be doing."

"Maybe, but your suspicion doesn't prove my dad has done anything wrong."

Remy's face reddened. She abruptly pulled away from Julia and slid off the bed. Julia was still trying to wrap her head around what Remy was saying when she pulled on a pair of boxers and a T-shirt and sat in the chair Julia kept in the corner of her bedroom. Putting distance between them.

"I realize that. I know it could be just as your dad said. That Dan's the son of some fisherman he used to know. I just don't buy it. There's something else going on, and I can't put my finger on exactly what that is."

"Why are you convinced it's not exactly as my dad said? Why do you have to assume the worst of him? He's a lot of things, but he's not the asshole you've made him out to be."

"No?" Remy smirked, and Julia wanted to leave and slam the door for dramatic effect. This was absolutely ridiculous.

"No, Remy. My dad can be frustrating, pompous, and controlling, but he's not underhanded. If you think this Bratton guy is up to no good, my dad has nothing to do with it."

"You're so blind from his love for you that you can't see him for who he really is," Remy said. "You didn't see the way he smirked at me when I asked him what he was saying about Jay."

"A smirk? Really? That's your proof that my dad is plotting against your family. Don't be a child, Remy." The moment the words left her mouth, Julia wished she could take them back. Tensions were high and she knew better than to let emotions drive her to say something that would only make things worse. This thing with Bratton had obviously been eating at Remy for some time and whatever happened with her dad was obviously enough to upset her.

Add to that the lingering pain from her injury and the frustration of not being able to be on the boat with her crew for weeks and Remy was understandably on edge. Julia needed to try to calm things down before they said more things they wouldn't be able to take back.

Julia sucked in a deep breath and slowly released it. Remy had been raised to believe the Claymans, especially Julia's dad, were horrible. She couldn't hold it against her when Remy thought he was the boogeyman.

"Let's not fight about this," Julia said as calmly as she could. "I'll ask my dad about Bratton and see what he says. I think I'll have a better read on whether he's telling the truth about their association. I'm sure this is just a huge misunderstanding. I know it's hard for you to see past your distrust of him, but he's not a bad man."

Remy stood and riffled through her bag for clean clothes. "While you're at it, why don't you ask him what he said to me in the parking lot."

"What are you talking about?"

"Just ask him. He'll know. I'm sure he'll play innocent on that one, too, but I know exactly what he was trying to say. He doesn't think I'm good enough for you, and I wonder if you might think that, too."

"What does that mean?" Julia asked.

"It means I thought you knew me well enough to know I wouldn't make accusations casually. Something's wrong with your dad and Bratton; I'll find out what it is. You can ignore me all you want, I don't give a fuck, but I'm not letting the Claymans screw with my family's livelihood anymore."

"What does that even mean?" Julia wanted to scream. Once again, the bullshit between their families was trying to tear them apart. She was sick of the ridiculous animosity between them. She wondered if thinking they could ever rise above it was a childish dream.

"It means I'm going to take a shower. Dylan is taking me to pick up a birthday gift for my mom while you're in the office. I'll pack my shit so I'm ready to go when you're home. I'm ready to get the fuck out of this place."

Julia wiped tears away as she watched Remy storm out of her bedroom and slam the door. The exact thing she'd wanted to do. She heard voices in the hall then the shower started. The last thing she wanted to do was go into her office, but she had to get it over with so they could get home. She needed to have a long talk with her dad about several things, and she wasn't looking forward to any of it.

CHAPTER TWENTY-FIVE

Remy felt strange knocking on the door of her childhood home, but she wasn't sure if she should walk in without permission considering how her relationship with her dad was. She'd never felt so isolated from her family before, which affected her more than anticipated.

Her mom answered in an apron, drying her hands on one of the same dish towels they'd had since she was a kid. Remy had this urge to wrap her arms around her mom and break down in tears, but she hesitated. An adult couldn't collapse in their mommy's arms because they were sad, could they?

Remy's moms' eyes lit up when she realized who had knocked on the door. "Come in out of the rain, sweetheart. You're going to catch your death out there on the stoop. Why in the world are you knocking on the door? I don't think you've knocked one time in your life."

Remy shrugged and luxuriated in the hug her mom offered so freely. She was still very fit for an older woman, but the softness and warmth of her embrace were the greatest things in the world. Remy couldn't help but remember her hugs healing broken arms and broken hearts like they were magic. She didn't want it to end, but when her mom loosened her grip, she stepped back and kissed her mom's cheek.

"I wasn't sure with Dad and all," Remy said.

Her mom waved her comment off and guided Remy onto the stool in the kitchen where she'd witnessed thousands of brownies, mashed potatoes, birthday cakes, and most importantly, crab, prepared since she was old enough to sit up on her own. A memory of watching Julia cooking in her aunt's kitchen hit her without warning, and Remy took a deep breath to hold back the tears that threatened to fall.

They hadn't spoken in several days, and Remy wasn't sure things between them would ever be the same. She'd acted like a complete asshole to Julia and she was so embarrassed of her behavior, but she wasn't ready to let go of what went down with Brian Clayman. Remy was taking a chance by talking to her dad about everything, but she didn't feel like she had a choice.

She'd talked to Jay about it and she knew he'd talked to their brother Pete, but she felt like she owed it to her dad to talk to him in person.

Remy's eyes widened at the plate of freshly baked cookies her mom had taken straight off the cooling rack for her.

"Man, do I have good timing, or what?" Remy took a bite of the hot cookie and swooned at the melted chocolate chips that burst in her mouth. Her mom made the best chocolate cookies on the planet and would fight anyone who disagreed.

"Here's your milk." Her mom slid a tall glass of cold milk next to her plate, and she suddenly forgot why she was even there other than this. Spending time with her mom had always helped to center her world, and she knew this was exactly what she needed at that moment.

"I'm not just saying this because of the cookies, Mom, but you're the best. I love you so much."

Her mom turned back toward the sink to hide the tears Remy saw her wipe from her cheeks. She knew none of them told her mom enough about how much they appreciated her, and Remy vowed to talk with her brothers about taking the time to do it more often.

Remy's dad had always been such a bigger-than-life figure, and she was sure that made her mom feel a little pushed into the corner.

Her dad might have made the money and most of the decisions, but her mom was the glue that held the family together.

"What brings you here, sweetheart?" her mom asked.

"Had I known there would be cookies, I wouldn't say this, but really, I wanted to talk to Dad."

"It's about time you two talked. He doesn't always show it, but he's torn up about all this. How are things with Julia?"

The mention of Julia's name brought back the sadness Remy was doing her best to ignore. They hadn't gone this long without speaking since their first date. Julia had become such an essential part of her life that this distance between them felt like a billion miles rather than only a few blocks. It hurt but wasn't something Remy could deal with at the moment. She had to focus on Bratton and not let anything else derail her before talking to her dad about him.

"Things with Julia aren't great at the moment."

"Oh, Remy, what did you do, sweetheart?"

"Jesus, mom, maybe she was the one who did something?" Remy was annoyed that her mom assumed she was the one that had caused their argument. It was mostly true, but it bothered her all the same.

"Was it her?"

Remy dunked her cookie in her milk and took a big bite of it before shrugging.

"Remington Miller, you apologize to that girl. Whatever you did, a sincere apology will hopefully go a long way."

"I plan on it."

"Stop planning and start doing."

"Yes, ma'am."

Her mom poured herself a glass of milk and took a cookie from the rack. "What are you talking to your dad about?"

"Just some boat stuff. It might not be anything, but I wanted to discuss it with Dad anyway. Just in case."

Her mom watched her wipe her hands on the napkin beside her plate and drink the last milk in her glass. She cleared the dishes to the sink and then took Remy's hand.

"Is everything okay?" her mom asked.

"Who knows? I'll tell him what I know and let him do whatever he wants with the information."

"You're a good kid, Remy," her mom said.

"The prodigal daughter returns." Her dad's deep voice broke through the calmness of the kitchen and immediately set Remy's nerves on edge.

"Not exactly, but I had hoped you'd spare a few minutes to chat with me."

Her dad rounded the kitchen island without acknowledging Remy's request and wrapped her mom in his giant arms. For a man with such a rough exterior, he didn't hold back when showing his wife how much he loved her.

"I missed you today, sweetheart," her dad said to her mom. "I'm sorry I'm so late. Peter had trouble with the winch on his boat and needed my help getting the old one off."

"Well, he came to the right place. These big muscles aren't just for show."

"Okay," Remy said, suddenly feeling weirded out. "Should I wait for you in your office, Dad?"

He waved a dismissive hand toward her and kissed her mom again. Nothing made her happier than seeing her parents so in love with each other, but it grossed her out when things started to get a little dirty.

Ten minutes later, Remy's dad entered the little house he used as an office in their backyard. It was the first time she'd been there since the day she'd told him she was going to work for the Claymans before the party. She didn't miss the irony that she was now there to say to him she suspected the Claymans might be just as bad as he'd always said. Well, not all the Claymans, but Brian, at least.

As per custom, her dad poured them each whiskey and pulled cigars from the box. This time Remy accepted one and allowed the sweetness of the cigar and the burn of the whiskey to prepare her for what lay ahead.

"We haven't seen you in a while, kiddo. Did you forget you have a mother?"

Remy leaned forward to gently tap the ash from her cigar.

"I didn't think I was welcome," Remy said.

Her dad smirked and ashed his own cigar before downing the rest of what was in his glass and pouring more of the golden liquid for each of them.

"I guess you should have thought about that before you did what you did. It shouldn't have kept you from visiting your mother, though. She's been worried about you."

No sense in arguing with him about something Remy agreed with. None of this was her mom's fault, and it was her bad that she'd failed to see past her anger to stop by and see her more often.

"You're right," Remy said.

With a perceived small win under his belt, her dad sat back in his chair. "What can I do for you, Remy?"

"I've come to talk to you about your new captain."

"Dan?"

"Yeah. Bratton."

"What about him?" he asked. "He hasn't put up the numbers I had hoped for, but he's just starting, and it takes time to get the feel of things when you're coming into new fishing grounds."

"It's not about that," Remy said. "I haven't heard about how his fishing has been."

"What is it, then?"

Remy cleared her throat and ashed her cigar again, buying herself a little time to deliver the speech she'd gone over several times before then.

"Has Jay mentioned anything about him to you?"

"He said there was some business with the logs a bit ago, but that doesn't mean anything. He's not the first guy to fuck up the logs, and he won't be the last. I don't think it's happened again since that one time. What of it?"

"Did you hear about him not measuring the crab?"

"I did. I don't like it, but Jay put Kel on board to make sure everything is okay. Why are you so concerned about this? You don't even work for us anymore."

"You're still my family. What if I told you I saw Bratton in Brian Clayman's office?"

Her dad revealed the slightest surprise before quickly masking it and taking another sip of his whiskey. He set the glass on the desk and cleared his throat before speaking.

"Did you ask him why he was there?"

"No," Remy said. "He took off as soon as I saw him. Brian tried to play it off with some story about how Dan was the son of someone he used to work with, and something happened to his dad or something."

"Is that so?" Her dad tapped more ash from his cigar into the tray. "Well, maybe that's all that's happening."

"I overheard Brian asking him what Jay did when he found out."

"Found what out?"

"I don't know," Remy said. "I can only assume he was talking about not measuring the crab because it wasn't long after that happened that I saw him in there."

"Are you sure this isn't about the fact that I gave him the boat and not you?"

"I'm only letting you know what I heard, Dad. I'm not completely sure what to make of it, either, but I thought you should know since the guy is responsible for one of your boats." Remy was done with this conversation and stood to leave. "Thanks for the drink."

"Sit down, kid," he said.

Remy folded her arms across her chest but refused to sit. Her dad chuckled and stubbed his cigar out in the tray.

"What does your girlfriend say about this?" he asked.

"I...we aren't really talking right now."

"Why is that?"

"I told her about my suspicions about Bratton and her dad, and she didn't believe me."

"Do you have proof that Brian's done something nefarious, or are you just making assumptions because Bratton was in the office with him and you heard him say something about Jay?"

"Well, no, I don't have proof, but I can't ignore what I saw and heard."

"You might be right. I think Brian Clayman's a dickhead, and the thing you heard him say about telling Jay does concern me a bit. But without proof, you can't expect Julia to choose your word over her own dad's."

Talking to her dad about Julia made her uncomfortable. Mainly because he was making excellent points about how Remy had acted like a real asshole.

"Out of all my kids, you're the most like me, and it pisses me off. You can be as stubborn as you want with me. Still, I'm warning you now, you keep up that bullheadedness with the women you date, and they'll always leave you wondering what the hell happened when they walk out the door. I learned that lesson the hard way with your mom, and it almost cost me everything. Don't make the same mistakes I made."

The wind was sucked from Remy's sails as she collapsed back into the chair.

"I won't." Remy thought of her argument with Julia and how, even though she was still frustrated that she didn't back her up when she raised concerns about Bratton, Remy also understood that she was wrong to expect Julia to blindly be angry with him when there was no proof that her dad had done anything wrong. It wasn't fair of Remy to put her in that position, but she wasn't exactly sure how to move forward yet.

An apology would go a long way. However, she still needed time to work out this Bratton thing before she did anything else, or things could blow up again. Julia had said she would talk to her dad, and Remy just had to trust her that she would do it.

"Look, I appreciate your concern and that you took the time to stop by and talk to me about it. I'll talk to your brothers and ensure we're all keeping a closer eye on Bratton until we know him better and are sure he's not taking us all for a ride."

Her dad stood and walked around the desk to take her into his arms. "Don't ever fucking scare me like you did. When we didn't know if you were alive...I just don't ever want to go through that again, kid. I love you."

The sudden display of affection took Remy off guard, and she had to think about how frustrating he was sometimes to stop herself from crying. She'd missed this. Love from her mom was equally important, and she'd never try to compare it to her dad, but it had always been easier won than affection from him. He hugged them. He'd always told them he loved them and showed them how much they meant to him, but it didn't come as often or as easily as affection from her mom. This made it even more emotional when he did.

"I love you, too, Dad."

He backed away and grabbed both of their now empty glasses to take into the house to be cleaned. "Let's go see if dinner is ready. Your mom's making lasagna tonight. I know that's one of your favorites, so you picked a good night to stop by."

She followed her dad out of his office and closed the door behind them. "Only because Mom makes the best lasagna in the freaking world. I don't know how she does it. It has crack in it or something."

Her dad laughed and placed his giant paw of a hand on top of her head and playfully ruffled her hair. She kept it so short it didn't do too much damage, but enough that she complained and tried to finger it back into place.

"Mom," her dad said when they reached the kitchen. "You need to show your daughter how to make your famous lasagna. It might eventually get her out of a jam with the girlfriend."

Remy looked from her dad to her mom, who also seemed shocked by what he'd said.

"Yeah. Um. It might take more than lasagna to get me out of the doghouse. "

"That bad, huh?" her dad asked.

"Maybe worse."

He shook his head and carried the lasagna from the kitchen to the dining room. "You've got a hard road ahead of you, kid."

Dinner was surprisingly pleasant as Remy and her dad had her mom laughing so hard she almost choked on her wine. She'd missed this. Things with her dad were far from perfect, but he was a good dad, which meant a lot.

When the last of the dishes were rinsed and put away, Remy put on her coat and slipped into her boots she'd left by the door when she arrived.

"I promise to be at Sunday dinner this week. Sorry I haven't been around. I won't make that mistake anymore."

Her mom brushed a lock of hair from Remy's eyes and stood on her tiptoes to kiss her forehead.

"I'm proud of you, Remy. Don't you ever forget that. We're proud of you and love you more than you'll ever understand."

Remy's dad handed her a food container he'd boxed up for her to take home to Andy and patted her on the back.

"Don't be a stranger, kid. We may disagree, but you're my kid, and I love you."

"Love you, too, Dad. Andy may want to marry me after she sees I'm bringing home mom's lasagna. It's her favorite meal in the world." Remy held up the food container as she backed out the door and waved to her parents before climbing into her truck. Remy's life wasn't going well at the moment, but she felt good that she'd at least started to patch things up with her dad.

CHAPTER TWENTY-SIX

It had been a week since their argument in Portland. She hadn't spoken to Remy since that day and the distance between them was constantly on her mind. She knew that at least part of the time, Remy had been out on the boat and very likely unable to call, but there had to have been opportunities.

She'd gone over and over their argument, and instead of giving her clarity, it just frustrated her more. How could she expect Julia to condemn her dad for something there was no proof he'd done? That was an unfair, ridiculous expectation. It pissed Julia off that she'd not only said the things she'd said but then disappeared once they were back in Elder's Bay as if their relationship meant nothing to her.

The cold shoulder pissed Julia off, but she also tried to put herself in Remy's shoes and gauge how she would feel in the same position. In a way, she was in a similar predicament. It wasn't that she would blindly believe her dad, no matter what it looked like to Remy if he said he had nothing to do with it. Still, she at least owed him a chance to explain his side of the story before she accused him.

Remy didn't trust Julia's family, especially her dad, which put her in a deficit when appealing for a bit of understanding regarding him. She knew him better than Remy and would be a much better judge regarding what he would and wouldn't be capable of doing.

He was a competitive businessman, but he'd never do anything unethical. That wasn't the man he was. Remy didn't know that, though; only time would prove that her dad had nothing to do with any shifty stuff Dan Bratton may or may not have done.

She'd been trying to reach her dad since returning from Portland, but he and her mom had taken a trip down the coast to see friends in Coos Bay for the week. Taking time away from the business was something her dad had never done before, so Julia took it as a sign that he was happy enough with her running this side of the company that he felt comfortable leaving her completely in charge for a few days.

That trust left Julia feeling proud in a way she'd never imagined. The idea that she would take over the company someday had always been a distant dream. Now that her dad was stepping away more and more, it was beginning to feel like a reality.

Julia looked up when the screen on her phone illuminated. She had hoped it would be a message from Remy, but her dad's photo appeared, indicating an incoming call from him. When she answered, she could hear road noise in the background and the faint sound of her mom singing along to Depeche Mode.

It always amused Julia that her mom was such a fan of the group. Not that *Violator* wasn't one of Julia's favorite albums of all time, but if she didn't know better, she'd never imagine her mom would even know who they were. It was like she had some secret life in her youth that Julia couldn't even picture. She guessed there were always things like that about a person's parents.

"Hey, Dad," Julia said, answering the call. "Are you guys on your way back?"

"Yep. Your mom wanted to brunch at that German place before we got on the road, so we're only just leaving."

"Well, it's worth it. Did she get the sauerbraten?"

Her dad chuckled. "Of course. You know, she says it's exactly like Oma's. I doubt she'll ever order anything else there."

"It sounds like you had a good time," Julia said.

"We did. Coos Bay is a nice town. It's growing, and new places are moving in. The casino and the dunes have brought a lot of tourists into town, and with them, new restaurants to feed those people."

"I doubt you have ever gone anywhere other than Captain's Choice, the German place, and the floating fish and chips place downtown."

"Why would we ever go anywhere else?"

Julia leaned back in her office chair, slipped out of her pumps, and set her feet on her desk. This was a nice distraction from work and thoughts of Remy and the Dan Bratton issue.

"I got your message, Jules. Sorry it took so long to get back to you. We had a busy week."

"No problem. It can wait for you guys to get home."

"Are you sure?" he asked.

"Absolutely."

"How about you come to dinner tonight? Your mom has wanted to try a new chicken enchiladas recipe, and you're just the victim—"

"Hey," her mom said.

"I mean guest she'd like to try it out on."

Julia smiled and relished the playful banter between them. Things could be so intense and frustrating with them at times, and there were moments like this that reminded Julia why she loved them so much.

"That sounds great. What time and what can I bring?"

Her mom's voice rose above the road noise and sound of the music. "How about six p.m. and a bag of limes? We'll put your dad to work making his famous margaritas."

"No complaints here. Dad makes the best margaritas on the planet. You'll have to teach me what magic you perform to make them tart."

"I guess I can trust you with my secrets. You're old enough now," Julia's dad said.

The mention of secrets reminded Julia of why she needed to talk to her dad in the first place, and it brought down her mood just a bit. She pulled her feet off the desk and slipped back into her pumps.

"Sounds good. I'll see you tonight."

"Okay, bye, sweetheart. Don't work too hard."

The line dropped, and Julia was again left alone with her thoughts. She stared at the picture of Remy she'd used for the lock screen on her phone. Remy had just returned from a trip and was still dressed in her rain gear and a ball cap, leaning against the door to the pilothouse with a cocky grin. She looked sexy and dangerous, and Julia's clit pulsed at the memory of the sex they'd had later that night.

Things between them were always pretty hot and heavy. Still, they were always a little dirtier after a trip, especially when they were apart for days. Julia had never been with someone who could be both gentle and rough. It was like Remy was everything Julia could ever want sexually, all packaged up in an intelligent, kind, sweet, incredibly hot person.

Of course, Remy had also been a complete asshole to her and said things that were difficult for Julia to brush off. They needed to talk.

What would Julia even say when they did? You were a complete dick to me, but I love you, and we need to work through this? Well, that was probably exactly what she needed to say. Julia also needed to speak to her dad about Dan Bratton before they could move on from this. If they could move on from this.

No matter how much she dreaded bringing up the situation with her dad, she needed him to reassure her that Remy was wrong. She didn't believe he would do something as low as screwing with another family's livelihood. That being said, somewhere in the back of her mind, a part of her would be heartbroken but not all that surprised if he did.

Julia shook her head. No, he wouldn't do that. He could be ruthless but not unethical. She'd lose all respect for him if she found out Dan Bratton was intentionally screwing with the Millers and her dad had any part of it. She wasn't sure she could get over that.

Julia sat in the den several hours later with her dad, enjoying her third margarita. She knew she should take it easy to keep a level head to discuss what she needed to bring up, but the temptation to allow the alcohol to make her braver was undeniable. Knowing she needed the courage told her that her confidence that her father wouldn't engage in anything underhanded was waning.

"Hey, Dad, can I ask you something?"

"Another drink?"

Julia shook her head and set her empty glass on the small table beside her chair. "No thanks. I'll have to drive home at some point, and I need to stop drinking these and start drinking water if I'm doing that tonight."

Her dad shrugged and poured himself another margarita from the pitcher. "You could always stay here tonight. You haven't slept in your room in forever. I don't know why we keep a room here for you when you don't use it."

"I use it when I come down here and don't have another house to stay in, Dad. You know that. Aunty won't be gone forever, and I'll be looking for a place to live."

"That reminds me," her dad said. "I talked to her last night, and she asked me to have you give her a call."

"What about?" Julia had talked to her aunt a few times while living in her house, but it had been a couple of weeks since they'd connected. Julia always reached out to her, so she was curious why her aunt wanted her to call.

"Don't know. She wouldn't tell me. Just said she wanted you to call."

"Okay," Julia said. "Back to my question. How do you know Dan Bratton?"

The surprised look on her dad's face wasn't missed by Julia. Whatever his relationship was with Dan, Julia got the feeling it was something her dad had not expected to discuss with her.

"He's the son of a guy I used to work with. Good kid." He downed the last of his drink and stood to pour himself another.

"Dad, take it easy. You aren't supposed to be drinking at all and certainly aren't supposed to drink an entire pitcher of margaritas."

Her dad waved her off. "I'm not. We've split these."

"Umm, not really. I had two glasses from the first pitcher and one from the second. That adds up to having an entire pitcher on your own. You have to start taking better care of yourself. The doctor—"

"I know what the doctor said, Julia. Stop badgering me. I'm a grown man."

She knew arguing with him was useless, so she returned to her line of question about Dan Bratton.

"Anyway, I've never heard of you working with a Bratton."

"Oh, sure. You've heard me talk about Cliff Bratton. He worked with me on the *Barbara J.*"

"No, you worked on the *Barbara J* with Uncle Tommy and Matt Kuzman. You've told me a million times about how you guys would play practical jokes on each other, and it pissed Papa Joe off."

He looked cornered and stood to fill his glass once more. Julia beat him to the pitcher and poured the last margarita down the sink in her dad's wet bar.

"You're all done," she said.

"Look here, young lady—"

"Stop. Tell me what the hell is going on. Remy said you told her the guy's name was Jerrod Bratton, and now you say it's Cliff. You tell me he worked with you on a boat that I know he didn't work with you on. She said she overheard you ask this Bratton guy something about Jay Miller. What the hell is going on?"

Her dad slammed his empty glass on the counter and returned to sit in his chair.

"You aren't going to leave this alone, are you?"

He pulled a cigar from the box on the table next to him and prepared it to be smoked. He offered it to Julia, but when she waved him off, he lit it and sat back to relax.

"I just want the truth, Dad. I need to know what's going on."

"Is this because of that girl you've been fucking?"

"What the fuck, Dad?" Julia was ready to turn around and leave. Her dad had never spoken to her like that, and the shock hit her like a slap.

"I'm sorry. I didn't mean that," he said. "I never worked with Jerrod Bratton. He was a friend of Uncle Tommy's, and Dan came to me looking for a job."

"He has a job."

"I guess the Millers have been less than hospitable to him, and he's trying to line something else up."

"So he came to you?"

He nodded and tapped his cigar on the ashtray. "He did. And I met with him as a favor to his dad."

"Uncle Tommy's old friend?"

"Yes, Tommy's friend. The Jay thing was just him telling me about something that happened, and I asked him what Jay Miller thought about it when he found out. Remy is obviously looking for a fire where there's no smoke."

The cloak-and-dagger stuff was weird, but her dad's explanation wasn't unreasonable.

"Why have you been so cagey about this? You could have told me he was looking for a job."

"Because you're dating Remy, and he works for her family. I didn't want you accidentally revealing something during your pillow talk. I thought I'd taught you better than to mix business with pleasure."

"We're professional, Dad. Besides, it's none of your business who I sleep with."

"It is when you're sleeping with one of my employees. Maybe it's time for you to head back to Portland. I'm well enough to take things over here. You've been a big help, but it's time for you to go home."

He was clearly trying to move her focus from Dan Bratton. Still, she wasn't exactly sure what else to say about that situation. She knew he wouldn't tell her anything else to help clear up the confusion, especially now that he'd provided a reasonable explanation. Julia wasn't convinced he was telling her the truth, but that was only a feeling. She needed more proof to believe her dad had done anything wrong.

There was no doubt that she had to continue spending more of her time here in Elder's Bay instead of returning to Portland. Even if her dad did come back to work full-time, which he wasn't ready to do, she couldn't leave him unsupervised.

"I wanted to talk to you about that. I think I'm going to stay in Elder's Bay longer. You could use the help, and honestly, I like being here. I never thought I'd say that, but I'm tired of living in the big city."

He stubbed out his cigar and sat forward in his seat. "Oh, sweetheart, you don't need to do that. Your old man can handle this and let you get back to the job we sent you to college to do. You're so good at the sales part and handling the business on the restaurant side. You don't want to deal with these grumpy old fishermen until I'm ready to step down and you have to."

"Actually, I think I do. Tessa's been doing an excellent job taking care of things in Portland. I've enjoyed getting to know this side of the business. I like working with the fishermen and being close to the water. It's been nice to slow things down a little."

"I thought you hated living in Elder's Bay."

"I did," she said. "I couldn't wait to get out of here, but now, it feels right."

"Is this because of that Miller girl?"

"Would you stop calling her that? Her name is Remy. I won't lie to you and say she has nothing to do with this, but I can honestly say that even if we weren't seeing each other, I'd still be making this move."

He picked at the stitching on the arm of his chair.

"Dad?"

"Fine, Julia. You can stay here in Elder's Bay. We'll discuss what your new role will be on Monday."

Julia didn't know if his attitude was because he didn't want her close enough to keep tabs on him or because he felt like he was being pushed out of his job. Either way, she wasn't prepared to hash it out tonight. She had planned to ask him about the other thing Remy had mentioned about something he said to her in the parking lot, but she decided that could wait. They'd talked about enough that night, and she had a raging headache.

"I'm going to go home. Please thank Mom for dinner."

He half-heartedly raised his hand to wave good-bye but didn't get up from his chair or look her in the face. She'd upset him; the best thing to do was give him space. Without another word, Julia picked up her stuff near the front door and left. Their discussion had been such an emotional drain that all she wanted to do was crawl into Remy's arms and have the warmth of her embrace make it all go away, but that wasn't something she could have at that moment.

Things between them were strained, and Julia needed to figure out how to improve them. She knew Remy wouldn't want to hear that she'd talked to her dad, and he had a reasonable excuse for why Dan Bratton was in his office. The fact that Remy would never accept that, even if it came from the woman she loved, was a whole other thing they'd need to figure out. She needed a large glass of water, ibuprofen, and sleep. She'd figure out the rest of it tomorrow.

CHAPTER TWENTY-SEVEN

The buzzer sounded to let Andy and Corey know it was time to push another crab pot over the side. They'd been at sea for two days, and Remy felt weary to the bone. Even when they were in port, she wasn't sleeping well. The situation with Dan Bratton had been bad enough, but the emotional distance she had with Julia was what had her tossing and turning through the night.

The time they'd spent apart over the last two days brought into focus just how difficult it would be when Julia moved back to Portland. Remy had never meant to get as attached to her as she had, but there was no denying how important Julia had become to her.

The navigation system indicated it was time for another crab pot to be dropped so she pressed the buzzer once again. Remy felt like she was on autopilot, just going through the motions of her life while her heart prepared itself to be broken.

She vaguely heard the door to the pilothouse open, but her mind didn't register exactly what the sound was.

"That's the last pot, skipper." The rain had picked up and Corey's wet weather gear was drenched.

"Hmm?" Remy's mind had been elsewhere and she'd completely lost track of the pot count.

"The deck is clear." Corey peeled off his jacket and hung it on the hooks in the overhang just outside the door. The boat swayed a little from the waves as he stepped into the pilothouse, pulling the door closed tight behind him. "Damn, it's picking up out there."

Remy handed him a dry towel for his face and hands then climbed back into the captain's chair and stared through the window at the dark clouds that had gathered.

"You okay, Rem? I know this stuff with Bratton and Julia has you on edge, but it's not like you to lose focus out here."

Remy entered the coordinates of their next destination into the navigation system. Both Corey and Andy had been her steady companions the last week. She hadn't opened up to them emotionally as much as she might normally, but they'd never left her side, nonetheless.

"I'm sorry, dude. I'm having a hard time. I need to pull my head out of my ass and focus on what I'm doing before someone gets hurt. I promise to do better."

"We've got you, cuz." Corey wrapped an arm around her shoulders as Andy climbed up the ladder from below decks with mugs of hot coffee for each of them.

"Thanks," Remy said, taking the warm drink from her.

"Talk to us, Rem. Maybe we can help you work through this."

Remy nodded before setting her mug down in the coffee holder she kept attached to the edge of her desk so it wouldn't roll around in the rough seas. "I was a complete dick to Julia and I owe her a huge apology."

"No argument here," Corey said.

"I thought you guys were supposed to keep me from doing stupid things?"

Andy choked on the sip of coffee she'd just taken. "We have to leave you on your own sometimes, Rem."

The boat shifted when a large wave hit them from their port side. They'd all been a little shook up after the wave that took out their radio and left them virtually alone in the raging waters of the Pacific ocean, but they were fishermen and had bounced back pretty quickly, all things considered.

"I miss her." The admission sounded pathetic, even to Remy herself. She'd created this mess and now she had to fix it. "I don't want her to move to Portland."

"Have you told her that?" Corey asked.

"She knows."

"But have you said the words? Sometimes she needs to hear you say it, even if you think she already knows," Andy said. "I suspect she isn't ready to give up on you, yet. She loves you. That doesn't just shut off because you're a dick sometimes."

"That's a relief because despite my best intentions, sometimes I can be a stubborn asshole. Not a good trait, and definitely something I'm working on, but—"

"Oh, we know, pal. You forget who you're talking to. Although, we can all be assholes sometimes. The key is to know when to apologize and to learn and grow from each experience. That's what makes us lovable assholes. We're trainable and our intentions are always to be better."

Remy and Corey laughed. Opening up to her best friends really had helped to settle Remy's mind.

"Get your gear on," Remy said." We're coming up on the first string we dropped this morning. Let's get these pots on board and get home. I'm tired of this weather."

"Roger that," Corey and Andy said in unison before stepping into the vestibule to don their wet weather clothes once again.

Four hours later, the seas were worse than they had been all day. The remainder of their pots were secured to the deck, and they were finally on their way home. Corey had gone below to try to get a little sleep because he and Brooke were going on a romantic weekend trip to Seattle with the few days off they had.

"Do you think that'll ever be us?" Remy asked Andy, pointing below where Corey was sleeping.

"Marriage?"

"Yeah. Committing yourself to the same person for the rest of your life," Remy said.

Andy shrugged and sipped from her mug of hot coffee. "Who knows. I hope so"

"Me, too."

The gear on the boat deck slammed against the rail when a particularly large wave hit them from the side.

"Can you go out there and make sure the stack is secure? It's moving around more than I like."

Andy set her coffee mug in the holder and put on her rain gear to check the pots that were secured to the deck. If there was too much movement, it could shift the weight on one side of the boat enough to cause them real problems in these large seas.

"PAN-PAN, PAN-PAN, PAN-PAN. A 406 MHZ EPIRB DISTRESS BEACON HAS BEEN RECEIVED BY SATELLITE. SIXTY NAUTICAL MILES WEST OF ELDER'S BAY. THE BEACON IS REGISTERED TO THE FISHING VESSEL *DETERMINATION*. KEEP A SHARP LOOKOUT FOR SIGNS OF DISTRESS AND ASSIST IF POSSIBLE."

Andy entered the pilothouse just as the radio had started the emergency address.

"Isn't that Bratton?"

"What the fuck? Yeah, it's Bratton. Jay's filling in for one of the crew this week who'd broken his arm." Remy immediately got on her radio and contacted her brother Peter, hoping he might have information about what was happening.

"Peter, this is Remy. Do you read me?"

"I hear you Remy. Did you hear that message?"

"I did. Is Jay on the *Determination* right now?" Remy held her breath, hoping Peter would tell her Jay wasn't on there and she was mistaken.

"He called me this morning before they went out and said he'd be on there today. Kel's on there, too."

"When was the last time you talked to him?"

"This morning," Peter said. "This weather has been pretty gnarly, so I had planned to check in on both of you, but the day just got away from me. How are you guys?"

"We're good. We should be back in a couple hours. Should we turn around and head toward them?"

"No. You guys get out of this weather. I know the Coast Guard has a cutter that will be there within the hour, and they've sent a helicopter to check it out. By the time you got there, the Coast Guard would already be on the scene."

"Roger that. We'll keep heading in. Will you let me know if you hear anything?"

"I promise I will. I love you, Remy. Tell Andy and Corey I love them, too."

"Will do, brother. We love you, too. Be safe."

"Roger."

Two hours later they had secured their boat and were heading into the office. Julia was waiting for them as soon as they made their way inside. She held her arms open and Remy gladly accepted her embrace.

"Are you guys, okay?" she asked.

"We're fine. Have you heard anything about the *Determination*?"

Julia scrolled through some text messages on her phone. "It sounds like everyone is safe."

"Thank God." The relief in knowing her brother was safe almost made her cry. "Do you know what happened?"

"Not yet," Julia said. "It sounds like the Coast Guard is bringing the crew back in the helicopter. Let's go to the air station so we can meet them when they land."

Remy took Julia's hand as they walked to her truck with Corey and Andy on their heels. The air station was only twenty minutes away and they could see the helicopter approaching when they arrived. They explained who they were to the guard at the gate, and they were escorted to the hanger and told to wait until they were able to get everyone safely inside.

"You okay, baby?" Julia asked as she squeezed Remy's hand.

"Yeah. Jay's safe and that's all that matters." She pulled her phone from her pocket and sent a text to her brother, dad, and mom, letting them know that she was there to meet Jay when he got off the helicopter.

Both her dad and Peter were still out on their boats, but they were due to arrive in port within the next couple hours. She knew they must be going mad with worry and was glad that at least she could be there for Jay when he was released.

She watched as Dan Bratton was led off the helicopter followed by Kel, another man she didn't know, and finally Jay. Her brother looked pretty shaken up and was covered in some black substance that looked like soot. The fact that the entire crew had been on the helicopter didn't bode well for the state of the boat. They wouldn't have left it until it was a total loss.

"Jay," Remy called to him as he walked toward another part of the building. She watched him say something to one of the coasties that were escorting them and then he jogged toward Remy. She met him halfway and allowed the tears to fall once she was in his arms.

"You scared the shit out of me, brother."

"Now you know how I felt," Jay said as he squeezed her tighter. "I'm so glad to see you, kiddo."

The others joined them, and the group followed where Dan Bratton and the rest of them had gone into the building with the helicopter crew.

Remy could see Dan talking to a Coast Guard officer in a conference room next to the waiting area where everyone else had gathered. He seemed upset and the officer took notes as Dan spoke to him.

"What the fuck happened out there, Jay?" Corey asked.

"Fucking Bratton. Apparently, he'd been falsely logging that maintenance had been done, but it hadn't. There was an oil leak in the engine room that nobody noticed until it caught fire. Things went from bad to worse in a matter of minutes and the boat was engulfed in flames before we were able to do anything other than deploy the life raft and abandon ship. Everyone made it off the boat, but it's a goner."

An Elder's Bay police officer came into the room where they all sat and someone escorted him into the room where Dan Bratton was still speaking to the Coast Guard officer. They all looked at each other in confusion as the sound of raised voices drifted out of the door as it opened to allow the police officer in.

"What's that about?" Corey asked.

"No idea," Jay said.

"Mr. Miller?" The police officer called Jay over and pointed toward a small office across the hall from where Dan was being questioned. "Would you mind answering a few questions for me?"

Jay nodded and squeezed Remy's shoulder as he walked past her, comforting her even when she knew he had to be freaking out inside himself. Why in the world would a civilian police officer be involved?

"I'm so confused," Andy said.

Julia rested her hand on Remy's thigh. The tentative contact was more than they'd shared in days and Remy's heart raced at her warm touch. She slid her hand over Julia's and gently squeezed it. They desperately needed to talk, but this wasn't the time nor the place for that to happen.

"Remy Miller?" The police officer's voice cut through the silence in the room and Remy watched Jay walk past him and back toward where they were sitting.

"He just has a couple questions about the Bratton stuff we've been talking about, Rem. It's fine."

Remy looked at Julia who just smiled and nodded her encouragement. "Just tell them everything you know, sweetie. If my dad really did have anything to do with any of this, he'll face the consequences of his actions."

She kissed Julia on the cheek and stood to follow the officer into the room.

"Good afternoon, Ms. Miller. My name is Detective Clark and I just want to ask you a few questions about Dan Bratton's association with Brian Clayman."

"Yes, ma'am. Please call me Remy."

"Thanks, Remy. Would you mind telling me your full name?"

Remy answered the first few questions identifying herself and how she knew Dan Bratton and Brian Clayman. She then told Detective Clark the things Jay had shared with her about the logs and what Kel had experienced with Dan not telling his crew to measure the crab. Finally, she explained what happened when she found Dan in the office with Brian Clayman.

Even after all her blustering about Brian and how angry she was that Julia dismissed the idea that he would be involved in something nefarious, Remy felt guilty for accusing Julia's father of something that if proven to be true could get him into trouble. She knew that was ridiculous and counter productive to feel that way, but her heart hurt for being put in this position.

When she was done being questioned, the detective led her back out to the room where everyone else sat and watched as Kel was brought in for questioning. She noticed Dan sat alone in the corner of the room. His head was bowed, face cradled in his hands. Remy had zero compassion for whatever stress he was feeling at that moment.

"Where's Julia?" she asked when she realized she wasn't where she was sitting before.

"They took her into the room where they were interviewing Dan," Corey said.

"Why?" Remy asked.

Corey shrugged. "No idea. They just asked her to go in there when Dan came out."

Remy sat in the cold hard plastic chair she'd sat in before her interview and looked toward the room where Julia was being questioned. She'd done nothing wrong, so Remy knew she had nothing to worry about, but she was anxious for her to be with her again. Remy's protective nature didn't like it that they were separated in a tense moment like this.

Andy was pulled into the room with Detective Clark when Kel was done, then Corey followed. Everything Remy's crew knew had been secondhand knowledge, so their interviews were short and when Corey was done, Julia was also released from the room she'd been in.

It had been a long night and by the time they'd dropped Andy, Corey, and Jay, Remy was left alone with Julia, unsure of whether she should drop her off at her house and go back to her own parents, or not.

"We need to talk," Julia said as they pulled away from Jay's house.

"I know."

"Can we save it for tomorrow?"

Remy nodded. "Of course."

"Will you hold me tonight?" Julia asked.

Remy was so happy she had to swallow past the lump in her throat. "Absolutely."

When they finally reached Julia's house, it was almost midnight. Not a word was spoken as they removed their clothes and prepared for bed. Once they were finally under the covers together, Julia scooted back to press her back against Remy's front. Remy wrapped her arm around Julia's waist and held onto her tightly until they both succumbed to the exhaustion of the day.

The next morning Remy woke up alone. She touched Julia's side of the bed and found cold sheets and nothing else. Her head felt heavy as she forced herself to get up and put on a fresh pair of boxer briefs and T-shirt that she kept in the girlfriend drawer Julia had given her.

It wasn't difficult to figure out where Julia had gone. The sound of clanging pots and cabinet doors slamming was a clear indication she was in the kitchen and if Remy were to guess, she wasn't happy about something.

"Morning," Remy said as she climbed onto a stool at the kitchen island. She was thankful for the distance the large surface provided between her and an obviously angry Julia. "Everything okay?"

"Eggs?" Julia asked. She held up a skillet in one hand and two eggs in the other. The move could be interpreted as a threat if she didn't know better.

"Sure. Can I help?"

Julia shook her head. She set the pan on the stove then gently placed the eggs on a kitchen towel that was neatly folded on the counter next to the stove. She placed her hands on the edge of the counter and bowed her head. Remy's heart sank as she noticed Julia's shoulders shake with sobs that seemingly came out of nowhere.

"Hey, hey, hey." Remy jumped up from the stool and rushed around the island to pull Julia into her arms. "It's going to be okay, baby. I've got you. Everything's going to be okay."

Julia's body relaxed into Remy, and they stood like that for several minutes, wrapped in each other's arms, until Julia was able to stop crying.

"Did something happen, sweetheart?"

"Oh, Remy, I just…"

"Let's go sit on the couch where I can hold you a little better," Remy said.

Julia turned back to the eggs. "Let me make you breakfast first."

Remy made sure the burners on the stove were off then took Julia's hand to lead her into the living room. "I'm just fine. Let's chat and then I can make you breakfast, or we could go out and have a nice breakfast at Sam's Diner. Whatever you want."

"Maybe Sam's?" Julia sounded like a lost child and Remy's heart couldn't take much more. She was ready to give her anything just to take that sadness away.

"I'll tell them to start making pancakes and to keep them coming until my girl is so full, she's grateful for remembering to wear stretchy pants. Don't forget to wear stretchy pants, by the way."

The soft sound of Julia's laugh made Remy want to give herself a high-five. "What happened, baby. Did something happen this morning or is this residual stuff from everything that happened last night?"

They sat on the couch and Julia practically climbed into Remy's lap. Remy wiped the tears from her cheeks with her thumb and kissed the tip of her nose.

"My mom called this morning. The cops showed up at the house early this morning to interview my dad. I guess Dan Bratton admitted to the detective last night that my dad had paid him to cause problems on your dad's boat."

"I knew it." The words were out of Remy's mouth before she could think about the ramifications of saying them out loud. "I'm sorry."

Julia sat forward and scooted over on the couch, just out of Remy's reach.

"I'm so sorry, baby. I shouldn't have said that."

"I know you think this is a time to celebrate your victory for being right, but my family has just been turned upside down."

Remy wanted to crawl into a hole and not come out until Julia somehow forgot any of this ever happened. There was a part of her that was satisfied to be proven right, but the cost of that was breaking Julia's heart and Remy would do anything to take that pain away from her.

"I'm a complete asshole, baby. I wasn't thinking. It just came out, but I'm so sorry you and your family are dealing with this."

"What was he thinking?" The confusion on Julia's face made her look so vulnerable. This was fucking horrible.

"I don't think he was thinking. Not with his logical brain. What did your mom say?"

Julia collapsed against the back of the couch and rubbed her red rimmed eyes with her hands. "She's beside herself. Charlie is with her now."

"Where's your dad?"

"He was still at the station when I talked to mom, but she said she thought they would be leaving soon. Our family lawyer was in the room with my dad during the interview and he told my mom that they couldn't hold him for anything. I think Dan is in deeper trouble as far as anything criminal, but Clayman Fisheries could get some heat for my dad's involvement. I think it matters where he got the money to pay Dan off with. If it came from the company coffers, then that's bad for the company. If it came from his personal account, I don't know. I need to find a lawyer to represent Clayman Fisheries. I don't trust our family lawyer to put the company first. Dad can keep Wally to represent his interests, but I have to protect the company."

"What's going to happen?"

"I don't know. I think a lot of that has to do with your dad and how far he wants to push this. He has every right to throw whatever he can at us, and I imagine he'll do just that."

Remy tentatively reached out and pulled Julia's hand into her lap. She didn't want to force her to allow contact, but she needed a connection between them, and she hoped Julia did, too.

"Unfortunately, since the boat sank, most of any evidence they might have gotten is on the bottom of the ocean," Remy said.

"I know your family has every right to try to bury Clayman Fisheries under so much legal crap that we'll never pull ourselves free. I don't blame them one bit. I have no idea how this thing with my dad is going to go, but please pass along to your family that I will be moving to have my dad removed from any role in the company effective immediately. Word travels fast and Tessa texted me that some of our vendors and clients have already been calling to insist I take full control of the company. I'm going to get dressed and go talk to my dad this morning. I'm incredibly sorry for everything, including not listening to you as much as I should have when you talked to me about Bratton. I didn't want to believe it."

"Julia. Sweetheart." Remy knew Julia was on the verge of a spinout. She couldn't imagine the pressure she must be feeling right now and to have to confront her own dad, especially with him recently being ill, must be torture. She pulled Julia across the couch and back into her arms. She felt her hesitation for a moment before relaxing into her chest and allowing herself to cry again. "I'm so sorry you've been put in this position. I'll get dressed and talk to my dad. He can be a hot head, but he can be a reasonable man when he wants to be. Once he realizes going after Clayman Fisheries will hurt you much more than it would hurt your dad, I think he'll be willing to give you a chance to make things right," Remy said.

"If you guys want out of your contract with Clayman Fisheries, just let me know. It's the least I can do, although if you want to stay on, we're more than happy to keep you."

The contract wasn't something Remy had even thought about. She didn't want to leave Julia without a captain, but she also felt the need to be with her family right now. Of course, her dad wouldn't have a boat for her to run now that Dan Bratton had sunk the only one the Miller's had available. What a mess.

"I'll need to talk to my crew and my dad. We're in port for a few days anyway, so it's not something that has to be decided right this minute. I love you. Thank you for being so considerate of my feelings about this."

"I love you. I'll always try to be considerate of your emotions, but even if you weren't my favorite person, it's the right thing to do."

"My girlfriend is a hot business lady."

Julia's laugh was lighter than Remy had heard her have in days. If there weren't so many expectations on them today, Remy would try to convince her to spend the day in bed. Unfortunately, breakfast and a few kisses were the best they could do for now.

"Let's get dressed and go out for those pancakes I promised you. We both have a long day ahead and we'll need pancakes to get us through it."

"You should have been a doctor."

"We'll play doctor tonight and I'll give you a thorough examination."

"I like the sound of that. I'm sure I can think of some parts I'd like you to check," Julia said.

Waiting for this evening to touch each other was getting more difficult by the minute.

"We better start putting clothes on or we'll never get those pancakes."

CHAPTER TWENTY-EIGHT

The sun had set when Julia arrived at her parents' to speak to her dad. Her brother's car was in the driveway, so she hoped his presence would be positive and not one more obstacle for Julia to overcome.

"Where's Dad?"

Her mom sat alone at the kitchen table with a mug of coffee. There was an unsettling silence in the house that Julia didn't remember ever happening before.

"Mom?"

"He's in his office," her mom said.

Julia's brother, Charlie, entered the room with a shawl and wrapped it around their mother's shoulders. Without a word, he wrapped Julia in an embrace and held onto her like she was the only thing keeping them afloat. She knew that wasn't all that far from reality. Charlie was her older brother, but he looked to Julia to lead the family. She'd always felt like it was her destiny to take over for her dad someday, but now that the time had come, she was scared.

The future was more uncertain than ever, and part of her just wanted to crawl under the covers and let the cards fall where they would. She knew that wasn't an option. Their family business was about much more than just her parents and brother. They employed dozens of other family members and a decent part of the town. In one way or another, Clayman Fisheries was part of the fabric Elder's

Bay was built on, and Julia knew it was up to her to ensure that they survived the mess her dad had gotten them into.

"I'm going to talk to Dad. Can you stay here with Mom?"

"Yeah. Of course. He's in his office, about half a bottle of Four Roses whiskey down. He threw something at my head the last time I tried to go in to talk to him. Beware."

"Charlie?" She waited for him to look up from his coffee.

"Yeah?" he said.

"A lot of things are going to have to change. I hope I have your support."

"Always."

Julia nodded and squeezed her mom's shoulder. "We'll be okay. I promise." She hoped she could deliver on that promise.

She gently knocked on the office door before stepping inside. Her dad was sitting at his desk, staring at a framed painting of his dad, who had started Clayman Fisheries many years before. Julia poured them each a glass of water from the wet bar and placed it in front of him before sitting in a chair on the other side of the desk.

"What did the police say?"

He downed the last of his whiskey and started to pour himself another glass before Julia took it from his hand and pushed the glass of water toward him. She placed the stopper on the whiskey decanter and returned it to the liquor cabinet.

"What did they say, Dad?" she asked again.

"There's an ongoing investigation. They told me to be available for questioning. I'm not to leave Elder's Bay until they've permitted me to do so."

"Did you do it?"

"Do what, Julia? Just come out and say it? What is it exactly that you think I've done?"

"Did you pay Dan Bratton to sabotage the Miller's boat?"

"No. Not exactly."

"What the hell does that mean?" She was sick of the twisted words and half-truths from him. It took everything to bite her tongue and not scream at him for acting like such a child, but she knew that as soon as voices were raised, he would shut down, and the conversation would be over. At least anything useful.

"Wally told me not to talk to anyone because anything I say to you can be used against me if this thing goes to trial."

Their family lawyer was right. She knew it but didn't know how to fix this if she didn't know precisely what he'd done. The only thing left for her to do would no doubt break both of their hearts and possibly destroy her relationship with her dad. She was putting the company before him, and the only comfort she found was that she knew if he wasn't the one on the receiving end of it, he would completely agree.

"I've contacted lawyers for the company, Dad."

"What lawyers? Wally's been our lawyer since your grandpa was running things. He's a damn good lawyer."

"This isn't about Wally's competence. The company needs separate representation that can't be connected to you in any way. I contacted a firm in Portland. They're sending someone by tomorrow."

"What time?" Her dad tapped his fingers on the desk like he had made a decision.

"What do you mean?"

"What time will they be there? I need to make sure your mom gets a suit ready for me."

"Dad. You aren't invited," Julia said.

"What do you mean I'm not invited? It's my damn company." He leaned forward in his chair like he was ready for a fight.

"Not anymore, Dad." Julia pulled an envelope from her purse and removed the papers the lawyers had emailed her before she came to her parents' house. "You're going to step down from Clayman Fisheries, effective immediately. You need to sign this paperwork to transfer control of the company and its holdings to me."

He stood so fast his chair slammed against the bookshelf behind him, and the crash of glass as different pieces of art he displayed came cascading down to shatter against the hardwood floor. Charlie rushed in with a wild look on his face.

"Are you okay, Julia?" Charlie asked as he eyed their dad. It was clear that he'd lost as much respect for the man as Julia had, and she had to swallow back the tears that threatened to fall.

"I'm okay. You can stay if you'd like. I've just told Dad that he needs to sign this paperwork to transfer control of the company to me. It's the only way to ensure his mistakes don't destroy everything."

Charlie walked to the desk and scanned the documents. When he was done, he pushed them in front of their dad and slammed a pen on them. "Sign it, Dad. You've done this to yourself."

"I never wanted this to happen. I wasn't trying to risk anyone's life. He was only supposed to be a nuisance. Slow down their production. Be a thorn in their side. It's not my fault the kid's an idiot."

"You just don't get it, do you, Dad?" Charlie asked. "This isn't the company Julia and I want to be part of." He looked at Julia, who nodded. "You either sign these papers, or we're taking you to court. We can't sit here and watch you destroy something that means so much to all of us."

"Dad. You made a mistake. It was a completely wrong-headed and foolish mistake, but a mistake nonetheless. Sign these papers and let me try to save Clayman Fisheries from being the pariah of this community. This is our only chance."

The first time Julia had seen her dad shed a tear was at her grandma's funeral. The second was when he picked up the pen and signed the papers in front of him. She knew what it took for him to relinquish control of the company to her, even if that was eventually what was supposed to happen, anyway. This wasn't how he wanted to go out, and she felt terrible that it ended this way. Whether he brought this on himself or not.

Julia gathered the papers and stuffed them back into the envelope.

"Dad?"

"Get out. Please. Both of you. I need to be alone."

Her heart ached to see him this way. Charlie took her hand as she picked up the envelope, and they left the office. No matter how things ended, she knew her relationship with her dad would never be the same. A part of her was mourning what seemed like the end of a chapter in her life.

"You okay?" Charlie asked.

"I'm not sure."

"You did the right thing, Jules. He'll see that, eventually."

She wasn't sure if he would, but it was done. She'd blown up part of her life. Now it was time to rebuild it in a way she could be proud of, not by tearing down and breaking the competition, but by helping build a better community for the town's good. It was up to her, and she hoped more than anything that she was up to the task.

CHAPTER TWENTY-NINE

The incessant beeping of a phone pulled Remy from a deep sleep. She and Julia had been up talking until late the evening before, and she was beyond exhausted. Remy opened her eyes enough to see it was six in the morning, then quickly buried her head under her pillow. Julia had said she needed to be up early but insisted Remy sleep as long as she needed.

The phone rang again and Remy realized that if she didn't answer it, she'd never get back to sleep. She sat up begrudgingly and looked at the screen of her phone.

She was prepared to ignore whoever was attempting to call her, but the four missed calls from Julia worried her enough to call her back without even listening to the voice mails she'd left.

"Remy?" She recognized the voice on the other end of the line as Julia's brother, Charlie. That he was answering the phone and not Julia sent a jolt of panic through her like a burst of electricity.

"Where's Julia, Charlie. Is she okay?" Remy was out of bed and pulling on her pants within seconds.

She heard his voice crack as he cleared his throat. "Yeah. Kinda."

"What the fuck do you mean, kinda? Is Julia okay?"

Remy braced for the worst but already felt herself losing her tether from the earth. She realized then that if something happened to Julia, she'd never recover. Life on earth seemed to stop as she waited for Charlie to continue.

"Our dad…it's bad, Remy. She needs you."

Her moment of relief knowing Julia wasn't the one hurt flowed into a pang of guilt, knowing how devastated she must be that her dad wasn't well. Things between her and her dad were strained, to say the least, but he was her dad. Remy couldn't imagine how she'd feel if her dad were the one who was ill. She'd be a mess.

"Where is she?"

"We're at Pacific Crest Hospital. He's in ICU. Come to the waiting room. She's been staring out the window since the doc came in to tell us how bad things are, and I can't get her to even look at me."

"I'll be there in five."

"Thanks, Remy. I'm really sorry about—"

"We'll talk about it later, Charlie. I'll see you soon."

Remy hung up before Charlie could answer and pulled on a jacket and boots before running for her truck. It was a short trip to the hospital from Julia's house, but it seemed like it took a lifetime before she was there and finally reached the room where Charlie instructed her to go.

She found Julia in the corner of the space, her body turned awkwardly to the side so she could stare out the window. The rain had started to fall on Remy's drive over, and she could hear the faint sound of ducks happily quacking in the puddles that gathered on the lawn below.

"Baby?" Remy knelt on the floor between Julia's knees and slid her hands along the tops of her thighs to rest on either side of her hips. Her voice stirred Julia's attention, and she looked down at Remy with the broken look of a lost little girl who was unsure where to find safety. Remy wanted to be that safety for her but knew she'd need to wait for Julia to ask for it.

"Remy?"

"I'm here, baby. Charlie called me."

Julia looked around the room as if only realizing there were others there besides herself. She cradled Remy's face and caressed the edge of her jaw with a delicate thumb. Tears spilled from swollen eyes, and Remy's heart broke at the pain she saw in them.

"You look tired," Julia said.

"I'm okay. You must be exhausted, too. Did you get any sleep last night?"

Julia nodded and turned back to the window. "Some. I kissed you when I left for work at five this morning, but you were pretty out of it."

Remy cleared her throat and pulled Julia's hand around to her mouth so she could kiss her palm.

"I love you, Julia."

A doctor entered the room and interrupted their moment. Remy knew from the look on her face that the news wasn't good. The doctor walked over to where Julia's mom sat and knelt before her. Julia watched from her seat near the window but didn't bother to get closer to them. Remy sat beside Julia on the small couch and wrapped an arm around her shoulders.

"Mrs. Clayman?"

"Yes," her mom said.

Remy couldn't hear exactly what the doctor said to Julia's mom, but she understood when she began to weep that it couldn't have been good. After a few moments, the doctor left the room, and they were alone once again. Charlie looked over to Remy and gave her a nod as he pulled his mother closer and held her while she fell apart.

Julia's attention was once again focused out on the window. Dawn was beginning to illuminate their view, and Remy could see the steady cresting of the waves in the distance as they rushed toward the shore. She wondered if the sight of the ocean gave Julia any of the comforts it gave Remy. The rhythmic movement of the water had always served to calm Remy like nothing else could. She would give anything to give Julia comfort just then but wasn't sure where to even begin.

"Sweetheart? What can I do?" Remy grabbed a box of tissues from the small table next to the couch and gave one to Julia before taking another to dab the tears from her own cheeks she hadn't realized had fallen.

"Just hold me," Julia said. "Please just stay with me."

"I'm not going anywhere," Remy said.

The four of them sat silently in the waiting room for an hour, until Julia's mom finally stood, picked up her purse from the floor, and walked out of the room. Charlie turned to Remy, and when she waved him on, he quickly followed after his mom. Remy kissed Julia's forehead and squeezed her once more.

"Is your car here?" Remy asked.

Julia shook her head and blew her nose into a clean tissue. "No. Charlie picked me up on his way to the hospital."

"Come on, my love, I'll drive you home."

An hour later, they were both cuddled together in Julia's bed. Neither had taken the time to do anything other than remove their shoes and pants before crawling between the sheets and holding each other. Sleep came much easier for them than Remy expected. When she woke, she heard the clanging of pots in the kitchen and smelled fresh coffee brewing.

The time on her phone indicated it was two in the afternoon, and she texted Andy to tell her what had happened.

Every muscle in her body seemed to ache as Remy slung her legs over the side of the bed and walked to the kitchen. She was still only wearing her T-shirt and boxers and hoped Julia was the only other person in the house.

"Hey," Remy said as she sat at the kitchen counter and watched Julia flit around the kitchen, making a much larger breakfast than they'd ever be able to eat. "Did you get any sleep?"

"Some. You?" Julia asked.

"Some. What are you doing, Jules?"

Julia stopped with a pan of eggs in one hand and a spatula in the other. She looked around the kitchen and then at Remy with an incredulous look. "I'm making breakfast."

"I see that."

A large glass of pineapple-orange juice, a plate of eggs, bacon, biscuits with sausage gravy, and a small bowl of fruit were placed in front of Remy.

"Biscuits and gravy?"

"It's your favorite, right?"

"Yeah, but…" Remy understood Julia was dealing with her grief in her own way, and it wasn't her place to question her process. "Thanks. This looks delicious."

Julia made her own plate and sat next to Remy at the counter. She pulled up a book on her kindle and began reading while they ate breakfast. Remy took that as a hint that she wasn't ready to talk about what had happened and accepted that Julia would speak to her when she was able.

By seven that evening, Remy wondered if Julia even wanted her there. Since they'd woken up that afternoon, Remy had only been another thing in Julia's environment that she refused to give her attention. They'd cleaned up after the breakfast feast in silence. Remy had followed Julia into the yard to pick weeds from the garden for an hour before a light rain forced them back into the house.

No words were exchanged when Julia plopped herself on the kitchen floor and pulled everything out of the cabinets, sorting them into piles to keep or give away. The only time they spoke was when Remy insisted she let her carry the boxes of donation items to her truck to be dropped off later.

When Julia began making another home-cooked meal, Remy wrapped her arms around her and held her tight until she felt the racking of her body from the sobs Remy knew needed to happen.

"Let's sit in front of the fire," Remy said as she led Julia out of the kitchen and into the den.

"But what about dinner? You must be hungry."

"I'm okay. I can order something to be delivered if we get hungry. You need to relax and let me take care of you. You can't keep going like this."

"I don't deserve to relax," Julia said.

"What are you talking about?" Remy guided Julia to sit on the couch in front of the fireplace before starting the fire and lowering the room's lights. "Why don't you deserve to relax?"

"I killed him. I don't deserve anything."

"What are you talking about, sweetheart?" Remy wiped the tears that had fallen onto Julia's cheeks. "None of this is your fault, Julia."

"You don't understand." Julia tried to pull away from Remy's grasp, but she held on and forced Julia to look at her.

"What don't I understand, baby? Talk to me."

Julia jerked away from her and buried her face in her hands. "You don't understand, Remy. I knew he was sick, and still, I pushed him. I left him no choice but to sign control of the company over to me and give up the one thing that meant anything to him in this world."

"You're wrong, Jules. There was no doubt that his family was the most important thing in your dad's life. Not the company. The company may have been how he defined himself, but he loved his wife and kids more than anything. I'm certain of that."

"Well, I was the one that forced him to lose everything, so I guess you didn't know him as well as me, after all."

The doorbell interrupted their conversation. Remy hesitated to answer, but the loud knock afterward left her no choice.

"I'll get it. We're not done with this conversation. I'll be right back."

Remy jogged to the door and looked through the peephole to find Charlie on the other side.

"Hey, Charlie." Remy greeted Julia's brother with a hug. They barely knew each other, but the man looked like he needed affection, so she was happy to offer it. She knew how much he loved Julia, making her feel a kinship with him.

"Hey, Remy. Mind if I come in?"

"Of course." Remy stepped aside to allow him access and took his coat to hang on the hook inside the door. "Julia's in the den. How is your mother holding up?"

"She's been baking all day. She refuses to sit down for even a minute. I suspect she'll just keep going until she collapses."

"The apple doesn't fall far from the tree. That's basically how Julia's been today, too."

Charlie nodded. "That's what I was afraid of. You said she's in there?" He pointed toward the den.

"Yeah." Remy led Charlie to the den and walked away to get each of them a glass of water.

When she returned, Julia was wrapped in Charlie's arms as they both cried. Remy set both of their waters on the coffee table in front of them. She sat next to Julia on the couch and watched the fire spark while Charlie comforted her.

"Julia, none of this is your fault."

"I—"

"No. I know how you think, little sister, and none of this is your fault. Beyond the guilt and embarrassment he felt about the Bratton thing, he hadn't slowed down on the drinking or smoking even a little bit. The doctor was clear with him about what that would do, and he ignored it because he was who he was. There wasn't anything any of us could have done to stop him. And he paid the ultimate price for his mistakes. This tension between you guys over the last few days was hard on both of you, but it's not what killed him. I know you want to take responsibility because you always do that, but you can't this time. This is on him, not you."

Charlie took tissues from a box on the table and handed one to Julia before blowing his nose on one of his own. Remy thought of her dad and how terrible he was on his own body. Things weren't exactly great between them right then, but she hoped he would take Brian Clayman's death as a warning to change his behavior before it was too late.

Remy walked Charlie to the door a few minutes later. She gave him her number since he'd had to use Julia's phone to contact her before and told him to call if there was anything at all she could do to help. He nodded and jogged to his car as it began to rain.

When she returned to the den, she found Julia standing in front of the fire with her arms crossed across her chest. Remy wasn't sure if she should touch her or not, so she stood beside her but kept her hands in her pockets.

After a few moments of silence, Julia finally spoke. "He texted me last night."

"Really?"

Julia nodded and pulled her arms tighter across her chest. "I didn't see it until this morning because I'd left my phone on the charger and hadn't checked it before we went to bed."

"What did he say?"

"He apologized and said he loved me. I meant to call him this morning, but decided to wait until mid-morning so I didn't wake him. The lawyers are supposed to be at the office this afternoon which is why I had to go in early today. I wanted to get my ducks in a row before they arrived. I guess I should probably call them before they leave Portland and head this way. There's no rush now that dad has died. We'll probably need to wait until the will is read before we get lawyers involved."

"I'm sorry this happened, Julia."

"Me, too."

Remy plopped down onto the couch. The entire situation felt like it had taken a few years off her life, and she was exhausted. She wished she could rewind the clock and had been more understanding when Julia struggled to believe her dad would be capable of something like that.

"I'm so sorry about our fight. I would have had difficulty believing someone if they'd accused my dad of doing something I knew wasn't right. I should have been more understanding."

"You were upset and as it turned out, you were right. I appreciate you not rubbing that in."

"I don't think he was a bad man, Jules. I believed him when he said he only wanted Dan to be a nuisance. Not that it makes what he did okay, but I really don't believe your dad ever meant for things to go as far as they did."

"I should have known he would do something like that."

"Not true. How could you have known? None of this is your fault."

Julia nodded, but Remy doubted she agreed with what she'd said. It was clear that Julia was determined to blame herself, and in her grief, there was nothing Remy could say to change her mind. She'd have to work through that in her own time.

"I talked to my dad's assistant this morning. I guess dad heard from a couple of vendors that your dad was buying a new boat. There was talk that some of our clients might sign with your dad when their contracts with us were up. Apparently your dad was offering them a better deal. With his feelings toward your dad and the fear of losing business, he hired Dan to go for the job as captain of the new boat. He asked some friends to vouch for him and it worked. Your dad hired him. It was all a ruse. Once Dan got the job, he was supposed to do a few things that would be a nuisance to your family, but he swears it was never meant to go as far as it did."

"Did Charlie know?"

"No. I'm sure of that. He was just as angry as I was when everything unraveled."

Remy nodded and rubbed a thumb across the palm of her hand for comfort. She didn't know what to say that wouldn't make things worse, so she kept her mouth shut and allowed Julia to speak.

"I haven't talked to your dad yet, but I'm going to offer him the boat you guys have been using as a replacement for the one Dan Bratton destroyed. It's a better boat. I can't do anything about the time he lost or the frustration he has caused, but hopefully the boat will be a large enough gesture that your dad will see I'm serious about putting this feud between our families behind us."

"That's...good. I'm sure he'll appreciate that."

"It's the least we can do," Julia said.

Remy nodded and reached out to tug on Julia's hand that hung by her side. She turned to Remy and gave her a sad smile.

"I think I need some time to think if that's okay?"

"Um, sure, yeah. Want me to order some food for us?"

"Sure. I'm not super hungry so get whatever you want."

"So, yeah. I'll—"

"I just need a couple hours to myself."

"I get it. Why don't I go pick up some of my clothes at Andy's and I'll grab us food on my way back. If you need me, I'll have my phone."

"Thanks for being with me today. I couldn't have gotten through the day without you."

"Of course. My pleasure."

Remy was hesitant to leave Julia alone, but she had to trust that she knew what it was that she needed. Soon she'd be back in Portland and Remy needed to learn to step back and allow Julia to ask her for what she needed instead of feeling like she should step in.

The thought of her going back to Portland made Remy's stomach hurt. They'd adjust. There was no other option but to adjust, but she hoped that someday soon they'd be able to be together all the time. Julia was her family and more than anything she wanted them to be together.

She kissed Julia's forehead one last time before going to their bedroom to get dressed. The last few days had drained her emotionally and she vowed to take Julia away somewhere nice when things settled down. They needed a beach, fancy drinks with little umbrellas, and each other.

CHAPTER THIRTY

A week later, Julia sat in her car, checking her lipstick in the rearview mirror one last time. She'd been in Portland for a few days dealing with lawyers and officially transferring that part of operations to Tessa. She hadn't been to Skipper's since the last time she was there with Remy, and the blast of music and heat from so many bodies pressed together reminded her why she'd stopped going.

Remy wasn't expecting her back until the next day, but she'd been able to wrap things up early and couldn't wait to get home to her. Now that everything was finalized, she was ready to tell her about the house and ask her to officially move in with her.

She thought Remy would be excited but a tiny part of her worried the events of the last few weeks might have eroded some of what they'd had. Julia had been admittedly distant after her dad's legal troubles and then his sudden death. Her natural reaction to withdraw and only depend on herself when things were hard wasn't always the best when you were in a loving relationship. For her part, Remy had been patient and kind through the entire ordeal.

It was a typical Friday night and the crowd of locals were already drunk and rowdy. She found her uncle Tommy sitting at the bar with some of her cousins, just like any other night after a week of back-breaking work on a boat.

"Hey, sweetheart," Uncle Tommy said when she approached him. He wrapped his arms around her, and for a moment, he reminded her enough of her dad that she closed her eyes and soaked up the affection he offered. "How's your mom holding up?"

"She's good." Julia raised a hand to the bartender, indicating she needed to order a pitcher of beer. "Some of the other widows of local fishermen have pulled her into their circle. They've kept her so busy I don't think she's had time to miss him yet."

"Your dad sure loved you both," Uncle Tommy said.

Julia nodded but didn't otherwise respond.

"He may have made mistakes, but he wasn't an evil man. He was an idiot sometimes, but he wasn't a bad man. We grew up in a different time. Things between the Millers and us were always competitive, and after that tragedy with our brother, your dad just couldn't let it go."

"Did you blame Frank Miller for Uncle Davy's death?"

"Nah." Uncle Tommy shook his head. "Frank and I were never friends, but we were friendly. He really cared for Davy. His death was hard on Frank, and I knew whatever had happened, Frank punished himself more than any of us could have."

The bartender set the pitcher she'd ordered on the bar and waved off her money when she tried to pay.

"I suspect you'll have a hard time paying for anything in this town from now on. You've done a hell of a job with the company, kiddo. I'm so proud of you. It's been good for business, and it's been good for the community."

The compliment was unexpected, and Julia bit her bottom lip to stave off any tears that threatened to fall. The last couple months that Julia had been in Elder's Bay, she'd slowly been trying to change the culture at Clayman Fisheries. There'd been complaints from vendors, even when she was in Portland, about her dad's behavior.

People loved her dad. He was a charming guy, but he could be a bit rough around the edges. She knew this contributed to some of their contracted boats threatening to leave and go to work for the Miller's. Now that the drama with her dad and Dan Bratton had settled down, and with the changes she'd made during her time in Elder's Bay so far, the worst of the bleeding had hopefully stopped. She kissed her uncle on the cheek and held up the pitcher of beer.

"I better get going. I have exciting news to share with my girlfriend."

Tommy smiled and tipped his hat to her. "You go get her, sweetheart. She's a good kid and a hell of a fisherman. You've got a keeper there."

Julia wound her way through the crowd to the poolroom in the back. Dylan had messaged her an hour before to let her know they were all at Skip's.

Just as it had so many months before, the laughter stopped when Julia walked into the pool room. Andy and Remy sat at a high table in the back, watching Corey line up his next shot. Dylan and Brooke were deep in conversation in the other corner, but both jumped up and ran to greet Julia when they saw her.

"Hey, Jules." They both hugged her, careful not to cause her to spill the beer she held.

"Hey, girls. You both look beautiful tonight."

"Holy shit, look at you." Dylan and Brooke stepped back enough to take in the form-fitting, midnight blue lacy dress Julia picked out for this very night, hoping it would stir something in Remy. If the look she gave Julia was any sign, she'd chosen well.

Remy slid from the stool she was sitting on and pulled Julia into her arms.

"Hey baby, I didn't think you'd be back until tomorrow."

"Can I take this for you?" Andy pointed toward the beer Julia had almost forgotten about.

"Yes, please. I thought you guys might be thirsty."

"Always," Andy said. She took the pitcher and topped off each glass.

"I'm finding it difficult to control myself. You look smoking hot in this dress. I say we ditch these fools and go back to your place so I can take it off of you."

"On that note…"

Julia smiled and glanced over at Dylan and Brooke, who both gave her an encouraging nod.

"Do you think we could find somewhere quiet to talk?" Julia asked.

Remy looked over at Andy and Corey, who were in a heated discussion about the fate of Daenerys Targaryen in *Game of Thrones* again. Julia had heard of the epic battle that followed the last season and how Remy's best friend and cousin had almost literally gone to blows over whether there were clues all along to the character's state of mind or if the writers of the show had gone off the rails and betrayed the fans. Thankfully, Julia's opinion aligned with Remy's, but they agreed never to discuss it with her crew.

"Yeah, let's get out of here." Remy downed the rest of her beer and turned to the others. "We're leaving."

"Call me tomorrow, Jules." Dylan said as Remy took Julia's hand and guided her toward the door.

Once they'd left the bar, Julia felt weirdly nervous about being alone with Remy. Possibly because she wasn't wholly confident about what she'd say. She was about ninety percent sure Remy would be thrilled to move in with her, but that pesky ten percent of doubt told her she might think they were moving too fast.

"Want to sit in my truck like the last time?"

"Do you still have that joint in the glovebox?"

"Yep," Remy said.

"I'm sold. You might have to help me get into the passenger seat. This dress isn't very forgiving."

Remy's hungry eyes made Julia wet as she took a moment to admire the dress she'd almost not worn. She feared it would appear a little too much for a night at Skippers, but apparently Remy approved.

"Fuck me, you're beautiful," Remy said.

Julia gave herself an internal high five. "Thanks." She allowed Remy to take her hand and pull her toward the back of the parking lot where her truck was.

When they reached the truck, Remy opened the door and picked Julia up, placing her in the passenger seat like she weighed nothing.

"Good?" she asked.

Julia nodded, and Remy shut her door to run around to the other side. Once they were closed into the tight space, Remy opened the glove box and pulled out the tin with the joint still in it.

"You know you're probably screwed if a cop pulls you over and finds that thing in your glovebox?"

Remy shrugged and took a long drag before handing it to Julia. "Probably. I took it to a party a year ago and forgot to return it to the house."

A gentle relaxation came over Julia, and she reached out her hand to rest on Remy's thigh. "I think I've smoked more pot since I've been back in Elder's Bay than I have since high school."

"Oh no, am I corrupting the homecoming queen? Because that's fucking awesome."

"I always knew you Millers were a bad influence." Julia tensed when she realized what she'd said. They hadn't really talked about the feud between their families since the stuff with her dad and Bratton had happened and she hoped the tease wouldn't upset her.

Remy giggled which set off a coughing fit as the smoke from the pot she exhaled burned her lungs.

"You okay?" Julia asked as she patted Remy's back.

Remy nodded and offered Julia the joint. "Want any more? I think I've had enough."

"I'm good."

"We're going to have to roll another one soon if we keep sneaking away to get stoned."

A truck parked next to them and Remy and Julia went completely still so they wouldn't be caught. Of course, the pot smoke Julia was sure billowed out of the partially open window was probably a clue that they were there.

When the voices of the men seemed far enough away, Julia peeked out the window to make sure the coast was clear.

"I think we're good," Julia said. She looked at Remy and found her smiling at her.

"What?" Julia pulled the visor down to check her face in the tiny mirror on the back. "Do I have something on my face."

"I'm so in love with you," Remy said.

This wasn't the first time Remy had said she loved her, but something about this time was different. The way she was looking at

Julia. The silly situation they were in. Everything about this moment filled Julia's heart with love.

"Move in with me?" Julia hadn't meant to just throw it out there like that, but she was tired of waiting for the right moment.

"What do you mean? I'm practically living with you now."

"I mean for real."

"I don't understand how it would be different from what we're doing now. I stay at your aunt's house every night when I'm in port. At least until you go back to Portland."

"It's not my aunt's house. It's ours. And I'm not going back to Portland."

Remy sat up in her seat and stared at Julia. She could tell the words were taking a minute to sink in and Julia waited patiently for her to respond.

"I don't understand."

Julia reached across the console and took Remy's hand in hers. "Well, I've transferred all my Portland duties to Tessa. I might have to go there occasionally for one thing or another, but from now on I'm working almost all the time in Elder's Bay."

"Seriously? Just like that? No waiting?"

"Nope." Julia's heart felt so full she thought it just might explode.

"Holy fuck," Remy said. She looked like she was in shock and Julia really hoped it was a good kind of surprise.

"What are you thinking?" Julia asked.

Remy lunged across the center console and practically climbed into Julia's lap. Since she was much smaller and wearing a very tight dress, the prospect of that was a little scary. "Easy, champ. I'm a delicate flower."

"You're my delicate flower." Remy kissed her so enthusiastically; Julia had a hard time catching her breath. "What did you mean about the house being our house?"

"Aunt Tina asked if I'd like to buy it. She honestly asked me several weeks ago, but I wasn't sure if I was going to be moving to Elder's Bay at that point. I'd told her I couldn't give her an answer right then and if she found someone else before I was ready to move out that I'd understand and find another place to stay. When I called her a couple of days ago to get an update on what was happening with it, she told me she hadn't listed it. She knew I'd need to eventually move to Elder's Bay once I took over for Dad, and with the way I'd talked about you she knew it was only a matter of time before I figured out I couldn't go back to Portland if that meant leaving you behind."

"Smart lady," Remy said.

"You can tell her yourself when she visits next week. We have paperwork we need to take care of, and she wants to figure out what she wants to take and what she'll leave for me. It sounds like she's met someone and is moving to Greece to be with her, so I don't think she'll be taking all that much."

"Who else knows?"

Julia's phone beeped and she looked down to check the message. She smiled and held it up so Remy could see that it was Dylan asking if she'd told Remy, yet. The phone beeped again, and Brooke was demanding she hurry and come back in so they could all celebrate.

"Dylan, obviously, and apparently Brooke and probably the rest of them by now. Should we go in and celebrate with our friends?"

"I love you deeply, Julia Clayman."

"And I love you, Remy Miller. Forever."

EPILOGUE

Remy squeezed Julia's hand while waiting for the winner to be announced. It had been a long three years filled with many successes and failures, but knowing they had each other had made any obstacles ahead of them seem manageable since they'd face them together.

"And this year's Oregon State University Generational Leadership Award goes to Julia Clayman from Clayman Fisheries in Elder's Bay, Oregon."

The crowd erupted in applause, and Remy beamed at her fiancée, who looked shocked to hear her name announced. Everyone knew Julia was the obvious choice, but she still had difficulty accepting the well-deserved praise and recognition she received for helping turn her family's company into a vital part of their community.

Clayman Fisheries had always been one of the largest employers in Elder's Bay, but under Julia's direction, it had become so much more to the families that lived in the small community. Remy's cheeks hurt from smiling as she stood to hug her.

The next few hours were a blur as she accepted the award, and they danced the night away with other award recipients from across the state. Her heart was whole, and after their wedding the next month, she would consider herself the luckiest girl in the world.

When they finally made it into an Uber that would take them to their hotel in Portland for the night, she shared the photo response her parents had sent after she'd won. Julia laughed at the Millers' exuberant faces, followed by a text saying they were proud of her.

The whole town was proud of her and Remy couldn't wait to get to the hotel, so she could show Julia just how turned on she was by a winner of the Generational Leadership Award. Remy hadn't realized that was one of her fetishes, but apparently, it was.

"You were amazing tonight, sweetheart."

"I love you and I love that you act like I've just won an Academy Award."

"This is better than a stupid Academy Award," Remy said. "Your dad would be so proud of you."

Julia looked out the window momentarily. Remy had come to understand it was something she did when she missed her dad. She wasn't as sad as she had been in the beginning. Time heals and all, but Remy still knew she missed him and wondered how he would feel about the woman and leader she'd become.

"Charlie texted me the same thing. He said he'll be at the barbecue Sunday with the girls. Mom has a community meeting she has to attend. She said she'll be late, but she'll be there."

"You realize that our moms have been meeting at the Crab Pot twice weekly to discuss the wedding."

"Oh, I know. Mom's been giving me all the updates. I'm afraid they've turned this into a much larger event than the small family get-together we had envisioned."

Remy kissed the engagement ring on Julia's finger. "Do you want me to make them stop? I'll drive to Vegas with you right now if that's what you want. I just want to marry you, and I don't care about the chaos. I know I won't see any of it when we're standing up there. I only have eyes for you. The rest of the world can fuck off."

Julia laughed. "You're so much more of a romantic than I ever pegged you as."

"Too much?"

"Just right," Julia said. "I wouldn't change one bit of it, and I can't wait to be your wife."

"Are you sure about hyphenating your name? I understand if you don't want to stir the pot with the last few of your cousins that can't let the feud go."

"Nope," Julia said. "I'm positive. I think it's about time we officially joined these two families and forced everyone to lay down their swords."

"I'll probably continue to watch my back, just in case."

"Those same cousins are still dependent on their jobs with Clayman Fisheries, so they don't have to like it, but they have to accept it."

"Especially after the babies start coming," Remy said.

"Babies? How many are we talking about? We discussed one little Miller spawn, but nobody agreed on multiples."

The driver stopped in front of their hotel, and Remy got out and held her hand to help Julia from the car.

"Thanks, man," Remy said before closing the door.

"Well, I guess I assumed there would be at least two. You love your brother so much, and I love mine. I want our kids to have that built-in support system you only get with siblings."

"If you're lucky," Julia added.

"They will be."

The glass elevator carried them to the tenth floor, and Julia slipped out of her heels when they entered their room.

"God, my feet are killing me. You have no idea what a femme woman must endure to look pretty for the butch stud she's trying to lure into her bed."

Remy removed her suit jacket and draped it over a chair. "Oh, really?"

"Really." Julia watched her with a fire in her eyes that Remy hoped would never dim.

"Well, I think I can speak for all the butch studs out there when I say, we appreciate every sacrifice you make." Remy toed off her oxfords and removed the tie from around her neck.

"Really?"

"Really," Remy said.

Julia plopped down on the bed with her legs hanging over the side. Her dress was so form-fitting that Remy assumed her movement was probably limited. The white button-down shirt she'd been wearing was the next article of clothing to go, which left her in a white undershirt and black slacks. The arms of the shirt fit snugly around her biceps. The hunger in Julia's eyes said that she had noticed.

The silk tie slipped through Remy's fingers as she untied the knot. Julia smiled as her hands were bound with the fine material before Remy knelt on the floor between her legs and pushed the dress that only came to mid-thigh up and over her hips, revealing the black lace panties Remy knew were for her benefit.

"Mmm, I love it when you wrap your pussy up so pretty for me."

The panties weren't removed but instead were pulled to the side so Remy could run a finger along the folds she could see were already wet for her.

"You're a very good girl. Your pussy is ready for me before I even touch you."

"Yes. For you."

"That's right," Remy said. "All mine."

Remy's finger circled Julia's opening and teased her with the tip. Not enough to satisfy her, but enough to elicit a moan from her lips.

"Please, Remy," Julia moaned.

The power Remy felt knowing Julia was hers made her want to strut around with her chest out like a rooster in a hen house. They'd weathered the storms, and they'd survive the ones ahead of them, but they'd do it together.

"I love you, Julia."

"Love you. Please. You're killing me, baby."

"How do you want it, sweetheart? Slow and romantic, or fast and rough?"

Julia moaned. "Fast. Rough."

"I was hoping you'd say that."

Remy helped Julia slide up the bed and then shed her shirt and slacks. She'd wanted nothing more than to be inside Julia all night, so she drove two fingers into her tight depths without any more preamble. Julia lifted her hips at the sudden intrusion but moaned her approval.

The spot Remy knew would immediately send Julia over the edge was just at the tip of her fingers, but Remy wasn't ready to bring her there quite yet.

"That's right, sweet girl, let me finger fuck you. Your pussy's so tight, and it's all for me, isn't it?"

"Yes. Fuck. You feel so fucking good."

Julia's legs rested on Remy's shoulders as she leaned forward to drive her fingers deeper.

"I'm going to come," Julia said.

"Not yet."

"Baby." Sweat dripped off Julia's forehead and trickled down the side of her face. "Can't stop."

Remy leaned forward until she almost had Julia folded in half and rhythmically drove her fingers into her pussy until she felt her walls spasm around her.

"Too much," Julia said. She reached out to push Remy back, but the energy that Remy had been building all night still needed an outlet.

Before Julia had completely come down from her release, Remy gently pulled her fingers out and helped her flip onto her knees. Julia's hands were still bound, so this position made her extremely vulnerable. Remy knew this was something she enjoyed in their sex life, so without hesitation, she moved to the side of Julia's body and rubbed her flattened hand against her butt.

"I told you not to come, didn't I?" Remy's voice was scolding, even though Julia knew it was only an act.

"Yes, but I—"

"I didn't ask for excuses." Remy hadn't realized how much fun this power play could be in the bedroom until Julia had asked her to spank her one night. They didn't do it that often, but when they did, Remy felt like the king of the world.

"No. No excuses," Julia said, panting to catch her breath through the excitement. "I'm sorry."

The hand rubbing Julia's butt cheek gave a gentle smack followed by a firmer one. "Do you think I should punish you?"

"Yes. Please."

Remy smiled and proceeded to spank her on the ass until her cheeks reddened and felt warm to the touch. She never did it hard enough to hurt her, but she knew Julia enjoyed the sting of Remy's hand against her skin.

When done, she leaned forward and kissed the abused area before rolling Julia back over and crawling between her legs.

"Poor, baby," Remy said. "You took your punishment like a good girl."

"Yes, ma'am." Julia was out of breath, but Remy could tell she was primed for another orgasm already.

The tie was removed from Julia's wrists, followed by the remainder of her clothes. Remy slid down the bed and draped Julia's tired legs over her shoulders before dragging her tongue from her opening, up to her distended clit. Julia was ready. There was no doubt about that.

"Somebody was turned on by being spanked," Remy said.

Julia laughed and covered her face with her hands in embarrassment.

"Shut up and do your job," Julia said as she tugged Remy's short brown hair.

"Oh, I like it when you get all bossy with me. Give a girl an award...."

A moan escaped Julia's mouth when Remy leaned in to suck her clit into her eager mouth. This is what she'd wanted all day. Remy loved everything they did in bed, but the noises she could pull from Julia's lips when she went down on her were more satisfying than anything. Even better than being on the ocean.

She took her time building Julia up. When she finally came, Remy relished in the knowledge that she'd been the one to make this beautiful woman lose her mind. There was absolutely nothing better.

When Julia tried to reciprocate, Remy convinced her to wait until the morning. This night was about Julia, and Remy was happy to postpone her orgasm until the next day. Right then, she only wanted to fall asleep with Julia wrapped up tight in her arms and their whole lives ahead of them.

About the Author

Angie Williams, winner of a third grade essay competition on fire safety, grew up in the dusty desert of West Texas. Always interested in writing, as a child she would lose interest before the end, killing the characters off in a tragic accident so she could move on to the next story. Thankfully as an adult she decided it was time to write things where everyone survives.

Angie lives in Northern California with her beautiful wife and son, and a menagerie of dogs, cats, snakes, and tarantulas. She's a proud geek and lover of all things she was teased about in school.

Books Available from Bold Strokes Books

Bones of Boothbay Harbor by Michelle Larkin. Small-town police chief Frankie Stone and FBI Special Agent Eve Huxley must set aside their differences and combine their skills to find a killer after a burial site is discovered in Boothbay Harbor, Maine. (978-1-63679-267-5)

Crush by Ana Hartnett Reichardt. Josie Sanchez worked for years for the opportunity to create her own wine label, and nothing will stand in her way. Not even Mac, the owner's annoyingly beautiful niece Josie's forced to hire as her harvest intern. (978-1-63679-330-6)

Decadence by Piper Jordan, Ronica Black, Renee Roman. You are cordially invited to Decadence, Las Vegas's most talked about invitation-only Masquerade Ball. Come for the entertainment and stay for the erotic indulgence. We guarantee it'll be a party that lives up to its name. (978-1-63679-361-0)

Gimmicks and Glamour by Lauren Melissa Ellzey. Ashly has learned to hide her Sight, but as she speeds toward high school graduation she must protect the classmates she claims to hate from an evil that no one else sees. (978-1-63679-401-3)

Heart of Stone by Sam Ledel. Princess Keeva Glantor meets Maeve, a gorgon forced to live alone thanks to a decades-old lie, and together the two women battle forces they formerly thought to be good in the hopes of leading lives they can finally call their own. (978-1-63679-407-5)

Murder at the Oasis by David S. Pederson. Palm trees, sunshine, and murder await Mason Adler and his friend Walter as they travel from Phoenix to Palm Springs for what was supposed to be a relaxing vacation but ends up being a trip of mystery and intrigue. (978-1-63679-416-7)

Peaches and Cream by Georgia Beers. Adley Purcell is living her dreams owning Get the Scoop ice cream shop until national dessert chain Sweet Heaven opens less than two blocks away and Adley has to compete with the far too heavenly Sabrina James. (978-1-63679-412-9)

The Only Fish in the Sea by Angie Williams. Will love overcome years of bitter rivalry for the daughters of two crab fishing families in this queer modern-day spin on Romeo and Juliet? (978-1-63679-444-0)

Wildflower by Cathleen Collins. When a plane crash leaves eleven-year-old Lily Andrews stranded in the vast wilderness of Arkansas, will she be able to overcome the odds and make it back to civilization and the one person who holds the key to her future? (978-1-63679-621-5)

Witch Finder by Sheri Lewis Wohl. Tasmin, the Keeper of the Book of Darkness, is in terrible danger, and as a Witch Finder, Morrigan must protect her and the secrets she guards even if it costs Morrigan her life. (978-1-63679-335-1)

A Second Chance at Life by Genevieve McCluer. Vampires Dinah and Rachel reconnect, but a string of vampire killings begin and evidence seems to be pointing at Dinah. They must prove her innocence while finding out if the two of them are still compatible after all these years. (978-1-63679-459-4)

Digging for Heaven by Jenna Jarvis. Litz lives for dragons. Kella lives to kill them. The last thing they expect is to find each other attractive. (978-1-63679-453-2)

Forever's Promise by Missouri Vaun. Wesley Holden migrated west disguised as a man for the hope of a better life and with no designs to take a wife, but Charlotte Rose has other ideas. (978-1-63679-221-7)

Here For You by D. Jackson Leigh. A horse trainer must make a difficult business decision that could save her father's ranch from foreclosure but destroy her chance to win the heart of a feisty barrel racer vying for a spot in the National Rodeo Finals. (978-1-63679-299-6)

I Do, I Don't by Joy Argento. Creator of the romance algorithm, Nicole Hart doesn't expect to be starring in her own reality TV dating show, and falling for the show's executive producer Annie Jackson could ruin everything. (978-1-63679-420-4)

It's All in the Details by Dena Blake. Makeup artist Lane Donnelly and wedding planner Helen Trent can't stand each other, but they must set aside their differences to ensure Darcy gets the wedding of her dreams, and make a few of their own dreams come true. (978-1-63679-430-3)

Marigold by Melissa Brayden. Marigold Lavender vows to take down Alexis Wakefield, the harsh food critic who blasts her younger sister's restaurant. If only she wasn't as sexy as she is mean. (978-1-63679-436-5)

The Town that Built Us by Jesse J. Thoma. When her father dies, Grace Cook returns to her hometown and tries to avoid Bonnie Whitlock, the woman who pulverized her heart, only to discover her father's estate has been left to them jointly. (978-1-63679-439-6)

A Degree to Die For by Karis Walsh. A murder at the University of Washington's Classics Department brings Professor Antigone Weston and Sergeant Adriana Kent together—first as opposing forces, and then allies as they fight together to protect their campus from a killer. (978-1-63679-365-8)

A Talent Within by Suzanne Lenoir. Evelyne, born into nobility, and Annika, a peasant girl with a deadly secret, struggle to change their destinies in Valmora, a medieval world controlled by religion, magic, and men. (978-1-63679-423-5)

Finders Keepers by Radclyffe. Roman Ashcroft's past, it seems, is not so easily forgotten when fate brings her and Tally Dewilde together—along with an attraction neither welcomes. (978-1-63679-428-0)

Homeland by Kristin Keppler and Allisa Bahney. Dani and Kate have finally found themselves on the same side of the war, but a new threat from the inside jeopardizes the future of the wasteland. (978-1-63679-405-1)

Just One Dance by Jenny Frame. Will Taylor Spark and her new business to make dating special—the Regency Romance Club—bring sparkle back to Jaq Bailey's lonely world? (978-1-63679-457-0)

On My Way There by Jaycie Morrison. As Max traverses the open road, her journey of impossible love, loss, and courage mirrors her voyage of self-discovery leading to the ultimate question: If she can't have the woman of her dreams, will the woman of real life be enough? (978-1-63679-392-4)

Transitioning Home by Heather K O'Malley. An injured soldier realizes they need to transition to really heal. (978-1-63679-424-2)

Truly Enough by JJ Hale. Chasing the spark of creativity may ignite a burning romance or send a friendship up in flames. (978-1-63679-442-6)

Vintage and Vogue by Kelly and Tana Fireside. When tech whiz Sena Abrigo marches into small-town Owen Station, she turns librarian Hazel Butler's life upside down in the most wonderful of ways, setting off an explosive series of events, threatening their chance at love…and their very lives. (978-1-63679-448-8)

Broken Fences by Jo Hemmingwood. Former army sergeant Seneca Twist has difficulty adjusting to civilian life until she meets psychologist Robyn Mason and has a place to call home. (978-1-63679-414-3)

Never Kiss a Cowgirl by Ali Vali. Asher Evans dreams of winning the National Finals Rodeo in Vegas, and Reagan Wilson wants no part of something that brings back the memory of what killed her father. (978-1-63679-106-7)

Pantheon Girls by Jean Copeland. Cassie Burke never anticipated the detour life was about to take when a meeting with a prospective client reunites her with a past love and reignites the star-crossed passion they shared twenty years earlier. (978-1-63679-337-5)

Roux for Two by Aurora Rey. For TV chef Chelsea Boudreaux and hometown boy Bryce Cormier, love proves as tricky as making a good pot of gumbo. (978-1-63679-376-4)

Starting Over by Nance Sparks. Jennifer has no idea if she can mend Sam's broken soul after the sudden loss of her wife, but it's never too late for starting over. (978-1-63679-409-9)

The Accidental Bride by Jane Walsh. Spinsters Miss Grace Linfield and Miss Thea Martin travel to Gretna Green to prevent a wedding, only to discover a scandalous passion—for each other. (978-1-63679-345-0)

Three Wishes by Anne Shade. A magic lamp, a beautiful Jinni, and a cursed princess make for one unbelievable story. (978-1-63679-349-8)

Undiscovered Treasures by MJ Williamz. For Cyl and her friends Luna and Martinique, life's best treasures often appear when you're not looking. (978-1-63679-449-5)